THE
CHILD

THE CHILD

THE RED LIGHT AND SHADOW

KEITH F. GOODNIGHT

Text copyright © 2013 by Keith F. Goodnight

Published by 47North — Seattle, Washington

www.apub.com

ISBN-13: 9781477807729
ISBN-10: 1477807721
Library of Congress Control Number: 2013936770

For Jennifer and Nagy

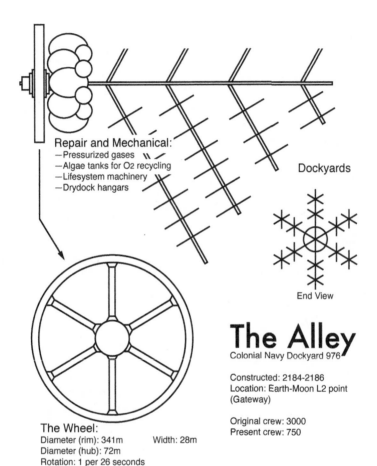

Repair and Mechanical:
—Pressurized gases
—Algae tanks for O2 recycling
—Lifesystem machinery
—Drydock hangars

Dockyards

End View

The Alley
Colonial Navy Dockyard 976

Constructed: 2184-2186
Location: Earth-Moon L2 point
(Gateway)

Original crew: 3000
Present crew: 750

The Wheel:
Diameter (rim): 341m   Width: 28m
Diameter (hub): 72m
Rotation: 1 per 26 seconds

This is what I think: I think it was all planned from the start. I think everything was arranged, all the parts put in place, all of us just following a script written by someone—some thing—long before.

Marta told me once that people seek explanations for tragedy, that they find villains or conspiracies because they can't stand the idea that sometimes terrible things happen for no reason. Is that all I'm doing now, trying to find meaning in a meaningless disaster?

No, it can't be. The level of coincidence, so many unconnected events . . . it defies probability. It didn't just happen. It was planned. It was deliberate.

The nightmare question is: How far back does the plan go? Has my entire life been manipulated? Was the whole of human history arranged to lead me to that fatal decision in the generator room? It's possible, judging by the things Brown said before he died. I wish I could believe he was wrong.

I know all this sounds like paranoid delusion. But you're already convinced I'm crazy, aren't you? I can't change your mind now, and I shouldn't even want to: My lawyer tells me that being insane is the only thing keeping me from the death penalty. So I won't try to be persuasive, to convince you I'm telling the truth. Believe me, or don't.

I'll just tell you what happened.

1

CHAPTER ONE

I grabbed a handhold to stop myself from floating right into the window. None of us liked working in freefall. We weren't trained for it like the Navy crew, but the only part of the base that had gravity was the Wheel. Comprising mostly living quarters and offices, the Wheel couldn't provide the empty volume needed to properly control our experiment.

We'd been working on the Alley, the Navy's main base at Gateway, for three months—ever since our project entered the experimental stage. While there were other places in the Colonies that offered enough space for our generators, the Navy's SciTech division had sponsored our project, and the Alley had the empty space. Built during the Independence War fifty years ago as a repair facility for the fleet guarding Gateway Transit Station, the Alley now stood three-quarters empty, serving only a small search-and-rescue squadron that patrolled the civilian shipping lanes. A crew of seven hundred and fifty occupied a base originally built for three thousand, and immense hangars stood empty and useless. But they provided plenty of room for our small group of thirty scientists, students, and technicians, and all of our equipment.

My position secured, I looked through the window into the hangar and studied the equipment. Everything appeared in order. The hyperfield generators crouched in the center of the vast, shadowy space, lit up in gleaming copper and silver by the spotlights we'd trained on them. Sparks of light escaped the connections of the fiber-optic cables, highlighting the strange geometry of the generators' spines and the spiderwebs of wire that held them together. They looked—well, they looked like nothing else in the Solar System. The closest analogy I can think of would be an Escher print of two metal sea urchins decorated with Christmas lights.

Some people find the appearance of hyperfield generators disturbing. They say there's something wrong about their shape, not meant for three-dimensional space, looking at them makes them feel queasy. I've never felt that way. I love the way they look.

But it wasn't the appearance of the generators that pricked my nerves with a tingle of anticipation. In a few minutes, I'd see the hyperfields themselves. That was the real treat.

Objectively, an active hyperfield isn't much to look at. Energy flows into our universe from hyperspace. Fascinating to physicists and vital to our technology, but as for its appearance—just blackbody radiation, a mundane glow no more exciting than a light panel or a candle flame.

But I've always looked at that simple glow not as a physicist, but as the ten-year-old boy I was the day Linda Ryder brought one of her prototype generators into the dark cold of Midway. Warm light had poured out of it like magic, and my mother had smiled, had even laughed, for the first time in my memory. Objectivity be dusted—hyperfields are *beautiful*.

The chance to admire them was a privilege of my research. Industrial hyperfields are surrounded by photoelectric panels, hiding them from view. They'd be too bright to look at directly anyway. But our generators were in the open, and produced a much weaker field: a warm firelight glow much like Linda's original prototype that had so captivated me as a boy.

From behind me I heard Drake Williams raise his voice. "Final call! Place your bets!"

I rolled my eyes. Of course, others had their own interests. Turning away from the window I looked over our control room, crowded with half a dozen people. We'd set up our control consoles in the OCC—the hangar office, "Operational Command Center" in the official jargon—and in contrast to the hangar, it barely had room for our usual team of three. Drake at the computer console, Kyoko Fujiri at the electrical engineering station, and myself watching the instruments and data recorders filled it up nicely. Today two of our grad students, Beth Willis and John Ikira, hovered near the back, and Commander Warren, the base CO, had also come to play spectator.

Drake had his handscreen over his head, its soft glow casting a blue light across his face as it displayed the numbers from his betting pool on the upcoming test.

"How's it stand?" I asked.

"The jackpot's over a hundred and fifty credits," he said. "Ten seconds is the clear favorite, but we've got some optimists today—there are bets placed all the way up to twenty."

Commander Warren frowned. "Dr. Williams, I *know* you are not promoting gambling on my base." The smile in his eyes contradicted his stern tone.

"Certainly not!" Drake looked very innocent. "This is purely recreational, Commander. Hypothetical money only."

"Very good." Warren folded his arms. "I'll put fifteen credits on eleven seconds—hypothetically, of course."

I smiled. Navy men had a reputation for gambling—despite regulations against it—and since we'd come aboard the Alley we'd learned the reputation was justified. The crew seemed to bet on everything from traditional games of chance to the next day's menu in the mess hall. Commander Warren, his official position notwithstanding, hadn't failed to place a "hypothetical" wager since Drake began his pool.

I didn't share the taste myself, but I liked to hear how the pool was running. The betting favorite reflected a consensus on our progress, and it could be surprisingly accurate. Today's predictions matched my own intuition that we were back on track after a run of disappointing failures.

Kyoko pointed at Drake's screen. "The simulation is finished," she observed. "We are ready to proceed."

"Kyoko, where's your entrepreneurial spirit? There's money to be made here!" But Drake had already shut off his handscreen, clipping it to his belt so it wouldn't float away, even while his free hand danced across his keyboard. Kyoko flashed him a cool look, then turned back to her own screen.

I pushed off from the window, and almost overshot as I swung around behind my own console, clutching hard at the rail to stop myself in time. Dusted zero-g conditions! Besides the bruises we collected from lurking metal edges, there was also the danger of crunching into delicate equipment. It had happened more than once.

But this time I managed to correct my overshoot before crashing and embarrassing myself. I attached my belt clips to the rail and breathed a sigh of relief. A chuckle from my right told me Drake had noticed the near miss.

"Okay," I said. "Kyoko's ready to go, Drake's closed the casino, and I didn't break anything. Let's run it."

I could hear the hum of cooling fans through the open door into the hangar, and a faint scent of ozone drifted in. Beth and John took out their handscreens, ready to take notes. Commander Warren nudged himself back toward them, out of our way.

Drake punched a few commands into the computer. Several screens on the wall blanked and reset. On my own screen, the instrument readings quivered restlessly around zero.

"All circuits test in good order," Kyoko said.

I nodded. "Start recording." I glanced at the chronometer on my screen: 0830 hours, Monday, August 15, 2231. The time stamp appeared on the graphs as they began tracing lines of data across the screen. Following protocol, I announced, "This is run number thirty-seven," although there was little chance anyone had lost track. "Okay, Kyoko, fire them up."

Kyoko switched on main power to the first generator. The lights dimmed at the sudden power drain. It takes a lot of energy to punch a hole into hyperspace, though very little to maintain it.

I watched the graphs oscillate as the hyperfield initialized. They settled down after a few seconds, and Kyoko said, "Alpha field is active and stable."

She hit power to the second generator. Again the lights flickered and then steadied. "Beta field is active and stable."

I allowed myself a pleasurable moment to just stare at them. About two meters across and perfectly spherical, the hyperfields glowed a warm yellow-orange. If I were in the hangar at that moment, I'd have felt the heat radiating from them, like that of a campfire—similar to the warmth that had washed over me in Midway that first time.

However, I couldn't go out there and enjoy it. It wasn't dangerous, but it would screw up the data. Hyperfields react to the arrangement of matter and energy around them; that's why we needed the space of a whole empty hangar for our experiments. A person drifting near would be an uncontrolled variable we didn't need, so I had to stay put and be content with the view through the window.

"Okay, Drake, you're up," I said.

"Beginning the run." Drake tapped his keyboard, and the generators crept toward each other on slender rails, in carefully graded motion almost too slow to see. The software now took control of adjusting the generator configuration, to keep the hyperfields stable as they moved closer to one another. They'd keep closing in on each other until their event horizons touched, bringing them into overlap.

At the moment of contact, an ordinary hyperfield would instantly collapse. But our fields would survive contact for a short time—ten seconds, if Drake's pool was any indication. Longer, if we were lucky.

Long or short, we'd have those seconds to record as much data as we could about what the contact did to the fields, and what happened in the overlap region.

Already I could see the graphs beginning to fluctuate as the fields protested their approach to each other. Nothing bothers one hyperfield so much as the proximity of another. But Drake's software stayed on top of the changes, keeping the fields stable—so far.

Around one minute before contact, with the fields less than ten centimeters apart, I noticed something strange. The readouts wavered and the variation increased in amplitude. I expected that as contact approached. But I didn't expect to see different instruments out of sync with each other, a sure sign the hyperfields were falling apart, before they had even touched.

"Dust!" I cursed. "The fields are collapsing!"

"I don't think so," Kyoko said. "Energy output remains constant. I see no sign of collapse."

"Constant?" I frowned. How could that be? My graphs were all over the screen, every one contradicting every other. Those readings *couldn't* come from an intact field, only the final chaos of a field in collapse. Unless—

I called up a new graph, one we rarely had reason to use: energy output charted across the electromagnetic spectrum. It should display a simple curve of blackbody radiation. Instead it showed a complex pattern of peaks and valleys. Each drop in output at one wavelength matched a rise in another, keeping total energy output constant. The hyperfields weren't collapsing. Instead they were—what? What the hell were they doing?

"Look at this!" I said. "Look at it!"

Thirty seconds remained until contact.

"Bloody hell," Drake said. "They've never done that before!"

Beth and John peered over my shoulder. I could hear them whispering excitedly to each other.

Suddenly, Beth said, "You can see it!" She pointed out the window. "Look! You can see it!"

I looked up from my screen to the window. My eyes widened, my heart beat faster: I was seeing the impossible.

The two fields rippled in strange patterns. In place of the yellow-orange glow I had always loved, waves of brighter light raced across their surfaces, flashing and changing colors like some metallic rainbow set on fire. The instruments went wild, pegged out by readings beyond their design limits.

Commander Warren was the only one who didn't know the significance of what he was seeing. His voice remained calm but interested when he said, "Professor, I thought hyperfields were always uniform."

I laughed, a little wildly. "So did I, Commander. So did I! Every known law of hyperfield physics says energy output should be the same for every point on the event horizon. This is—this—" I turned briefly to meet his eyes. "This is new!" I would have jumped up and down if it were possible in zero gravity.

The hyperfields were shining now, lines of brighter light contrasting with lines of shadow, chasing each other across the two fields. There was a pattern to the rippling waves, something familiar, and I realized I was seeing the multidimensional shape of the true hyperfields, projected in ripples of light and shadow onto the visible spheres.

It was incredible, impossible! I'd seen that shape in my imagination a hundred times. I'd played with it in my mind, turning it this way and that, visualizing how it must look, how I could change it, what math would describe it. But I had never seen it with my eyes. No one had. No one ever could. The only visible part of a hyperfield was the plain sphere of glowing heat radiation. Until now.

I had no idea what the instruments were reading. I couldn't tear my eyes away from the spectacle outside the window. Neither could the others. We all stared, colors sweeping across our faces.

Even the usually controlled Kyoko betrayed her excitement, unconsciously lapsing into her native Japanese. "*Kirei*," she whispered. "Beautiful."

All of a sudden the light swirled, rippling and crisscrossing into complex moiré patterns of prismatic color. A single shining point, the glaring blue-white of an electrical arc, sprang into being directly between the two hyperfields. I knew at once what it meant.

"Contact!" I shouted. "They're in contact!"

"The fields are holding." Kyoko's voice shook.

Drake pumped his fist, and muttered under his breath, "Go—go—go—"

I forced myself to look down at the screen. The instrument readings were meaningless numbers I'd never seen and couldn't interpret. All I could understand was the time index counting upward from the moment of contact.

"Five seconds," I said. "Ten . . . fifteen! Twenty!"

The point of light at the fields' intersection grew brighter. It was so bright it was hard to look at and still increasing. I could feel the heat even through the window. Outside, the generator frames glowed red-hot, and the noise of the cooling fans had risen to a scream.

"The energy output is rising," Kyoko needlessly observed. "But it doesn't seem to be coming from either hyperfield—"

"It's coming from the overlap region!" I said. I had instruments aimed at that point.

Drake looked at the time. "Thirty seconds since contact!"

Our hyperfields had never remained in overlap for more than twenty-one seconds without one or both collapsing.

The glare from the overlap point now washed out the light from the fields themselves, but they were still rippling in the same patterns as before. Was I mistaken, or were the ripples getting more pronounced? They were starting to become unstable.

Forty seconds. Fifty seconds. One minute. And still the fields remained.

"The energy continues to rise!" Kyoko said. She had to shout over the noise of the cooling fans. "Dave, this is getting out of control; the heat will damage the generators. We should shut down—"

"No, keep it going!" I roared. "We can rebuild the generators if we have to! We may never collect data like this again!" But the data wasn't really on my mind. I wanted to see what would happen.

Commander Warren moved back against the far wall. I was aware of the movement, but paid no attention.

"The software's on top of every flicker," Drake said. "We're doing it! Sustained overlap!"

But even as he ended his sentence, there was a flash from outside so bright and sudden that I thought for a moment something had exploded, even though there was no sound or concussion. Then, silence and sudden darkness. The hyperfields were gone: Both had collapsed at the same moment. The cooling fans had stopped; their circuits must have blown, and smoke curled around the generators, which still glowed bright red. I could smell burned plastic and hot metal. In the OCC, now dull and dim, half the screens had gone blank.

There was a sort of collective sigh, and then everyone exploded into cheers and applause.

"Ninety-three seconds! Ha!" Drake pounded his fist on his console. "Ninety-three! They'd have kept going forever if the generators hadn't burned out!"

Kyoko shook her head, already reestablishing her normal calm. "No, it was not stable. The energy kept increasing, with no sign of leveling off. Even the sturdiest industrial generator would have burned out." Her eyes met mine, and I caught a glimpse of a rebuke in them. If the hyperfields were my baby, the hardware was hers. She thought we should have shut down before the generators were damaged.

I looked around the room. Beth and John looked rather giddy as they compared notes. And Commander Warren was waiting by the electrical panel, his hand resting on the main circuit breaker that supplied the generators. He'd been ready to cut the power since the moment I ignored Kyoko's warning. For a moment I thought he had, but then I saw the breaker was still closed. The generators had burned out before he'd had to act.

I gave both Kyoko and Warren a nod, not quite an apology but acknowledging that perhaps I'd been a little too enthusiastic.

"Where'd all that extra energy come from?" Drake asked.

"The overlap," I said. My screen hadn't shut down. I scrolled back over the readings. "The alpha and beta field kept a constant total output right to the end, despite the local variations. It was in the overlap . . . these readings look almost like a third hyperfield formed there."

"A *separate* hyperfield? Without generator circuitry?" Drake shook his head. "Is anyone keeping a list of how many impossible things just happened?"

I laughed. "Linda Ryder used to tell me that to work in hyper-spatial physics, you have to believe six impossible things before breakfast. She was quoting an old book, I think." I stared ruefully at the screen. "One thing's for sure. We just threw out everything we thought we knew about hyperfields."

"Good-bye, Ryder equations," Drake said. "Hello, Williams-Harris-Fujiri equations."

"No, no, Harris-Williams," I replied.

Kyoko interrupted. "If we are to discuss priority, I believe alpha-betical order is fair."

That would make it Fujiri-Harris-Williams. I grinned at her.

Commander Warren cleared his throat. "You're all overlooking the most important question," he said. "Who wins the pool?"

Everyone laughed, and looked at Drake. "Obviously, the house keeps the money," he said.

From the back of the room, John snorted.

"Nice try, Drake," I said.

"Well, how about—"

The sudden wail of an alarm siren interrupted whatever Drake was going to propose. We all turned to the window, sure that something had happened in the hangar. But Warren pushed over to the nearest live screen and called up the intercom.

"Warren here," he said. "What's happening?"

A faint tinny voice answered over the intercom, "Sir, this is Lieutenant Peterson, control deck. We've received a distress call from a passenger liner approaching Gateway on the Belt run. They report engines disabled and they're losing atmosphere. We're tracking them and they're coming in ballistic. I've signaled all hands to rescue stations."

I unclipped from my console and pushed back, looking at Warren. "What—"

But the Commander held up a hand, stopping me midsyllable. He spoke to the intercom. "Very good, Lieutenant. Prep all ships and launch recon ASAP. I'll be right there."

I exchanged a look with Drake and Kyoko. Both had already left their consoles. We all knew what "losing atmosphere" meant: not the engine failures or futzed nav systems that the Alley dealt with every few days. It meant something catastrophic had happened.

The transition from our experiment to the Navy's emergency was too sudden, like a whiplash curve in a roller coaster. The screens still showed our data; smoke still curled from the generators. Now this.

It paralyzed us for a moment, as we tried to figure out what to pay attention to. But the Commander suffered no such confusion. "Professor, I'll have to ask you to get all your people back to the Wheel. We may need the dockyards clear for rescue operations."

"Right. Commander, if we can be any help—"

"Thanks, but the best thing is to keep out of the way." Warren swung himself through the door. Pulling himself effortlessly along the handholds, he vanished down the corridor.

I was still trying to catch up with the sudden turn of events. For one dizzy moment, it actually seemed the two were connected, the experiment and the accident. As if the hyperfields wrecked a spaceship at the same moment they burned out the generators. But that was just crazy.

I shook myself, clearing my head. "Shut everything down. Let's get back to the Wheel."

A distant thunder echoed along the Alley's superstructure as the first of the rescue squadron launched. The crew wasn't wasting time.

CHAPTER TWO

The wreck of the *Lunar Explorer* must have been the worst disaster the Alley's rescue squadron had ever dealt with. It may have been the worst ever to befall any civilian spacecraft in history; the final death toll was over two thousand. Maybe there were ships that suffered worse losses on the day of the Catastrophe forty years ago, if any passenger liners were in flight when it happened, but I don't know.

We gathered in an otherwise unused rec center that we'd made our own in the three months since we came aboard the Alley. It was a big, comfortable room, two decks high for a spacious feel, with pastel-colored walls instead of the usual military gray. Couches lined the walls; clusters of comfortable chairs formed conversation pits or circled around game tables. At one end, a door led to a small theater.

We connected the movie screen and most of the table screens to the Alley's com channel and listened to the chatter between the control deck and the rescue squadron. The video rotated between a tactical display and views from the cameras on board the rescue ships.

Knots of conversation formed and broke up again, but mostly everyone watched the screens and listened to the com traffic, waiting to see how it would all turn out. Charles Peretta kept up a running commentary for anyone who'd listen. He was a fan of spacecraft design and always ready to rattle off statistics about ship classes and engine specs. When we heard the ship's call sign mentioned on com, Charles looked it up in the registry and found out it was the *Lunar Explorer*, capacity twenty-seven hundred passengers and crew.

The Alley had responded to plenty of distress calls in the months since we'd been on board: sending out a tug to tow a freighter with engine failure, or a shuttle to pick up some amateur crew who had managed to disable their pleasure yacht. But almost three thousand people on a ship losing atmosphere—that was different.

The rescue effort went badly almost from the beginning. Warren scrambled the Alley's entire complement of ships. Six recon fighters led a formation that included four shuttles, three cruisers, and three tugs. But within minutes of their launch, they lost their fix on the target. The *Lunar Explorer* had sent no message after the original distress call, and the recon ships couldn't detect a trace of it anywhere.

"That just shouldn't happen," Charles explained. "Every ship has a TID—that's a transponder, sends out ID, position, ship status—and it's sealed in its own black box. It should keep transmitting even if the entire ship is destroyed."

Over the speakers we heard the recon pilots complaining about heavy EM radiation interfering with their sensors. The tactical display changed to reveal the increasing uncertainty of the *Lunar Explorer*'s location. It had shown a line indicating the ship's projected course, and a flashing dot for its current position. Now the line was a cone, spreading out from the last established point of contact, while the dot expanded into a larger circle with each passing minute. Meanwhile the rescue squadron approached the area like the hour hand of an old-fashioned analog clock.

In the rec center, we wondered if the ship had simply blown to fragments too small to detect. I found myself near the back of the room with Drake, Kyoko, Beth, and Charles. Drake called up the tactical display on his handscreen, and traced the lines of the navigational plot with his finger. Beth watched the screen, twisting her hair nervously. We debated ways the Navy might try to find the ship, bandying about suggestions with the confidence of armchair experts.

"You know, before the Catastrophe, they would have been able to just see the *Lunar Explorer*," I said. "Sunlight used to reflect on ships' hulls; they could see ships in orbit from the surface of the Earth."

"If the liner still has any running lights, or even interior lights, they've got a good shot at picking it up visually," Charles said. "The computers will be going over the camera images for any moving points of light." He frowned. "But if they've gone dark, they might never see them."

"That's horrible." Beth shuddered. "Think of being trapped in t-total darkness, all those people, with, with the air leaking out . . ."

"There'd be emergency lights," Charles said. "Battery powered, self-contained—even if the ship's power is down, there'd be light to see by."

"Enough for the computers to spot?" I asked.

Charles shrugged. But the most interesting suggestion was Drake's.

"It occurs to me," he said, "you could use a hyperfield as a sensing device."

I cocked my head. "You mean, calculating backward from the way they respond to matter and energy?"

"Why not? Make a very twitchy field, something like our experimental models, and write software to analyze the shifts, calculating a map of the field's surroundings."

"There's an idea." I was intrigued. "It'd give you a full 3-D map of everything around it, insides of boxes, behind walls . . . nothing would be opaque to it, it could see through anything, and it could do it without X-rays or other radiation. Think what doctors could do with something like that—"

"Think what the Navy could do with it today," Drake said. "No problem with EM interference; the program would just tell them where the ship is."

Kyoko frowned, her eyes distant. "It is an interesting idea, but I think it could not be done. The changes are complex and over-lapping. There would be too many possible solutions to the calculations, even if a computer could be programmed to perform them."

"Six impossible things before breakfast?" I asked.

There was a sudden burst of chatter from the speakers as several of the squadron pilots tried to talk at once. After a moment, the single voice of the flight leader came through.

"Base, we have detected ED beacons. Multiple ED beacons, strong signals."

The Alley's flight control officer responded. "Flight, how many beacons?"

"Base, we have six ED beacons. Repeat, six."

Everyone looked at Charles.

"What's an ED beacon?" Drake asked. "Escape pods?"

"Lifeboats," Charles answered. "On a ship, they're called lifeboats."

Someone across the room asked, "Well, how many people do they carry?"

Charles took a deep breath. "A ship of the *Lunar Explorer*'s class carries thirty lifeboats, each of which can hold one hundred people."

"Thirty." Drake stared. "And they've only found six?"

"Maybe they're still launching." Charles didn't sound confident.

With the beacons providing a navigational fix, the rescue squadron now closed in rapidly on the site of the disaster. Static hissed over the com channel. In the rec center, no one talked. The story was reaching its climax, and no one believed it would have a happy ending. At most six hundred were saved, out of twenty-seven hundred people.

The flight leader called in, his voice broken by the interference. "Base, I have visual on target." The screen changed to a view from the squadron leader's camera.

Chunks of the picture kept dropping out or falling to pieces. It looked like only about a third of the signal made it past the interference. But it was just enough to transmit an image: the tumbling silhouette of the *Lunar Explorer* surrounded by a halo of glowing red.

"Leaking drive plasma," Charles said. "That explains the interference. That stuff puts out static like you wouldn't believe."

"Base . . . no interior lights . . . target." The flight leader's voice crackled in and out of audibility. "There . . . extensive cloud of debris and . . . am closing on—*holy God*!"

The ship's tumble had brought the far side into view. I don't know how it looked to the pilots, but the static-ridden picture on the screen was clear enough to draw a gasp from everyone in the rec center. Beth swayed, and pressed both hands against her mouth. Someone whispered, "Oh God."

Half the *Lunar Explorer* was gone, simply ripped away, as if the ship was an animal torn in half by a predator. The hull was twisted and peeled back. The guts of the ship spilled out of the wound, trailing off in a mass of crumpled decks and tubes and cables. The wreck bled clouds of gas, shimmering red and orange. I'd never seen a ship damaged like that, not even in video files from the War.

"Bloody dusted hell," whispered Drake. "What could cause something like that?"

Charles tried to answer. He cleared his throat and tried to sound judicious. "Well, the, uh, the damage runs from bow to stern. It's the port side that's . . . if there was an explosion in the drive system, you'd expect damage concentrated aft . . . It looks more like . . . like . . ." He threw up his hands, looking pale and shaken. "Oh dust, I don't know. I've never seen anything like that."

Beth turned away from the screen. "They're dead," she said. "They're all d-dead."

My impulse was to answer with some hopeful comment. But the image on the screen countered any optimism. Beth was right and we all knew it.

◀   ◀   ◀

By that evening the Alley had 587 new temporary civilian residents—the total number recovered from the six lifeboats. The rescue squadron had taken the lifeboats in tow and brought them back to base, not having the capacity to ferry that many people all the way to the nearest Colony. They'd have to wait for a larger ship to dock with the Alley and take them on their way, which would take a day or two.

So the survivors came on board. Our research group stayed out of the way and saw very little of them. The crew settled them in quarters near the infirmary, far from our block of cabins and offices. I only encountered one group of survivors, the evening of their arrival on my way back from the mess hall. I rode the elevator down to deck 5, where all our cabins were, and heard a babble of high-pitched voices. When the elevator doors slid open, I found myself in the midst of about a dozen kids (I would later learn it was exactly a dozen). They must have just arrived on another elevator.

They looked around eight or nine, although a few looked younger still, perhaps no more than five. They stared at everything with wide eyes, chattered among themselves, and didn't seem traumatized at all. I didn't know what things had been like on board the *Lunar Explorer*, but since none of them were injured, they might not have understood the full extent of the disaster.

It's strange to remember that I met the children that first night and didn't think a thing of it. I didn't pay much attention except to avoid blundering into them. I don't recall seeing Andrew or Laurie, or Nia, or any of the other names or faces that I'd be poring over in desperation within a few days. At the time, they were just a bunch of kids.

Three of the Alley's crew tried to steer them into a corridor. I recognized Lieutenant Montoya, the supply officer who managed our use of the Navy's facilities, and Brown, a nondescript little steward who worked in the mess hall. There was also a medic I didn't know.

And there was a woman, in civilian clothes. She had dark hair and gray eyes, and looked around thirty years old. She had a pale face and a distracted expression. I could tell she tried to be in charge of the children but wasn't up to it. It was the crew that kept the group moving.

Montoya kept up a steady stream of talk, holding the children's attention with war stories told in a tour guide's voice as she led the group. She nodded at me when I came out of the elevator. Brown, bringing up the rear, smiled pleasantly and said, "Good evening, Professor Harris." Then he turned his attention back to the children, frowning as if something puzzled him.

What would have happened if I had pulled Brown aside, right then, and asked him what was bothering him? But it's futile to speculate now.

I went one way, toward my cabin, and they went the other, and that was the end of the encounter. I did wonder, for a moment, why they were here instead of with the rest of the survivors, before realizing they'd gone in the direction of the Admiral's Suite, an old flag office from wartime. It must be the only cabin on the Alley large enough to keep all twelve kids together. With that tiny mystery solved, I thought no more about it.

◀　◀　◀

Freefall is as fun to play in as it is painful to work in, and on my way back from the hangar Tuesday morning I indulged myself in some childish antics. After an almost sleepless night, maybe I was a little punchy that morning. Whatever the motive, I launched myself down the corridor with a reckless leap, grinning as I found I could sail straight down the length of it without needing to fend myself off the walls. When the right-angle turn into the main thoroughfare approached, I reached out to grab a handrail and let my momentum swing me around, then grabbed a ring on the towline and let it pull me down the new corridor.

"Ha!" I laughed aloud at my success, then with an embarrassed smile looked over my shoulder to make sure no one had been watching. Any of the crew would have laughed to see me feeling proud of so simple a maneuver; the aerobatic freefall skills of the Navy put us scientists to shame, even after three months' practice.

But there was no one there; it was still early. I had given up the effort to sleep around 0600 that morning: There was too much on my mind, between the results of our experiment and the disaster. A fitful doze was all I had managed. So instead I went to check over the generators, and found they weren't as badly damaged as they first appeared after run 37. A lot of wires with fried insulation, but the number of vital components that needed replacing was few. Good news to start the day.

The towline pulled me down the corridor toward the Transfer Room, the connection between the sprawling dockyards and the Wheel, and my favorite place on the Alley. It was just a big cylindrical space at the center of the Wheel—in fact, the chamber actually was the axle on which the Wheel spun.

The outer wall of the Transfer Room was divided between the dockyards and the Wheel. Two rows of handholds ran on either side of the seam, constantly passing each other as the Wheel deck rotated. A person could grab hold and be pulled across, into gravity or out of it. Gravity this close to the center was a mere fraction and the hop was easy in either direction.

I liked the place for a nice little illusion it presented. Every child knows gravity in the Colonies comes from rotation, but now that I stood on the Wheel side, it looked like it was the dockyard that rotated—and was the home of mysterious forces. If I'd left some object floating in the dockyards in zero-g, it would appear to orbit some unseen center of gravity.

I always thought the Colonies should have rooms like this, to take children for their first relativity lessons. I stood looking back for a moment, letting my mind wander.

Then I heard a laugh, a child's giggle, but not the delighted sound of a child who's just encountered some new wonder or seen something funny. Rather it was the disturbing laugh of a boy who has just pulled the wings off a butterfly or a soon-to-be bully who has just pushed a classmate down, discovering power for the first time. The laugh sent a crawling sensation up my spine.

I looked around, but I was alone in the chamber. I looked up, toward the dockyard corridor. The lighting had changed; the corridor went dark, and the lights in the Transfer Room took on a reddish tinge. The hatch looked like a black shadow surrounded by a red halo. It reminded me, unpleasantly, of the way the *Lunar Explorer* had appeared on the rec center screen, wreathed by its lifeblood of drive plasma.

I bumped my head and opened my eyes. Suddenly, I was on my back on the deck, beneath the handholds. I sat up. The light was normal white, the corridor as bright as it should be, and there was no sound of giggling. I must have fallen asleep while standing there. I'd let my mind drift, and it had drifted further than I'd intended.

I guess I got even less sleep than I thought.

I shook my head to clear it. I was lucky the slight gravity had made my fall so gentle. I'd probably pay for that sleepless night later in the day; back when I was a student I could pull an all-nighter without consequence, but in recent years a migraine was the usual price. Oh, well.

The strange little dream had already faded. By the time I clambered down the ladder to the main Hub deck, I'd forgotten it completely. I wouldn't remember it again until much later.

CHAPTER THREE

I arrived at the mess hall in time for breakfast and found it busier than usual. I didn't see any of the survivors, but a lot of extra uniforms crowded the room, I suppose displaced by the new arrivals using the other hall. The Alley kept only two of its ten mess halls open. The rest remained unused, like the many empty rooms that marked the Alley's decline from its wartime status.

Stewards bustled around, keeping up with the extra crowd, and the sound of murmured conversation mixed with the clinking of silverware on plates. I could smell coffee and bacon in the air, but knew only the coffee would be any good. I don't know what it was about the Alley—or maybe it was the whole Navy—but they had great coffee and lousy food. I looked over the shoulders of the crewmen in the serving line and saw the bacon was as greasy as ever, and the scrambled eggs as dry as if the cook hadn't bothered to add water to the powder they came from. I skipped it all and poured a cup of coffee, adding a lot of sugar to give the caffeine something to work on.

I found an empty table, took out my handscreen, and called up the data file for yesterday's run, starting a couple of statistical analysis routines. I didn't expect to find out much from them but had to start somewhere. While the computer chewed on the numbers, I sipped my coffee and people-watched.

The next table over, a group of pilots discussed the rescue mission. Those who had actually flown it narrated the details while the others offered critiques. All seemed to regret that they hadn't found more survivors. If only they'd had more time . . .

The dark-haired woman I'd seen before with the children arrived escorted by a steward—it was Brown again—who guided her through the line. She also passed on the bacon and eggs but picked up a plate of fruit slices and a glass of water. Brown left and she stood there wavering, looking from the uniform-crowded tables to the empty ones, apparently uncertain whether she wanted company or not. She settled for the compromise, approaching the table where I sat alone.

"Do you mind if I join you?" she asked.

"No, that'd be great. Please." I waved at a chair.

She put down her tray and sat facing me. "I'm Marta Federova," she said, extending a hand.

I shook it. "Dave Harris."

She fiddled with her food but didn't eat any. Her pale, tired face had no expression and her gray eyes were shadowed. I wasn't sure whether I should make conversation or not.

Suddenly, she laughed, a jagged sound. "Do you mind if I join you," she repeated. "That's a pretty inane thing to say at a time like this, isn't it?"

"I'm not sure there's any good thing to say."

Looking up, her eyes found focus. "I saw you yesterday. In the corridor."

"Yes."

She played with her food some more.

"I wasn't all there yesterday. I got a knock on the head somehow. The medics say I'm okay." She delivered this information in a flat monotone.

Then she seemed to grow more alert. She cocked her head and gave me an inquiring look. "You weren't on the *Explorer*."

"No," I said.

"But you're not in the Navy?"

I shook my head. "I'm a professor at Star City University. Physics. Some colleagues and I are using the Alley's facilities for a project."

"The Alley? Is that what they call this place?" Marta looked around.

"Yeah," I said. "It's just a nickname. Officially, it's 'Naval Station 976' or something like that. But everyone calls it the Alley."

"Oh." She seemed to lose interest; her eyes lost their alert expression. But after a short silence, she snapped back into focus. "Why do they call it that? The Alley?"

"I don't know. I don't think I've ever heard. I know it goes back to the War, that's all."

"Well, it's pretty big for an alley. Huge."

I shrugged. "Pre-Catastrophe architecture. Aren't they all?"

She nodded and picked at her fruit slices. "I got lost looking for the mess hall. The steward had to show me the way."

Another long silence, a fading of interest, and then again an abrupt return. "They've put us in this big suite they said used to belong to some admiral and put a bunch of cots in it. They said it was the only cabin large enough to keep the kids together."

That confirmed my guess the night before. "How are the children? I hope they didn't also get lost on the way here?"

I succeeded in drawing a faint smile. "They're eating in the suite. That steward arranged to have their meals brought there, to avoid having to herd them all over the place. They'd wander off, get lost, like you said."

"But you sneaked out to eat alone?"

This time it was a real smile. "I think I'm justified taking an hour off. I mean, there's supposed to be three of—" She broke off. Her eyes lost focus and she stared at nothing. The smile was gone.

I understood now what she was seeing during those distracted moments, and I mentally kicked myself for taking the conversation back to the accident. Unsure what to say, I let the silence stretch.

Again Marta was the one to break it. As before, she pulled back from her thoughts, her eyes focused, and she was present again. "So you're a physics professor? What's this project you're working on out here?"

"We're working on new hyperfield technology. We want to make two hyperfields overlap."

"Ah." She nodded. "Is that a good thing?" A gleam in her eye revealed a trace of humor, barely discernable behind pale fatigue.

"I guess it depends on what you're interested in."

She leaned forward on her elbows and rested her chin on one hand, her expression showing a bright interest. "Tell me about it."

I hesitated. "I don't want to bore you."

"No, no, it's fascinating. Tell me what your overlapping hyperfields will do for you."

"Well, quite a lot, scientifically. There's a lot we can learn about hyperspatial physics by studying the overlap of two fields. There're also practical benefits, if our theoretical models are right. Drake Williams—he's one of my colleagues on the project—has simulations on a method of generating electricity directly from an overlapping network of hyperfields. No photoelectric panels, no light or heat emitted, the energy would come through in the form of electrical potential. And Professor Assagiri at New Tokyo has a model of overlapping hyperfields that can produce kinetic energy, to drive a spacecraft. No rockets, no fuel, the ship would just go. One of his former students is also on the project, Kyoko Fujiri. And there's other—"

Marta yawned.

I leaned back. "Now, I knew I'd bore you. You have to be cautious around professors: We're all programmed to speak in fifty-minute lectures."

"No, I was just up all night." Without warning, her face went blank again. She spoke, quietly, as if addressing someone not present. "I'm afraid to sleep. If I had been in my cabin when it happened—"

I didn't know what to say. "Well, maybe you should try."

She cut me off and was back in the present. "No, I want to enjoy my new and exciting phobia for a while." She laughed, one sharp bark. "Tell me how you got interested in hyperfields."

I shrugged. "I've just always been fascinated by them. I saw Linda Ryder's first public demonstration in Star City, in the Midway District. I was ten years old and I'd never seen light like that before. I remember my mom telling me it was like the Sun used to be. It was the first time I ever saw her smile . . ."

Now it was my turn to drift into memory, but with an embarrassed laugh, I was back. "So I was hooked. Hyperfields were all I wanted to hear about for years after that."

"Ten years old . . ." Marta gave me a long, speculative look. "You must have been born right before the Catastrophe."

"Yeah. I turned forty-one this past June. I was one of the last children born before it happened."

"I'm on the opposite side. I was one of the kids born after, very likely conceived the same night you found your life's work. So there's a connection between us, if you like."

"Birthday in February 2202?" I guessed. "Drake and Kyoko were both born the same month that year."

"It was quite the baby boom." Marta cocked her head. "What was it like, growing up in the Dark Years?"

That's a question only asked by those who will never understand. People around my age share that secret. Older people get it, partly, but they knew the light of the Sun before. People younger have no idea. How do you explain what it's like being a child in a society that believes there's no future? Going to schools that close down each grade behind you because there aren't any younger kids coming up? I just shrugged and gave my standard answer. "I took it for granted. It was dark, and that was normal. It was cold, and that was normal. There wasn't enough food, and a lot of people got sick and died, and all of it was just—normal."

"Children adapt to things," Marta said. "My kids are handling it better than I am."

I was confused until I saw her eyes lose focus. She was in the wreck of the *Lunar Explorer* again. "It doesn't seem to have affected them at all," she mused. "There was some yelling and crying when it happened, but once that passed . . ."

"Do you, er, know if any of their parents survived?"

She blinked. "What? Oh! Of course, you wouldn't know. None of the children had family on board. They're all orphaned or come from abusive homes. We're taking them back to Star City. A lot of young families move out to the Asteroid Belt looking for all the new jobs, but it's dangerous work out there. Between accidents on the one hand, stress and isolation on the other, the Belt's got a big problem with kids who've lost their families—or need to lose them before they get hurt worse."

"So you're with Colonial Services then?"

Marta nodded. "Child Welfare Agency. We bring groups of these kids back to the Colonies on a regular basis. Too often. Too many. This is the third run Jenny and Tom and I have—"

At once she was back in the accident. Something kept pulling her back there. I had the impression there was something she didn't want to face, but couldn't leave alone. Was it just the shock? Flashbacks caused by trauma? It wasn't a comfortable conversation, and I was afraid of saying the wrong thing, making it worse. The best thing I could do was follow her lead.

After a moment, she was back again. "Tell me more about your project. You want to make hyperfields overlap and do all these marvelous things. Are you sure it's even possible?"

"Oh yes. We know a few types of naturally occurring hyperfields, and they overlap all the time. The human brain generates a natural hyperfield of its own, called the neurofield. It doesn't do anything; it's so weak it's barely detectable, but it has an event horizon with almost a meter radius." I held out my hands to show the size. "You and I are overlapping our neurofields right now."

"Why, Professor, I hardly know you." There was that humor again, a gleam in her eyes that wouldn't allow itself to be completely buried. "So, have you succeeded in copying my overly friendly brain with your fields?"

"We've done it for short periods of time. The neurofield is an important model system for us; we've based a lot of our design on what little we know about it. Just yesterday we had a very successful test. We got the fields to overlap for ninety-three seconds."

"Oh, wow," she said. She looked very impressed—except for that teasing gleam in her eye. "Soon you'll be driving that no-rockets spaceship all the way across the *room*!" She grinned, different from the faint smiles she'd managed until then, one that changed her whole face.

I had to laugh. "Well, we've got to start somewhere."

Then it was gone and she was back in the accident. "There was a lot of flaming gas all around the *Explorer* when we looked back from the lifeboat. I suppose that was the rocket fuel?"

"I suppose."

Marta was silent for a very long time, staring into the distance, and this time she didn't come back or change the subject. Finally, whatever it was she was suppressing came out.

"There was no warning. It was after dinner. I took the kids for a walk along the lifeboat deck. Jenny and Tom said they were going to play cards in one of the lounges. They left. There was a crash and then a screeching, tearing sound, and we were thrown off our feet. The children screamed. I did too." She paused, then without a breath rushed on in a headlong burst: "All the lights went out, and we were in total darkness, and this wind began roaring down the deck so hard you couldn't stand up, and my ears started to pop. I knew it must be the air going out and I thought, I'm going to die here, right here when the last of the air goes. Only, then, the wind died down, and I could still breathe and then some lights came back, and I could see that bulkheads had come down over the corridors. That must have been why the wind died down but there was still a breeze. The air was still leaking out. Some of the crew came around and they grabbed people and threw them into the lifeboats. There wasn't any order or reason to it; they just grabbed whoever was nearest. They grabbed the children and threw them in and threw me in after them, and then we launched. When I looked back there were flames and the whole liner had just been completely torn apart."

She saw it again as she spoke; I could see it in her eyes, as if it was still right in front of her. She had to gasp for breath when she finished speaking, and she gave a shaky laugh.

"Sorry," she said, as if she'd burst into loud sobs and was embarrassed about it. Her gray eyes sparkled as if with tears, though her cheeks were dry.

"It's all right," I said.

She looked better. Still pale, and now even more tired than before, yet somehow healthier. She looked down at her plate as if noticing her food for the first time, and began eating.

"Rehydrated, bleah," she complained as she ate an apple slice. "They're never as crunchy as when they're fresh." But she didn't slow down.

"Yeah, the food here's awful."

"How long have you been here?"

"Three months."

Marta clucked her tongue. "Poor boy." She finished the last of her fruit plate. "I think I could sleep now."

"I should go too," I said. I showed her my handscreen. "I have some results I need to go over. We have a lab meeting coming up."

"Thanks for talking to me," she said. We both stood up.

"If I see you around the next few days, I'll bore you with more professor talk."

She grinned, a comfortable expression, as if she wore it all the time. "I'll get revenge with tales of government paperwork."

She waved and walked away.

◀ ◀ ◀

"Dr. Harris!"

Anne Lindsey, my newest grad student, had not yet learned to call me Dave. She came out of the grad students' office at the same moment I stepped out of mine. Tom Markov emerged right behind her, and I suppressed a smile. My senior grad student, Tom had attached himself to Anne within a week of her arrival. Near as I could tell, they thought no one had noticed they were a couple. But they were hardly ever seen apart.

"Going to the lab meeting?" I asked.

"Yeah," Tom said.

I paused while they caught up to me before we all continued toward the conference room.

"I can't believe I missed the experiment yesterday," Tom said. "Of all the days to decide I'd just stay in my office working on my paper—"

"I'm going to show the video in the lab meeting," I said.

"Not the same." Tom sighed dramatically. "There were really patterns of different energy all over the fields?"

"Yeah."

"I thought that was impossible," said Anne. "I thought the equations said they had to be uniform."

"They do." We turned a corner, and I saw a couple of Drake's students going into the conference room ahead of us. "Obviously the Ryder equations are incomplete in some way. They can't just be wrong, or else—"

"—or else someone would've noticed it before," Tom finished.

"Exactly." I thought about it, slowing to a stop midcorridor. If I could have seen my own face, I bet it would have had the same distant, unfocused look I'd seen on Marta's.

I thought out loud. "Uniform energy emission over a spherical event horizon is a *finding* of Linda's work, not an initial assumption. Obviously the underlying field geometry is not spherical, it's very complex . . . that's what projected onto the energy horizon during the run . . ."

"How do you know, Dr. Harris?" Anne asked.

I came back to the present. "It's *Dave*," I said, not for the first time. "And I know because that's what it looked like." I laughed. "I know we can't publish based on that, but I'm confident when we analyze those patterns, that's what we'll find."

I started walking again, my students trailing. Once inside the conference room, everyone took their usual seats. The lab meeting didn't provide any answers to our momentous experiment, but we managed to define the questions, and formed a plan for what to do next. Kyoko and her electrical engineering team would have to design new instrument arrays. Drake's group would chew on simulations to find what variables in our hyperfields had produced the novel results.

After the meeting, Charles Peretta headed off to the hangar to repair the damage to the generators. John Ikira went with him to assist.

We never saw them alive again.

CHAPTER FOUR

The lab meeting used up the morning. It was a little after noon when I returned to my office, a large but plain room with a metal desk and screen, a couple of chairs, and a single window. The office had one touch of personality: a fabric bulletin board mounted on one wall, with a few antique memos from the Alley's wartime heyday still stuck to it.

As I went to put my handscreen on the desk, it slipped from my fingers, landing on the deck with a clatter. My clumsiness reminded me I was working on too little sleep, though so far I'd managed to avoid the expected headache. I had another analysis program I wanted to run, and maybe after that I'd sneak back to my quarters and take a nap.

But as I bent down to pick up the handscreen, I felt something strange. Just a faint sensation, a sort of mental vibration. It wasn't a physical feeling, more as if my thoughts quivered for a moment.

Its strangeness caught my attention, and I paused midreach, frowning as I puzzled over it. And then, with no more warning than that, the full effect hit like a bomb going off in my face. That's how sharp, sudden, and painful it was. As if I'd been waiting in total darkness and silence, when without warning a searchlight blinded my eyes, a thousand sirens screamed in my ears, and electric shocks crawled up and down my skin. The needle smell of ammonia stung my nostrils and my tongue burned.

I remember screaming at the sudden agony, but that's all I remember of those first few minutes. I must have recoiled on instinct and hit the back of my head against the deck or a wall, because a painful lump formed there later.

What—What— I couldn't think. I couldn't do anything. There was only the shrieking in my ears and the light in my eyes and the electric fire on my skin. I was lying on my back. I curled up in the fetal position, clamping my eyes shut and pressing my hands over my ears, but nothing could block out the glare or the noise.

What's happening? I screamed the question in my mind. I may have screamed it out loud, I don't know. Had there been an explosion? A fire? A collision? Perhaps the Wheel was tearing itself apart. I tried to think through the pain. Escape pod. I had to get to an escape pod. I had to get *out.* Out of my office, out of this fire or whatever it was. Surely I couldn't survive long in this—

Slowly, I realized there was no fire. The pain subsided. It still hurt, but not so bad. The sensory overload continued; but it wasn't killing me. Was it growing less, or was I just getting used to it?

Piece by piece, a strange kind of coherence emerged from the chaos. The harsh glare and shrieking sounds began to take on shape, as if my mind was learning, one step at a time, to make sense of them. I *was* getting used to it.

My eyes were clamped shut, but I could see. I saw my office in every detail. I could feel the size of my office. I felt the prickly sensation of electric current traveling in the wires in the walls. More than that—I saw corridors and rooms beyond it, and others beyond them, until the entire Alley was visible to me. I didn't see through the walls, I saw *around* them. Across the outer bulkhead, I felt space, empty against the Wheel's skin. I tasted . . . roast beef in the mess hall, salt water in the algae tanks, cold metal decks and walls.

There was no perspective, no spatial relationships. I saw behind me as well as in front, saw objects from both sides at once, saw distant things as large as nearby ones. Everything looked like a bad imitation of a Picasso painting.

Glaring lights and black shadows crawled over everything, and the colors were . . . *wrong*. Somehow not like the colors I knew. I heard distant screams and shouts jumbled with the noise of machinery, alien in tone. There were sounds I couldn't identify, sounds that made me sick to hear, sounds not meant for our Universe.

The pain was all gone now, and I didn't seem to be in any immediate danger from—whatever this was. I could think again. But what could I make of this multisensory kaleidoscope?

I've had a stroke, I thought. That must be it. It was the only explanation. These could only be hallucinations. Brain damage—some ruptured artery spraying blood through delicate brain tissues, creating these distorted images.

That meant I needed help. I needed a doctor. I had to get someone's attention. But could I even call out? The world was a jumble. The Picasso illusions overrode everything. I tried to concentrate. I felt my heart pounding: a familiar, real sensation that I held on to.

I flailed out with one hand and hit the floor at my side. That helped. It was another bit of reality. I forced myself to open my eyes.

Yes! That helped more, much more! I could see the drab walls of my office. There was that antique bulletin board. The lightpanels in the ceiling glowed. It looked normal. I could *see* that it looked normal, and the Picasso-world—well, it didn't go away. It was sort of pushed to one side, and then it changed.

I cannot possibly describe what it changed into. There are no words in any human language for it. No longer sight or sound or taste or touch, it became as different from all the familiar senses as a color is different from a musical note. So it became an *other-sense.* And while it still told me about sounds, shapes, and their substance, it did so in an *other* way. It still danced at the edges of my normal senses, wanting back the territory it had lost. I knew it would take my sight and hearing away from me again, if I let it. I had to concentrate on the real world.

I lay on the floor, limp. When I tried to shout, I managed no more than a croak. "Help! Help me!"

No one came; but I doubted I'd called loud enough to be heard. I turned my head and saw my handscreen lying a short distance away where I'd dropped it. I could call the intercom, call the infirmary. Propping myself up on my elbows, I reached for it.

It leaped at me! The moment I reached for it, it jumped up off the deck and threw itself at my hand like a missile. I recoiled with a shout, falling back to the deck, and instantly the handscreen changed course in midair and hurtled away, even faster, striking the far wall hard enough to shatter.

I stared at it, shaking. *What the dust! What the hell! What just happened?*

The ruined screen lay inert on the deck, as if it hadn't just come to life and attacked me. Maybe I imagined it; maybe I actually threw the screen without knowing it. My astonishment cost me my concentration, and the other-sense roared back, replacing my eyesight with Picasso-world again. I had to fight it off a second time, but it was easier than before.

I had to get out of my office where this nightmare had struck me. I'd find help outside. I didn't even think of trying to call for help on the desk screen above me; I just wanted *out.*

Gripping the edge of the desk, I pulled myself up to my knees, feeling dizzy and on the edge of fainting. My vision wavered for a moment, not with ripples of blackness but with ripples of Picasso-world. Standing was out of the question; instead I crawled to the door.

Here I looked up at the door panel. *I will press it with my fingers*, I told myself. *It will not do anything by itself. I will reach out with my hand and press it with my fingers.* I repeated that mantra to myself over and over as I stood on my knees to reach the button.

It worked. Whether the flying handscreen had been all in my head or not, the door control worked normally. I half crawled, half fell through the door as it retracted.

"Help! Someone!" No answer. The corridor wasn't usually busy but there should be someone near enough to see me lying there, if not hear my feeble call.

I struggled up and looked around. There to my left someone lay against the wall. He was in the fetal position, hands over his ears, eyes shut, his face twisted in an expression of pain.

Whatever was happening, it wasn't just happening to me.

I recognized him. It was Jack Elliott, one of our technicians. I gasped. For a second, I thought he was on fire. He had an aura around his head that at first seemed like white flames. But my eyes saw nothing: The white fire only appeared to the other-sense, an illusion of Picasso-world.

I crawled to Jack and grabbed his shoulder. He flinched but didn't open his eyes.

"Jack! Listen to me! Focus on my voice!" I shook him.

He made no sign that he heard me. I tried again.

"Open your eyes. That makes it better. You'll be able to see again. Try! Can you hear me?"

I kept trying but couldn't get him to respond. He hadn't gotten used to this, this effect, whatever it was, the way I had.

"Okay Jack, I'm going to find help . . . hang on, someone will help . . ."

But what help could I expect to find? Seeing Jack, I realized what the other-sense had shown me from the beginning: This effect was all over the Alley.

Everywhere in Picasso-world I could see—sense—people sprawled or curled up on the decks, running blindly, flailing at nothing. Sounds of crashing and shattering, incoherent shouts and screams, came through the other-sense. All was panic and disorder; I could not sense anyone unaffected throughout the whole base.

And everywhere, objects flew around by themselves, exactly as my handscreen had done. Some people were surrounded by storms of such debris. Doors and heavy bulkheads bent and twisted under invisible forces, as if a million poltergeists had arrived to haunt the Alley. Here and there fires sprang up, without any source. If this other-sense was more than a hallucination, then I knew I alone was able to function. Which meant no one was in control of the Alley.

If this didn't stop soon, we were all dead. It could only be a matter of time before this effect damaged something that would kill us all—lifesystems, main power, who knew what. I felt a fluttering hollowness in my gut. Maybe it already had.

I suppose it was the fight-or-flight instinct that let me struggle to my feet, wobbly but without falling over. I had no idea what to do, but knew I had to do something.

I looked around and tried to take stock. I want to say the air was filled with a roaring sound overlaid by loud sirens. I want to say the lighting flickered and distorted, half dark and half lurid red. But none of that was true; it was all the other-sense bleeding into my eyes and ears. The reality was the corridor was silent, the lighting normal, and if not for Picasso-world frizzling my mind, everything would seem calm and quiet.

I left Jack and staggered down the hall, keeping one hand against the wall to steady myself. Ahead was a cross corridor leading over to where Drake and Kyoko had their offices. I seized on the idea that if I could get through to my colleagues, then together we'd think of something. It didn't deserve to be called a plan, but it was better than standing there.

I rounded the corner and saw someone else sprawled on the floor. His head was in flames, and at first I thought it was an illusion like the white-fire around Jack. But after a split second I realized, with a jolt to the stomach, real fire engulfed his head and shoulders.

"God!" I turned back around the corner to find an emergency fire station. But as soon as I spotted one, the extinguisher tore loose from its bracket and leaped at me. I recoiled and it actually turned in midair to fly away, exactly as my handscreen had done. Flailing desperately, I managed to grab ahold of it, then ran back to spray the flames. The fire extinguished easily, but all that remained of the man's head was ash. Even the skull had been consumed, and yet the fire hadn't touched him below the shoulders. My throat clenched at the smell of burned meat. But there was hardly any smoke, not enough to activate the fire suppression system, and I couldn't see any source for the fire. I didn't know who it was. His clothes were civilian, so he was one of our research group, but with no face left, I couldn't recognize him. In shock, my knees gave out, and I collapsed to the deck. The fire extinguisher hit with a metal clang and rolled away.

What the hell is going on? I thought. *Just what the dusted hell is going on here?*

◀ ◀ ◀

I sat stunned for a while. This was a nightmare, a nightmare! Other-senses and flying objects and auras and fires—it was time to wake up.

But there was no waking up.

Jumping to my feet, I lunged for an intercom panel on the wall and got to it before it had time to yank itself out of the wall or do anything unnatural. I jabbed the fire code and the alarm siren echoed up and down the hall.

I liked it. It was better that it sounded like an emergency. Quiet in the real world, while the other-sense raged with noise, was just too confusing.

I waited, but nothing happened. No voices on the PA. No rush of emergency personnel to the scene. The alarm continued. I called up the control room, Commander Warren's office, the infirmary, the com center. I tried Drake's office and Kyoko's and everyone else I could think of. Nothing. Only the squeal of malfunctioning electronics from one call that all at once cut off. The other-sense was right. I was the only one.

I could tell that my colleagues were in their offices and labs, although I couldn't recognize anyone. I saw them all front and back, inside and out.

Everyone I sensed had a white-fire aura, like Jack had. Almost everyone. Here and there, across the Alley, a few people had none—the motionless ones, even down to their still hearts. The white-fire was a sign of life, displayed to the other-sense. How long did any of us have?

Ahead was Kyoko's design lab, and someone stood in the center of it, flailing. It was probably Kyoko herself. I ran there, reeling from

44

side to side as if I were drunk, ignoring my dizziness in my eagerness to reach her. I thought I could get through to Kyoko. She was my colleague. We'd worked together for years. Together, we'd find a way to put an end to this madness.

I came through the door and into a whirlwind. Wrecked and overturned tables and chairs were shoved against the walls, rattling as if trying to escape. In the air, flying debris formed a shrapnel storm of wires and circuit boards, shards of broken screens, keyboards, and drawing tablets, and daggers of wood that had splintered from the furniture. It all hurtled back and forth, bouncing off the walls and lunging at the figure struggling in the center of the chaos.

It was Kyoko. She ran in little circles, arms outstretched, eyes squeezed shut, screaming incoherently. The shrapnel kept striking at her and then rebounding. Her clothes were torn and blood streamed over her face from a cut on her forehead.

"Dust!" I swore. "Oh, God." It was horrible to see Kyoko like that. She was always so controlled.

The white-fire enclosed her head, brighter than Jack's and sending out lashing tendrils of energy to strike at the flying objects. That's what kept them flying: I was seeing—or rather other-sensing—the power I'd used on the handscreen and the extinguisher. Except Kyoko had more of it, and it was entirely out of control.

"Kyoko!" I shouted. "Kyoko, listen to me! It's Dave!"

She gave no sign that she heard.

"Kyoko, you're the one making these things move! You can make them stop! You have to calm down to make them stop!"

I tried to reach her, but when I got close, something shoved me back, soft but inexorable like a wall of pillows. I slid backward across the floor, fetching up against a wall beneath the remains of a table.

Beth lay making soft whimpering noises near the wall nearby. Like Jack, she'd curled up in the fetal position.

"Beth, can you hear me? Beth?"

No answer from Beth either. I cursed under my breath. I had to reach Kyoko first, before she killed herself.

I worked my way back to her, staying low, crawling on the floor. That kept me below the whirlwind and hopefully below Kyoko's force. When I got close, I stood up and grabbed her. Those tendrils of energy pushed me away, and she struggled physically in my arms, but I held on tight.

I put my mouth right next to her ear and whispered, in as calm a tone as I could manage, "Kyoko, calm down. Kyoko, calm down. It's all right. Calm down."

If she'd persisted, she'd have managed to push me away. That force was unnaturally strong, but all at once it ended. She went limp in my arms. Off-balance, we spilled to the floor. Debris rained on the deck for a few seconds as the whirlwind ceased, and her white-fire aura retracted, becoming more like the others I could see, around Beth, around Jack, around most everybody else.

"That's good, Kyoko," I said. "That's good, stay calm. Can you talk to me?"

But she remained unresponsive and wouldn't open her eyes. I tried for several more minutes, with no luck. Then I tried to get through to Beth, all without result.

I could do nothing for them. Unless I found a way to wake up from the nightmare.

I sat on the floor and tried to think. What could I do? I had no clue what caused it, why I alone could handle it, or how to fix it. I didn't even know if it could be fixed. For all I knew, the cause had already stopped, and all this was permanent damage.

The other-sense wouldn't let me think. Wild impressions clamored for attention, creeping into my normal senses. I didn't know how long I could suppress it before I lapsed back, ending up right where I started, where everyone else still was. I wished I could just—

Try to use it.

I froze. The thought came as if from outside. I'd been fighting to ignore the other-sense. I assumed that to stay in control I had to concentrate on ignoring it. But use it? Use it how?

The answer that came was definitely my own, though I had the feeling I was just filling in the details of someone else's idea: *To find a light source, use your eyes. To find what's lighting up the other-sense, use it.*

It made sense. And I had no other ideas. With some reluctance—I wasn't sure I'd ever be able to come back to the real world—I closed my eyes, and let the other-sense take over.

It's data, I told myself. *View it objectively. Analyze it!*

With my eyes closed, Picasso-world flooded back. The effect had the entire base in its grip. The whole Alley was spread out before the other-sense. It was way too much detail to comprehend, but I found I could focus my attention on this or that part. Everywhere, people running, sprawled, or curled up. Flying debris. Structural damage all over, getting worse.

The white-fires contained emotions. It surprised me to realize it; it wasn't like I could feel people's emotions, rather that their aura showed them the same way a facial expression would.

There *was* a source. I could tell. Something was lighting up the Alley for the other-sense. What was it? Where was it? I searched. One of the white-fires was brighter than all the others. Was that it? I studied it. It was wrong somehow. It hurt to sense it, and I had the idea it was more red than white, although it was really an . . .

other-color, if that makes sense. I couldn't detect any emotion in it, nor could I tell anything of the physical person it came from, if it was a person. It was too bright. And it wasn't far away. Over in the direction of the VIP cabins, near the Admiral's Suite where Marta said they'd put the children. I hoped they were all right; that red light felt dangerous. But it wasn't the source of the effect. I kept searching.

From one aura I actually picked up words. I couldn't quite tell if they were spoken aloud or just thought: *hurts like when I was a child and the misharen—* And also: *Eiralynn is—*

I could make nothing of either phrase. But that word *Eiralynn* drew attention to itself; it pulled on my mind somehow. For a moment I thought it was "eight tall men"—it sounded like that, or rhymed with it, but that wasn't it. It was definitely *Eiralynn*. The word had a color to it, red and fearful. But it meant nothing to me.

The aura with the strange words wasn't the source either. What was?

Without warning, the deck lurched underneath me, knocking me off-balance so I sprawled out on the floor. A gigantic metal groan filled the air, followed by an electric hum so loud and deep that I felt it more than heard it, pushing on my eardrums and vibrating under my skin. The deck shuddered, and then came another jolt, so hard it sent me, along with Kyoko and Beth, sliding against the wall.

They didn't react, but I struggled to all fours, gasping with new fear. There could be only one explanation for that motion.

The Wheel had wobbled on its axis. And it continued. The deck rolled in a deep rocking motion, and superimposed on the roll was a constant shudder.

Was it possible the power Kyoko had displayed earlier could have moved so huge a mass? I didn't think so. More likely something had happened to the controls, attitude thrusters firing out of sequence or something. Whatever the cause, I was out of time. There was no way the Alley could withstand this kind of stress for long. The electric hum must be the overstressed maglev bearings, the groaning sound of the Wheel's superstructure twisting under the strain. If it didn't stop, the base would tear itself apart. The crew needed to take charge *now*.

I had to see the answer. It was there. It was right in front of me. *Use your eyes to find a light source, use the other-sense to find—*

I got it! It was so obvious, like any puzzle after the solution is revealed. Something was lighting up the Alley for the other-sense. It was fanning those white-fires around everyone's heads until they were bright, destructive, and out of control. I could sense nothing from the source directly, but I could tell the direction it came from. It was out in the dockyards, in one particular hangar, not far from the Wheel. Our hangar.

And with that, the ideas dropped into place like falling dominoes. Obvious.

A hyperfield could drive a spaceship without rockets.
A hyperfield-based sensing device could see through anything.
Six impossible things before breakfast.

It was our generators. I took off running.

CHAPTER FIVE

Our offices lay about halfway between two of the six spokes that connected the Wheel's main decks to the Hub. I had no idea whether spoke D or E was closer. I ran for E out of habit since our mess hall on deck 3 was off the spoke E elevators.

The deck stopped shuddering, but the swaying continued. Combined with my own dizziness, it kept me reeling from one side of the corridor to the other, rebounding off the walls. I fell more than once, but picked up and ran again. Most everyone I saw was curled against the walls. I didn't stop or try to reach any of them. One man—a crewman, not anyone I knew—sat babbling nonsense words in a loud voice. The other-sense gave me flashes of more junk storms like the one that had surrounded Kyoko, but I didn't stop to help there either.

What if the shaking stopped because the Hub's torn apart, leaving the Wheel spinning free? I thought about how the atmosphere would rush out next—

Alex Montgomery, one of Drake's grad students, passed me in the opposite direction. He was running, eyes wide, screaming at the top of his lungs. A cloud of shrapnel followed him. I hit the deck, letting the storm pass over my head. A few meters farther down, a door suddenly bulged outward into the corridor, as if it were a piece of soft plastic someone was shoving from behind. The power this effect produced—was it that strong?

I heard more screaming, thuds, and crashes. The auras of fear, panic, and pain that I felt with the other-sense threatened to overwhelm my mind, but that wasn't the worst. I came face-to-face with another of Drake's students, Eric Ivanov, who turned to face me and opened his mouth as if about to speak, then burst into flames, fire spraying out of his mouth and eyes, jetting at my face. I recoiled. His hair burned, and I could see his skin blackening. I froze, stunned. Then I tackled him, throwing myself on top of him in hopes of smothering the flames. The fire went out easily enough, but by the time I acted, it was too late.

I suppose if it had kept burning, there would have been nothing left of his head but ash, like the other body I found. But instead his charred features remained, black and withered, empty eye sockets staring upward, lips drawn back in a snarl. Like before, there was almost no smoke. But the burned smell thickened the air and clung to my scorched shirt.

I left him lying there, and ran on, although every impulse was to stay. After a lifetime of civilized behavior, it felt wrong to pass by so much pain and suffering, but no officials were on their way, and I couldn't help Eric now. I couldn't help anyone, except by reaching the generators and shutting them down. So I ran, with clenched fists and an imagination filled with images of fire consuming Drake, Kyoko, Tom, Anne, and Beth and—

Reaching the elevator lobby, I hesitated. Above me I could sense the metal column reaching a hundred and seventy meters up to the Hub.

Did I dare take the elevator? If the spoke was bent or twisted after the Wheel's wobbling, if even some minor damage had occurred, if the elevator stuck while I was in it, that would be the end.

There was no one to come get me out. I'd sit there until the Alley came apart, while the effect raged on and my friends who weren't already beaten to death by flying scrap burned, one by one.

Or I could climb the emergency stairs, the equivalent of fifty-six decks. I was no athlete and I wasn't sure I could make that climb even under the best conditions. I *was* sure it would take a long time, even with the gravity diminishing as I climbed.

With the other-sense, I tried as best I could to study the elevator shaft above me. It seemed clear and open, but I couldn't really tell. The other-sense was powerful, but it was a sense, not an engineering report. I wouldn't recognize a mechanical fault in the shaft even if I "saw" it.

It would have to be the stairs. The risk of the elevator was too great, though I hated the time it would take: My mind filled with pictures of the Wheel finally tearing itself to bits while I made the long climb.

I entered the closet-size stairwell to the left of the elevators and looked up at the steep metal steps rising in flights to a vanishing point overhead. Our offices were on the outermost Wheel deck, giving me the longest possible climb.

As I started, I tried to pace myself but that mental picture of the Wheel coming apart around me drove me on. The stairwell echoed with the sounds of groaning metal and the electric hum of the bearings from far above. I was panting by the time I reached the inner bulkhead of the Wheel. Five decks climbed and fifty-one to go. Already my legs ached, my heart pounded.

Above the bulkhead the stairwell opened out into the spoke itself. The interior was hollow, a honeycomb of support girders in triangular bracing patterns, and the stairs switched back and forth as they climbed between them. I could see the whole climb ahead of me extending up to a tiny hexagonal patch, all I could see of the outer Hub bulkhead.

The noises from above echoed off the walls and girders. Clangs and bangs and metallic screeches surrounded me and yet I couldn't tell where any of it came from. I smelled ozone, but I could neither see nor sense any obvious electrical shorts.

Up one flight, turn around, up the next, and on, and on.

Ignore the pain in your legs and the burning in your chest, I told myself. *Keep going.*

The bottom of the shaft dwindled as I climbed while the top came no nearer. The gravity lessened as I climbed but the stairs became steeper, designed for the lower gravity. I forced myself to climb faster. I wasn't sure which screamed louder for me to stop, my lungs or my legs. Finally my legs gave out, and I fell, gasping for air, to the grating. I would have to rest before going on.

I'll bet the crew does this climb in one go without even raising their heartbeats, I thought. I always knew I'd have to pay for my sedentary life one day. I just thought it would be in a doctor's office, receiving news of a bad heart. Not climbing for my life and the lives of countless others on an out-of-control space station.

I looked over the edge, and tried to compare the distance above with that below. Maybe I'd climbed twenty or so decks. I was as far from the noise of confused minds and their poltergeist whirlwinds as I could be. I sensed them below, all those white-fire auras, and I sensed more above, but here, halfway between Wheel decks and Hub decks, all were distant. I was alone. During the entire effect, the other-sense had never seemed more calm and orderly—almost *right* somehow—than it did at that moment.

After my breathing eased somewhat and my heart's pounding wasn't quite so labored, I hauled myself to my feet and started up again, with a jabbing protest from my legs that made me groan aloud. I moved on autopilot, my mind wandering, trying not to think of the pain in my muscles. Up one flight, turn around, up the next.

I heard a hissing sound above but paid no attention to it, nor did I notice the smell. Every breath burned now, so the extra sting didn't attract my attention until I climbed right into a cloud of fumes spraying out of a damaged pipe. Panting, I took in a full breath of the caustic vapor. It burned my eyes, mouth, and throat. Gagging, I doubled over coughing, and lost my footing, making me tumble down the stairs to the next landing, where my head struck a guardrail hard enough to send shooting stars across my eyes. The clang of the impact echoed through the spoke. I was lucky I didn't go over the rail and hit the Wheel deck far below.

Between savage coughs, I gasped for air. My eyes watered, stinging. Whatever that gas was, it was no part of the lifesystem. I half crawled and half slid down two more flights, until my breathing eased and I couldn't smell the gas anymore. When I stopped coughing, I looked back up.

The gas formed a white cloud across the stairs. It jetted from a burst pipe, and the force of the spray carried it across the steps and out into the interior of the spoke. It didn't disperse much, and whatever it was must have been heavier than air because I could see it trailing downward, like a stream of water coming out of a hose.

I'd have to hold my breath while I ran through the cloud. If it really was heavier than air, I'd be able to get above it and breathe again.

But there was no chance of holding my breath until I rested some more. I waited while I watched the cloud, worrying that it might spread in my direction. When I smelled its sharp, stinging scent, I knew I was out of time and had to try.

I took a couple of deep breaths and, squinting my eyes against the burning, I leaped up the stairs, into the cloud and as far past it as I could go before I let the breath explode out of me. I gasped for air. It was clean: I'd made it past.

I climbed again. It was impossible to rebuild my momentum, I could only trudge upward. But I'd climbed more than halfway now—the gravity was down to 0.5 g and would offer less of an obstacle.

The stairs grew steeper, eventually becoming a ladder. No more landings and back-and-forth flights; it was a straight shot up a tube of safety bars right to the Hub. I used my arms as much as my legs now, pulling myself upward fast enough to feel the Coriolis force pushing me sideways. Off to the far side of the spoke, a cluster of torn electrical cables sparked furiously. I wasn't looking up when I banged my head again. A solid deck barred my way: the underside of the Hub. I'd made it.

I climbed onto a landing to my right. Above it, the hatchway stood open. It should have been closed, but I could see that the frame had twisted. Gravity was just a fraction now, and I only had to grab the edge and pull myself up to the Hub deck.

Elevator bank E and its parallel flight of stairs opened into the center of the Observation Gallery, a huge open space nicely decorated for visiting VIPs, three decks tall, stretching from one side of the Hub to the other and about a quarter of the way around its circumference. The outer walls were entirely transparent, and apart from the orderly forest of support girders, the whole Gallery was open floor space.

Here in the Hub, where the Wheel's wobble had impacted the bearings that should have kept it in place, I saw the worst damage I'd seen yet. One entire wall had been shoved inward into a bow shape, warping the transparency. The girders along that side were bent and twisted, and the deck had crumpled into accordion folds.

I could see the housing of the maglev bearings outside at the top of the window. When the Wheel wobbled, it must have shoved the Hub wall against it, crushing the wall inward. If those transparent walls had been glass, they'd have shattered. But the air was still: No rush of air blew from any breach into space. Still, it must have been close.

If there was another jolt like the last one—the bearings had held up this long, but couldn't hold up forever. Someone must stabilize the platform, and soon. I could sense that the people nearby, the officers in the control room and the crew out in the dockyards, were as badly off as those I'd left below.

Time was running out. I couldn't stand gawking at the damage; I had to go.

I jumped for the handrail above the stairs, easily catching it and swinging myself up to the mezzanine. After climbing another ladder I found myself between the maglev bearings themselves.

Here the hum wasn't a sound but an earthquake. I saw no damage, but I had no time to puzzle over that. One final ascent, effortless now in gravity so slight I could barely feel it, and then I reached the Transfer Room. I grabbed a handhold and let it pull me into zero-g, then kicked off for the circular opening of the main corridor. The towline wasn't running, so I pulled myself along by the handholds.

There were lots of crew in the corridor, all of them in the same condition I'd seen before. Instead of lying or crouching on the deck, they floated. I had to push my way around them. I didn't encounter anyone with a debris storm around him, but I did see one burned body, the ashes just hovering where there had once been a head.

It was ahead of me now, the source of the effect. My hyperfield generators were somehow boosting those white-fire auras we all had. Now that I drew close, the effect grew stronger. The other-sense became more vivid, more insistent, and it started to leak into my normal senses again. I felt it, saw it, tasted it, alien and wrong. And it began to hurt again, the same pain as before, what seemed like ages ago when it hit me in my office.

I suppose if I could have observed myself with the other-sense, I'd have sensed my own white-fire getting brighter and brighter as I got closer to the source, and as the pain mounted, I worried that I might burn like the others. It struck me those real fires might have come from the white-fires getting *too* bright.

I turned a corner and felt a breeze behind me, pushing me along. Somewhere up ahead, what I feared most had happened: There was a breach. Air was leaking into space.

No time, no time! I had dawdled, speculating about the Alley's damage and what the other-sense was doing, and now it was too late. Even if I could bring the effect to a halt, how long would it take the crew to recover? To respond to the damage? Maybe never. Maybe the generators had already destroyed the brains of the victims.

My panic made me clumsy, and as I grabbed for handholds in frantic haste, I missed them as often as I caught them. I bumped into the wall and tumbled, bouncing off the opposite wall at an angle, flailing for a hold.

I moved against a shock wave of energy now, blasting into my mind and pumping up the other-sense into an outraged scream of meaningless noise. My ears roared and blackness darkened my peripheral vision. Every push forward took an effort, as if the effect was trying to keep me away, to prevent me from shutting it down. By the time I turned the last corner and saw the hatch to the OCC ahead, I was trembling and panting harder than I had been during the climb. The pain was deep in my head, my senses scrambled. I smelled metal burning, heard the electricity in the cables.

Charles and John floated limp in the middle of the OCC, and there were no white-fires around their heads. Both were dead.

I looked out the window into the hangar and saw nothing. The generators looked dark, with no sign of any active hyperfields around them. Was I wrong about the cause? No—I could *sense* it, I could *feel* it. It all came from right here, so close I was burning. I was too close and couldn't stand another second of the pain.

With dimming eyes I saw the consoles were live, their indicator lights green as if they were running an ordinary hyperfield test. I thrashed my hands at the controls but couldn't work the keyboard. I couldn't even see the buttons in any way that made sense, yet I still slapped at them futilely. I was fading fast. It wasn't just hurting me, it was damaging me. I couldn't stay conscious under it for long. I was too close. Sight and sound were gone, even Picasso-world had broken down in blasts of thunder and lightning behind my eyes.

It was killing me.

I made a wild leap away from the console, searching with my fingers for the power breaker. I pictured Commander Warren waiting there during our last experiment, run 37, with his hand on the switch ready to cut the power. Where was he now? No, *I* needed to pull it. Warren wasn't here. I couldn't think. Where was I? I wanted Warren to—

No! Think! Pull the breaker! Shut it down!

I felt the panel beneath my hands, soft and alien. I felt my fingers sink into the metal, but that was just the other-sense. I struggled to feel what was real.

Where's the switch, where's the switch, WHERE'S THE SWITCH?

Nothing felt like it was supposed to. I flailed at every button I could find, with no real idea what I was hitting.

And then I found the right one. With cataclysmic suddenness, it was over. The other-sense ended. No bang, no fade, it just stopped. I felt blind and deaf. The pain was gone, but so was every other sensation. I floated in dark silence, disoriented and exhausted, my head spun, and then I lost consciousness.

CHAPTER SIX

Was I awake? Was I even alive? I couldn't tell. I floated in darkness and silence, touching nothing, without sensation. Cogito, ergo sum. If I could ask myself the questions, then I must be both alive and awake. I stretched out full length but still didn't touch anything. I knew where I was now: still in the OCC, floating somewhere in the middle of the room. I must finally have hit the main power breaker, not just for the generators, but for the whole hangar. There were no lights, the PA speakers were dead, all the consoles dark.

The other-sense was gone, and nothing hurt but the muscles of my legs and an ache from the bruise on my head: normal pains, almost comforting. But what about the Alley? Had everyone else— recovered? I needed to get out of the OCC. I tried again to reach a wall or console or something, but couldn't. It's hard to get moving in freefall without something to push off from. The instinct when adrift in freefall is to swim in the air, but air isn't thick enough. So I held still and waited to drift into something. It shouldn't take long; the OCC wasn't that big of a room.

I could hear something. A distant ringing in my ears . . . it dawned on me that it was the sound of the Alley's alarm signal, drifting down from the nearest working speaker. It had sounded when I first pulled the fire alarm back down in the Wheel. Had nothing changed, then?

But then—a voice. Oh blessed, wonderful relief! I couldn't make out the words, but I could tell it wasn't a recording. The tone and rhythm sounded like someone giving orders. It didn't sound like Commander Warren, but it was someone in control. I sighed as the tension drained out of me. We might still be in danger, but at least someone was back in command of the base.

I bumped into something and grabbed at it, feeling cloth over softness. It was a body, either Charles or John.

It was the stuff of a horror video, alone in the dark with two dead bodies. I'd felt horror enough during the effect, seeing Eric burn, seeing Kyoko screaming in the center of a whirlwind. But not now. I was done with horror for the moment. What I felt was a sudden, overwhelming rage. This body in my hands, one of my friends. Back in the Wheel, others were dead, still more injured. All because of my generators. My work. How could it have happened? How was it possible?

I wanted to put my fist through a console. I wanted to go out into the hangar and smash the generators to bits with a hammer. I wanted to scream at the top of my lungs. How could I not have seen it coming?

I held the body, my fingers clenching its clothing, and took a deep breath. The spasm of rage passed as suddenly as it began, leaving behind a hollow ache in my chest. I closed my eyes, needlessly since it was dark. I pulled the lifeless form close and whispered, "I'm sorry. I'm so sorry."

Then I pushed off against the body. A second later, I touched one of the walls and grabbed for something to hold on to, finding one of the handholds that sprouted from the walls of all zero-g rooms. I heard an ugly, inanimate sound as the body bumped into the opposite wall.

"I'm sorry," I said again.

Keeping hold with one hand, I turned my back to the wall, peering into the darkness.

I saw a thin seam of light, just visible as my eyes adjusted. It had to be the door into the corridor. It must have closed behind me after I entered during the effect.

Carefully feeling for one handhold after another, I made my way around the room toward that seam of light. It would have been quicker to just push off toward it, but I didn't want to risk losing my bearings again. I tensed each time I put out a hand, dreading the feel of soft flesh instead of metal, but encountered only bundles of cable or the corners of consoles.

Finally, my fingers closed around a metal rod I recognized as part of the door's hinge system. With power out, I'd have to use the manual latch. I felt around, found the latch, and pumped the handle. The door slid open.

The light I'd seen through the seam in the door came from the intersecting corridor ten meters away. The lights here by the hangar were out, like those inside. I pulled through the hatch and then looked back. The open door gaped like the mouth of a cave or a tomb, the dark gate of a graveyard tomb where vampires or zombies might lurk. But this tomb held a monster of another kind, one that could bewitch people so their senses went crazy and their heads burst into flames. I shuddered, and turned away quickly.

Pulling myself toward the light, I found an intercom panel. The clock display showed 1427 hours. I couldn't believe it—barely two hours since it had all started! I would have guessed I'd spent longer than that on the climb up the spoke alone. Could it be that an entire day had passed, and it was 1427 hours again? Surely not.

As I reached the panel, the sirens cut off and the voice on the PA stopped, ending a series of cryptic announcements issuing orders in jargon I didn't really know. "Stand by for further instructions," the PA concluded. The only sentence I understood.

I heard voices, very distant, far off down the corridor. I noticed the breeze had stopped and guessed the people down there must be a damage control party, and they'd already sealed the breach.

I called in and got a young officer—by the sound of his voice no older than his early twenties. He sounded like he was barely hanging on as he stammered his way through a series of obviously scripted questions, probably part of some disaster protocol. He asked me if there were any wounded at my location. Were there any open fires or atmosphere leaks? That sort of thing. I answered, telling him there were two dead but no wounded, but when he started to say it would take some time before anyone could get to me, I departed from his script.

"This is where it started," I said.

There was a moment of silence.

"Uh, say that again?"

"This . . . effect, whatever it was, it was caused by my hyperfield generators."

Another pause. I heard a babble of voices in the background calling out reports and orders.

"Uh, Professor Harris, your location is—oh yes, that's the hangar assigned to your research project." The officer paused, I imagined to collect himself.

His confusion didn't surprise me. Just the opposite. I was surprised that he or anyone else could function at all. This wasn't a collision or fire or some kind of accident anyone could anticipate. Everyone had just had their brains scrambled for two hours. And yet down the corridor a crew had already plugged an atmosphere leak, other parties no doubt were working on repairing other damage, and this kid might be getting by on habit and a prewritten script, but he was getting by. Wasn't that what the combination of planning and training was supposed to do anyway? Score one for the Navy, and I was glad of it.

After a few seconds the officer resumed, "Do I understand you to say that your equipment caused this emergency?"

"Yes."

"Will you stand by while I pass on that information?"

"All right."

There was a much longer pause, and when the officer came back he said, "Will you please come to the control deck immediately? Commander Warren wants to speak to you."

I'll bet he does, I thought. Aloud, I said, "On my way."

◀   ◀   ◀

The Commander stood in the center of a different kind of whirlwind. Officers and crew crowded the control deck, their voices filling the air, speaking with purpose—an altogether different sound from the shouting and screaming during the effect. Although at first glance, this new chaos seemed almost as bad. Everyone talked at once, shouting reports and asking questions on a dozen different priorities. From what I could overhear, the Alley was off-station, tumbling end over end, and one or more ships had torn loose from their moorings and crashed through the dockyard structures. Automatic bulkheads had prevented too much atmosphere loss but a few minor breaches remained—likely the cause of the breeze I'd felt before.

Warren's attention flicked this way and that, somehow listening to it all and issuing orders on every different crisis in the same crisp, level tone, as if he was organizing a routine shift change. I was amazed at his composure. Here was a new perspective on a man I'd known primarily as the genial, interested host who liked to bet in

Drake's pool. I knew he was the commanding officer of a rescue station but I hadn't seen him at work in a real emergency before. I was glad he was in charge; I'd have been utterly overwhelmed.

Warren leaned over the shoulder of Lieutenant Peterson, the one who'd reported the *Lunar Explorer*'s distress call the day before, and studied a diagram on Peterson's screen. It looked like an orbital plot. The Commander looked up and nodded as I approached, his eyes cold when they met mine, and then he returned to the screen.

I had to wait my turn for his attention. I didn't mind, not expecting our conversation to be enjoyable. While I waited, I looked around.

I'd visited the control room a few times before, and thought it showed the Alley's decline from wartime days more clearly than anywhere else. Rows and rows of consoles once busy with operations for an entire Colonial fleet stood empty, with only one corner of the room remaining active to monitor the Alley's own operations and that of its little rescue squadron. Now junk strewed the floor, screens had shattered, spaghetti tangles of wire trailed between the broken pieces.

"How reliable is this?" Warren asked.

I turned back to him, but he was talking to Peterson.

"It's preliminary, Commander," the officer replied. "Based on only fifteen minutes' plot so far."

"Very well. Continue."

Peterson switched his screen to a scrolling text display. "Gateway station and FLEETCOM-LUNA are both tracking us and trying to refine our new orbit. We're falling away from the L2 point at a bad angle for any ships on the Gateway routes to match orbits. If these numbers hold, our next window for a safe rendezvous is about eight days from now. The *Yamato* and the *Britannia* can reach us in a few hours if they use emergency acceleration, but only if they start in the next fifteen minutes. Even if they do, they couldn't leave again until that window opens in eight days."

"So we can't get the civilians off any sooner either way." Warren frowned, and cursed under his breath. "Dust it, I wish we could—tell FLEETCOM I do not request the *Yamato* or *Britannia* meet us with emergency acceleration. There's no point risking their crews when all they can do is join us for a week's ride."

"Sir," Peterson acknowledged.

Warren straightened up and regarded me with an expression hard enough to break rocks. In a tone of voice that must have been passed down from drill sergeant to raw recruit since the days of the Roman legions, he said: "Did you know something like this could happen?"

"No," I said.

I thought: *I should have. Somehow, I should have known.* But I didn't say it.

Warren kept me nailed down under that hard glare for several more seconds. It was an effort to meet his eyes. Finally, his expression softened just the tiniest amount. "All right, I'll accept that. Can it happen again?"

"No. I pulled the power breaker to the whole hangar. The generators can't possibly activate now."

"Okay, Professor. What's the story?"

"I don't know, yet. The generators got turned on somehow."

"Somehow? Weren't you there?"

"No, I was in my office when it started. We had two technicians working on the generators, Charles Peretta and John Ikira, but they'd have no reason to activate any hyperfields. I don't know how it happened."

"What do they say?"

"They're dead."

"Burned?"

I shuddered. "You know about the burn victims, then? I saw two. But Charles and John were just . . . dead." I frowned, disliking what I had to say next. "As for the effect the hyperfields produced, that's a mystery. I have no idea what they did, or how."

"Then why do you believe your equipment caused it?"

That was the hard question. I knew I couldn't talk about other-senses and Picasso-world without sounding utterly crazy, and unless someone else turned up with similar experiences during the effect, I had no evidence, other than the fact the effect ceased when I cut the power.

I tried to keep it simple. "I could feel the direction it was coming from, somehow. It got stronger as I got near the hangar, and when I shut down the power everything stopped at once."

"You felt the direction." Warren stared at me. Around him the shouting of reports and requests continued, and I knew he was impatient. A number of officers hovered nearby, waiting their turn with the Commander.

"It's a long story," I said. "Maybe we should talk about it later—"

"We'll talk about it now, I think. You seem to have *felt* a lot. I don't remember anything but pain and some kind of nightmare. I sure couldn't have gone from here to the hangar under my own power. But you came all the way from the Wheel?"

"It flattened me at first," I said. "Like everyone else, I guess, but for some reason I—I don't know, I got used to it. Before you ask, I have no idea why. I didn't see anyone else who recovered. Maybe you'll find someone. Anyway, I got better. And like I said, I could feel the direction it came from."

Warren frowned and looked out across the room toward the windows that overlooked the dockyards. He took a deep breath.

"Professor, we have thirty-four confirmed dead and we're still searching. More than two hundred injured. The base has sustained considerable damage, and we've fallen off the L2 point into what looks like the worst possible orbit for making any rendezvous, or for having the Alley return to any location where it can usefully function. There's a very real possibility we'll have to abandon this facility."

He turned back to face me. "There will of course be an inquiry, and when it's done, heads will roll. Mine, almost certainly."

"Yours?" I protested. "Commander, this was my equipment. It's no one's fault but—"

"I'm in command here, Professor." Warren's tone indicated that was all the explanation needed on that score. "Your head will likely be on the chopping block too, if you're right that your generators were the cause."

"I know," I said.

"Before you fall on that sword, Professor, you'd better have more to say than just that you had a feeling."

"I hear what you're telling me, Commander," I said. "I am going to find out exactly what happened here—and why."

"Then I won't keep you." Warren's attention shifted away from me as completely as if I'd never been in the room. "Mr. Fisher, I want that status report on thruster capacity—"

Even as a civilian, I felt an impulse to salute. Instead, I turned and left.

◀ ◀ ◀

After all my worries about the elevators on the way up, I entered one going down without even thinking. But then again, if it got stuck now, there'd be someone to get me out. I only realized I'd taken the wrong elevator when I emerged back on Wheel deck 5. I'd come down spoke A, stepping out into the center of the *Lunar Explorer*'s survivors' quarters.

People wandered up and down the corridors, dazed. Some huddled against the walls or sat curled up, as lost as any I'd seen during the effect. The chaos was so bad I thought for a moment the effect had returned. A second disaster coming right on the heels of the *Lunar Explorer* crash was just too much for them. Doubly traumatized, the result was sheer panic.

Medics and other crewmen tried to calm everybody down, but they were too few.

Cabin doors stood open, and I could see broken furniture and debris scattered across the floors. In the corridor too, signs of damage were everywhere. Including one scorch mark on the floor where a body had recently been removed. It was hot and stuffy in the pressing crowd, and a thick smell of sweat and fear hung in the air.

I pressed back against the elevator door as it closed behind me, and stared at the scene in horror. *All of this is your fault*, I told myself. The hyperfields were my invention. Linda Ryder's originals had been used for thirty years without causing anything like this. Only mine.

I should have expected it. Somehow I should have known it could happen. Now all I could do was figure it out after the fact, when it was too late to do any good. Maybe I should just call it off, shut down my research, and get a job in some bank. I couldn't kill anyone that way.

I thought about retreating back up to the Hub, going across up there to the elevators that came down near our offices. It was probably quicker than walking halfway around the Wheel, and I'd avoid all this mess. But I didn't. Feeling like it was a kind of penance, I shoved my way into the crowd, and made myself look at every detail as I went along.

Crewmen hurried up and down the corridor, often assisting injured survivors, twice pulling someone on a gurney. I walked close to the wall to stay out of their way.

Hearing a whimper, I looked around. I'd just passed a cross corridor. It looked deserted; I saw no medics or crewmen. I heard the whimpering again. It was a woman's voice. I followed the sound.

The corridor ended at an intersection with another hallway, just a short stretch with cul-de-sacs at either end. No cabin doors, just a series of storage lockers. I suppose that's why no crew had checked the area.

After the mayhem of the crowd, the short corridor was almost oppressively quiet. The soft whimpering echoed. A woman huddled in the corner at the end of the hall to my right. She had her knees drawn up, her head bowed down over them. Her arms were folded over her head as if she was shielding herself from falling debris. Her Navy uniform told me she was crew, not a *Lunar Explorer* survivor. The uniform had no rank insignia, meaning she was enlisted rather than an officer. Someone in the maintenance crew perhaps, caught by the effect in this little-traveled storage area.

I hesitated, looking back. Should I try to get a medic? She didn't look injured, and I'd seen plenty like her back in the crowd. The medics were leaving those in her condition alone while they attended to the more obvious injuries. I went to the woman's side and crouched down.

"Are you all right?"

She gave no response, just kept whimpering and rocking back and forth. She really seemed just like the people I'd passed during the effect, and I wondered if I could get through to her now that it was over.

The name on her shoulder patch was Pierson. "Crewman Pierson. You're all right, it's over now. Come on, let me take you where you can get help. Can you stand up? Pierson?" I tried to keep my voice calm.

I was oddly determined to get through to her, as if the whole mess would get better if I could just help *one* victim, just one. And with no need to race for the generators, I decided to stay and keep trying.

At first, I did no better than during the effect. But after I'd called her name for what felt like a long time, I heard her whisper something I couldn't make out.

"What did you say?" I leaned in to hear.

"Don't make me see it again."

"See what?"

"I won't look. I won't, I won't. I don't wanna see it again," she said, her voice a little girl's frightened whine.

What had she seen that so terrified her? Had she experienced the other-sense that I had, or was it just some nightmare? I stopped myself from asking, certain it'd be the wrong thing to do.

"It's gone now," I said. "You won't see it again. Come on, let's go somewhere you can get some help."

She sobbed. "If I open my eyes it'll be there, I know it will. Don't make me."

I sighed. "All right. You don't have to. You just stay there. Everything will be all right."

I couldn't think what else to do. At least I'd gotten her to respond. I'd tell one of the medics about her, so she wouldn't be overlooked.

71

"On your feet, crewman! Attention!"

My heart skipped a beat when the unexpected voice shouted right behind my ear. I jumped, whirling around.

It was the woman I'd met at breakfast. Marta Federova. She had a medic's tunic pulled over her shirt and a large bruise marked her forehead, but otherwise she seemed all right. In fact, she seemed a good deal better than before.

As our eyes met she flashed a quick smile, then looked sternly at the woman on the floor.

"I said get up! Move it!" Marta's clear voice was no match for Warren's gravelly tone, but she still managed a passable drill sergeant shout. "What do you think you're doing, lying around on the floor during an emergency? Didn't you hear the alarm?" There wasn't a trace of gentleness in her voice; she barked out each syllable like a slap.

Pierson looked up, eyes wide, mouth gaping. "I—I—I—"

"Don't sit there stammering at me. Get on your feet! What's your station at general quarters?"

"F-f-fire control. Wheel deck three section fifteen." Pierson scrambled to her feet and stood at attention, shaking all over but trying to hold herself together.

Marta's eyes flicked to the shoulder badge. "You don't look injured, Pierson, why aren't you there?"

"I, I'm sorry, I just—it was just—"

"Look at me, Pierson." Marta stepped closer and looked the woman in the eyes. She softened her voice, but kept her crisp military tone. "Eyes front. Look at me. You with me now?"

"Yes. I'm sorry, I was—"

"Don't apologize, just stay with me. Now. Are you injured?"

"N-no. I don't think so."

"Good. Then get to your duty station. Move it."

72

"Yes, ma'am." Pierson managed an uncertain salute, then ran down the corridor.

I watched the whole scene in silent amazement. As Crewman Pierson vanished around the corner, Marta dropped her military act and grinned at me. Again I noticed the expression fit her face with easy familiarity. "Honestly Dave, have you never seen a video? You slap people who're hysterical, you don't croon at them."

I groped for something to say. "I—was that—shouldn't we have taken her to the infirmary or something?"

She shook her head. "They've got enough real injuries to deal with, and this is still a Navy base at emergency stations, remember? She's on her feet. She's not bleeding. They'd send her to her post anyway. Best thing for her, really. Best thing for hysteria is just to snap out of it and do something."

"I'll take your word for it."

"That'd be smart, since you clearly have no clue." Her grin and a mischievous gleam in her gray eyes took the sting out of her words, and despite my mood, I had to answer her infectious smile with one of my own.

"I guess I don't. So, are you all right?"

"I got off easy," she said. "I slept through it. Never knew anything was wrong until a crewman pounded on my door to see if I was okay. So I missed the big brain fry and got some good rest as well. Ironic, isn't it? I escape one disaster by being awake and another by being asleep." She seemed positively chipper, in stark contrast to everything else going on.

"And you've been recruited by the Alley's medical staff."

"They were slammed. I spent a couple of summers in college working at the psych office of the Navy hospital in New London, so I volunteered. I'm helping out where I can—you know, rescuing

floundering physicists from hysterical crewmen, that sort of thing."
She grinned again.

"What about the kids with you?"

"They've stuck a steward from the *Lunar Explorer* in with them.
Teresa's her name. She's doing okay—also slept through the party—
so I left the kids with her. They're all right too." Marta paused, and
looked thoughtful. "A little peculiar, actually. They *weren't* asleep,
but none of them seemed hurt. When I woke, they were laughing
and talked about it almost as if it was some kind of game—about
how they could make things fly in the air. But all the adults I've
talked to say it was pretty unpleasant."

"It was," I said.

"All the junk lying around, you'd almost believe the kids weren't
imagining the bit about making stuff fly. Everyone must have been
pretty wild under its influence to create such a mess. Our quarters
are the same, everything's tossed up. Thankfully none of the children were injured. They talk like they loved it."

I thought about the differences in brain function between asleep
and awake, between a child and an adult. Had anyone studied differences in neurofields in those cases? It occurred to me that could
be important in figuring out how this happened.

Marta seemed to read my mind. "You're expecting to be in on
the investigation of all this, aren't you? This had something to do
with your experiment."

Her tone was interested rather than accusing, but I felt like the
prime suspect in a murder mystery.

"Yes," I admitted. "The generators switched on somehow. I don't
know how, but they affected our minds."

"What happened, did they affect those brain hyperfields you
told me about?"

She was a quick study. I nodded. "That would make sense, but I don't know how or why."

"It wasn't your fault."

I shrugged.

"You can't be blamed for something no one imagined could happen. Look, I don't know anything about physics but I haven't lived my life in a bottle. I know we use hyperfields for energy, and no one's ever said anything about them causing hallucinations."

"Ordinary fields, yes. My new ones appear to be a bit more dangerous—"

"Which you couldn't have known." Marta's voice was stern. "Do I have to give you a kick in the pants like I gave Pierson, or are you going to remember that?"

I smiled a little bit. "I promise."

"Good." She looked back down the corridor. "I really should get back. Tell you what. I'll meet you for dinner tonight, assuming they actually manage to have food by then. Same mess hall where we met this morning, right?"

She was so energetic she almost left me breathless. So different from this morning, as if the effect had energized her. Had it? Some strange consequence of sleeping through it? She stood waiting for my answer. "All right. See you then."

And I was surprised by how much I suddenly looked forward to it.

◀ ◀ ◀

I found Drake and Kyoko in the rec center where we'd watched the rescue operation. A lot of the group was there, all looking pale and shocked. Kyoko had cleaned the blood off her face, but dried stains still marked her shirt. A livid bruise ran down one cheek, and her eye on that side was swollen half closed. Drake appeared uninjured.

"Dave, you're all right!" He jumped to his feet. "We couldn't find you. The medics came through taking a head count, asking about injuries. You weren't in your office."

"I was in the OCC, then I went to see Commander Warren."

"The medics wouldn't tell us anything about what was going on. You went to the hangar? Did you see Charles or John? We haven't found them."

"Yes." I fell into a chair. "They're dead."

Drake sat back down. "Hell. Dusted hell."

Kyoko said nothing, but put her head down. Beth choked back a sob. Charles and John were both in Kyoko's lab group.

"Is anyone else missing?" I asked.

"No." Drake spoke slowly. "But . . . Paul, Ellen, and Xian were taken to the infirmary. They're pretty banged up. And . . . and three others are dead."

"Three?" A heavy weight squeezed my chest. "I saw . . . only two. Eric was one of them . . . he burned. Someone else burned?"

"Mark Perrin."

Mark was my postdoc. The weight constricted my chest tighter.

"The other is Anne Lindsey," Kyoko whispered.

"Anne? Oh, dust." I looked around for Tom, but he wasn't in the room.

I recalled congratulating Anne on joining the team, not long before we moved from the University to the Alley. I chose her out of more than fifty applicants.

"They found her in her quarters," Drake said. "It . . . it was like she was battered to death by her own furniture." He looked up, an angry, baffled expression in his eyes. "How does something like that happen? She was alone. Even if we were all tearing around like maniacs, how'd she get so beat up alone? Did she do it to herself?"

I understood she must have been surrounded by one of those whirlwinds of debris, like Kyoko. But unlike Kyoko I hadn't come to stop it. Could I have? Did I pass right by Anne while she was dying?

Dust. Bloody dusted hell.

It seemed Drake and the others remembered none of it. "It doesn't make any sense!" he said.

"No, it doesn't," I said. "But we're going to make sense of it."

CHAPTER SEVEN

That night I had the dream for the first time. I stood in the center of a vast, open flatness, a perfect geometrical plane stretching to infinity. Above, the sky was dark, but directly overhead glared a savage red light, filling half the sky, agony to look at, but I couldn't look away. A shadow blocked my view of the source but somehow didn't stop the red light itself from burning me like the heat of an open furnace.

There was nowhere to hide from the Red Light and the Shadow, no shelter anywhere on that infinite plane. I ran, trying to at least get out from under it, but as long and hard as I ran I never actually moved, and the light stayed overhead, pinning me down.

Then, it changed. I looked up, and the Shadow had become the wreck of the *Lunar Explorer*, bleeding its cloud of glowing drive plasma as it plunged out of the sky directly toward me. I cowered, falling to my knees and raising my hands over my head as if that could ward off the impact of megatons of shredded metal. But the crash of metal never came. I looked up again.

The Shadow had become a hyperfield generator, and the Red Light, the glow of an active hyperfield. But it wasn't the friendly glow I'd loved all my life; instead, it was an angry snarl with ripples of blood and fire. And the generator—the generator was wrong somehow. The interlocking mass of field coils and spires and cables seemed normal enough, but something was—it wasn't a hyperfield generator at all, it was alive, some horribly bent and crippled organism waving tormented and broken legs in the air while the hyperfield around it spat fire, intending to burn me to ashes. This time I screamed and covered my eyes, but again I was unharmed.

I didn't dare to look a third time, but something forced me. My hands fell away from my eyes. This time what I saw I could not comprehend. The Shadow was still a living creature, but it was shapeless and amoeboid, sending out thick ropy tentacles, blacker than space, to writhe and bask in the Red Light. And the light both came from and went into it; they were somehow one. One malevolent organism, the Red Light and the Shadow together. It burned my mind to perceive it; merely to know it existed caused pain, a lethal thought that crawled like insects inside my skull.

And then—I couldn't stop myself from screaming when I knew—*it was aware of me.* It looked down on me, it saw me, and the blunt force of its malignant glee froze me with terror. This time I couldn't cover my eyes or turn away but remained paralyzed, staring into it.

A voice came from it, high and clear and utterly alien, stabbing needles into my ears as it spoke words I didn't understand but have never forgotten: "Mi'vri! Alan ayanvishar! A simai lansar ire ayangemar a ima lan a'ayan y'poro. Eiralynn ayansar a lanres ra'ayan seshar!"

Then my paralysis broke and I ran. Even though there was nowhere to run, I fled in blind panic across the empty flatness. Death would have been better than to keep seeing It, to be seen by It, to hear Its voice again. But there was nowhere to hide, and liquid tentacles of shadow crawled out of the Thing and spilled over me, drowning me in darkness.

I jolted awake in bed, screaming, the sheets soaked in sweat. Every muscle tense and frozen, while the sweat chilled against my skin. The fear persisted, even after I understood it was only a dream. Still afraid to move, in case the Red Light and Shadow noticed and came back, I shivered, staring at nothing while I tried to make myself believe it wasn't real. But other thoughts insisted: *No, it is. It is real. It's out there somewhere, somewhere—Outside.*

That word, *Outside,* summed up the whole nightmare in a single concept. I had seen something from Outside, infinitely removed from anything that was or ever should be in this Universe.

After a while I forced myself to break the nightmare's spell. I turned my head and the clock showed 0413.

It had been hard to fall asleep in the first place, though I'd expected to be out the moment my head hit the pillow. Surely after such a day, exhausting physically and emotionally, and not sleeping the night before, fatigue would conquer all. But my mind was too full: of questions, of horror, of anger. Anger about Anne and Mark and Eric and Charles and John. It all stormed through my mind and kept sleep at bay for long, turbulent hours. Then, when sleep finally came, the Red Light and the Shadow refused me any rest.

I tried to sleep again, rolling away from the clock. I made myself relax and breathe slowly, rhythmically, but all that accomplished was turning the sweat-soaked sheets clammy and cold. Finally, I got up and stumbled over to the other bed—the Alley's cabins were originally built for two crewmen to share—but although the dry sheets were at least comfortable, I managed no more than a fitful doze.

When the alarm pinged, I dragged myself out of bed feeling only half alive. After a shower and a shave, I felt a little better, but not much. I could swear the gravity had increased. I felt it pulling at my arms and legs and when I sat down, I sagged into the chair as if most of my bones had been removed. I stared at a spot on the wall until my eyes closed of their own accord, and then the intercom chimed.

Shaking myself, I straightened up in the chair and hit the button. The screen lit up. It was a video signal. A crewman with the shoulder badge of the coms department said, "Professor, Commander Warren would like to speak to you. Please hold."

A Navy logo replaced the image for a moment. I yawned. Then the video blipped on again with Warren's face on the screen. He looked tired too, and he hadn't shaved, but his eyes were as hard and alert as before.

"Professor, there's something you might be interested to see," he said. "This is the video file from the security camera in the main control room, recorded yesterday at the time of the emergency."

Off camera he punched a button, and the screen switched to a silent view of the control deck. It was a cheap low-res picture but I recognized Warren at the back of the room. Officers manned the few control panels normally in use.

Warren's voice resumed while the footage played. "We have cameras in all sensitive areas, of course. We didn't go over the files yesterday, but overnight the security department reviewed them all. Here it comes."

I watched. Everything looked normal. There was no warning before everyone on camera suddenly jerked, as if simultaneously slapped in the face, with no apparent cause. In the background, Warren crumpled to the floor in convulsions. A couple of officers curled up into the fetal position, like many I'd seen at the time. Two men jumped up and started running, waving their arms, bumping into consoles and bulkheads and each other, taking no notice.

Then some small object—I couldn't tell what—flew up off one of the consoles and danced in midair. It struck one of the officers and leaped away, and as if that was a cue, the whole room came alive. Consoles shattered and some tore loose from their moorings. Pieces and shards flew into the air. It took a few minutes to build, but soon the debris storm was in full force—two storms in fact, one centered on each of the men who were up and running around. I shuddered, flashing back to the scene with Kyoko.

Something must have hit the camera at that point, because the picture broke up into digital noise. Warren's face came back on the intercom screen.

"We've got similar scenes from everywhere we had a camera," he said. "I have to say it's the damnedest thing I've ever seen. I thought we did the damage ourselves, thrashing around. Now I see this . . . disembodied force sweeping through my base. What the dust was it, Professor? What did your machines do?"

"I think we did do the damage ourselves," I said. "I think we did it with our minds."

He frowned at me. "Care to explain that?"

"The human brain generates a hyperfield—you know that, right? Somehow that natural field interacted with my generators' fields and produced—well, I don't know what to call it. Telekinetic seizures, maybe."

"How is that possible?"

"I don't know yet. But it happened." I told the Commander the whole story of my experience of the effect, filling in the details I'd skirted the day before.

He listened without interrupting, but a crease between his eyebrows deepened as I spoke, and when I finished he said, "If I hadn't seen that video—"

"I know. Believe me, I'd like it a whole lot better if I could dismiss the experience as a dream."

"Yeah. Speaking of bad dreams, Dr. Cole tells me a large number of the crew are reporting they had nightmares last night. You?"

Cole was the Alley's chief medical officer. "Yes. Nothing that made sense but it felt pretty nasty. How about you?"

Warren was amused by the question. "I haven't been to sleep yet. I've ordered Cole to schedule exams for the whole crew. Maybe these nightmares are just a result of stress, but I want to know if my crew's suffering from brain damage."

"I don't know, but I have an idea where to start," I said. "There's a group at Star City University studying the neurofield. We collaborated with them early in our project. Can you reopen the com channels? I'd like to contact them."

"I want to keep coms secure right now," he said. "We're still in a state of emergency, and we've got half the United Colonies jamming the bandwidth with questions about the liner accident. Cole can call this group you mention on official channels if he needs to."

"Well, that's fine, but I need to talk to them for my own research," I persisted. "I've got files on the neurofield, but only on the physics of the hyperfield itself, not the biology. If we're going to make headway figuring out—"

"—then the doctor is the one to ask. I want the civilian lines closed for now."

I took a deep breath. "Well, how about just a single line, a secured channel that only my group can—"

"Professor, my priority is to restore this base to safe and normal operations. Unless you're going to tell me you suspect an ongoing hazard that you can spot and the doctor can't, then *it can wait.*"

I almost told him I suspected just that, in the hope of getting him to agree. But the generators could do no further harm without power, and if there were any medical consequences of the effect,

Dr. Cole would spot them before I did. The Commander was right: There was no hurry. However, knowing that didn't make it easier to swallow, and I fought to keep my voice level as I said, "Understood, Commander. I'm sorry to be pushy."

He allowed his expression to grow more friendly. "Don't worry about it. I know you civilians can't help yourselves. I assume you'll be inspecting your equipment today?"

"As soon as I can."

"I've posted guards on the hangar. I'll notify them your people have authorization to enter. I trust you'll take all necessary safety precautions."

"Of course."

Warren signed off.

I leaned back and ran my fingers through my hair. During the conversation with Warren, especially watching the video, I had woken up a bit, but now just an instant's idleness and I started to sag again. I longed to crawl back into bed.

I tried to apply some common sense. The Navy was sure to convene a review board, or board of inquiry—whatever they called it— to investigate the damage and loss of life. If I knew anything about such inquests, they'd be painstakingly thorough, spending months covering every detail before issuing a report that'd be hundreds of megabytes in text alone. Meanwhile, such radically new hyperfield phenomena would give physicists around the Colonies enough meat for years of future research.

So what hurry was there? What difference could it possibly make if I got some needed hours of sleep before I started? None. It would be better if I just got into bed and postponed the whole day. That's what I should do. But I sighed and dragged myself to my feet. We'd start by looking over the generators.

THE CHILD

◀ ◀ ◀

The smell of coffee and the familiar sound of plates and silverware made the mess hall seem almost normal. As if nothing out of the ordinary had happened. Monday—the worst disaster in civilian shipping. Tuesday—a brain-scrambling effect almost destroys the base. Wednesday—scrambled eggs and bacon. Surreal routine.

I looked around for Marta but she wasn't there. She hadn't appeared at dinner the night before, either, although the mess hall did open (prepackaged sandwiches out of some emergency crate). I spotted Drake and Beth at our usual table, but it looked empty without Charles, John, and Kyoko. At least Kyoko was all right; I'd pinged her on the intercom before leaving my cabin, and arranged to meet her later in the OCC to start checking the equipment. But she didn't show for breakfast. I also looked for Tom. I hadn't seen him since the lab meeting, and he wasn't here either. I wasn't sure what I'd say the next time I saw him, since he and Anne weren't officially a couple. Should I bring it up? I was sure he must be having a hard time. Probably alone in his cabin . . . I'd have to go find him soon.

For now, I grabbed a double cup of coffee, and despite my disdain for the Navy's cooking took a plate of overcooked eggs, before joining Drake and Beth at the table. Conversation came in fits and starts. We tried to talk about other things, but only one topic held our minds and we kept drifting back to it, then lapsing into uncomfortable silence. I understood a little better now the nature of my first conversation with Marta.

Drake and I finally settled into a discussion of the technical issues, allowing us to stay on the topic at hand while skirting the unpleasant realities.

"We have to take as our working hypothesis that the Effect did something to our neurofields," I said.

Somewhere during the conversation, "the Effect" had acquired a capital letter, audible whenever we said it.

"I suppose that's the least impossible of the impossibilities," Drake said. "Hyperfields do react strongly to the presence of other hyperfields, so I can see it's more likely the Effect messed up our neurofields than that it affected us in some unrelated way. But the neurofield is supposed to have no function. If tampering with it affects the mind to that extent, why has no one ever noticed so much as a twinge from being near hyperfields before? And even if we accept that neurofields were affected, it still doesn't get us to . . . to that." He gestured at his handscreen, which displayed Warren's security video.

I'd described my experience of the Effect to the group the night before, after finding them in the rec center, but Drake had been skeptical. He insisted it was all a hallucination, until this morning when I told him to call up the video and see it for himself.

He replayed the video, watching with a sour expression as if hoping it would be different the second time. "What is it you think this shows, or that you experienced? Clairvoyance? Remote viewing? Telekinesis? You know what garbage all that ESP nonsense is, Dave."

"I do. So we have to be careful using those words. No one started reading palms or gazing into crystal balls. We have phenomena that *resemble* some of the claims of the psychics, but were artificially produced by a technology that never existed during the centuries people believed in that stuff. The similarity could be a coincidence."

Beth picked rather listlessly at a stack of soggy Navy pancakes, and didn't join the conversation. It wasn't unusual for her to be quiet, but today she was more so than usual.

"So let's put it this way instead," I continued. "Under the influence of the Effect, our brains received information about our surroundings, from some source other than our normal senses—the *other-sense*, as I've been calling it. Apparently my brain had some unique ability to interpret it; *why me* is a question we can ask later. But a lot of people were producing energy, some in the form of fires, others in the form of kinetic energy to move objects. Do you see where I'm going?"

Drake leaned back. "No."

I ticked off on my fingers. "One—sensitivity to the surroundings. Two—emission of energy."

Drake got it. He straightened in his chair. "Hyperfield properties."

"It's what I realized when I finally saw the Effect came from our generators. What happened to us can, at least in principle, be explained by known hyperfield properties."

"*Known* is a bit of an exaggeration," Drake said. "For the kinetic energy, I expect you're thinking of Assagiri's theory, that hyperfields could be used as a spaceship drive—"

"Yes, and as for the other-sense, it was you who proposed using hyperfields as sensing devices."

"Kyoko was right to be skeptical about that. It'd require fiendishly difficult calculations, if it's even possible at all. The same for directing hyperfield output into kinetic energy at will." He paused, then smiled lopsidedly. "I have a lot of admiration for our brainpower, Dave, but I don't think even our mighty neurons could solve those problems, within a few minutes of the start of the Effect."

"Not everyone's brain did," I said. "Apparently I was the only one who gained a coherent other-sense, and it seemed to me like only a few people had those debris storms around them. Only a few people produced kinetic energy that way. In some people, the energy was just heat, and . . . well . . . fire." I trailed off. So much for staying on the safe, technical side of the topic.

Beth looked up with dark, painful eyes. "Some people," she said, her voice somewhere between a whisper and a moan. "Some people. Two of them were Mark and Eric. Don't talk about them like data points."

"I'm sorry," I said.

"Yeah, me too," Drake said.

Another awkward silence. The sound of voices from other tables seemed loud; there was even a burst of laughter from a group of crewmen nearby, a jarring sound, out of place. Didn't they know their crewmates had also died? But it was a big crew, maybe no one they knew. Or maybe they were trading fond and funny stories of those who were lost.

"Anyway," I said slowly, easing back into the conversation, "the neurofield exists. The brain generates it, for whatever function. If the brain is able to work with it in this way—"

"That's a big if, Dave," said Drake. "And it joins a long list of others."

"Oh, I agree." I counted on my fingers again. "*If* using hyper-fields as sensors is a solvable problem. *If* they can be used for kinetic energy—that's an untested model. *If* it's possible for our hyperfields to trigger exactly the right change in the neurofield, and *if* brains, adapted to the normal neurofield, could handle an altered one. That's all *if* the generators affected our neurofields at all. We don't even know that, though it's plausible." I stopped, and had to smile. "Well, I could go on, but I'd run out of fingers before I ran out of *ifs*. It's all just speculation right now. It fits the facts as we know them. It's a place to start, is all."

"Here's an alternative," Drake said. "Like you said, only you had experience of the other-sense. What if it was just a hallucination—more lucid than the rest of us got, but still a hallucination."

"The security video—" I began, but Drake interrupted.

"I know. But hear me out. What if the generators did produce a field that produced kinetic energy, but directly. Not through our brains. The movement of objects on that video looks pretty random to me. So it knocks us out, tosses the Alley around—and the rest was imagination."

I thought it over. Strange as it was, my experience during the Effect had a reality to it. I didn't doubt it. Should I? And yet—

"I knew the generators were the cause, and I was right. It got worse as I got close, and it stopped when I shut them down. How'd I know that, if the other-sense wasn't real?"

Drake shrugged. "You knew our experimental generators are based on the neurofield. Subconsciously, you jumped to the conclusion that the generators were causing what you call the other-sense and incorporated it into your hallucination. It was a lucky guess."

"Lucky guess?" My face showed my incredulity.

"Okay, say you were able to sense a directionality to the Effect. That's still a long orbit away from all this psychic stuff. And far more plausible."

"But, but why?" Beth flushed as Drake and I turned toward her, but she kept going. "Why is that more plausible than what Dave said? Y-you're looking for lucky guesses and hyperfields that move objects *and* affect our brains, and Dave is saying, 'Let's be careful with those words.' But why? It's so much simpler than all of that, isn't it?" She stopped, took a deep breath, and plunged on. "Nothing improbable had to happen here. The generators only made our neurofields stronger or more sensitive. Our brains didn't have to learn how to use them because they already know. What if this is the neurofield's true function, and has been all along? Psychic power, ESP. And, and before people tried to use scientific-sounding words, they called it second sight or, or even magic. People have believed in these things for thousands of years. What if the Effect didn't make something new, but only woke up something very, very old?"

Running out of steam, Beth looked down at her fingers, her face bright red, and finished hesitantly, "I . . . I just think . . . that might . . . make sense, is all."

"You're right, it does," I said. "If we concede there's some truth to those old beliefs, then what's happened here becomes easier to explain. Be we do need to be careful. Just saying ESP is no substitute for a proper scientific description of how it actually works, and those words carry a lot of baggage. A lot of—"

"A lot of dust," Drake said flatly. "Dust clogging the filters, that's all that is. Whatever the resemblance between the Effect and a load of old superstition, it can't be anything more than coincidence. If there was any truth to that psychic stuff, there'd have been evidence before now."

"People have claimed evidence over the years," I said. But I shook my head. "I know, I know. Between bias, wishful thinking, and outright fraud every such study has been discredited. Still, I wonder how long it's been since a serious scientist even looked? If only crackpots are trying, then of course you only get crackpot studies." I stared into the distance, suddenly thoughtful.

"It's significant *that* only crackpots are looking," Drake said. "Rational people notice there's no evidence for any of it."

"Absence of evidence is not evidence of absence," I said.

Drake snorted. "A slogan made up by pseudoscientists and religious kooks to justify clinging to their nonsense."

"It's not nonsense," Beth said, so softly I could barely hear her.

"We'll see," Drake said. "It's going to take a lot before I jump on board with a bunch of palm readers. I'll give you any odds you want on that bet. If there were real psychics, they wouldn't be posting celebrity gossip or sitting in little booths at Independence Day fairs. Real psychics would be gambling, picking the right stocks—they'd be rich, and they'd be running the world."

"Maybe they are," I said with a laugh. "Haven't you ever wondered how the really rich got so lucky?" But something drew my eye away from Drake, across the room, where the stewards were bustling over the serving table. With a frown, I added, "Or maybe the real psychics don't want to be noticed."

CHAPTER EIGHT

After breakfast, I met Kyoko at the hangar at 0900, as we'd arranged. With her were her postdoc Leo Hayes—her only postdoc now, Charles had been the other—and three technicians, one of them Jack Elliott, who I'd last seen curled up on the floor outside my office. Beth had come with me from the mess hall.

I was unprepared for seeing the generators again. I wouldn't have expected to see or feel anything unusual—maybe a little less enthusiasm, given fatigue and the circumstances, but that's all. But with my first look, I finally realized why so many people found hyperfield generators disturbing.

The hangar, always shadowy except for our work area, looked positively sinister with angular patterns of dark and light folding themselves over the equipment. We'd brought in portable lightpanels since the power was still out, and they cast harsh shadows. As for the generators themselves—they looked like angular insects, bristling with hundreds of gleaming stingers, crouching ready to leap on their prey. And they *did* look wrong, somehow, just as a lot of people had always claimed. The geometry was somehow unnatural. Nothing should really look like that, I thought for the first time.

I remembered my nightmare, the generator coming to horrible, crippled life, and I shuddered, suddenly having a wild impulse to rush forward and smash them. It wouldn't take much to wreck the fragile needles of metal and glass and ceramic beyond repair. They'd never hurt anyone again. That would teach them.

My reaction to them startled and disturbed me. Surely I was more rational than this. These were inanimate objects, machines incapable of any motive or deliberate action. They weren't malevolent; they didn't do anything on purpose. But I looked at them and I thought, *You killed my friends.*

I was punchy from another sleepless night, that was it. That, and the shock of it all. If we'd all been on board the *Lunar Explorer,* I'd be angry at spacecraft right now. So I told myself to put it aside, move on, and get to work.

"Let's start by taking images of everything," I said, keeping my voice carefully neutral. "Orthographic and holographic, every angle you can think of."

"Yes," said Kyoko, "and multiple images of these components, please." She pulled up a parts list on her handscreen and synched it to Leo's.

"Anything that looks damaged as well," I said.

I watched Leo and the others work, and every time they went near the generators for a close-up shot, I winced. I didn't really notice I was doing this until a growing ache in the back of my neck made me realize I'd gone taut as a violin string. My eyes started to water, and I realized I hadn't been blinking. In fact I'd been watching them work as if they were the poor fools in a monster movie about to get sliced.

This was ridiculous! What was I afraid would happen? Did I think the generators would spring to life, metal spines lunging like scorpion tails—

Stop it! I took a deep breath, let it out slow, and forced my muscles to relax.

I turned away, mostly to prove to myself that I could, that I didn't *have* to keep watching as if I expected trouble, but as I turned, I caught a strange expression on Kyoko's face. It was a dark, smoldering frown as she kept her eye on the work. I realized she felt the same way toward the generators as I did. Seeing me look at her, she hid her expression straight away, but as our eyes met, we each knew the other's thought and traded half smiles of understanding.

"It is foolish to resent them," she said. The bruise she'd received in the Effect had darkened to a more pronounced purple down the side of her face. "They only behaved as their physical natures required of them."

"I guess somehow we expected better of them," I answered.

Kyoko sighed. "One cannot expect loyalty from a device."

It made perfect sense Kyoko and I would feel the same; the generators were hers as much as mine. More so, really. I'd conceived of the new hyperfields, but she'd designed and built the hardware that brought them to reality. They were our children.

Then I had to smile, as I wondered where Drake fit into that metaphor.

Kyoko looked at me quizzically.

"It's nothing," I said.

"We must find out how the generators got so out of control. Why would Charles and—" Her voice caught and she suddenly became very interested in studying her handscreen. She continued without looking up. "Charles and John must have activated the generators. But why? They had no reason to run any new experiments."

"I don't know," I said. "If they had some idea they wanted to test out, they knew I'd be happy to put it on the schedule. They wouldn't do it off the books. Unless—"

I had an idea on the tip of my mind, but it vanished as Leo approached. "I don't see any visible damage to either generator, except some fried insulation on a couple of wires."

"There was damage when I was here yesterday morning," I said. "Minor, but visible. You're sure they're clean now?"

"Yeah."

"Hum." I thought it over. "So Charles and John had finished with the repairs before they—before the Effect started. Whatever they did should be logged. We need to get the power back on in the OCC, start up the computer. We'll need the data files from the Effect itself too."

"Yeah, good," said Leo. "We also need to get the juice back on for the self-diagnostics on the gen—"

"No!" Kyoko and I interrupted at the same moment, causing Leo to blink in surprise and stare at us.

"That could alter the state of the generators," I continued. "Presumably the configuration's been altered, given the . . . *different* results. But the generators might automatically reset to default on power-up and we'd lose their altered configuration."

"Well, what of it? The computer log will have recorded whatever their settings were."

"If the computer log worked properly, which we don't know since we don't know what malfunction caused all this. We can turn on the power to the OCC, get the lights back on, but the lines to the generators stay dark."

Leo persisted. "Look, we can start up the computers first, bypass the power-up routines, keeping everything as is, then connect the generators."

"No."

"It's just that we need the self-diagnostics to tell us the state of the components."

"You can test them manually."

"Manually? But that would take hours, and there's really no reason—"

Leo's persistence wore at me. I was tired and the headache I'd expected yesterday had finally arrived. What really bothered me, though, was that he was right. It made sense to power up the generators to check their status. I was making up excuses to cover the fact I just didn't want to give them power. Ever again.

But Kyoko came in on my side. "I agree with Dave. It is not wise to connect the power supply again until we are sure exactly how and why the hyperfields initialized."

Leo kept on. "Well, if it's a safety issue we can—"

"Just do it the way I tell you, all right?" I didn't quite shout, but heads turned.

Leo spread his hands. "Fine, whatever you say."

I regretted my irritability at once. "Sorry."

Leo shrugged. "Yeah. I understand. No problem." He moved off toward the OCC.

I rubbed my eyes with one hand and let out an unhappy sigh. If there had been gravity, I'd have gladly sagged into a chair. It's funny how even with no gravity, I still missed the familiar gesture.

"Hum," I said again. "What were we talking about before?"

"How the generators activated," Kyoko said.

"Right." I tried to recover the thought I'd had before Leo arrived, but it was gone. "The computer logs ought to tell us something."

"H-hey, um, I found something interesting," Beth interrupted. She showed Kyoko her handscreen. "Some of, of these servos have changed. I mean, from the way they were set for run thirty-seven."

Kyoko took the screen from Beth, and I looked over her shoulder.

"I looked at some of the calibration marks," Beth continued. "I know just looking isn't very accurate, but I, I could see they were far off from where they should be."

There are two ways to alter a hyperfield's configuration: Either change the voltage of various components, or move the components into different positions. Servos on the generators' frames handled the latter function. Beth had noted the approximate values of those she'd checked, and she was right—they weren't where we had left them.

"This would change some key field variables," I said. I tried to picture the consequences in my head, but my mind was too woolly.

"They must have, maybe bumped into the generators while they were replacing parts," Beth said. "Moved some of the arms."

"And just stumbled on another radically new hyperfield, with properties never seen before?" I shook my head. "We're missing something."

Just then the regular hangar lights came on; Leo had reset the breakers. I looked immediately to the generators, half-sure I'd see them spring to life, but no lights gleamed around the fiber-optic connections. They were still power-down. Leo might have argued with me, but he would never have connected their power without permission, any more than Charles or John would have run an unauthorized—

"That's it!" I exclaimed. The elusive idea had popped up again, and this time I grabbed it.

"What?" Kyoko asked.

"Maybe how the generators activated. We shut down in a hurry on Monday. The distress signal sounded for the *Lunar Explorer* and we shut everything down. What if we missed something? We were distracted. Maybe we just shut off the consoles but not the generators."

"I believe we were thorough," Kyoko said.

"But if we weren't—if the generators were still trying to run a hyperfield program . . . the fields collapsed on Monday because components of the generators burned out. Then yesterday, Charles and John replaced the components, and as soon as they did—" I spread out my arms, indicating all that followed.

"Field activation is a specific procedure," Kyoko said. "I'm not sure it could happen that way."

"I—" I hesitated. "I found Charles and John in the OCC, not out here in the hangar. So—" I talked it through. "They notice the generators are live, and for some reason the computers have started field activation. They head into the OCC to shut it down, but they're too late."

"It's horrible," Beth said. "Like it was a trap set for them."

I glanced quickly at the generators. A trap, yes. Again they reminded me of predatory insects waiting for unwary prey—but if I was right, they didn't set that trap. We did. I did. A single moment of criminal carelessness.

It felt right to blame myself, bitter though it tasted.

"I'll check the run file," I said. "We'll see what it says."

I pushed over and swung myself through the door into the OCC. I fastened my belt clips to the rail at my console. A polite "Please wait" message showed on the computer screen while it booted up. Obviously it wasn't supposed to be shut down by just cutting off its power, and the system had to run a set of self-diagnostics before letting me in. After a minute or so, the screen flickered and filled with graphs: instrument readings taken during the Effect. Some of the lines were flat, probably damaged instruments Charles and John hadn't yet replaced or that were damaged during the Effect. As for the rest of the data—the numbers were crazy, the graphs all over the map. I'd never seen numbers like that for an active hyperfield before, not even during run 37, and I was unable to visualize their significance as to the nature and shape of the field itself.

Something bizarre, that's certain, I thought.

The time codes showed the Effect had lasted around two hours, not a day and two hours, but I'd figured that one out already. Drake would have to run these numbers through his simulations to see if we could make anything of them.

Meanwhile, I wanted to know whether we'd properly shut down after the last test run. I called up the file for run 37 as well as the user input log to see what repairs Charles and John had done.

I found contradictory information. The file for run 37 showed we did shut everything down properly. I was wrong about that part. But the file for the Effect (the computer called it run 38, thinking it was just another experiment) said the generators *were* already live when Charles and John started logging replacement parts. So, the trap was set, just as I'd guessed. But when was it set? And how?

I scrolled back through the file. If the operating system worked as it should have, run file 38 wouldn't have begun with the Effect; it would have begun whenever the generators were activated. Scrolling back, and—there! The file began with a normal startup routine, and the time was Tuesday morning, just after I'd come around to have a look at the damage from run 37. After I left, someone must have come in and started up the generators. But why would anyone do that?

More to the point—who? The file didn't display any record of the commands entered to activate or run the software. I checked the user ID to see who was logged in at the time.

No one. No one was logged in.

I looked up and out through the window. Kyoko and her team clustered around the generators, sinister spiders gleaming in the hangar lights. But I wasn't angry with them. No, not anymore. Now, I was scared to death of them. Because, according to the run file, only a few minutes after I left, the generators started up and ran a perfect field activation routine—*by themselves.*

CHAPTER NINE

One way or another I was going to figure out what happened. There had to be an explanation, and I would find it.

I showed Kyoko the run files, and we agreed to physically disconnect the generators from their power supply, as an extra safeguard beyond keeping a breaker switched off. We decided to call an extra lab meeting that afternoon, and then I left her and her group to get on with their measurements. I needed to go see the doctor about contacting the researchers at Star City.

The infirmary was on Wheel deck 3. As I rode the elevator down, I felt the increasing gravity drag on every muscle. Slumping against the wall, my eyelids felt heavy. Keeping busy and talking had kept sleep at bay, but the idle seconds in the elevator made my head nod.

Dust! I needed to sleep. But there wasn't time. I had too much to do. The elevator stopped and I shoved myself back into motion, blinking hard and trying to look alert, at least.

Dr. Cole reminded me of Commander Warren. I found him surrounded by a cloud of subordinates and, like Warren, paying attention to every report and request at once. Every bed in the infirmary's main ward was occupied, and that was a bad sign, since like everything else on the Alley, it was built for wartime capacity.

The medical staff must be overwhelmed, I thought, and stopped just inside the main entrance, sure the doctor would have no time to talk to me.

But as soon as he spotted me, he approached with his hand out. "Professor Harris, just the man I was hoping to see—yes nurse, I saw the report, just carry on—come to my office, won't you, Professor?"

He pumped my hand vigorously and led me through a corridor. Most of the doors to the exam rooms were open, and I could see patients also filled those beds, many who looked like they sustained more severe injuries. We passed a glass-walled ICU with patients on life support. The unpleasant yet familiar hospital smell of antiseptic tainted the air.

Cole noticed me looking around. "We've got the worst cases in here, but if you're wondering—they're all going to make it. We've lost all we're going to. Here's my office."

It was a smallish room with a standard-issue desk and a couple of chairs. A screen on one wall traced what looked like heartbeat rhythms, I suppose from the ICU patients. The room felt like the doctor didn't use it much. Hesitating at the door I asked, "How many total . . . ?" and let the question trail off.

"Final count was forty-one dead," he answered. "A little over three hundred injured, including both crew and civilians."

"Are you—can you handle them all?"

"Sure." He shrugged. "The Alley's a rescue station, remember? I've got a much bigger staff than needed for our regular crew. For the most part they're idle except for disaster drills—which paid off yesterday. We got lucky, if you can call it that: We were prepped for hundreds of wounded from the *Lunar Explorer* but it turned out the survivors were mostly uninjured. The extra beds we set up were still ready after yesterday's excitement. We got a little slammed at first but we're on top of the situation now."

Cole didn't resemble Commander Warren so much after all: He talked a lot more. I sat down as he continued.

"So I gather you believe all this was caused by your hyperfield equipment. I'm trying to assess if this caused any damage to anyone other than the injuries we're seeing, but I don't know what to look for."

"I'm afraid I don't know either," I said. "We're assuming the generators interacted with our neurofields, but I don't know anything about neurofield biology. I hoped you might."

"No." He shook his head. "I've been reading some papers on the neurofield this morning—well, skimming them anyway." He gestured vaguely at a small screen on his desk. "No one seems to know what the dust the brain's doing with a hyperfield in it. There's some work on the nerve pathways that create the field, but they don't know much even about that. On the medical side, the database has a few records of hyperfield-related injuries, but nothing puzzling. Industrial accidents, that sort of thing. An industrial hyperfield is white-hot and people who get too close suffer burns, not hallucinations or seizures, or whatever it was—" He sighed, letting a touch of frustration show. "See, I don't even really know what it did to us. No one remembers enough to describe it, so it's hard for me to know where to start."

"Well, I can help with that, at least a little." I launched into an abridged version of my adventure, focusing mostly on the symptoms I'd felt and witnessed.

Cole listened thoughtfully, stroking his chin. "Well. I've seen the security videos, so I know the physical phenomena were real, but I wouldn't be too sure about this *other-sense* of yours. Perceptions in an altered mental state aren't reliable."

"Maybe, but I think hyperfield properties could plausibly explain it."

He shook his head. "In terms of hyperfield physics maybe, but you're positing a very sophisticated interaction between the neurofield and the nervous system, something not likely to develop so quickly."

That was more or less the same objection Drake had raised. I hesitated a moment, then with a casual air said, "There's an idea floating around that we may have discovered the basis of psychic powers."

"Oh, you're thinking *that's* what the neurofield is for?" Cole grinned unexpectedly. "I'm going to find this a very confusing Universe if it turns out I have to add tarot cards to my diagnostic equipment." He laughed, not mockingly but as if he genuinely enjoyed the idea. I had to smile in return.

"Well, maybe not," I said. "But the people to ask about it are at Star City University. There's a group in the neuroscience department who we collaborated with early in our project. They were researching the function of the neurofield, and we wanted to know its parameters as a model system for our generators. We pooled our grants to fund taking measurements of the neurofield in volunteers. I want to call that group, but the Commander has all the civilian coms closed down."

"Would this be Rothberg and Wilson?"

"Yes."

He nodded. "They wrote the papers I looked up this morning. I'll put in a call, see if they have any insights."

"In the meantime, if you want to look for unseen damage caused by the Effect, you might try measuring people's neurofields, see if they're different from normal."

"I don't have any equipment for that," he said. "No medical reason for it, until now."

I frowned. "We might be able to modify our instruments . . . I don't know, the neurofield is a very weak field and the equipment we brought with us isn't meant for it . . ."

"I wouldn't know what to do with the data anyway."

"I suppose not. Well—" I stood up to leave, but swayed as the whole room spun around me and my eyes went dark. I had to sit down again fast.

"Looks like you didn't sleep any better than anyone else last night," Cole said.

"No. Nightmares."

"It's most likely just a reaction to the shock, nothing unexplainable. What'd you dream about?"

I picked one from the list of images the Red Light and Shadow had formed. "I dreamed the hyperfield generators had come to life and were spitting fire at me."

The doctor chuckled. "You don't need to be a psychologist to get the symbolism there. I wouldn't be concerned unless it persists or other symptoms crop up. Stop by the dispensary on your way out. I've got them handing out a mild sleep aid. More of an anxiety suppressant than a sedative—it should shut down any nightmares and help you sleep through tonight."

"Thanks." I stood up again, more carefully this time.

But as I turned to leave Cole said, "Something else occurs to me."

"Yes?"

"Have you ever heard of spontaneous human combustion?"

I stopped, my attention riveted at once. "It sounds like a good name for the burning deaths during the Effect." My skin crawled at the memory.

"It's an old superstition," Cole said.

I stared. "You mean it's happened before?"

"It's *believed* to have happened before. Rather like ESP. Mostly during the nineteenth century, but there were alleged cases well into the twentieth. Bodies burned to ash, almost no smoke produced, no fire alarms set off. Animal tissue will burn like that, under the right conditions. The fat acts something like the wax in a candle. I'd have said that would be enough to explain the strange phenomenon: Some perfectly ordinary accident catches someone on fire, conditions are right to produce the unusual burning pattern, and if the ignition source isn't obvious, people make up a scary story. But now—"

"—now maybe it's not just ESP that's more real than we've believed," I finished. "It makes you wonder what other old legends are waiting out there."

◀ ◀ ◀

Lunch was a vaguely beige pasta dish with bits of alleged chicken. It was the kind of thing that Charles, I remembered with half a smile, used to call goop du jour. After the steward slapped a mound of it on my plate, I grabbed another double cup of coffee and found a seat.

I'd picked up a handscreen I found lying in one of the labs since mine had broken during the Effect, and I needed one in order to keep working. I'd return it to its owner at the lab meeting that afternoon. Although the screen's personal directory remained locked, the lab password got me into the project files, which was all I needed.

I knew what I had to do: Find some seam in the Ryder equations where they could be unfolded, making room for new complexity. For thirty years of industrial use, for three months of our own project, every hyperfield acted exactly as the Ryder equations predicted. So whatever was missing from those equations must normally cancel out, affecting the results only in the rarest of circumstances. We'd stumbled across those circumstances in runs 37 and 38, the experiment and the Effect. Something we added before Monday's test, either in the software or in the generator design, evoked that hidden complexity. If I went over exactly the changes we'd made, I ought to be able to see where I had to modify the equations.

It was futile. My eyes locked on the screen while the equations scrolled meaninglessly past, and my mind drifted. Now and again, I'd start back to attention and try to focus on the problem, but then I'd drift again. My lunch sat uneaten on my plate, no great loss.

Then someone stuck a hand between my eyes and the handscreen. I jumped and looked up. Marta grinned at me, retracting her arm from across the table. She sat back.

"Ah, there you are," she said. "Sorry, but I got tired of repeating *Hi, Dave* over and over."

"I didn't hear you." I shrugged in apology. "I guess I was kind of absorbed in my work."

"No, you were asleep."

"I was?"

She nodded. "Your eyes were open and you weren't drooling or anything, but trust me—you were gone."

I put down the handscreen and rubbed my eyes. "I guess I'm a little tired."

"*Pfft!*" Marta's exclamation was half laugh, half exasperation. "A little tired, right. You and everybody else. I don't know if I'm on a Naval base or the set of a zombie movie."

"It's these nightmares. I suppose you didn't have any?"

"Just another benefit of sleeping through the party. Teresa's the same, and I've met some other people from the *Explorer* who also slept through it all and they're okay too. More so than the average, anyway." She studied my face for a moment. "Meanwhile you look worse than the average."

"I didn't sleep much the night before, either," I admitted.

"You and me both. The difference is, I caught up last night. So why aren't you in bed now?"

"I don't have time. There's too much to do. I have to figure out what happened."

"Sure, but do you have to figure it out today? You're not on the crew; it's not like the lifesystems will fail or we'll drift into deep space if you work it out later."

She made a theatrical gesture of looking all around. "Or is there a doomsday clock counting down somewhere and I've missed it?"

I had to smile. "No, no doomsday clock."

"No. So—I'd let you get on with torturing yourself, but I'm an interfering busybody. It says so right on my ID card: *social worker.* So tell me this: Won't your research go faster if you're actually awake for it?"

I laughed wearily. "I suppose."

"So take the day off. Start tomorrow."

"I really can't."

"Uh-huh." Marta took a bite of her pasta, made a face, and put down her fork. "You weren't kidding about the food here. Speaking of—sorry I stood you up for dinner last night."

"It's okay," I said. "I figured you had to look after the children."

"Actually I'm hardly being allowed to. They've assigned a couple of medics and that mess steward, Brown. He's giving them lunch now. I think they're afraid I'm too traumatized to be trusted with the task."

"Are you?" I suppose it was fatigue that made me tactless. But Marta didn't seem to mind.

"I suppose I should be. Most of the *Explorer* survivors are just this side of catatonic. But I've always bounced back fast from trouble."

A strange expression crossed her face like a passing ghost, but was gone before I was sure I'd seen it. She shook her head. "I miss Jenny and Tom, but I'm okay. I was a wreck when we met yesterday morning. Today I'd say you're the wreck. You really should give yourself some time to rest."

"I'll be fine. I've pulled all-nighters before."

"*Pfft!* You really are clueless if you think that's all that's going on. Right now, Dave, you're feeling guilty about surviving because that's what survivors feel, plus you're pissed off because your beloved babies betrayed you—"

"What?"

"Come on, I was out of it yesterday, but I wasn't dead. I saw how your eyes lit up when you talked about your hyperfields. They're your babies. You raised them to do all these wonderful things, but instead . . . Do you know this quote: 'How sharper than a serpent's tooth it is to have a thankless child'? Of course you're angry, and you want explanations—right now. The bad news is that you could solve the scientific problem down to the last decimal point and it wouldn't give you the explanation you want. That explanation doesn't exist, and it'll take time to realize that."

I started to get angry, but not at the situation, at Marta. What business of hers was any of this, anyway? Besides—she came a little too close to home for comfort. Only a couple of hours earlier I had been thinking about how the generators were like my children.

"You know," I said to her, "when you said that *you* were okay just now, I believed you."

Marta grinned and leaned on her elbows, chin in one hand. "Yes, but that's because you're more gullible than I am."

"Gullible? Then you're not okay?"

"Now you're trying to change the subject."

"Or you are."

"No, you are."

I was about to say something else, and then I just started laughing at the whole childish exchange. I laughed a good deal more than it really deserved. I suppose that was a sleep-deprived mood swing. But at least it felt good.

Marta leaned back. "Now that's better."

I shook my head as the laughter passed. "How did you do that?"

"I'm really good."

"You know, you're not what I imagined a social worker is like."

"Oh, were you expecting something like this?" Marta leaned forward, her eyes growing wide and dewy while her brows knit together in a concerned frown. Her whole face changed as she took my right hand between both of hers. I felt a little static shock run up my arm.

"David," she breathed. "I can see you're hurting. I'm *here* for you, let it all out."

I gaped at her, speechless. The room grew a few degrees warmer. Then suddenly she dropped her pose and her habitual grin reappeared. She released my hand and straightened.

"I can also do the heartless bureaucrat," she said. "You know, the villain in dramas where the heroine is a plucky young single mom trying to raise her child by herself."

Marta's face pinched into a narrow, disapproving pucker and her posture turned stiff. The impression was so complete I'd swear even her hair tightened up. "Professor Harris, this is a very serious situation. I shall have to file a report, and if I do not see signs of improvement, action will be taken." Then she resumed her old self again. Once more I laughed.

"That's all video drama stuff." She waved a dismissive hand. "Me, I'm a smart-ass. I have been since high school and I have it down pat. Don't mistake it for therapy; it's just a way of lightening the mood."

"It worked," I said.

"Of course it worked, I told you I'm really good." She grew serious. "But listen—you really should take a few days off, you and all your group. It's not just a matter of lost sleep. You've lost friends, and it takes time to deal with that. It's advice, not orders. I'm not your therapist and I'm not your mommy." She displayed a sly version of her grin. "So eat your veggies and go take a nap."

"I'll think about it, I really will." I looked down at my plate. "Meanwhile, there are no veggies here."

She tilted her head. "What is it with you and the food here? I admit institutional food is always sad, but you have an especially snide attitude toward it."

"I don't know. I just hate bland food. I guess it goes back to my childhood, growing up on pressed algae cakes and stored rations. Once they managed to replant the orchards and gardens and reclone the livestock, I never wanted to touch any of that again." I smiled. "You might think I'd have some nostalgia for that kind of stuff." I looked at my plate and shook my head. "No."

She had a speculative look in her eye now, as she studied my face. "It really all goes back to hyperfields for you, doesn't it? They gave you light and warmth, made your mom smile—and they empowered the Colonies' chefs as well!" She laughed, a sound like running water, different from the brass of her normal humor.

I puzzled for a moment. Had I mentioned my mom's smile to Marta? Well, I must have—I remembered her smile clearly whenever I thought back to that day.

"They make everything better," I admitted. "Or . . . they used to. Until yesterday."

"You'll get back to where you were," she promised. "It'll just take time. Meanwhile, no veggies but eat your goop du jour."

I started. "What did you say? Why did you call it that?"

"It was just a joke." Marta was puzzled by my reaction. "Sorry, it just came to me."

"Charles Peretta—he's one of our group who died in the Effect—used to say that. I was thinking about it a few minutes ago." I frowned. "You just caught me by surprise."

We finished eating, neither of us with much enthusiasm, then both stood up at once. Marta jabbed a finger at me.

"You going to rest now?"

I sighed. "No."

"I figured. Tell you what, walk me back to the Admiral's Suite and I'll introduce you to my kids. I promise not to keep talking like a textbook on grief counseling."

"That'd be nice," I said, then hastily added, "Meeting the kids I mean, not—"

"Not me shutting up?" She laughed. "I expect that'd be nice too. No worries. Let's go."

I followed Marta out the door, but as we left my eyes strayed to the chronometer on the wall. Recalling her joke about the doomsday clock, I half expected it to show a bright red countdown. But my mind was wandering again. Did I have any actual reason not to take Marta's advice? None! The emergency was over, the research would go on for years anyway, and I was sure everyone in the group must be feeling as tired as I was. At the lab meeting, I'd tell them we were closing shop for a few days. After all, there wasn't any dooms-day clock.

CHAPTER TEN

The Admiral's Suite was filled with the kind of chaos that only a dozen small children can create. Papers covered with scribbles littered the floor and every horizontal surface, while a number of the kids bent over blank sheets earnestly producing more. Toys were scattered everywhere, and the kids who weren't drawing were in constant motion, chasing, tumbling, and climbing over the furniture. High, clear voices filled the room with a loud chatter.

Marta smiled at the scene but I was in no condition to appreciate it: As we'd approached the room my headache had blazed, pounding mercilessly at the back of my skull. It was bad enough to blur my vision, a clear message to take Marta's advice and get some rest. I'd just hang on until the lab meeting, I told myself, then I'd head back to my quarters for a nap.

Meanwhile, I tried to look as cheerful as I could while Marta introduced all twelve children by name, none of which I remembered. Marta herself beamed at them with an entirely non-smart-ass smile.

"Are you Marta's boyfriend?" one boy asked me.

She answered before I could. "No, we're just friends."

"He *is* your boyfriend! You went off to lunch and had smoochies!"

This earned him a chorus of giggles from the other kids. But Marta said, "Sadly, no. No smoochies for me." She leaned down to the boy and her smile returned to her normal grin. "But I promise I'll work on it."

The children surprised me: They seemed entirely normal. Hadn't Marta said they were all orphaned or abused?

She must have noticed my expression because, as the children went back to their playing, she said, "Were you expecting sad little faces covered in dirt like in *Oliver Twist?*"

"I guess so."

She shook her head. "Children this age aren't that obvious. They don't act depressed like adults do, at least not for long stretches. There's no force in the Universe that'll stop kids from playing when they get together; it's a biological imperative, as much as language or walking on two legs. Child abuse is hard to diagnose unless you're an expert. It's often missed—or imagined when it isn't there. To get it right, you have to know what to look for."

She bent down and picked up one of the abandoned drawings, glanced at it, then handed it to me. "For example."

It was signed "Laurie, age 7" in big block letters. A stick figure family stood under a half circle that probably represented a lifesystem dome. A line of brown marked the ground, and the sky was a dense black scribble at the top of the page. Five-pointed stars filled the white space between sky and ground. Laurie's self-portrait was a little stick figure with curly blond hair and a triangle-shaped blue dress, but the parents were strange. The mother was ill-defined, vague, drawn all in gray. Her face smiled, but she had no eyes. The father was a nightmare, his head enormously out of proportion to the body, even for a stick figure. His whole face was colored bright red with a black mouth open in a scream displaying jagged monster teeth, vaguely reminding me of my dream of the Red Light and the Shadow.

"Dust," I muttered. My headache seethed.

"Art therapy's been used with kids for centuries," Marta said. "They don't draw how things look; they draw how they feel—like the way they always put the sky up out of reach, rather than extending it to the ground."

"How do you do this job? See stuff like this and not—"

"Burn out? Now you know why no one acts like those tear-streaked softies in video dramas. Lay yourself open like that and you'll burn out in a week. But here's the good news that makes this job worthwhile: All these kids will be okay. Just in the last couple of decades, with the discoveries in cognitive science and neuropsychology—we've got therapies they couldn't dream of twenty years ago." She waved the drawing. "This is what these kids feel like for now, but not for long. For the first time in history, we can fix a broken mind like we'd fix a broken leg, and it'll heal just as well. We get these kids back to the Colonies, and they'll all be okay."

She paused for a moment, her eyes shining, and then laughed as she put her shields back up. "Of course, people are still people. Some of them will grow up to be jerks. But they'll be *healthy* jerks."

I recalled how she said I looked when I talked about my hyperfields. I guessed it was similar to how she looked talking about those new therapies. I felt a kindred spirit, but she was luckier—her work hadn't turned Frankenstein.

Nor will it ever, I thought. She'd chosen her love more wisely than I had.

◄　◄　◄

I intended to keep the lab meeting short. When Kyoko and I had decided to call it, we'd expected to get everyone assigned to the new task of investigating the Effect, but now that I'd resolved to take Marta's advice, I planned to tell everyone to take the next few days off.

116

A part of me still wanted to demand speedy answers, to get on the research right now and figure out how my hyperfields had malfunctioned so wildly. But I told myself no. Marta was right. I was exhausted, emotionally as well as physically. We all were. I—we—needed to take time to cope with what had happened.

I paced up and down the conference room, holding off sleep with movement. I didn't want to start nodding off in front of everyone. At least my migraine had faded to a dull ache after I'd left Marta and her kids.

Everyone drizzled in around 1300. There wasn't much conversation. People settled around the table, slumped in their chairs, or leaned on their elbows, their faces pale and expressionless.

I sighed, and resisted the urge to collapse into a chair of my own. A few days' rest—just one good night's sleep, really—and we'd all be better.

I was just going to tell everyone to go rest, but Drake came in with news. "I checked the software logs after Kyoko called this morning," he said. "Have a look at this."

He displayed a text file on the wall screen. Heads turned to look. Drake rubbed the back of his neck and yawned, then shook his head.

"Sorry." He pointed at the screen. "The run files show the program output and hyperfield activity, but this log preserves an internal record of everything the software does—inputs, outputs, every variable—for debugging purposes. Here's the time index where the run file begins, where the generators started up before the Effect with no one logged in. That was a little after 0700. We must have had a system crash of some kind, because the log is corrupted. It's unreadable."

I took his word for it. The raw log file was a mass of cryptic numbers and names I couldn't have easily interpreted anyway. But where he pointed, I did see a series of unusually jumbled lines, a string of random characters and numbers as if some animal had crawled over the keyboard.

A system crash? And only minutes after I'd left the hangar. If I'd stayed a bit longer, would I have seen something happening, and been able to stop it?

"These logs were received from several consoles around the OCC around the time of the Effect," Drake continued. "You can see they're just nonsense, but the computer reacts as if they were legitimate commands. It responds by updating a series of internal variables to alter the hyperfield configuration. Unfortunately, those lines are also corrupted—there's no way to tell which variables it changed or what values it changed them to. Then it launches the run software and tries to start the hyperfields. But they won't initialize—the generators are still damaged. I'm guessing one of the commands it received earlier must have set up a loop because the computer just tries over and over again to launch the hyperfields until finally— bingo."

"And no one logged in?" I asked.

"It could be one of these data lines is a user log-on, but there's no way to tell."

Alex Montgomery, one of Drake's grad students, spoke up. "If no one was logged on, where'd these inputs come from?"

Drake shrugged. "Hardware fault? System error? That's something we'll have to try and trace."

"Why don't you try sending the file to the Alley's coms department?" I suggested. "If the corruption isn't random, their decryption software might be able to untangle it."

"Not a bad idea." Drake made a note on his handscreen.

"Hold on, back up." Alex looked skeptical. "You're calling this a system error? A random malfunction produces valid parameters for a radical new hyperfield? Can you imagine the odds against that?"

"What's the alternative?" Leo asked. "That someone logged on, entered the commands, and then messed up the logs to hide their tracks?"

"Why not?" Alex said. "The Alley's the main Navy base at Gateway. Maybe smugglers—"

"Smugglers who know more about hyperfield physics than anyone in the Colonies? That's hardly more likely," Leo said.

"Maybe one of us was paid to—"

"All right, that's enough!" I interrupted Alex. "We can stop that train of thought right there. None of us could have done this on purpose. None of us knows how it could be done, yet. We're not going to point fingers at each other like suspects in a locked room mystery. This was an accident, and we'll figure out how it happened."

There was a silence. Then Kyoko gave a gentle *ahem*.

"Another matter," she said. "These corrupted files will deprive us of information about the precise settings applied to the generators. Many of the analysis programs need that data."

"Can't you calculate backward from the data in the run files?" asked Leo.

"Only by assuming the fields were produced in accordance with the Ryder equations, which is the question at issue." Kyoko's eyes met mine. "We will need to power up the generators to obtain information on their settings from the self-diagnostics."

"Yeah." I looked away. "Yeah. Well, we'll deal with that later. For now, we're going to put all this aside for a few days. We lost friends yesterday. I think we're all still in shock about that. And I know no one slept last night. We're taking time off, to rest and to . . . start coping. So everyone get some sleep. Or get together and talk. Whatever you need to do, and we'll come back to this later."

As the meeting broke up, I called Drake and Kyoko over to talk about whether we should schedule a memorial service. I figured the Navy would have one, but should we have our own? We were thinking it over when Beth approached.

"I was th-thinking," she said. "Are we going to try and, and measure people's neurofields, see if they're different?"

Kyoko looked thoughtful. "I am not sure we have the right instruments. The neurofield is a very weak field, far weaker than our test fields."

"I mentioned the idea to the medical officer," I said, "but as he pointed out, we wouldn't even know what to do with the data."

"Well, well, I was thinking we might do ESP tests and see if, you know, if there's a correlation. M-maybe a stronger field means stronger—"

"And the lunatic fringe weighs in again!" Drake cut her off with an open sneer.

Beth wilted.

"Drake!" I said, dismayed that he'd be so harsh.

He seemed surprised himself, and at once turned apologetic. "I'm sorry. I shouldn't have snapped like that. Bad day all around, Beth, I'm sorry."

She nodded, not answering.

"I think it would be interesting to see such results," said Kyoko to her student, "but they are perhaps better gathered by the neuroscience group back at the University."

Most everyone had filed out of the room by now; only a couple of conversation clusters remained. Belatedly, I remembered my borrowed handscreen. I held it up. "Anyone missing their handscreen? I picked this up in the lab; mine got broken in the Effect."

Those still present looked at each other. It was Tom, sitting alone and silent at the conference table, who finally answered. "That was Anne's."

"Oh." I looked at it. "Okay."

Tom got up and made for the door. I stopped him at the threshold. "Tom," I said. "Listen. I know that you and Anne were . . ."

"Yeah," he said.

"How are you holding up? If there's anything I can do to help . . ."

He looked at me with a strange, closed expression. "It'd be nice if I could say, well, we all knew the risks. But we didn't, did we? No one ever told us there were any risks, did they? You'd think someone ought to have warned us." His eyes glinted with accusation.

"I didn't know it could happen," I said. "I'm sorry."

"I guess you know now, don't you?" he said. "Too bad it's too late."

He turned and left before I could say anything else. I just stood there, silently agreeing with him.

◀ ◀ ◀

I went back to my office and brooded uselessly for a while. For the moment I was too sullen to sleep. I should have known. I blamed the hyperfield generators—some random malfunction and they turned into killers—but ultimately it was my fault, not theirs. Somehow, I should have known what they were capable of.

At one point I turned my chair and stared out the window, watching the stars turn, and thought about what Cole had told me about old myths coming true. I used to like ghost stories and local legends, those crazy reports that turn up on the newsnets every Halloween. I liked them not because I believed them, but because I didn't—the way a roller coaster is fun because you know you're not actually plunging to your death.

There was that story last year from out in the Asteroid Belt, a delightful source of creepy shivers. Prospectors claiming to have seen some huge, man-shaped, fur-covered creature walking around on the surface of asteroids, living in vacuum with no pressure suit. The Beast of the Belt, they called it. There had even been a flurry of reports about some hysterical family that claimed the Beast had come up to their lifesystem dome and pressed itself against the windows, glaring at them with red eyes.

What if something like that turned out to be true? I couldn't explain that with hyperfield properties, however hypothetical. It would mean all bets were off; science and reason were in vain, and any outlandish thing could be true. What if I saw some shaggy ape-man clambering among the dockyards? What if it heaved itself into view right outside the window, staring at me? Its red eyes glowing, shadows at their center.

Oh, this is no good! I was making my skin crawl, and not in a pleasant, Halloween-shivers kind of way. I blanked the window because I couldn't shake the feeling that I might see the Beast at any moment. I stood up and headed for my cabin. High time I tried to take that nap.

◄　◄　◄

I walked down the corridor but something was wrong. I passed a crewman and stopped, startled, and looked back over my shoulder.

It was so faint I couldn't be sure, but I thought for a moment I had seen—sensed—the white-fire aura around his head.

I shook my head. Just my imagination. If the Effect was back, I'd know.

I startled myself again by arriving at the rec center. It was the opposite direction from my cabin. I must have started down the corridor the wrong way, been so tired I didn't notice. *Wonderful*, I thought, *you're walking in a daze now.*

I heard a lot of voices inside and smelled beer. It sounded like the research team had taken advantage of the time off. Perhaps they were holding a wake (if not an official one). I went in.

Everyone was there. I saw Drake sitting with a group of officers, playing cards, stacks of chips piled in front of him. Kyoko and Beth sat at another table, a small crowd around them. Everyone seemed cheerful. Maybe I should be reassured, but still I felt something was definitely wrong.

I saw the white-fires now, and the walls had a hint of transparency, as if I could see through them. No one else seemed to notice anything wrong.

I went over to the table Kyoko and Beth occupied, as the crowd around them laughed and clapped at something. Beth wore glittery robes and gold jewelry, looking like a carnival palm reader, and she dealt out cards with strange pictures on them. I wondered what they were.

She looked up at me. "These are tarot cards, Dave. I thought you recognized them. I'm telling our future."

"How did you know what I was thinking?"

"Telepathy, of course. Don't you understand yet that it's all true?"

She put down a card with a picture of a tower exploding.

"What's that one mean?" someone asked.

"I don't know," said Beth. "Who's got the book?"

"I do." Kyoko consulted her handscreen. Her face was pale and her voice gray and listless. "The Tower struck by lightning. Sudden change or revelation. It can also mean downfall."

"I like the revelation meaning best," said Beth. "Maybe we'll succeed in our research and all win Nobel prizes in magic."

"Beth," I said, "you know, even if hyperfields can explain ESP, I don't think that extends to occult stuff like this."

"Oh, we're just playing," she answered. "Besides, it's all true. Everything has always been true. Even *that's* true, see?" She pointed to a window—which was odd, because the rec center never used to have windows.

But as I puzzled over how the window got there, a shaggy face suddenly appeared, with red goggle eyes and a goblin grin full of jagged monster teeth. It extended a lolling tongue and licked the transparency, laughing madly as it pointed at me with one long-clawed finger.

I reeled backward and tried to scream, but no sound came out. I closed my eyes. *It's not real, it's not real.*

"Beth," I managed to whisper, "Beth, I think we're hallucinating. It's the Effect, the Effect is back."

"The Effect's over, Dave," Beth said. "You're stuck in this world now."

"Play another card," said someone else.

I turned away, not opening my eyes until I knew I wouldn't have to see the Beast again. Behind me, I heard another tarot card slap onto the table.

Beth said, "Oh! Death."

"Good," said Kyoko in her flat, dull voice. "I'm so tired."

Clearly the Effect was happening again. Different this time, but still altering everyone's minds. I ran over to Drake, clutching at his sleeve like a panicked child.

"Drake! Listen, something is happening—"

He glared at me, angry. "Don't interrupt the game, Dave! Nothing is happening here! Nothing except that Beth's gone insane. It was bound to happen sooner or later. Look at her over there, believing things all over the place. Like that, for example." He pointed at the monster in the window. "Do you think that's real? Ha! It's not even a hallucination, because hyperfields don't cause hallucinations. Show me the peer-reviewed paper that says they do, and then I'll believe I'm hallucinating what I think I'm hallucinating."

I turned, looking for someone to make sense. Brown the mess steward sat nearby holding some kind of sculpture resembling a crystal bowl, with a spire sticking up in the middle of it.

"What's that?" I asked.

He looked up at me. "This? This can't help us, Dave. Sharu is too far away. It's up to you, and you'd better hurry because Eiralynn is—Eiralynn is—"

"What?" I grabbed his arms and shouted in his face. "Eiralynn is what?"

His face had gone blank and he just kept repeating over and over: "Eiralynn is—Eiralynn is—"

I let him go and rubbed my eyes.

Gotta think. Gotta think. The Effect was getting worse, becoming more like the first time. I had to find Commander Warren. We might all be in danger. I could see right through the walls now; the other-sense was in full force. There was something outside, in space, besides the shaggy Beast. Something red and glowing, with darkness at its heart.

I fought down panic. I had to find someone I could talk to. I had to find—Marta!

She was there, in a corner of the room, surrounded by the children. They were all bent over drawing pads, scribbling furiously.

"Marta!" I cried. "Help me! I need help!"

She looked up and a cold red light gleamed in her eyes. "I can't help you, Dave. It's too late. You should have worked faster." She spread her arms to indicate the children. "It owns them now."

I rushed over and looked at what the children had drawn. Every page was the same: a solid field of red with a horrid black shape at its center.

"The Red Light and the Shadow!" I screamed, losing all control. "The Red Light and the Shadow! Why did you draw it? Where did you see it?"

In perfect unison, the children looked up and pointed toward the wall.

It was there, the Red Light and the Shadow, huge and flaming, rushing toward the Alley.

"It's Eiralynn!" yelled the children.

Brown finally completed his sentence: *"Eiralynn is COMING! Eiralynn is COMING!"*

I froze. I wanted to run but I couldn't. I could only wait as the tidal wave of red fire and black shadow engulfed the Alley, deck by deck, room by room.

Whoosh! Part of the dockyards vanished into fire.

Whoosh! The Hub fell into the Shadow and was no more.

It started to eat its way down the spokes. The Shadow poured itself eternally into the flames around it, and the Red Light trailed back into the darkness at its heart. Liquid, oozing and alive, engulfed the deck just above me, then poured down.

I must run. I must escape! But I couldn't move! I could only stand there, helpless, while it forced its way down my throat and in through my eyes and ears, and its voice called out, cold and dead yet alive, right beside me, "Vai Eiralynn ayansar! Ayan namar! Ayan namar!"

I woke up screaming.

I sat up in bed, shuddering, then I slumped forward, burying my face in my hands. *God*, I thought. *Bloody dusted hell.*

I looked for the chronometer. Fifteen minutes had elapsed since I lay down to nap. Just fifteen minutes.

CHAPTER ELEVEN

Trying to nap did no good. The Red Light and the Shadow came at me in one disguise after another, never more than a few minutes after I'd closed my eyes. After a few attempts, I gave up. And by then I was too scared to try again.

I could have taken Dr. Cole's pills, but I wanted to save them for the night. So I got up, shrugged back into my clothes, and went to my office. I tried to work but my concentration was shot. I stared dully at a screen full of equations, waiting for some flash of inspiration that never came.

I started when the ping of the intercom broke the silence. Commander Warren wanted to talk to me—the second time that day a call from the Commander had interrupted my dozing. Briefly, the absurd thought that he was doing it on purpose crossed my mind, but that made about as much sense as that nonsense about the Beast of the Belt.

Anyway, he was doing me a favor—if I'd fallen entirely asleep, the Dream would have come back.

Warren's face on the screen showed no sign of the fatigue he must be feeling. If he'd tried to sleep at all he must have had nightmares like everyone else, but he seemed unchangeable, as if he were carved out of granite. He probably hadn't tried yet.

"We're on top of the damage," he told me, "and I'm starting to work on a preliminary report about this mess. Have you found out anything?"

"Not much," I admitted. "It appears some kind of computer malfunction triggered the generators. They went into start-up mode on their own, and when my people replaced the damaged components, well, that was it. As for the Effect they had on us, the physics behind it, that's still a mystery." I sighed. "Not one likely to be solved soon, either. This is radically new hyperfield behavior. Scientists could be chewing on it for years before we understand."

"I hear from Cole that you're thinking this has something to do with ESP."

"It's an idea we've talked about." I explained briefly.

The Commander listened, then frowned. "I don't know, Professor. I don't know how that would look on an official report."

"I don't think it would look too good in a peer-reviewed paper either, but we may be stuck with it." I spread my hands. "Even if it's true, it doesn't help us explain the physics."

"This has been a strange couple of days," Warren said. "You know we still have a shipwreck to investigate as well. The computers have been running a forensic simulation based on the images our ships recorded. You know what the preliminary conclusion is?"

"What?"

"Collision with 'a large object probably of natural origin.'"

It took me a moment to interpret the dry, neutral phrase. "Wait—you mean an *asteroid*?"

"A small one, maybe a few dozen meters across, but that's the first read. The *Lunar Explorer* struck something, not quite head on, and it stripped away nearly half the ship as it went by."

I gaped. The odds against such an encounter were—astronomical, to be literal about it. Outside of badly written action videos about space pirates, meteor "storms" don't exist. And even if the one-in-a-million chance did occur—

"Why didn't the ship's nav systems detect the object before the collision?"

Warren smiled grimly. "According to the flight recorder, there was a malfunction in the ship's radar systems right before. Bit of a coincidence, isn't it?" Unaware that he was verbalizing my own thoughts, Warren continued, "What are the odds against meeting a large asteroid in the first place? And at the one moment when the nav systems will miss it—"

"About like the odds of a computer crash producing a radical new hyperfield by accident."

The conspiracy theories raised at the lab meeting earlier that day sprang into my mind. I frowned. No, it was ridiculous to even think about that.

But Warren was thinking about it. He gave me a sharp look. "Are you suggesting some connection?"

"No," I said at once. "It was just a stray thought. Even if you imagine some plot—"

"Yeah. To be honest, Professor, it occurred to me. I don't like coincidences, and two such bizarre accidents in succession is a big one. If some saboteur on board the *Lunar Explorer* shut down their nav systems, and then tampered with your generators . . ." He sighed. "But it's all nonsense. Who would benefit from both events? Who could know there'd be an uncharted meteor heading for collision? Who would know how to modify your equipment?"

"No one," I answered. "There's no one in the Solar System who knows how to create the Effect we experienced yesterday. That much, I can tell you for sure."

"Yeah." He shook his head. "No, as nice and tidy as it would be to put all this down to some criminal mastermind, it won't hold up. How do you plan to proceed in your investigation?"

"I've told my people to knock off for today and rest. We—they're all in shock over the people we lost, and no one has slept, with the nightmares. When we get back to it—" I paused. Here was the point I didn't want to face. We needed to know exactly how the generators were set during the Effect, and given the corrupted computer logs, there was only one way to find out. Kyoko had mentioned it in the lab meeting. I didn't want to do it, but she was right. It was the logical next step.

I continued, "We've learned all we can from examining the generators as they are. Next, we'll have to restore power and use the self—"

"No."

Warren's reply was so flat and final it caught me off guard. I paused for a few seconds before speaking again. "Commander, we need—"

"Professor, what are you thinking? Five minutes ago you told me some malfunction triggered your generators on their own. Now you want to plug them in so it can happen again? Not a chance."

It had never occurred to me that it might not be my decision how to handle my equipment. I felt my toes being stepped on, and it annoyed me. I thought to myself, why, I could have just let Leo power them up this morning and Commander Warren would have been none the wiser! And nothing bad would have happened, of course not.

It wasn't as if I *wanted* to connect the generators again. I wasn't proposing it recklessly, as the Commander seemed to think. I hated the idea of letting those machines get power again, but I knew that's what we had to do. The truth was, I felt pretty good about myself for facing my irrational fears and setting them aside. Only here was Warren thinking *he* knew best how to handle *my* equipment.

Trying to sound reasonable, I said, "Commander, we can take any necessary precautions to prevent—"

"The necessary precaution is to keep those machines disconnected. The risk of turning them on again is unacceptable."

"We need that data. We can't proceed without it."

"Then you'll just have to wait before you proceed. If the Navy decides the research is worth the risk, then once we get these civilians off the base and the crew prepared for any emergency, you may continue. Until then, my decision is final."

I plead diminished capacity for what came next. Lack of sleep, the emotional shock of recent events—and perhaps, the early rumblings of what was soon to come. But whatever the cause, I let myself get angry; and then I let it run away with me.

"I don't think that's your decision to make, Commander."

Warren's face changed, subtly, but it should have been enough to warn me off. "I think you'll find it is, Professor."

"This is my project and how I conduct it is up to me," I snapped, stupidly digging the hole deeper. "My use of the Alley's facilities was approved by the Navy and you were *ordered* to cooperate! The rest is my business, not yours!"

Warren didn't raise his voice. But his tone was a slap in the face. "It became my business when your equipment killed forty-one people under my command, *Professor*. You'll find that my orders—*if* you bother to read them—direct me to extend 'all cooperation that is consistent with the safe operation of your command.' It is my judgment that any further use of your equipment is inconsistent with safety and so it will not be done, under any circumstances."

I still didn't wise up. "Commander, you're being completely irrational! We can easily make certain that no—"

"Since you clearly do not understand, Professor," Warren interrupted, "I have no choice but to declare the hangar containing your equipment off-limits to all civilians. That specifically includes every one of your people, Professor Harris. You're out. That's it."

"But you can't do that!"

"Complain to the Navy. Complain to the President, if you think it'll do any good—once I reopen civilian com channels, that is, which I don't anticipate doing anytime soon. Until higher authority says otherwise, I am in command here. If I tell the guards at the hangar to shoot to kill, *they will do it.* Do I make myself clear?"

Too late, far too late, I woke up. What the dust did I think I was doing? I tried to get control of myself. With an effort, I bit back my next angry retort and said, "Yes, Commander."

"Good." Warren closed the intercom link immediately. The damage was done.

I stared at the screen—now showing my equations again—while I trembled with stupid fury. Who was I angry at? Warren? Myself? *What was I thinking?*

I tried to calm down. It didn't really matter. We were going to lay off for a few days anyway. I'd go to Warren and apologize and patch things up somehow. In eight days—no, seven now—the relief ships would arrive and they'd take the civilians off. Then there'd be a chance to revisit the issue, with the advantage of rest and a little distance to keep the discussion friendly.

Meanwhile, the equations on my screen might as well have been hieroglyphics. I cleared the screen with an angry slap at the keyboard.

I needed to regain my equilibrium somehow. Think pleasant thoughts, I told myself, as if those were so easy to come by just then.

On an impulse, I opened the library directories and searched for an image of Linda Ryder's first public hyperfield demonstration on May 23, 2201, in the Midway District of Star City.

The library produced the picture used in all the histories and biographies. In it, Linda leans over a console, located to the right of a high platform supporting her generator. She is frowning in concentration at whatever readings the instruments are giving her. Linda's husband sits at the console. He was an electrical engineer who worked with her to build the generator. The console itself is a haphazard affair of trailing wires and stacked instruments, each piece built in Linda's lab through trial and error.

The hyperfield dominates the picture. At its center, the generator crouches, not too different in appearance from my own models. The hyperfield it's producing glows a warm yellow-orange, bright at the center, trailing off to deeper orange at the edge. Its glow bathes the faces of Linda and her team. A few photoelectric panels stand to one side of the field, capturing enough of its light to power the generator circuitry and sustain the field—for that's the point of the demonstration. But most of the light spills freely across the crowd, gazing wide-eyed and openmouthed at the wondrous sight.

As always, I looked through the crowd hoping to see a glimpse of my own ten-year-old face, but as usual, I didn't find it. I was there somewhere, though, on that day.

I remember my friends and I used to sneak above decks in Midway to pick our way across the frozen squares of former parkland, and stare at the ice-draped skeletons of trees. I liked to look up at the ribbon of cold stars, far overhead, seen through the vast transparency that used to let in the sunlight, before the Catastrophe. Before the sun went out.

In those days, in the heart of the Dark Years, the only warm, lit places in Star City were the algae farms. They produced both oxygen and food, and to sustain those vital functions the tanks received almost all the energy that could be squeezed from the unreliable fusion reactors. The dormitories, where we all lived and tried to shut out the darkness, got only enough light and heat to keep them habitable.

Midway, and other above-deck areas of the Colony, got nothing. What had once been the most expensive living space in Star City stood empty, a wilderness dark, frozen, and dead. And strictly off-limits, which was why my friends and I liked to sneak up there.

On the day of Linda's demonstration, though, I went to Midway with full permission, with my mom by my side. All the grown-ups were buzzing about this new hyperfield thing; most seemed to think it wouldn't work out. My teacher had tried to explain how it worked to my small class of last-born kids, but I didn't really get it.

Lights mounted on poles lit up the strange machine on the platform, including the people working on it. Everyone's breath made white fog, visible in the light. I looked up, but the ribbon of stars was washed out.

Only Linda and her colleagues knew what we were about to see, having already seen it in her lab. She began a speech explaining her invention to the crowd, but I paid little attention. Grown-ups making speeches bored me; I wanted to see something.

Then she and the others did things at the console. My teacher had said the hyperfield would be a bright light. I didn't expect much since I'd seen lights before.

And then—*magic!*

A glowing orange ball swam into existence around the generator, brightened, then turned yellow. It got brighter, and then brighter still. Heat poured off it, heat I could feel on my face and through my coat even while the cold of Midway bit at the back of my neck. My idea of being warm was curling up in front of a little wall vent to catch puffs of hot air. *This* was being warm! And the light, it was huge. I'd learn its exact size in school later. Not all that big really. But to me then, it was huge.

When I looked up, I saw something I'd never seen before: the far side of Midway, the buildings and parks on the opposite side of the cylinder, six kilometers away, just barely visible in the orange light. In that moment, I finally knew how it must have looked in daylight, before the Catastrophe.

The crowd gasped, and then sighed, and then *believed*. Cheers and applause erupted. My mom grabbed me and hugged me, not in the desperate way she did when she couldn't stop crying but with joy. She wasn't crying, she was laughing and *smiling* and then she was crying too, but it was a different kind of crying, and it was really good.

I later learned the reason why hyperfields were important: They were small. How simple a quality to be so vital! A fusion reactor was a giant thing, surrounded by massive shielding, expensive in raw materials—and those in the Colonies were dangerously unreliable as well, constructed in frantic haste during the year between the astronomer's warning and the final Catastrophe. They'd had to cannibalize a lot of smaller stations to build fusion reactors for the Colonies and even so they couldn't build enough to replace the delicate photoelectric wings that had captured the pre-Catastrophe sunlight. A hyperfield generator, by contrast, used only trivial amounts of metal and silica, and produced only what we wanted from it—light and heat. No radiation, no waste.

It's no exaggeration to call it miraculous technology. But the practicalities pale in comparison to the euphoria of that moment in Midway. I sometimes wonder if it was something primal: In its color, light, and heat, the hyperfield wasn't that different from a bonfire, the sort of thing humans had gathered around to ward off the night since the dawn of time. Whatever the reason, everyone there knew, from the moment Linda flipped the switch on, that everything was going to be all right.

As for me, I was hooked. Linda's demonstration set my life path. I dedicated myself to those light-bringing, heat-giving, Mom-smiling miracles.

I was Linda's last grad student. She retired after I got my degree, and died a few years ago. She was only sixty-seven, but her health was never good. Like everyone of her generation with any expertise in physics or engineering, she'd worked on the fusion reactors during the Dark Years. Radiation poisoning from those days left a legacy that finally took her.

Now I looked at Linda's picture and thought, how would she handle this? Certainly not by feeling helpless because her results didn't fit a known set of equations. Linda wrote her own equations.

Only days earlier, as the rescue effort for the *Lunar Explorer* progressed, I had been excited by the prospect of doing the same thing. New math, a new set of equations, perhaps bearing my name into history. What scientist wouldn't be pleased by the prospect? But every time I looked at my data on the screen, all I did was brood over how to make Linda's math fit.

Did I need new math? If so, I'd follow Linda's example and find it. Marshenko's original hyperspace theory had languished for a hundred years, a curiosity viewed as a dead end by most physicists, until Linda resolved its contradictions and derived her equations.

Linda's work must represent only a partial derivation, a special case within a more general theory of hyperfield physics, the same way that Newtonian mechanics represented a special case within general relativity. Could it be Marshenko's original theory held the answer? Part of the way Linda made her hyperspace theory consistent was to dismiss certain faulty assumptions of Marshenko, and then see if the theory could be reworked without them. The data proved her right, but . . . perhaps at least some of Marshenko's errors weren't errors after all. Somewhere in the list, was there something Linda should have retained?

The thought felt promising. Linda's key insight had been—

The door chimed. "Come in."

The door slid open to reveal Marta standing outside. She jabbed a finger at me with a mock-parental frown. "I knew it! I knew you wouldn't take the day off like you were supposed to!"

Her arrival broke my train of thought, but I was glad to see her. "I tried, honest," I said. "Nightmares, right away."

She grew serious. "Sorry." She came into the office, looking around with mild curiosity, then sat down. "The medics are handing out pills—"

"I have some," I said. "But I want to save them for tonight. So for now—no napping."

"Well, it's dinnertime so I thought I'd look you up and see if you'd like another of our mess hall trysts."

Surprised, I checked the chronometer. Sure enough, they'd been serving dinner for the last half hour. "I lost track of time," I said. "I had no idea it was so late."

"Did no one ever tell you that being an absentminded professor's a cliché?" She cocked her head to one side. "You must come up with something more original."

"How about a mad scientist?" I shrugged. "Angry scientist, anyway. I may have just wrecked my project by getting in a shouting match with Commander Warren."

"Ah, well, a certain amount of venting is to be expected. Still, my advice would be to pick a target other than the guy who can have you thrown out an air lock. I suggest yelling at your students."

I smiled. She always made me smile, one way or another. "Right, because that's what good teachers do."

She grinned. "So, dinner? Before they stop serving?"

"Yes." I shut off the screen and followed Marta out, oblivious to the fact that I had just dropped the thought leading straight to the solution of the entire hyperfield mystery—or at least, to the scientific conundrum. I wouldn't come back to it until it was too late.

CHAPTER TWELVE

As we walked toward the mess hall, Marta said, "True or false, hyperfields are perpetual motion machines."

"False," I answered.

"But," she persisted, "doesn't a hyperfield produce enough energy to keep itself going, plus a lot left over?"

"The field doesn't create any energy. It's a conduit to hyperspace through which energy flows. The principle is the same as the water wheels they used to have in preindustrial times. The current of the river provides enough energy to turn the wheel and to grind grain or do some other work. A hyperfield is like poking a hole in a dam and putting your water wheel in front of the stream that pours out."

"Except we didn't build the dam."

"Right, the dam in this case is inherent in the structure of space-time. We just make the hole, which is actually an electromagnetic field created by the generator."

"See, back in college I had this philosophy professor who said hyperspace was just a construct physicists made up to—" Marta deepened her voice to sound remarkably like an aging and very pompous lecturer, "rescue their version of reality from the epistemological implications of true perpetual motion."

I knew she was just teasing, so I played along. "Your mistake was listening to a philosopher talk about science. They're very jealous of our success."

"Oh, he wasn't an antiscience type. He loved science. He thought you were making it all up, of course, but he admired the creativity."

"I *wish* we were making it all up," I said. "It would be so much easier."

"Okay, so here's a thought. You punch a hole into hyperspace and all the energy pours out. What happens if there are people—or something—living there?"

I smiled. "Hyperspace isn't a *place*. It's not an alternate Universe like you see in fantasy videos. It's an aspect of our own space-time, just a bit more complicated than the three dimensions our senses can perceive. No one lives there because it isn't a *there* at all."

"I see." With a wicked grin, Marta sprang the trap: "Then tell me again where the energy comes from?"

I could have launched into a lengthy explanation. Instead I laughed. "I'm caught! I've been making it up as I go!"

"Good, I'm glad we settled that," she said. "Because if there was someone living in hyperspace and we kept punching holes and taking energy, well, it occurs to me they wouldn't like it."

She made me laugh again. "I'd better not bring that up in a lab meeting, people might just believe it. They were halfway to formulating a conspiracy theory about smugglers today."

"Of course they were. People always look for villains when something bad happens. That's why you get lawsuits, pontificating politicians, everyone pointing a finger at someone. The human mind craves meaning; even the most sinister conspiracy is more comforting than the idea that bad things just happen, for no reason."

I thought this over for a few seconds, but before I replied I heard Drake call out, "Dave! Have a look at this!"

We stopped at the door of the mess hall, and turned around to see Drake waving his handscreen as he came toward us.

"What is it?" I asked.

"I've been running simulations this afternoon, using the data from the run files—I know, we know the physics we have is wrong, but I thought the sims might at least tell us something useful—"

"Weren't you supposed to be taking the day off?" I interrupted.

Marta looked at me and lifted an eyebrow. "Weren't *you?*"

I raised my hands. "Touché."

Drake stopped, noticing Marta for the first time. He looked from me to her and back again. I made the introductions, adding, "Marta was a passenger on the *Lunar Explorer.*"

"Oh." Drake hesitated as he searched for the right thing to say. "Er, you got out all right, then?"

Without a moment's pause, Marta deadpanned, "No, I was still on the ship when it blew up."

It took Drake a few seconds, then he relaxed and grinned. "Fast work, Dave. But picking up disaster survivors? Seems a little desperate."

Before I could say anything, Marta replied, "Dave and I have been secret lovers for years."

My exclamation was somewhere between a laugh and a protest as I felt the room get a little too warm again.

"That's excellent," Drake said. "Maybe you can help me out. The grad students have a pool going on just when Professor Lives-in-His-Head here will get snagged by someone. Give me the inside tip and I'll cut you in on my winnings."

"You don't really have a pool on that, do you?" I asked.

Marta laughed and leaned in toward Drake confidentially. "Let me know where the big money is and I'll see what I can do."

It was time to regain control of this conversation. I cleared my throat, "Drake, you found something in these simulations?"

"Yeah." Drake passed me his handscreen. "If this is right, during the Effect our alpha and beta generators both maintained active hyperfields."

I looked.

"Look at the field radius," Drake said.

I looked again. "Ten kilometers! That would enclose the entire Alley."

"That would make sense, wouldn't it?" Marta asked. "That's how they affected everyone."

"Well, yes, but . . . hyperfields of that size? From our little generators?" This was another impossibility, like the ripples of energy swirling over the fields in run 37. How could the event horizon extend so far beyond the hardware? I tried to picture it in my head, a new field somehow expanding outward . . . perhaps a kind of *unfolding* as it . . . no. It was gone. For a moment I thought I could see it, but the image fell apart. It just couldn't happen.

In line at the mess hall, I studied Drake's simulation. "Total energy output's not much higher than our normal settings," I observed. "That low an output dispersed over that large a radius . . . there'd be no light or heat strong enough to detect. No effect but *the* Effect. It hangs together . . ."

"Still," said Drake, "a ten-kilometer radius from one-meter generators? Are we up to six impossible things yet?"

I shook my head. "It's after breakfast. I'm afraid the allowance goes up."

Marta tilted her head. "Are you talking about *Alice in Wonderland*?"

"Is that what it's from?" I asked. "It's something Linda Ryder used to say when I was her student: To work on hyperfields, you have to believe six impossible things before breakfast."

"Turns out that's not a joke, it's a statistic," Drake grumbled. "I should start taking bets we'll see a field shaped like a cube instead of a sphere. We've got huge hyperfields, hyperfields with ripples in them, hyperfields that make people go crazy—not to mention all the psychic nonsense."

"Psychic? What's this?" Marta's eyes widened with interest.

As we reached the head of the line, I explained my guess—and Beth's spin on it—while Brown handed out plates of something meant to be lasagna.

Marta grabbed a salad as well. "Wow, my philosophy professor would love that."

Drake frowned. "Your philosophy professor?"

"I was joking with Dave about an old professor back in college, one of those guys who says science is just a human construct, no real truth to it, that sort of thing."

"Yeah?" Drake turned angry fast, a little too angry too fast. "Ask him how we managed to get out here, to build the Colonies, if we only imagined that technology would work. Ask him to step out of an air lock without a pressure suit and see if he can construct a reality other than the one Science says will kill him. Philosophers are just wasting their time. Science has learned more in five hundred years than philosophy has worked out in five thousand! Psychic powers, ghosts and goblins, religion, philosophy, it's all the same fluffy nonsense! If people don't like that, too bad, it's the truth!"

Drake kept ranting, his face getting redder and his voice rising slowly to a shout. Conversation around the room fell off as heads turned. I listened with mounting worry: This sort of diatribe was all out of character for Drake. I knew he was a Skeptic—with a capital

S—but he'd never seemed especially passionate about it before. Usually, he was as easygoing as Kyoko was controlled. His manner made no sense. I guess it made none to him either because just as I was about to interrupt his tirade, he caught himself and blinked, his face falling in almost comical surprise and embarrassment.

There was an awkward silence as he seemed to be thinking of something apologetic to say, but it was Marta who found the right way to break the tension. "Wanna bet?" she said.

Drake laughed nervously. "Yeah, I'll give you good odds."

The dangerous mood vanished like mist out of a cooling vent, leaving him shamefaced. "Look, I'm sorry. I don't know why I went off like that . . . bad day, I guess."

"You don't have to apologize," Marta said. "Dave just picked a fight with the base commander."

"What's this?" Drake looked at me.

"Thanks, Marta," I said. We exited the serving line and found an empty table while I explained. "Warren denied permission to reconnect power to the generators. I argued about it and managed to get us banned from accessing the equipment at all."

"Oh, we're all just brilliant today, aren't we?" said Drake. "Who's Kyoko yelled at?"

"Don't know." I couldn't imagine Kyoko losing her temper. But then, I wouldn't have expected Drake to either.

◀ ◀ ◀

The Observation Gallery maintained dim lights to allow a clear view through the transparencies, and with its high ceiling and tasteful decor to welcome visiting dignitaries, many thought it had a romantic atmosphere. But I swear I was just thinking of the view.

When we stepped out of the elevator, Marta noticed the damage along the side where the Wheel's wobbling had crushed in the wall. "You know, I've heard your story, but I hadn't thought how dangerous the situation must have been. This place could have torn itself apart, couldn't it?"

"Well, it didn't." I didn't want to dwell on the Effect. "The view's better on the other side anyway."

My mood had improved somewhat during the evening. We had gotten through dinner without anyone else losing their temper, and then had found some others in the rec center and gotten together a game of cards. Marta had given Drake a run for his money, but I lost badly—it seemed everyone could tell when I tried to bluff. I normally did better, even though I didn't have much taste for gambling. Fatigue had ruined my poker face; I could have easily dropped off to sleep right there at the table, but I wanted to wait until my usual bedtime to get back on a normal cycle.

After the game broke up, I suggested to Marta we visit the Hub. I can honestly say I wasn't looking for romance: I was too tired to want anything but sleep. But she was good company and I thought I could keep my eyes open a little longer. So here we were.

I led the way over to the undamaged side of the chamber, where the transparencies looked out over the dockyards.

"This is a huge room." Marta looked around curiously. "What is it, three or four stories up to that ceiling?"

"It's something like that," I said. "The Hub's got three decks, not counting that mezzanine, but this is the only deck used for anything but passing through." I pointed. "Up there, see those ladders? They go up to a deck between the Wheel's bearings, and then above that is a big cylindrical room called the Transfer Room, used for moving over to the freefall section."

"We came through that on our way from where they docked the lifeboats," Marta said. "But not through this gallery, just ordinary rooms and corridors. You don't often see space like this outside of the original Colonies."

"The Alley was built pre-Catastrophe, like they were," I said. I enjoyed playing tour guide. "They were rich enough to build cathedrals in space if they wanted to—and they did."

"I suppose it was abandoned completely during the Dark Years."

"I don't know, but I'd think so."

We walked past the theater-like rows of upholstered chairs and stood side by side, looking out at the view.

"Wow, that's magnificent," Marta said.

Massive, rounded shapes rolled by as we rotated with the Wheel. The docking array's extended network stretched out overhead, illuminated in the darkness by running lights and glowing windows. Out beyond the hangars, machine shops, and lifesystem tanks the stars wheeled, cold and indifferent, beyond all troubles.

"You imagine you'd be looking *down* on it, after coming up in the elevator," Marta said. "But of course the axis is still above us. Can you picture what it must have looked like during the War? Huge fleets of ships coming and going, and all bright in the sunlight?"

"I've heard the Alley was to have been the launch platform for the attempt to retake the Colonies in Lunar orbit," I said. "They had the entire Colonial fleet here ready to attack the Terrans, and then—"

"Then the Catastrophe," Marta finished. "It's a brush with history, isn't it? If they hadn't called off the War this might be a famous place."

We spoke in hushed tones, though there was no one around we might disturb. It just seemed to fit the setting. After a minute or two, as if reacting to the same invisible cue, we both turned to sit down next to each other in the front row of chairs.

"The Colonies are so huge you don't feel them as things that had to be built. But something like this really lets you see the kind of resources they had, the abundance . . . just fifty years ago." She shook her head in wonder.

"We'll be that rich again. Thirty years of hyperfields, we're still in the infancy of the technology. In theory, if you could build a generator that wouldn't be vaporized, the total energy you could get from a hyperfield is enormous. In time, we'll have more energy than the Sun ever gave us."

She turned from the view and smiled, leaning toward me with both elbows on the chair arm between us. "Do you suppose hyperfields could be used to bring back the Earth? Suppose a bunch of satellites orbiting Earth with hyperfields strong enough to thaw out the air, make it habitable again?"

"Sure they could." I smiled back. "Someday they will. I wonder what it was like to stand in an open field with a blue sky overhead. I bet the old pictures don't do it justice."

She leaned closer, and I leaned too. "So, you'd better get right on that," she whispered. "Don't keep me waiting."

We moved still closer, and my own voice became a whisper. "I'll start tomorrow."

But whatever would have come next never came. I saw something out of the corner of my eye. Something that looked like—

My head snapped around. I jumped to my feet and ran to the window, leaving Marta just as startled and confused.

"Did you see that?" I cried. "Did you see it?"

Frowning, Marta came over. "What?"

No. I did not see that. It was just a mistake.

It was a discoloration on a support strut. A trick of shadow given the illusion of motion as the superstructure rolled past the windows. It certainly was *not* a huge, fur-covered, man-shaped Beast clambering along a girder between two hangars, hunched over as it slouched its way along.

"Did you see it?" I repeated. I needed Marta to say something like, "You mean that guy in the pressure suit?" so I could believe I'd made a mistake after all.

But she said, "I didn't see anything." She looked at me questioningly, waiting for an explanation.

I stared hard out of the window, pressing my hands against it like I was trapped in a bottle. But the rotation had already carried it out of view—if it had been there at all. No, it had to be nothing.

"For a second, I thought—" I began to say, but caught myself. I couldn't possibly say what I thought I'd seen or she'd think I was nuts.

Marta was about to say something else. But before she could, someone screamed. A man's voice, shrill with terror.

We both jumped. My heart hammered and my first thought was, *Someone else saw it! It's real!* But I followed that with a more rational, *No, it can't be. It must be something else.*

"What now?" Marta asked, turning toward the sound.

An officer came hurtling down the ladder from the inner Hub deck, actually launching himself downward faster than the faint gravity would have pulled him. We lost sight of him for a moment as he crashed with an audible thud into the mezzanine deck, then reappeared at the edge and tumbled over the rail, landing in a heap a short distance from us.

I made a move toward him, thinking he must be injured, but he scrambled to his feet and looked around, eyes wide and staring. When he spotted us, he shouted, "You two! Don't just stand there! Run! Run! It's coming, didn't you see it? Don't you know? Run for your lives!"

My knees went weak and I could feel the blood draining from my face. It was hard to make my voice work. "What's coming? What did you see?" I thought I knew and dreaded hearing it confirmed.

But he didn't describe a fur-covered ape-man. His answer made no sense at all. "Wires!" he screamed. "Wires everywhere! Lines of force and they can't be measured! Don't you understand?"

He charged us, waving his arms. Without thinking, I moved between him and Marta. But she put a hand on my shoulder and stepped around me, holding her other hand out to the officer, who staggered to a halt a few feet from us.

"It's all right," she said. Her voice was very calm. Soothing. "We're all right. Tell us what's happened."

"Don't you know? How can you not know? It comes out of the wires, all blue-white with needles! Don't you understand? It's *electrical!*" His voice rose to a shriek as if this was the most terrifying thing possible.

"I understand," Marta said. "Look, there's no wires. But let's go over there by the wall where we're safe, until we can get some help."

She tried to lead him, but he yanked back and yelled at her. "Help? Help? There's no help! Lines of force in electric needles and the Spark Man coming! Civilians evacuate! Rescue stations! Civilians evacuate!"

He made a sudden lunge and grabbed Marta, pulling her off her feet and trying to drag her away. But he lost his balance and toppled over, kicking his feet as if still trying to run. I leaped for him and tried to pull Marta clear. All the while he kept shouting about evacuating the civilians, a man made of sparks, and needles in wires.

I wrapped my arms around Marta and we rolled free of him. He jumped up, glaring at us. "You must evacuate! Orders are orders! They can't be measured!"

Suddenly he hunched up his shoulders and batted his hands as if something had grabbed him from behind around the neck. Shrieking in absolute terror, he whirled around and around, trying to shake off his imaginary attacker, presumably some sort of electrical man made of sparks.

"Get it off me! Get it off me! Wires! Lines of force!"

I got to my feet and pulled Marta farther away. "Find an intercom panel, call security," I gasped. "The code's—uh—just enter zero-zero-one, that's the control deck."

Marta went. I circled the officer, staying clear of his thrashing. I was afraid he'd hurt himself—or us, if he tried to "evacuate" us again. I hoped Marta found the intercom fast.

All at once, he stopped struggling and went limp, falling to the deck. His screams became miserable, hopeless sobs. "Make it go away. No more, no more. Too many wires."

Marta reappeared at my side. "I called. They're coming."

She knelt down and spoke to the officer in low, soothing tones.

Security arrived in moments. They took charge of the whimpering officer. A medic showed up after another minute. The guards held the madman while the medic gave him some kind of injection that made him fall unconscious at once.

"Bloody dusted hell," I said, something I normally only thought, but I wasn't thinking of politeness just then. "What happened to him?"

The medic glanced at me. "Not just him."

I stared. Marta asked the question. "There've been others?"

"Three," said the medic. "In the last hour."

Breath rushed out of me as if I'd been hit in the stomach. I knew what this meant.

There really was a doomsday clock, and it had started ticking.

CHAPTER THIRTEEN

The pills did not work. The Red Light and the Shadow attacked, over and over, all night long. I suppose it was accumulated fatigue that let me get back to sleep each time, for a few minutes before I jolted awake once again, until my mind and body felt like shattered glass. The only reason I didn't give up trying was because I had to be able to work in the morning. I had no more time for rest and recovery.

Maybe I would have been able to sleep without the Dream if my good mood had persisted. But it was gone, blasted to shreds. Marta had tried to suggest the breakdowns the medic mentioned didn't mean anything. Maybe a few people already had psychological problems, and the trauma of the Effect just pushed them over the edge. She didn't really believe it, though. Neither did I. This was a sign of permanent damage from the Effect, and that meant there would be more to come.

But that wasn't what terrified me, what brought the nightmare storming back, what powered the doomsday clock now ticking away inexorably in my imagination. No, it was the fact that I had seen the Beast of the Belt outside the Observation Gallery window. That memory carried with it a thought, written in letters of fire across the front of my brain: *I'm next.*

It might already be too late. If I was seeing things like that, I might be only a hair away from raving in wild-eyed madness until a medic came to sedate and carry me away.

No one must know. Thank God I hadn't told Marta about it. I must not tell anyone.

So I tossed and turned in bed, forcing myself to breathe slowly and evenly after each gasping escape from the Dream, until my heart rate slowed and I could try to sleep again.

If I hallucinated the Beast, why did I also dream of the Red Light and the Shadow? Wasn't one nightmare enough?

The alarm pinged. 0700, Thursday morning. I hadn't slept much and yet I gave up the struggle with some relief. The face that stared back at me from the bathroom mirror had pale skin and hollow eyes. I swayed on my feet, but after a shower I both looked and felt more human. I had gotten enough sleep that I didn't feel any worse than the day before. But no better either. Coffee. I needed coffee.

◀ ◀ ◀

Everyone else looked better and talked about how the pills had helped. I almost complained they hadn't worked for me, but didn't. Perhaps that was another symptom, like the hallucination in the Observation Gallery. It was better kept secret.

As the day got going and I became more awake, I was inclined to dismiss my night fears about going crazy. I'd only seen a shadow out of the corner of my eye, and that was thin evidence for believing I was going insane. Such worries belonged in their place among the nightmares, not in the light of day.

Still, I didn't mention it to anyone.

I tracked down Kyoko and we put our heads together about how best to measure people's neurofields. It seemed like the logical next step. The problem was that our instruments weren't designed for such a weak field.

"We can modify them for a lower detection threshold," Kyoko said, "but at a cost to precision. If there are subtle changes, we may miss them." She looked fine. Everyone got a good night's sleep but me.

I rubbed my eyes. "Maybe it's a waste of time. No one knows enough about the neurofield to make anything of the data anyway. Even if our neurofields changed under the influence of our hyperfields, they should have changed back the instant the Effect ended. A permanent change in the neurofield would only happen with a permanent change in its generator."

"The generator of the neurofield is the brain," Kyoko said. "Any changes there are perhaps better detected by medical equipment than via hyperfield measurements."

"Blast all this anyway!" A wave of petulance washed across my mind. "Maybe those guys were already nuts."

Kyoko pursed her lips and spoke slowly, thinking as she talked. "You know, if Drake's simulation is correct about the size of the hyperfields, then they were in almost complete overlap for the whole duration of the Effect, and remained stable. Our project has succeeded."

"How about that. Hurray us." I ran my fingers through my hair. "Not the way we wanted it to, huh?"

She nodded.

"I'm going to talk to Dr. Cole again. Find out if there's some nice, ordinary explanation for the incidents last night. We can always hope. Otherwise . . ."

"If we do wish to take these measurements . . ." Kyoko was still considering the problem. "The best way to measure an extremely weak hyperfield is to measure its influence on a stronger hyperfield that we *can* record with precision. Nothing affects one field so much as another in proximity, yes? I propose we use our alpha generator, creating an especially unstable field while the test subject takes the place of the beta."

I laughed, one humorless bark. "That might be hard to arrange."

Kyoko didn't understand; apparently word of my blowup with Warren hadn't circulated yet. I explained.

She at once offered the same excuse for my behavior as everyone else, including myself: "Surely he will understand you were not yourself. We were all in shock, and without sleep yesterday."

"Maybe he will, but I doubt that'll change his mind on the safety question."

"If the medical officer finds these mental breakdowns yesterday cannot be explained otherwise, we will have good reason for him to reconsider."

"Yeah." I stood up and stretched; my limbs felt heavy and cramped. "Find Drake, talk to him about what we'd need to set it up like you suggested. I'm going to try and find Dr. Cole."

◀ ◀ ◀

Nothing seemed to have changed in the infirmary. It wasn't full of raving maniacs in straitjackets, anyway. Maybe the officer last night and the other three that the medic mentioned were isolated cases after all. I made straight for Cole's office.

The door stood open and I saw the doctor talking to Commander Warren. I paused at the threshold, and knocked.

Warren looked around, then nodded a brief greeting. "Professor Harris." His voice was cold, but not overtly hostile.

"Commander Warren. I want to apologize for yesterday, I was way out of—"

He cut me off with a brisk wave. "Case of impaired judgment. Forget it." Despite his words, his tone remained cold. "Come to see what more damage you've caused?"

I took the remark without protest; after all, he was right. "Yes." I looked to the doctor. "These four people—"

"Nine," said Cole. "Five more cases overnight."

"Dust!"

He waved me into the office. "Don't stand there in the door. Come in, sit down."

Two chairs faced Cole's desk, but Warren stood near the wall rather than sitting. I hesitated for a moment, then sat down. Cole glanced from the Commander to me, noticing the tension, but didn't comment.

"I don't suppose there's a chance these breakdowns have some ordinary explanation?" I asked. Warren made a derisive noise.

"You mean like post-traumatic stress? No." The doctor shook his head and gestured at a report on his screen. "The symptoms are all over the map, but are closer to paranoid schizophrenia than anything else I know of. Schizophrenia results from brain defects that can be detected by holographic imaging, but no such damage is present in any of the nine patients. Psychoactive drugs can mimic it, but all nine blood tests are clear. And yet brain *activity* is consistent with a schizophrenic state." He paused, and took a deep breath. "The bottom line is, something I can't detect is acting on my patients' brains the same way a very nasty drug would."

"Something like the neurofield," I said. "The Effect damaged our neurofields."

"Can't say yes, can't say no." Cole spread his hands and shrugged. "I'll add this detail though: No antipsychotic drug we've tried has had any effect on these symptoms. None."

"I want to measure the neurofields of people on board. A random sample, anyway. See if there are any changes from normal."

"We don't know enough to interpret whatever you might measure."

"Not medically, perhaps," I said. "But maybe if we figure out how the fields have changed, physically, that'll help us figure out the physics behind the Effect itself." I shrugged before adding, "And maybe then I can work out a way to change the neurofields back to normal."

"It's all pretty thin, isn't it?" Cole observed. "Maybe, maybe, if, maybe, hope so."

"Yeah." Another shrug. "It's the only thing I have left to suggest."

Commander Warren had been listening to the conversation as motionless as a statue. Now I turned to face him. "Commander, to take the measurements I'm talking about, we'll need access to our equipment, and not just for inspection. We'll have to run a hyperfield."

He crossed his arms. "You know my view on that."

"Yes, and again I'm sorry about yesterday. You were right to put safety first. But this will be safe, Commander. We'll be using a standard field configuration, nothing experimental. And we will physically disconnect the power cables whenever the generators are left unattended, so there's no chance of them starting up again on their own."

Warren frowned, and was silent for a long moment. Finally Dr. Cole weighed in.

"I think it's worth the risk, Commander. Right now, I can't treat this condition or tell who else is at risk. I'll have my people keep looking for the cause, of course, but we're not a research lab. We should pursue every avenue possible to put an end to it."

"All right," the Commander said at last. He looked like he'd just eaten something rotten, and then jabbed a finger at me. "No risks. No experiments. Just take your measurements. Clear?"

"Yes," I said.

"I'll notify the security detail you're authorized to resume your work. And I will tell them to have one man standing by at the breaker with orders to pull it if he so much as gets a headache. Do you have a problem with that?"

"No."

There was a commotion outside, the sound of shouting voices, and then someone called the doctor's name. Cole jumped to his feet and out the door, and Warren and I followed.

Two crewmen held a third, struggling wildly and shouting at the top of his lungs. A medic tried to get close enough to give him an injection. Cole rushed in to help.

"The time of Holy Convergence is upon us!" the new victim shouted. "You are all spinning by the power of Almighty Rotation but the Holy Convergence will unfreeze the oceans! The oceans! Call on the power of Holy Convergence!"

Warren turned to me. "Work fast."

◀ ◀ ◀

The job of modifying our equipment for neurofield measurements would fall mainly to Kyoko's group. The modifications wouldn't need much in the way of new software or theoretical calculations. I was glad enough of that because Drake seemed more interested in arguing with Beth than getting to work.

Their bickering started when I called a lab meeting that morning—our third in as many days—to bring the whole group up to speed on the latest developments. News of the mental breakdowns had spread. No one needed to ask why I'd canceled the "take some time off" plan I'd announced only the day before. We needed to figure out exactly what the Effect had done to us.

The brief session broke up as Kyoko called her group into a smaller meeting of their own to plan their modifications, but Beth approached me before they left.

"D-Dave . . ." She was even more hesitant than usual. "I, I came up with this, uh, little program I th-thought we might want to, to use . . ." She held out her handscreen, which showed an array of distinctive icons.

"What is it?"

"It's, well, it's a test for ESP."

Drake, who was standing nearby and had overheard, snorted and rolled his eyes in disgust, but perhaps remembering his embarrassment at dinner kept any remarks to himself.

For my part, I viewed the whole psychic business as a side issue. Interesting, certainly, and if it was true it helped explain the symptoms of the Effect. But the symptoms were what they were. Calling it ESP didn't get us any closer to answers.

However, I found myself annoyed by Drake's attitude and, more for that reason than any other, I gave Beth an interested smile and asked, "How does it work?"

Encouraged, she answered with more confidence. "Well, it's a simple program, really. It runs on two people's handscreens. One person sees an icon, and the other sees this screen with all the choices and, and tries to guess which one the other person is seeing. The program scores whether they guess right or not." She glanced briefly at Drake and, with a touch of defiance, added, "I made it blind so it won't be biased or, or give any feedback between the two people. The computer scores it all internally, so neither of them knows whether the guess was right or not."

"Interesting, but why have two people at all? Why not just have the computer pick a choice internally?"

"I thought of that." Beth nodded. "With a one-person test, the computer choosing an icon internally and not displaying it, that's just a number. Not even a number, it's, it's voltages on microscopic memory circuits. So I thought, even a clairvoyant sense couldn't tell one microcircuit from another. So, so with two people it's really testing telepathy."

Drake could no longer contain himself. He exploded, "Oh, what's the matter? Not confident your magical second sight can unravel a simple computer? Not much of a mystical power then, is it?"

Beth surprised us both by drawing herself up and glaring right into his eyes. "It's not a mystical power at all!" Her face flushed red, her stammer grew more pronounced, and her voice quivered. I'd never seen her angry before. "It's a—a—a—physical phenomenon. A p-part of *known* hyperfield p-properties that, that might be a, a *physical, scientific* mechanism for ESP! So, so, so I'm trying to test it *rationally*! Is, is that okay with you?"

Part of me was glad to see Beth stand up for herself instead of wilting. Another part was disturbed: Was no one acting like themselves anymore? Thank goodness for Kyoko, as steady as ever. She moved not quite in between Beth and Drake as they glared at each other.

"Let us all be calm," she said. She gave Drake a cool look. "I believe the results could be interesting." Turning back to her student, she continued, "You plan to correlate the results with our neurofield measurements?"

"Yes," Beth said.

"Our work modifying the generators must come first, but I see no reason why you should not collect this data." Kyoko glanced at me for confirmation.

"Sure," I said. "Sounds interesting."

Drake stood silent as Kyoko and Beth left the conference room, and when they'd gone he tried to make light of the whole thing. "You with Warren, me last night, Beth now—I'd better start a pool on who's going to lose their temper next."

"I think Beth had provocation," I said. "Why don't you lay off her? You've made your opinion clear."

But Drake couldn't let it go. "I just don't want to see this project turned into a joke," he said, and his eyes rumbled with anger. "And believe me, that's all this ESP dust will turn out to be."

◀ ◀ ◀

"I think it's a circle," the woman with the coms badge said.

"No, don't tell me, just, just enter it, in your handscreen and, and then let me know to go to the next one." Beth couldn't hide her excitement, and I could see over her shoulder that the communications officer had guessed right.

"Keep it up, Lieutenant," said a crewman. "Get that voodoo going!"

"Twenty credits says when it's my turn, I score above fifty percent," said another.

Beth's test asked twenty-five questions, with five choices for each question, so any random guess would have a twenty percent chance of being correct. Unless the crewman really was psychic, he'd just made a poor bet.

All that morning rumors flew up and down the labs: Half the crew was now confined to quarters, raving mad. One lunatic had tried to destroy the lifesystems. Another had gotten on coms and told the relief ships to turn back, so now it would be weeks before we had help. Warren was crazy. Montoya was crazy. It didn't start with the Effect, it was a contagious disease brought over from the *Lunar Explorer*. The Navy had a saboteur in custody who had crashed the *Explorer* and set up the Effect.

That last one came too close to paranoia for my comfort. Despite what Marta had said about how it was normal to look for villains, to believe something like that, you'd have to be . . . I didn't let myself finish that thought.

Everyone agreed on just one thing: This was no minor aftershock of the Effect, finished with a few people going crazy. Everyone expected it to spread. We believed this despite the fact that the actual number of cases was still quite small. There was something in the air. I have no idea what it was like to stand on the Earth and hear the distant rumble of an approaching thunderstorm—but I imagine it would be similar to what everyone was feeling that morning.

On top of that, no one had forgotten that of the thirty members of our research project, five now lay in the morgue beside the other victims of the Effect.

So, in that gloomy atmosphere, Beth's ESP test had the unexpected benefit of lightening the mood. She made the rounds testing anyone who'd agree whenever Kyoko's group gave her some free minutes. People took it as a lark. Most agreed to give it a try, smiling and talking over their scores. Those who scored high fielded joking requests for investment advice and gambling tips. Beth carried good cheer on the wings of her enthusiasm for the topic, and if no one exactly took her seriously, no one except Drake was openly hostile either.

By lunchtime she'd managed to hit most of our research group, but it was in the mess hall where she really scored. The crew treated the whole thing as a game of chance and, true to the Navy's prime pastime, Beth soon had a flock of eager volunteers waiting their turn, making side bets on their scores, and laughing in a friendly way over the whole thing.

She was so swamped that when I passed by her table, she called out to me for help. "There's all these people waiting to, to do the test and, and I'll never get to them all—"

"You know, these are probably not the people whose neurofields we'll be measuring. How do you plan to get your correlation?" The plan was that Cole would pick a list of test subjects based on some standard protocol for random sampling. I figured we'd check all of our own people as well, once we got under way.

"Well, it's just a baseline," she said.

I smiled. "Okay." Beth pointed me to the right directory and I called up her program on my, or rather on *Anne's*, handscreen. Then I whiled away the lunch hour giving the test to anyone willing to take it from a pudgy, middle-aged physicist instead of a pretty, young grad student.

I didn't keep an exact count in my head, but I guessed that by the time we had to get back to work, we'd added thirty or forty more data points to Beth's sample, on top of those from our research team. And just to finish off, before we left, I gave the test to Beth herself, and she gave it to me. I didn't even bother to check my score. It was just a bit of amusement, and that was all.

After lunch, I headed back to my office, where I'd been at work most of the morning with my own students, and Beth made for the elevators, studying her handscreen as she went. But just as I reached my door, I heard Beth calling my name. Turning around, I saw her rushing down the corridor toward me, face flushed with excitement, eyes shining.

"D-D-Dave!" she stammered. "I, I, I did a graph on, on the scores of the ESP test! Look at this! Look!" She held out her handscreen.

I expected to see a more or less normal distribution of scores, centered around an average of twenty percent. But the graph didn't look like that at all. It showed two distinct peaks. One was where it should be, around the 0.2 mark on the x-axis. The second, smaller peak rose around 0.6. The two peaks did not overlap; they were distinct. And there was one outlier, a single perfect score all the way at the end of the chart.

Beth breathlessly awaited my reaction. "What do you think?"

I glanced at the graph and added up the scores in each peak. "Well, the graph suggests about a third of us are psychic. But you know, Beth, people haven't been taking this very seriously. It could be some of them were playing tricks, getting a look at your screen somehow."

"Well, you t-tell me," she answered. "Look what happens if I separate the data by who gave the test."

She entered a few commands on the screen, assigning colors to the data points: blue for the tests she'd given, red for those I had. Then she showed me the graph again.

The colors separated perfectly into the two peaks: Beth's blue group formed the normal, twenty percent peak and the sixty percent peak was entirely red. Except for—that one perfect score. That was blue.

"The, the only people who took the test from you," Beth said, "were Navy crew. They were all placing bets with each other! If any of them had tried to cheat, the others would have called him on it right away! And, and the statistical routine says the difference between your set and mine is highly significant."

I frowned. What sense did this make? Even if a third of the crew were psychic, why would they all end up taking the test from me? Unless—belatedly, I got it. Now I understood why Beth was watching me with such avid fascination. My eyes focused on that single perfect score that Beth had given.

"That's right!" Beth said, as if—just as if she could read my mind. "That's *your* score! You scored p-perfect! And anyone who took the test from you, they did forty points better on average than random. You read my mind, and they read yours! It's telepathy! Dave, you're *psychic*!"

CHAPTER FOURTEEN

If Beth had showed me an unusually high score, I'd have been intrigued and excited. Even if I was alone at sixty percent, I'd have something to think about. But a perfect score? *Perfect?*

"It's a mistake," I said to Beth. "A computer glitch, something wrong with the handscreen I used, I don't know . . . Beth, I didn't read your mind. I just guessed."

"Maybe that's how it works, you know, unconsciously. I took the test from you and I'm there in that sixty percent group, but I didn't know that I was picking anything up from you; I just guessed too."

I grasped at straws. "Maybe you're the psychic."

"Me and everyone else who took the test from you? You're the one with the perfect score."

"Beth, I would *know*. I couldn't go through life with abilities that pronounced and never notice, not even if it works unconsciously. I don't have any history as a good guesser, or being particularly intuitive, or anything of the sort."

"B-but it makes such perfect sense," she protested. "Don't you see, this is, is why you could handle the Effect. You already had ESP, so you could handle it getting stronger."

I opened my mouth to argue, but then froze as I remembered Marta coming up with "goop du jour" right after I'd thought about Charles saying it. And she'd also guessed how I had been thinking of the generators as my children. No—I didn't need any mind reading to account for that, it was an obvious metaphor. And why couldn't two people come up with the same joke about the Navy's food?

But the thought came, *How did everyone know you were bluffing at cards last night?*

Because I'm not a good card player, I answered myself.

Maybe so, but you're not that bad.

Beth noticed my sudden confusion but—as if to provide a reassuring counterexample—she did not read my mind. "What is it?"

"Nothing," I said. Then, a little more sure of myself, repeated: "Nothing."

It had to be nothing.

◀ ◀ ◀

A few hours later, Kyoko called to say they were ready to start taking measurements. That meant creating a hyperfield with the alpha generator. Not just reconnecting power to the instruments and self-diagnostics, but actually starting up the generator and producing a hyperfield, for the first time since the Effect.

I had already been to the OCC earlier in the morning, before the whole business of Beth's ESP results came up: I had gone to watch Kyoko's group start setting up for our planned measurements. I felt I had to be there, on guard, just in case something happened. While they reconnected the power cables, my eyes locked on the generators: gleaming metal insects, squatting there with bristling stingers.

Warren hadn't joked about his orders to the security detail: A guard hovered by the breaker panel, his hand actually resting on the switch. But the Commander's concerns and my fears proved equally groundless. Leo plugged in the cables; the computers read the generators' self-diagnostics, giving us the data we'd wanted yesterday; and that was that.

I left Kyoko and her people to begin the work of moving the beta generator out of its nest of instruments, making room for the test subject who would take its place. Then I returned to my office, where I had called my own students in for a brainstorming session.

We usually crackled with ideas in such meetings, but today the conversation had been dull. The ideas limped along, going nowhere. Eventually I put the meeting out of its misery. Lunchtime brought the ESP test and a whole new puzzle to distract me as I tried to work on my own, until word came they were finally ready in the OCC.

Now, Kyoko's call meant it was time to head back there. This time not for merely plugging in a cable. This time the alpha generator would return fully to life.

My thoughts spun my head as I made for the elevator. Distracted, I strode along the corridor, head down, and almost ran into a wall as it jogged to the left. But I sensed the near collision and looked up in time. I turned, following the corridor, finding myself facing a row of windows looking out to the stars. And there it was. Outside, staring back at me, a hairy, laughing goblin face, red eyes gleaming, mouth stretched in a lunatic grin that revealed multiple rows of jagged teeth and a long, lolling tongue.

All the breath went out of me in a whoosh that failed to become a scream only because my vocal chords wouldn't work. In a convulsion, I hurled myself backward, slamming against the far wall with a painful thud. I flattened myself against it as if I could push right through the wall and away, staring with wide eyes and an open mouth.

But there was nothing there. Just the wheeling stars and my reflection in the window, pale and shaking, looking like someone who had just stepped on a live electrical wire. Maybe it was just my own reflection I had seen, my reflection and a touch of daydream.

But I couldn't dismiss it as just a shadow in the corner of my eye, not this time. I had looked right at it and seen it in too much detail to mistake it for something else.

It was real. The Beast was real or it was a hallucination—a full-blown, you're-going-nuts hallucination. Those were my choices: Either I was mad, or the Universe was. For a moment, I wasn't sure which would be worse.

I let go of the wall and crossed the corridor to the window. Slowly, unable to stop myself, I looked out. I looked from side to side, up and down, even pressing my cheek against the transparency to try and see around the edge to the outside wall. Nothing.

But I heard something. A rhythmic clicking: *tik-tik-tik-tik . . . tik-tik-tik-tik.* I knew what it was. Yes, it was the sound of claw-tipped fingers, somewhere outside clinging to the bulkhead, drumming impatiently, waiting for me to turn away, so it could come out. That's how it would act, of course: never showing itself to my face, always watching from behind my back, never allowing me more than brief glimpses when I happened to catch it by surprise. Waiting for its chance to—to—

Stop it! I tried to clamp down on my thoughts. Was I really considering the idea that this impossible Beast might be real? I knew that such a creature could not live in the vacuum of space. Hyperfield properties might explain ESP, but nothing could explain something like that. It was a hallucination. I experienced a hallucination. Nothing more. That ticking sound? Nothing—those "claws" were probably no more than a wobbly fan inside the air vent now chilling the sweat on my forehead. It was a momentary lapse, that was all. Obviously I was not immune to the aftermath of the Effect;

I had symptoms, that's why my imagination ran away so easily, if only for a moment. But as long as I understood that's all it was, as long as I *knew* what was real, then I was still sane.

A new fear struck. I whipped my head around, looking one way and then the other. What if someone saw me, recoiling in terror from nothing, peering through the window—acting crazy? They might already be calling the medics, to come with their inexorable grips and hypos full of sedatives. Dr. Cole had already told me he couldn't do anything about the symptoms; I would be taken to lie somewhere in a drugged haze until . . . But there was no one.

I headed back the way I came, until I reached a bathroom a few doors down, heading straight for the sink to splash water on my face. Running my fingers through my hair to straighten it out, I let the adrenaline rush slowly bleed from my system. After a few minutes, the face in the mirror looked almost normal, except for the fatigue that I couldn't hide.

I took a deep breath, and continued to the OCC, keeping my eyes averted from every window I passed.

◀ ◀ ◀

The beta generator's frame stood empty and skeletal, its components moored in careful order some distance away. Only the instruments remained fully intact, surrounding the frame. The alpha generator crouched in a pool of light, glittering with little blue highlights from the fiber-optic cables. I might have hoped the business about the Beast would distract me from my paranoia about the generators. No such luck. I could almost hear the generator whispering to me: *Go ahead and put me to work, Dave. Let me make a nice little field for you. My stingers may be sharper than a serpent's tooth, but I won't sting YOU again.* So now it was this *and* the Dream *and* the Beast. My neurosis count was up to three.

We planned to have the alpha generator running by the time the first subjects arrived. In the OCC, I exchanged a glance with Kyoko. "Are we ready?"

"Yes," she said. "The software is running and the instruments all show clean readings."

"The Effect can't happen again," I said to myself as much as her. "There's only one generator now and it took both to create the Effect."

"Do we know that? Both were on. Perhaps one alone would have sufficed."

"We're using plain vanilla field parameters."

"Yes." She took a deep breath. "Initializing hyperfield."

I held my breath. The lights flickered.

And for the second time—a nonevent. The field was so weak it could barely be seen, but it was there, a faint trace of an orange glow. And nothing else happened. All the variables on my screen showed steady, and the computer affirmed that run 39 had begun (I'd forgotten to announce it, but that didn't really matter). I was almost disappointed.

Kyoko turned toward me, unable to hide the relieved smile that broke through her careful calm. "It appears we will not become psychic again today."

I smiled back. "No."

She checked her screen. "The hyperfield is steady."

"Okay, we're running. Now we just need the guinea pigs."

The first subjects arrived at 0230 precisely, three crewmen and one officer, a woman with security insignia. They stopped just inside the hangar door, finding handholds with unconscious ease, as far from the generators as they could get, studying the alpha generator with suspicion as I emerged from the OCC to greet them.

If I believed Beth's opinion about my ESP, then I was the last person who should be trying to reassure our guests. I'd probably broadcast my own dislike of the generators directly into their heads. But the absurdity of the thought made me smile again and, in combination with the alpha generator's docile cooperation, I felt a weight lift off my chest.

As I approached, the crewmen formally announced, "Reporting as ordered." But I waved a hand.

"Relax, we're just civilians here, no need for protocol. We shouldn't have to keep you for long." Kyoko and I had talked it over: Based on our older studies with Rothberg and Wilson at Star City University, two minutes' recording should give us a reliable set of numbers. Cole's protocol would send us an initial sample of forty subjects to test, and after them, we wanted to measure some of the actual breakdown victims. Add a couple of minutes to get each subject in and out of position, and at that rate, we had hours of work ahead of us—but it wouldn't take long to see if a pattern emerged.

"Do any of you have questions?" I continued.

The security officer—Lieutenant Engstrom, by her shoulder patch—asked, "If this is a medical check, why isn't it in the infirmary?"

"We're trying to measure neurofields—that is, a weak hyperfield that the brain generates—in order to see if the Effect caused any lasting changes to them." I avoided the word *damage*. "The infirmary doesn't have the equipment to measure hyperfields, so we're using ours."

"These neurofields are why people are going crazy?" asked a crewman.

"It's possible. We want to compare healthy people to those who've been affected."

"So what are you going to do to us to get these measurements?" The second crewman had nerves in his voice.

"Nothing. You just have to wait by the generator for two minutes. You can hang on to that frame, and those instruments will record everything."

"So it won't feel like that brainstorm again?"

I shook my head. "No. You won't feel anything more than you're feeling right now."

"All right." He didn't seem entirely reassured.

I checked my handscreen. "First up is Crewman . . . Berziel. Am I pronouncing that right?"

"Yes, sir." It was the nervous crewman.

Leading him around the alpha generator, I showed him how to worm his way inside the beta generator's frame. As he settled in, we heard voices and turned. Beth had arrived and was talking to the others.

"Oh yes," I said. "After you're done our student there will have a little test for you."

Berziel's tension subsided. "Is that the psychic test I heard you were doing?"

"That's the one."

"So you guys think we all have ESP now?"

"Well, if the Effect did that, you'll never lose at gambling again." I didn't mention that he'd never be able to bluff in poker, either.

Berziel grinned.

"Okay," I said. "You're in position. Try to remain motionless. Everyone else has to clear out; our own neurofields will mess up the results, but you'll hear me on the intercom when the two minutes are up."

I found Dr. Cole in the OCC. He must have arrived while I was getting Berziel into position. "Have you started? I want to see the results."

"Have there been any more—"

"Ten since we talked. Not counting the one that came in while you were there."

"Okay." I gritted my teeth as I turned back to the console. Ten more? The rate of people going insane had increased. "Okay. Let's find out how to put a stop to it."

"The instruments are already recording," Kyoko said. "I started as soon as you moved clear."

The lines on my screen were noisy, and the variables flickered. The neurofield was so weak that at first the margin of error dominated. But as time elapsed the mean values steadied. At two minutes the computer pinged and stored our first data point under Berziel's name.

I hit the intercom. "You're done, you can come out now. Be careful not to touch the sensors."

While the crewman slid clear of the frame with the typical freefall grace of any Navy man, I called up a file of neurofield data from our previous study and compared.

"It looks normal." The deviations from one file to another were trivial.

Cole pointed. "This number is different."

"That's overall field strength. Our previous study showed neurofields vary a lot from person to person. Berziel's above average, but within the normal range."

"Well, you can't tell anything from one data point. Maybe we're all above average now. Isn't your theory that the Effect strengthened the neurofields, providing energy for the telekinetic symptoms?"

"Yes." I unclipped from the console and went to the door, checking my handscreen as I moved. Berziel was taking Beth's test, grinning as he did so.

"Lieutenant Engstrom, you're next," I said.

◀ ◀ ◀

The afternoon grew monotonous, as one crewman after another moved into position, hovered there for two minutes, then moved out.

By the time we'd finished with ten out of the planned forty subjects, I knew we weren't going to find anything. They were all normal; only their field strength varied, and within the normal range. Nevertheless we kept at it. Scientific methodology doesn't allow expectation to substitute for actual data. And I'm the first to say, *Rightfully so.*

But that afternoon it started to seem like needless grunt work, recording routine numbers over and over while, elsewhere, the ranks of the insane grew one by one.

Cole was called away about ninety minutes into our tests. The students and technicians in Kyoko's group had returned to the Wheel after the first few trials (except for Beth, who stayed and tested the ESP of the subjects as they finished). Even the security guard let his hand drop from the breaker switch, and just waited at his station, watching the proceedings without much interest.

We got a bit ahead of schedule, and finished the sample a little after 1800 hours. Beth had something of a backlog, but those waiting to play her game were entertained enough. Kyoko was about to shut down the hyperfield but I stopped her.

"I want to go out there and get measured myself."

"You? Why?"

I was embarrassed even to mention it, but I pressed on. "I got a perfect score on Beth's ESP exam. So . . ." I shrugged. "Let's just see."

I unclipped from the console and stretched. Kyoko watched me curiously as I left the OCC.

I waved at Beth. "Would you go help Kyoko? We're going to measure my neurofield."

Her eyes went wide. "Yes! Oh, this will show something, I, I know it will!"

She vanished into the OCC at once. I glanced at the four crewmen still waiting for the ESP test. "She'll be right back."

I crawled into the frame and waited. The alpha field glowed harmlessly to the side. I imagined I could feel the slight heat off it, but I knew it was really too weak for that.

Through the OCC window, I saw Beth take my console and watch the numbers. As the seconds crawled by, her eyes went wider and wider. The intercom was off, but I saw her mouth open into a *Wow!* that it didn't take a lip-reader to understand, and I knew Kyoko well enough to detect her astonishment in the flicker of her eyes and a twitch of one eyebrow.

"What is it?" I asked.

They couldn't hear me, but Kyoko must have seen my lips move because she turned on the intercom. "Dave, according to these readings, your neurofield . . ." She hesitated.

"What? What does it show? Is the configuration different?"

"The basic neurofield parameters are normal, the same as all the others. But—the field strength is enormous. An order of magnitude greater than the high end of the normal range . . . Dave, your neurofield is stronger than the present setting of the alpha generator."

Beth smiled, eyes shining, her thought easy enough to read with or without telepathy—*I knew it!*

◀ ◀ ◀

In the end, Beth was disappointed by her test results. After she excluded my perfect ESP score and strong field as outliers, any correlation between the other data points vanished. The cluster of normal field strength figures and the cluster of normal ESP scores had no connection to one another. I was a unique phenomenon. But I remained stubbornly hung up on one fact: If I was psychic, I would know. There had to be another explanation.

At dinner I linked up with Marta again. I told her about the neurofield results from the crewmen, saying nothing about my own.

In the evening, we went back and measured the neurofields of ten actual mental breakdown victims. Cole and a group of medics brought them in under as mild a sedation as possible to keep them controllable. Do I have to mention that they, too, all had normal neurofields? Another dusted dead end.

Cole sighed. "Well, it was a long shot that we'd find anything."

"It still has to be a result of the Effect, some kind of related damage," I insisted. "It's a ridiculous coincidence if people are going nuts for some completely unrelated reason."

"Perhaps if we increase the sample size," Kyoko said, "we will uncover some subtle effect, presently masked by the margin of error."

I shook my head, depressed about the whole prospect. I had been so sure we'd find something. But the only standout result was mine, and it told us nothing of real value.

I rubbed my eyes. Tonight, would the Dream finally let me sleep? Or would I spend another night caught between fatigue and nightmare, drowsing off only to jolt awake until I faced another drag-eyed, staggering day? I smothered a groan.

"We'll just have to get back to the physics," I said. "Try to figure out—"

"Why don't you just shut up?"

I turned, surprised. It was Leo. He'd come with us to the OCC, an extra pair of hands in case any of the patients got out of control. Now he looked angry.

"Leo? What—"

"Oh, sorry Dave," he said. "I wasn't talking to you. It's just that this guy keeps blabbering on and on *and on* and I wish he'd just *give it a rest!*" He pointed toward a corner of the room, where there was no one.

My eyes met Cole's. "Leo," I said, "there's no one there."

But he paid no attention. He unhooked his belt clips and launched himself with sudden, furious anger at the empty corner.

"*I SAID SHUT UP!*" he shouted. "*SHUT UP SHUT UP SHUT UP!*"

Cole and a couple of medics closed in. They had him under control in a few moments, a quick injection causing him to subside.

Kyoko had left her station, pressing back away from Leo and watching the scene with wide, horrified eyes. Her face had gone chalky gray. I imagine I looked much the same.

Leo was the first of our group to go under. He wouldn't be the last.

◀ ◀ ◀

Back in my cabin, I kept my eyes downcast until I blanked the window. If I never looked out into space, then I'd never see the Beast. Then I wouldn't go crazy, wouldn't have to face being surrounded by my own group of medics, my eyes going blank and passive under the sedative injection. With the window opaque, my sanity was safe.

But as I lay in my bed I heard, from the other side of the bulkhead only inches from my head:

Tik-tik-tik-tik.

Tik-tik-tik-tik.

Tik-tik-tik-tik.

Tik-tik-tik-tik.

CHAPTER FIFTEEN

To say the nightmare came back again would be redundant.
The night *was* the nightmare. The minutes crawled by while I tossed
between sleep and wakefulness, the two blurring together until I
didn't know if I dreamed the Red Light and the Shadow or the maddening ticking of claws beside my ear. The two shared each other,
and only my body's craving for sleep kept dragging me back under
to face their conjoined terror. Over it all was the high, alien voice
from the Red Light and Shadow repeating its taunt in that unknown
language, only one word standing out from the others: *Eiralynn—
Eiralynn—Eiralynn—*

Around three or four in the morning alarms shattered the
silence and a voice on the PA announced: "Security breach! All
security personnel report to stations! All civilians remain in your
quarters!"

The noise of the alarm cut through dreams, voice, ticking, and
all. I jerked up from bed, my heart pounding hard. What's happened
now? I thought.

Possibilities crowded my mind: the latest madman running up
and down the corridors with a weapon. Or standing poised over
some vital control panel, threatening to destroy us all. Or someone
just hit the security alarm because the voices in his head told him to.

I threw on some clothes and staggered to the door, almost falling over, the room spinning and rocking. It took a few moments to
realize it wasn't the Wheel wobbling, it was just me.

The alarm still shrieked, and the recorded PA voice repeated its message. I had no intention of remaining in my quarters as ordered; I had to find out what was going on.

But the door would not open. It was locked from outside. Then I remembered, they told us as part of our briefing when we came on board that all door locks on the Alley could be controlled from a central location, for security. They'd also said they didn't anticipate the feature would ever be used.

My cabin all at once became very small and stuffy. Claustrophobia wrapped clammy tendrils around my arms and legs and set them trembling. I came close to panic, and had to fight the urge to scream and pound on the door.

Instead I sat down and made myself take deep, slow breaths. *Calm down. Calm down.* I waited while my heartbeat returned to normal and the shaking of my limbs subsided. Why wouldn't the alarm stop shrieking? Surely all the crew must be at their emergency stations by now. Unless they'd all gone crazy. Unless none were left to turn it off. In that case, there'd be no one to cancel the alarm, no one to unlock the doors, I'd be stuck in this little cabin forever . . .

I couldn't call anyone. The intercom screen would only show the message "Intercom System Reserved for Emergency Personnel." I couldn't even listen to the com channels to figure out what was going on.

The alarms cut off, leaving behind a smothering silence. I tried the door again, but it was still locked. The security alert hadn't ended; someone had just turned off the sirens. At least that meant someone out there was still doing something.

In the prolonged silence, drowsiness soon dragged at me again. I didn't want to sleep, I wanted to know what was happening. And if I slept, I'd only meet the Red Light and Shadow again, and the—

but I no longer heard the Beast's claws ticking against the outer bulkhead. As soon as I noticed its absence, I expected the sound to return, but it didn't.

I'm stuck here, but it's free to move off somewhere else.

No. The Beast wasn't real. I must remember that.

I dozed, letting my head nod, but shaking myself awake every time I sensed my thoughts drifting into dreams. I had to stay awake to respond. I had to stay awake to avoid the nightmare, I thought, hovering in a sort of equilibrium of exhaustion. My dizziness gave the cabin an almost comfortable rocking sensation, like swinging in a baby's crib. My eyelids closed. I had to be awake in case anything happened. Like a call to the escape pods. It was warm. It was quiet. Had to stay awake.

The cabin light began to turn red. There was a shadow in it. A voice came over the PA, but it was neither a recording, nor an officer. It was cold and alien. The voice of Eiralynn. "Ayan namar! Ayan namar!"

I jolted awake. And so it went, over and over and over, for the rest of the night.

◀ ◀ ◀

Around 0730 in the morning, the PA announced the end of the security alert. I went immediately to the door. This time it opened.

Up and down the corridor, people emerged from their cabins. Most had already dressed, a few wore bathrobes or pajamas. All looked tired, worried, and haggard, except for Drake, who seemed more annoyed. I saw my students Tom Markov and Aaron Parvik, and my surviving postdoc Harold Norman, appearing from their rooms farther down the hall. People gravitated into small knots of conversation, every topic the same: "Do you know what happened? Have you heard anything?" No one had.

I went to the Admiral's Suite to check on Marta. I saw no sign of any disturbance along the way.

Another headache came on, and by the time I reached the VIP cabins, my temples pounded in time to my heartbeat. But I pinged anyway, and Marta answered. When she saw it was me, she stepped out into the corridor and let the door slide shut behind her. She wore an oversize Navy-issue gym shirt and shorts, presumably in lieu of whatever nightclothes she'd lost on the *Lunar Explorer*. She looked pale, tired, and rumpled.

"Are you all right?" I asked.

"The children are finally asleep," she said. "The alarms woke them up and they got panicky. It was too much like the alarms on the *Explorer*. We—they thought the base might be about to blow up like the ship did."

"You're all right otherwise?"

"What happened? What was the emergency?"

"I don't know," I said. "I came to see if you were all right."

She ran a hand through her hair. "I could use some coffee. I might even be willing to eat some of that Navy food."

I managed a smile, though my headache was getting worse. "Sure."

She looked down at herself. "Give me a minute to put some clothes on."

I tried a joke. "Don't bother on my account."

She gave me a pale, absent smile, and vanished back into the cabin.

After a few minutes, she reappeared, not only dressed, but completely reassembled, so that I half wondered if I'd only imagined her disheveled fatigue a moment before. She gave me her trademark grin. "You look well dusted, Dave."

"Well, I wouldn't want to give anyone a false impression."

She gave me a quick sideways look. "Bad night, huh?"

"Yeah. How about you? How are you doing?"

"Oh, I'm fine," she said, but it wasn't a real answer, so I stopped asking the question.

I thought of her Marta-as-usual manner now compared to the pale figure who had first answered the door. Suddenly, I had a very strange impression: I seemed to see both versions superimposed on one another, just for a moment. The image had an other-sense quality to it, but that had to be imagination—the other-sense ended with the Effect.

I shook myself and the vision faded. Would Beth call it a psychic experience? But it didn't take any kind of ESP to guess that Marta's demeanor now was at least partly a pose. She'd half admitted it herself, when she implied her smart-ass persona was something she chose, a pose like her video-drama impersonations. Tired Marta. Smart-ass Marta. Dedicated-to-the-children Marta. Was Real Marta in there somewhere, and if so did she ever let anyone see her?

Forget it, I thought. *You're a fine one to wonder about hiding things, and it's none of your business anyway.* As we walked to the elevators, my headache faded, so I focused on being glad about that at least.

◀   ◀   ◀

In the mess hall we found Lieutenant Montoya surrounded by a group that included Drake and most of the students. Kyoko and

Beth sat at a table nearby, listening in. I hadn't seen Montoya since before the Effect, when she'd guided Marta and the kids to their quarters. She looked okay and she spoke in a crisp voice, delivering an obviously prepared statement: "It appears that the medical staff overlooked a number of mental breakdowns among the *Lunar Explorer* survivors. During the midwatch a number of these individuals began wandering the corridors shouting and awakened others. Apparently a rumor spread that the Alley was being evacuated, and a number of the survivors crowded the elevators up to the Hub, searching for the pod stations.

"When some wandered into the command center, Lieutenant Leighton—the officer of the watch—called a security alert. The midwatch is a skeleton crew, so he decided calling extra security to duty was necessary for crowd control. Security and medical staff soon restored order, and the emergency is now over. Commander Warren has assigned additional security and medical officers to the civilian quarters, to prevent any recurrence and ensure that any new mental patients receive prompt treatment."

Marta frowned all the way through the lieutenant's account, glancing my way now and again as if to judge my reaction. But it was Drake who openly expressed his skepticism after Montoya departed.

"*Soon* restored order? The alert went on for hours."

Marta said, with her frown drawing lines between her eyes, "Can it be that bad already?"

"Well," I said, "surely it's no surprise the survivors were on the edge of panic, with all that's happened—"

"But the crew so overwhelmed that people actually wandered into the command center without being stopped?" She shook her head.

I tried to distance myself from the alarming picture she called to mind. "Look. The Alley's crew is seven hundred and fifty people. As of last night, there were only twenty-five cases."

"There'll be more now," Marta said.

"Plus however many were injured in the Effect," Drake added.

"Even so," I said, "there just can't be so many that they're in danger of losing control of the base."

"Wanna bet?" asked Drake.

"Not yet," said Marta.

The knot of people that had surrounded Lieutenant Montoya broke up, and re-formed in a line for the serving table, which we joined along with Beth. Kyoko stayed at the table, head down as if half asleep, but then I saw she was writing something on her hand-screen. I slumped against the wall, shuffling sideways whenever the line moved.

"So the Navy is posting guards and sending out lieutenants with reassuring statements," I said. "Meanwhile, we've got nothing."

"Surely not," Marta said. "What have you been doing with yourself the last three days?"

"Three days?" I blinked. Was it three days? I counted in my head. The Effect happened on Tuesday, the day after run 37 and the *Lunar Explorer* wreck. Now it was Friday morning. Three days since the Effect. I couldn't figure out if it seemed longer than that, or shorter. Only that it didn't seem possible this was the same week that began with Drake's pool betting on eleven seconds for sustained hyperfield contact.

I was drifting. I could've fallen asleep right there leaning on the wall, so I stood up straight, shaking it off.

"I've been chasing dead ends," I said. "The physics are a mystery, the Ryder equations have only one solution, Cole can't find any physical cause for the breakdowns, and all the neurofields we measured are normal."

"But, but what about you, Dave?" Beth interrupted.

Marta stepped in before Drake could say anything. "What's this? Dave, have you been holding back juicy news?"

In a breathless rush, Beth explained her ESP test, the neurofield measurement, and her conclusion: "So Dave is psychic!"

"But I'm not," I protested. "Beth, I'm not. I can't explain your results, but I couldn't be psychic and not know it."

Marta thought it was hilarious. "I don't know, Dave, you are awfully transparent . . ."

We reached the serving table.

"Good morning, Professor," Brown said, just like every day since we'd arrived at the Alley. There's something timeless about an Imperturbable Waiter. I couldn't picture Brown going mad, or running around in circles being chased by flying junk.

Marta got a fruit plate and a cup of coffee. I took only coffee. Drake piled his plate high with formerly powdered eggs and greasy bacon. How could he stand that stuff? We all went over to the table where Kyoko still worked at her handscreen. She looked up as we joined her, and put the screen aside. She looked tired and had worry lines on her face I didn't recall seeing before.

"You have to admit, Beth's story all hangs together." Marta leaned back in her chair, tipping it up precariously on two legs.

"Except, to repeat myself, *I can't read minds.*" I felt a little annoyed at having to make this point over and over. "It would be a strange sort of telepathy if it only works on someone who's staring at an icon on a computer screen."

"*Pfft!* What's your standard of comparison?" Marta grinned. "Put it this way: It only works on someone who's concentrating on trying to send a simple image to you. Sounds more sensible that way, doesn't it?"

"No," said Drake.

"We have so much evidence now—" Beth ventured, but Drake cut her off.

"You have *no* evidence! You did your correlation and apart from Dave, you came up with nothing. Dave's score was an isolated fluke—he's right here denying that he has any ESP. Clearly the explanation lies elsewhere."

"I, I have Dave's story about the Effect," Beth replied. "Not just his, his clairvoyance but also he *saw* others with telekinesis and the security video shows he was *right*. And it wasn't just Dave's own score—fifteen people who took the test *from* him also scored high!"

I watched the two of them, Drake and Beth, poised against each other like opponents in a high school debate tournament. "Look. Beth, I basically agree with you," I said. Drake opened his mouth to object but I held up a finger and he waited. "There's something to this ESP connection. But my evidence is subjective, my own experience during the Effect. By that same standard, I disagree that I'm psychic. I couldn't have the level of ability your test suggests and not know it."

"Maybe you have it out of order," Marta suggested.

We all turned to look at her.

She grinned at being the center of attention. "Beth suggests you had a lucid experience of the Effect because you were already psychic. What if it's the other way round? You are now psychic because you had a lucid experience of the Effect. It left you with a boost. Maybe from now on you *will* start to notice it."

"Then, then why was Dave lucid for the Effect?" Beth asked.

Marta shrugged. "I suppose there was something different about him. That strong neurofield you talked about, maybe. But it didn't do anything until the Effect switched it on."

"I still can't read minds," I said, but thought briefly of my vision of the two Martas.

"Well, let's try a—" her grin widened, "a thought experiment. I'll think of something and you tell us what it is." Her eyes took on a distant expression, and then focused directly on mine with comical intensity.

"You're thinking this is all pretty funny," I said. "But I don't need telepathy to see that."

She laughed. "Fair enough. But I really do have something in mind. Give me a guess."

Drake rolled his eyes. Beth watched eagerly. Just to stop Marta's teasing, I tried, but nothing came to me. I shrugged. "No, I don't get anything."

"Just guess."

I raised my hands helplessly. "Honestly, I have no clue. It could be butterflies for all I know."

Marta's chair came down on all four legs with a thud. Her eyes widened, and her laughter died out. "That's right." Her surprise was obvious.

Beth gasped and folded her hands as if in prayer. But Drake barked a derisive snort.

"You're making it up," he said. "It's a joke. You'd have said whatever he guessed was right."

"No," she said. "I did think this was just for laughs, but a butterfly was the image I had in mind."

Drake snorted again. "We're supposed to just take your word for that?"

190

"Okay. I'll try again, but I'll whisper to you what I'm thinking. Or I'll enter it on a handscreen."

"Forget it. I'm not going to waste my time watching you do cheap magic tricks." Drake got to his feet and leaned over the table. "Will you people at least try to remember we're scientists? Rational people? There is *no such thing as ESP*. There's no evidence for it and anyone who claims to have evidence is either gullible"—he glared at Beth, then turned to glare at Marta—"or a *liar*."

Marta didn't react to the insult, just calmly returned his stare. After a few seconds, he muttered a curse under his breath and stalked off, leaving his breakfast untouched.

I needed to break the awkward silence, so I said, "He's been getting angry about this since the subject came up. It's not like him."

Marta shrugged.

"Why won't he just admit the obvious?" Beth wondered. "I mean, I know a lot of people have believed silly things about ESP in the past, but we have evidence now."

"Oh it's not that," said Marta. "It's the outrageous injustice that silly people might turn out to have been right. He's picturing a be-jeweled carnival palm reader saying 'Told you so' while he has to sit there and take it."

She laughed, then caught my expression and said, "If you're afraid he's next on the psychiatric list, don't be. Getting mad and going mad aren't the same thing."

I smiled back, but her explanation didn't reassure me. Marta didn't know Drake; she didn't see how unlike him his recent behavior was. He had changed. In view of current events, that was ominous.

"The interesting question . . ." Marta tilted her chair back again and became thoughtful, "is *why* the silly people have believed this stuff for so long."

"What do you mean?" I asked.

"Well, crackpot ideas are always with us, but they come and go. Everyone swears the latest quack medical idea *absolutely* works, but it's forgotten as soon as the next one comes along. Or remember a few years ago, when everyone thought your personality was determined by the position of your Colony when you were born? All those books on how to find the perfect mate using orbital charts? When's the last time you heard anyone talk about that?"

Marta's chair hovered on the edge of toppling as she leaned even farther back, her eyes gazing unfocused at the ceiling.

"But ESP isn't like that. It's not a fad. People have believed in it for centuries, millennia even, in every human culture. The words change. One culture says it's evil, another says it's a gift of the gods. One says it's magic, another invents pseudoscientific terms. But the basic list of mind powers—telepathy, telekinesis, clairvoyance—stays the same. All throughout time. Skeptics explain it with a vague appeal to human gullibility, but that doesn't explain why this one idea persists while others come and go."

"It's because it's real," Beth said. "It's been true all along."

"And yet—no evidence. Not in a thousand years of searching. At least, not until now. Why?" Marta's eyes focused and she looked at Beth. "I think you and Drake are both right."

"What?" Beth and I spoke at once.

Marta smiled. "What if ESP is a vestigial trait like our appendix or wisdom teeth? There's this neurofield in our heads, right? It doesn't do anything now but maybe it did, once upon a time. Back before language, maybe. I don't know. ESP is gone now, but deep in our subconscious we still retain a trace of instinct, a knowledge that it's *possible*. Do you know, on Earth there were flightless birds that still spent time preening their useless wings and even tried to flap them in the breeze? And there were blind animals adapted to living in caves. I wonder if those animals, every now and again, felt a pricking from their vestigial eyes and knew that somewhere, somehow, there was light?"

She blinked, and came back to the present with an embarrassed laugh. "Well, I usually don't get so romantic. I got caught up in the moment."

"Where have you been for the last three days?" I demanded. "I've been trying to figure this out and you've had all the answers!"

She laughed again. "I'm just thinking aloud. Anyone could sit here and speculate and come up with something just as good."

"Oh, you're as bad as Drake," Beth said. "You're, you're still just avoiding the obvious. Talking about vestigial traits and subconscious instincts, just another way to, to deny the truth. It was *here* during the Effect. And Dave *has it now*. My test, and his neurofield being so strong, and, and, and the butterfly!" She turned to me, almost pleading. "You *have* to see it's true. You saw it during the Effect, you said you had your other-sense. You can see it again. I know you can."

Brown passed by with a broom and, noticing Drake's abandoned tray, retrieved it. I watched him and the other stewards bustling about the mess hall. It was easier than meeting Beth's eyes.

"Beth . . ." I sighed. "I just don't know. It doesn't help us figure out the physics in any case, and that's what we're really after."

"No." Beth's manner had changed. I couldn't put my finger on it; it was subtle, but she was different. She spoke with a quiet and unnerving conviction. "This isn't about physics. Not anymore. It's about ESP, it's all about ESP. Dave, you're the one with the power. You're the only one who can open the mysteries. You must be the one to find the path to the other side."

Beth's psychic fixation had just gone from uncomfortable to disturbing. She stared at me with a kind of religious ecstasy in her eyes, and every trace of hesitancy or stammer had vanished from her voice. It was like someone I didn't know was sitting there.

Marta regarded her with carefully impassive eyes.

I desperately needed to change the subject, and casting about for a reason I spotted Kyoko, who had remained silent through the whole conversation.

"Kyoko? You haven't said a word since we sat down. Are you all right?"

She looked up, then down again. She held up her handscreen. "I was just working on this list of damaged components we removed from the generators and need to inspect."

I saw a vagueness in her eyes. "You don't look good," I said. "Maybe you should go try to get some more sleep."

"No, I must return to work." She stood up and swayed, putting a hand to her forehead in a distracted sort of way.

Now I was worried. She looked dead on her feet, far worse than anyone else. "Kyoko, you're not well. I want you to get some sleep, or else go see the doctor."

She blinked as if she had trouble understanding me. "I . . ." She staggered suddenly and had to grab the back of a chair to keep from falling. I stood up and moved to her side, grabbing her arm to help. Marta came around the other side. Beth watched with wide eyes.

"Okay, that's it," I said. "You're going back to your quarters and we're going to make sure you get there."

"Per . . . perhaps you are right," she said, and even as bad off as she was, I could tell the concession cost her. Even now she wouldn't abandon her professionalism: She held out her handscreen, her arm shaking. "Beth, please go to the lab and conduct these tests, and I will try to join you this afternoon."

"A-all r-right," Beth said. She was herself again, alarm over Kyoko pushing aside whatever delusions were growing in her mind. She looked at me, and I didn't need telepathy to read the thought in her eyes: *Help her.*

"Go on, Beth, Marta and I will take care of Kyoko," I said.

She nodded, then turned and fled the room.

Kyoko walked to her cabin mostly unaided. Marta and I stayed on either side of her, Marta making encouraging but meaningless conversation. When we reached her door, Marta went inside to help get her into bed. I waited in the corridor, alone with my thoughts.

I'd counted on Kyoko to remain steady. At least she didn't seem to be growing irrational. But was this fatigue just a matter of the overnight alarms, or something worse?

Drake, Beth, and now Kyoko. Alarming behavior in each. And I could add myself to the list, walking around unable to look at a window for fear of seeing the Beast. Four out of four, all on the edge.

Was *everyone* this badly off, just trying to hang on, hiding it from one another? If so, no wonder a minor disturbance among the *Explorer* survivors had exploded into a riot, and no wonder the crew let it get out of hand. If that's how it was, there couldn't be much time left before everything fell apart.

CHAPTER SIXTEEN

While I waited outside Kyoko's cabin, I spun the situation in my head. Was there any way forward, anything I hadn't tried? I could only think of one test we hadn't tried yet that might be helpful, might get us useful data, and it was a test we didn't dare run.

Maybe Dr. Cole would come up with some treatment. Maybe he already had. Maybe with time the victims would just recover on their own.

Maybe the Sun will light up tomorrow and the Earth will be covered with daisies.

I sighed, and tried not to sag against the wall. When Marta finally emerged, I said, "I'm going to the infirmary to get an update. Come with me."

Marta frowned. "Me? What for?"

"I need your help." I laughed nervously. "I'm running out of colleagues."

"Don't be silly. Kyoko was just tired—I think she's lost more sleep than just last night—and Drake and Beth have their little fetish but they're not crazy yet. Neither are you. And I don't know anything about your research."

"You've got insight into the psychological side of all this, I don't. I'd like to hear what Dr. Cole thinks of this vestigial ESP idea of yours—maybe it'll help find a treatment."

"I appreciate the compliment, Dave, but do you really think a social worker's going to have better ideas than a doctor and a physicist about how to treat a medical problem caused by physics?"

"You have so far."

"*Pfft!* I spouted some hot air is all. Who knows if it's right?"

"Let's ask Cole."

She hesitated, and I realized she was trying to think of excuses. "I have to get back to the children. It's one thing for me to sneak out at mealtimes while the stewards are there. It's another to just abandon them."

"I'm not asking you to join the project staff, just come talk to Dr. Cole with me." A thought struck me. "Hey, you're not afraid of doctors, are you?"

She started, but said, "Don't be silly."

"You are!" I grinned, delighted to have guessed correctly.

But Marta didn't smile and I understood something else: As much time as she spent guessing what other people were thinking, she hated to have the tables turned.

"I admit I don't like them very much." She sighed. "Remember how I usually meet them, okay? It's when I'm taking custody of an abused child who, in spite of everything, is still screaming to go back to Mommy and Daddy. I'm doing the right thing, the doctors are doing the right thing—it still feels lousy."

She's lying. The thought zinged across my mind, but that wasn't it. She hadn't lied so much as omitted. She'd only said half, and the half she left out was important.

What are you hiding?

Something that was none of my business, that's what. I mentally kicked myself for even thinking of invading her privacy.

"I can understand that." Then, looking for something else to say, I came up with: "But you've worked with this bunch of doctors already—"

"Yeah." She sighed again. "Because the aftermath of the Effect was *so* much more comforting. Well, I pitched in when they needed me, I guess I can do it again."

Now I hesitated. "If you really don't feel comfortable—"

"Don't get all contrary on me, Dave."

And that was that.

◀ ◀ ◀

The infirmary was—well, a madhouse. As before, patients filled every bed in the main ward. But instead of the quiet wounded, most of the patients were strapped down, struggling and shouting. Only a few slept, perhaps sedated. The medics remained in constant motion just below panic level, and even as Marta and I arrived, two security guards appeared at the far end with a fresh victim shouting inane babble.

"It's still getting worse," I said.

"I thought it would be," Marta answered. Her eyes swept the scene and her shoulders hunched with tension. "The crew was too good sorting us out after the *Explorer* rescue to have allowed that riot to get started last night."

I spotted Cole talking to a group of medics. He saw us at the same time and, without pausing in his instructions, raised one hand pointing toward his office. I led Marta that way. In the office, she sat down at once, crossing her arms. I paced up and down. Neither of us said anything.

The doctor joined us after five or ten uncomfortable minutes. "We're up to fifty-two cases," he said without preamble, dropping heavily into his chair. "That's about three an hour since the last time we talked."

"Is that crew or—"

"Crew. The civilian count is lower, though I suspect there are more cases there than we've diagnosed. They're not sitting at duty stations where someone will notice right off if they lose it."

"That's how the panic started last night," Marta said.

Cole turned, noticing Marta for the first time. I made a quick introduction.

"Dave's trying to recruit me as his psychology advisor," she said.

"Hum. Well, you're right. We let the cases among the civilians pile up unnoticed. It was an oversight. But we've got medics and security stationed there now. We're confining nonviolent cases to quarters, whether crew or civilian, and focusing our attention on the rest. We should be able to stay on top of things for a while. The problem is, the rate is about to spike."

"How do you know?" I asked.

But Marta nodded. "You've got symptoms in people who haven't broken down yet."

"Yeah." Cole leaned back and rubbed the side of his face. "We've been doing brain scans on as many crew as we can find time for ever since these breakdowns began. I told you the patients have brain activity consistent with schizophrenia, but no physical cause, right? Good. Well, we're seeing similar activity in almost everyone we test. The progression is consistent and alarming: You could almost set a chronometer by the extent of the abnormality."

"I guess it was too much to hope that we'd be past the peak," I said.

"We're not even in the foothills yet. The schizophrenia-like brain activity causes overt symptoms of depression, anxiety, auditory or visual hallucinations, and eventually delusions, all getting worse as the underlying activity builds up. Some people are more susceptible than others; that's the way it is for any medical phenomenon, and it's those early victims we've seen so far. But everyone will give in sooner or later. Not everyone will have a distinct psychotic break; some will just slip seamlessly into insanity. But best I can figure, we've got two, maybe three days before everyone affected goes completely under."

There were five days until the relief ships arrived.

"I've—" I caught myself, and changed what I'd been about to admit. "I've noticed my friends acting strangely."

"I imagine they'd say the same about you."

I almost denied it. But that would have given as much away as openly talking about the Beast.

"There is one pattern I've discovered," Cole continued. "One group of people who are not affected."

My eyes widened. "Who?"

"People who were asleep during the Effect. I first noticed last night. The midwatch—that's midnight to zero six hundred hours—was on duty when the panic broke out last night. I realized I had no cases of insanity from them. The Effect started around twelve thirty hours. It occurred to me almost everyone on midwatch would have been asleep at the time. A lot of the evening watch also—that's eighteen hundred to midnight. I looked into it, and it checks out. The pattern holds perfectly: Everyone asleep during the Effect has no symptoms now. None. Everyone else . . ."

Marta uncrossed her arms and leaned forward, elbows on her knees. "Yes, that would follow."

Instantly, she had our complete attention. Cole leaned forward on his desk as if to imitate her pose. "Follow what?"

"Something I talked about with Dave and the others," she said. "Just speculation, really, but it fits with what you've found."

"Let's hear it."

So Marta sketched out the theory she'd shared earlier, finishing with, "So if Dave wasn't psychic before, but is now, the Effect did leave a permanent mark: It woke up the vestigial ability."

"But only in Professor Harris," Cole said. "How do you get from that to everyone going insane?"

"Why is a vestigial organ vestigial? It's on its way out the evolutionary exit door. The machinery is atrophied, the parts falling out of place or getting used for other things. This neurofield is still there, but the sense organ that responds to it is now shot. Then the Effect does something to the neurofield, makes it stronger or who knows what, but whatever it does forces that atrophied sense organ to listen to it. For Dave, that's what he calls his other-sense. For everyone else, it's just garbled signals. Couldn't that be the source of the abnormal brain activity?"

"But didn't Professor Harris's measurements show all the neurofields are normal?" Cole glanced at me for confirmation.

"Yes," I answered, "I'd hoped to see something different, but in hindsight it makes sense. Hyperfields don't have memories. Once the Effect was over, the neurofields would go back to normal, unless some physical change in the brain had happened, something that altered the neurofield's generator, so to speak."

"I haven't found any physical changes in the brains of those affected," Cole said. "Just the abnormal activity, with no detectable cause."

"That's where the sleeping part comes in," Marta said. "If I learn to play the piano, you wouldn't be able to see any physical change in my brain, would you? Maybe learning is all the change that happened. The Effect lit up the neurofield, and the brain learned to listen to it. Now it can't unlearn the new skill. Like finding the image in a hidden picture puzzle: Once you've seen it, you can't go back to not seeing it. Meanwhile, those who were asleep learned nothing."

"Ignorance is bliss." Cole laughed briefly. "You're right, it's all very speculative. It hangs together by its internal logic, but so might other explanations."

"No, it doesn't hold up," I said, with great reluctance. Now I would have to explain why.

Marta smiled. "What'd I miss?"

"The psychic sense worked with me during the Effect. The butterfly example and Beth's test say it still works. The machinery isn't shot. So, by your hypothesis, I shouldn't have any symptoms."

She became concerned. "But you do? I'm sorry."

"How bad?" Cole asked.

I hesitated. I had no reason to be embarrassed, or to fear I'd be rushed off in a straitjacket. Everyone except the lucky sleepers had symptoms, and they weren't all being locked up, at least not right away. I should just tell them. But I couldn't. I couldn't bring myself to admit I'd seen an ape-man outside the window, and had heard its claws stalking me all night. So I tried to minimize the whole thing.

I said, "Nightmares about a Red—well, that doesn't matter, but nightmares your pills didn't stop. And . . . well, I've acquired a phobia about looking through windows."

"Hum." Cole gave me a very doctorish look, which, under the circumstances, made my skin crawl. "Well, her theory could still fit. Maybe ESP works for you, but not as it should."

"If Marta's right, what do we do about it?"

Marta and Cole looked at each other. She said, "Shut it down somehow?"

"Easier said than done," the doctor answered. "I suppose . . . if we knew exactly which brain structure creates the neurofield and the psychic sense organ that goes with it, and it's not doing something else we can't live without, I could try and target it. I have a basic oncology unit on board, used to destroy tumor cells without damaging surrounding tissue." He shook his head. "Dust, even speculating about something like that might prove I'm crazy."

"Even if I'm wrong overall," Marta said, "something in the brain connects to the neurofield, and that seems the most likely bit of the brain to be causing the trouble now. At least it's somewhere to look."

"Maybe," said Cole. "It's a question of finding the right brain cells and *knowing* we've found them."

"Dave, could you maybe use your hyperfields to suppress the neurofield itself? Give the ESP organ nothing to listen to?"

"Human hyperfields don't collapse on overlap. If the Effect *did* boost them, then I suppose some field configuration could possibly suppress them. Depends on whether I can figure out the physics of it, which I haven't so far."

"The fact is," said Cole, "we don't even know if we're on the right track with any of this."

I collapsed into the one empty chair and rubbed my temples. The conversation had come around to the thought I'd had outside Kyoko's quarters, to the one test I absolutely did not want to perform. I could not believe what I was about to say. "It all comes down to this: We need data. Specifically, the only data we have left to collect—what happens to a human brain, and its neurofield, while actually under the influence." I took a deep breath and against every screaming instinct I had, finished: "We have to repeat the Effect."

◀ ◀ ◀

The next conversation involved Commander Warren, and took place in his office just off the main control deck. His first reaction to the idea was entirely predictable: "You're insane." By that time, that wasn't just a figure of speech.

Warren had a new executive officer. The former XO was "in his quarters," which seemed to be the new euphemism for "had gone insane." His replacement was Lieutenant Leighton, duty officer of the midwatch. I didn't have to ask why Warren picked a midwatch officer for the post.

Both Warren and Leighton listened quietly while Cole and I—mostly Cole—explained the proposed test. The commander's frown deepened as we talked, until his eyes almost disappeared beneath lowering brows.

"You're talking about putting this entire command at risk to try something you don't even know will help," he said.

"Drake's simulations showed the Effect covered the entire Alley," I said. "We can adjust the parameters to reduce field radius, keep it inside the hangar, while leaving the other parameters intact."

"So you say. But you admit you don't understand it, so how can you promise your settings will act like you expect?"

"It's the only way forward we can see," Cole said.

I added, "We've measured everything we can think of measuring. This is the last data we can gather: Repeat the experiment. See what it actually does."

"Maybe we should just wait," Warren said. "We have the midwatch crew ready to take control. You produce this Effect again, we could lose them too."

Leighton cleared his throat. "Commander, the midwatch is a skeleton crew of mostly junior officers. It's a custodial shift. Even with most of the evening watch joining us, that's not enough to keep control if the other thousand people on board are all nuts, not for the five more days it'll take for the relief ships to arrive. If the doctor has a shot at discovering a treatment, I think it's worth the risk."

"And it's better sooner than later, if it can be done at all," Cole said. "Commander, because of the *Lunar Explorer* disaster, my entire staff was on call at the time of the Effect. None of us slept through it. Neither did you. In two days, there will be none of us left. Meanwhile we had five more cases just while Dave and I talked this over. Five in less than an hour. The rate's picking up; they're going nuts before we can get to them all. Security's already losing control of the situation. The crash is coming, Commander, and we have no way of knowing if the damage, once done, can be reversed. I'd rather stop it before it gets that far."

Warren paced the room, arms folded. "You know, if some smuggling ring set out to take down this base, they couldn't have done a better job." He stopped and glared at me. "Are you considering that? That this might have been an act of sabotage and you're playing into their hands by doing it again?"

"Sir, it's unlikely that any smuggler would have the specialized knowledge needed to engineer these events," Leighton said.

"It's exactly what smugglers or pirates would want to do," Warren muttered.

"Commander, you wanted me to—" Leighton cut himself off with a glance in my direction. He carefully rephrased. "In my opinion, Commander, smugglers are not likely to be involved here."

Cole and I exchanged a look, understanding the scene perfectly. Part of Leighton's job was to keep an eye on his commander's mental state. Was Leighton prepared to actually take command if Warren got too bad? Perhaps he should take command now. After all, he was most likely immune and the Commander wasn't. But who was I to comment? I was being stalked by the Hairy Beast from Outer Space and was still determined to stay at my job.

"Who do you plan to make your guinea pig?" Warren asked. "Maybe you've forgotten that a number of people died during the Effect. Who do I ask to take that kind of risk?"

"Me," I said. "I will."

He didn't expect that. "You?"

"It's the obvious answer," I said. "I survived it once, I'm least likely to be hurt by it a second time."

"I'm no scientist," said Leighton, "but wouldn't this psychic business mean your data is not typical?"

I turned to Cole, who answered. "Our hypothesis is that Dave's strong neurofield is responsible for his different reaction. We're hoping that corresponds with stronger activity in the brain centers we want to find. That might make them easier to detect in him."

"It's a start," I said. "If we learn something useful, we can decide how to go on."

Warren frowned and paced. Part of me hoped he'd refuse. Then I wouldn't have to sit right between my two thankless children while they were, once again, given their serpent's teeth. But I had to do it. They were my responsibility.

Warren knew that. I think that's why he finally said, "Go ahead."

CHAPTER SEVENTEEN

There was some routine grumbling from Kyoko's group about "Take the generators apart, put them back together again," but not much. There was more concern that I was going to kill myself, or perhaps had already gone crazy.

Beth had no such worries. "It's a brilliant idea! Open yourself to the power, and you'll learn everything!"

Drake, for once, confined his skepticism to the work. "We don't know the physics! How can you be sure changing the radius won't change everything? If we even *can* change the radius."

And Kyoko, back at work after a few hours' sleep and looking enormously improved, said, "It is the obvious experiment, and we will no doubt gather useful data. But should you be the one to subject yourself to such risk?"

Rebuilding the beta generator took most of an afternoon's work for the electrical engineering group. They also had to set up an extra array of instruments, since this time the test subject wouldn't be sitting in place of one generator but rather in between them. Then Dr. Cole's staff had to squeeze in among the increasing clutter a package of their own instruments that we hoped would show exactly what part of my brain lit up when the Effect altered my neurofield.

I didn't hang around to watch. I stayed in our lab section down in the Wheel, checking on the rest of the research group, and the news wasn't good. By the end of the afternoon, Daniel Green and Victoria Martens from Drake's lab, Carol Pierce from Kyoko's, and my own postdoc Harold Norman had all joined Leo *in their quarters*. That phrase called up the memory of those early morning hours locked in my cabin during the security alert, how the room had grown small and stuffy, how I had no way of knowing what was going on outside. To be locked up like that again, this time with no hope the door would ever open . . . there seemed less and less of a difference between being in your quarters and being buried alive.

Marta had gone back to the kids. She was in her quarters but only in the harmless sense. She didn't need to fear that phrase; having slept through the Effect, she was immune. She'd begged off going with Cole and me to see the Commander. "I'm just another disaster victim to him. It'll sound better coming from you and the doctor." But she had promised she'd come when we were ready to try the experiment.

I thought about going to her and telling her about everything. The Beast, the Red Light and Shadow, the generators looking like insects. She could help. She was immune. She could watch me to make sure I didn't succumb.

But I couldn't do it. No one must know. It wasn't embarrassment. Why should I be embarrassed? I'm sure everyone was hiding something equally strange. No, it was the fear that she'd say, "You'd better go to your quarters." Once I was locked up in there, the Beast would come and drum its claws on the outer bulkhead, and there'd be no getting away from it.

But then there was the alternative: Attaching my belt clips to some frame halfway between the alpha and beta generators and waiting for them to spring to life. I remembered the pain of the Effect. I remembered the people who burst into flames. And I couldn't help picturing the generators rearing up on insect legs, field emitters transformed into scorpion tails . . .

So those were my choices: Face the generators and the Effect again. Or wait until I finally went crazy and heard the door seal behind me.

Kyoko pinged on the intercom. "We are ready."

◀ ◀ ◀

Other than the medics setting up equipment for Dr. Cole, and the ever-present security guard with his hand on the breaker box, there were no crew anywhere near our hangar. Warren had ordered them all to keep "a safe distance," though what that might be I had no idea.

By now it was early evening. Cole said they had one hundred and nineteen confirmed mental breakdowns among the crew alone. Add to that the number unable to return to duty after the Effect (I'd checked with the doctor, trying to make the question sound casual) and the doomsday clock had counted down to five hundred and fifty crew still working. Of that number, only around two hundred were mid- or evening watch and "safe."

The hangar looked a mess. Kyoko's group had slid the generators back on their rails, as far apart as they'd go, to make room for the new cluster of instruments. Cables straggled irregularly out from the rat's maze of wires and components stuck in between Cole's apparatus and Kyoko's elaborate but more elegantly designed generators.

She didn't like it. "It is a sloppy, improvised design, so disorderly. If there is a malfunction, it will take hours just to untangle the wires."

"It'll be fine," I said. I had more worries for myself than for the instruments.

You survived the Effect once, you can survive it again. But then I thought about how much it had hurt.

I clipped myself to my console next to Drake and Kyoko, both at their familiar stations. During the afternoon, Drake had had his computer simulations search for settings to shrink the hyperfields while keeping the other parameters intact. I'd worked on the same goal, but from the other end, applying the Ryder equations on the settings we got from the self-diagnostics. When we checked in with each other, we'd come up with the same answer. Reassuring as far as it went. We just had to hope the non-Ryder properties of the fields, whatever those were, would follow the same pattern.

Through the window, I saw Cole and his staff finish setting up in the hangar, and the doctor pushed off toward the door of the OCC.

Marta arrived at the same moment, entering the OCC from the corridor and coming straight to my side. "You okay? You ready for this?"

"Yeah," I lied. It didn't matter if I was ready or not; I had to do it. "Maybe you shouldn't be here, maybe you could keep a safe distance like the crew . . ."

She echoed my earlier thought when she asked, "Do you have any clue what a safe distance would be?"

Drake answered for me. "There's not one. We shouldn't be doing this."

"The farther away, the better your odds," I said.

"*Pfft!* I want to be here."

"And I want you to be safe."

"Aw, that's cute. I win."

I put my hands up and surrendered. The truth is, I was glad she'd be there.

According to plan, first we'd activate the hyperfields on a program that would automatically shut down after five seconds—just in case whatever happened was bad enough that the guard couldn't even pull the breaker.

As we set up for the run, the scene was strangely normal. Drake ran the debugging sims, Kyoko primed the generators. Even the faint whiff of ozone drifting through the open door was familiar. Encouraged by the normality, I tried to lighten the mood.

"Do you have a pool on the results, Drake?"

He gave me no answering smile. "A pool on what, how long it'll take you to burst into flames?"

So much for that. "Right," I muttered.

"It'll be okay," Beth said. "I know."

"Generators are ready," Kyoko said.

"Start recording. This is run number . . ." I had to check my screen. "Forty."

"Initializing alpha field . . . alpha field is active and stable . . . initializing beta field . . ."

I tensed. Here's where it would happen, if it happened.

"The software's running," Drake said.

I felt nothing. Yet another nonevent to make my fears seem foolish. Outside, I could see no hyperfields, but my screen showed they were live, and exactly the radius we wanted: overlapping where the new instruments waited. The spot where I'd be, next time.

Five seconds, and the computers shut it all down.

"Did anyone feel anything?" I asked.

No one had. I looked around the room with a relieved smile. "The settings worked. The Effect is confined to within the field radius."

"Or it just didn't happen at all," Drake muttered.

"It did," Beth replied. "Dave is right."

"I didn't see anything," Drake said.

I read my screen. "Field strength was high but . . . energy output almost zero." I groped for understanding, and wished I could visualize these new fields the way I used to do the old ones. "I think this new field design acts like a kind of facilitator for other hyperfields. That's where its energy output goes, rather than into heat or light." Mostly I was making that up. But it made a kind of sense, given my readings, and if what the Effect had done was to strengthen our existing neurofields.

We spent a few minutes examining our five seconds' worth of data from run 40, just to see what conclusions we might draw.

And now I was out of reasons to delay. "Right," I said in a false hearty tone, "my turn."

I unclipped from the rail. Cole moved forward, another medic in his wake. "We'll need to connect you to the activity monitors."

"Right."

The hangar never looked so large, or so dark, than when I pulled through the OCC hatch. My eyes wandered to the far end, to the vast clamshell door that could open to admit a docking spacecraft, and I wondered if the Beast was crawling around out there looking for a way in—*No!* Of course not, because the Beast wasn't real. It wasn't the true threat.

The generators made the Effect. Indirectly, they made the Beast, and sent the Red Light and Shadow to haunt my dreams. What would they send me now?

Hello children, Daddy's home, I thought as I approached, and fought down a hysterical laugh. My mouth was dry, and my heart pounded as if it was trying to escape my chest. I clipped myself to the frame between the generators. Cole and his assistant closed in.

They attached a few leads to my arms, chest, and forehead. "Vital functions," the doctor explained. "I don't want to be caught off guard if you have an adverse reaction."

I winced as something sharp stabbed my fingertip, held in place by a little elastic band. "Sorry, blood chemistry," Cole explained. After a few seconds it didn't hurt anymore.

Amid all these preparations, two images swam up from my memory, both from history texts of my school days: one, an early astronaut being prepped for his launch. The other, a criminal being strapped into an electric chair.

Which one are you? I had no answer to that question except: *I'll find out.*

Cole took a long look at his handscreen. I caught a glimpse of traces on the display I assumed were my heartbeat. He shook his head. "If you don't relax you'll give yourself a stroke before we even start. Are you sure you want to do this?"

I laughed without humor. "No. Got a better idea?"

He sighed. "We'll shut down immediately if anything goes wrong."

At his direction, I leaned my head back into a cradle that he then tightened. The clamps were soft but inexorable. I felt a rush of claustrophobia and took deep, steady breaths until it passed.

"Okay, let's do this. Run forty-one."

It won't be a nonevent this time, I thought.

Everyone went back into the OCC. I couldn't turn my head but I looked around as best I could by rolling my eyes. The generators gleamed on either side of me, shards of light sparkling from the fiber-optic connections. I listened to the hum of cooling fans. The ozone smell was stronger out here.

Through the window I saw Beth take my place at the instrument screen. Kyoko had the intercom on, so I could hear when she said, "Initializing alpha field."

The lights flickered—like they flicker in old movies when the warden pulls the switch on the electric chair—but all I felt was a strange little vibration. I recognized it as the same odd sensation that had provided the only warning of the Effect. So that's what that was: the first hyperfield starting up.

"Are you all right?" Cole's voice on the speaker.

"Yes," I said. "Go on."

"Initializing beta field."

And just like that, I had the other-sense back. I braced myself for it, expecting the same blast and sensory overload as the first time, but it wasn't like that at all. I seemed to pick up right where I left off, able to understand it side by side with my other senses. There was only a little pain, like the pain of turning on the lights after a while in a dark room. It was mild and soon passed.

The other-sense was more powerful than eyes or ears or anything normal. It showed me everything! I could explore the hangar, test the thickness of the outer hull, feel the vacuum of space outside. Exhilaration! What did it matter that I couldn't turn my head amid the medical sensors? I could look behind me without moving!

"I'm fine so far," I said. "I've got the other-sense. There's no pain. Don't shut it off. I'm okay."

I could sense everyone in the OCC and outside in the corridor. The other-sense showed them back and front, inside and out, all at once. I couldn't recognize anyone; it was too different from faces seen with eyes. Around their heads were the auras I called the white-fires, but they were different now. During the Effect the auras had blazed up, wild and uncontrolled. They glowed softer now, calm bubbles of energy in strange shapes. I understood: They were people's neurofields. They were hyperfields! Not as hyperfields looked, even in my imagination, but as they *really were*, one field sensed by another. Oh, what a wonderful thing to perceive them, not inflamed by the Effect, but as they should be, and they were just so beautiful, so very much more than the simple, warm glow I'd admired all my life.

All fear and resentment of my generators ran out of me. What a wonderful gift my children had given me now! Everyone should see this. Kyoko and Beth and Drake, Marta and Cole and . . . they'd love it! *Thank you*, I thought. *Oh, thank you!*

Someone was talking. It took a while to notice. The white-fires kind of vibrated along with the words and made it hard to pay attention to the version that came through my ears.

"Dave! Dave, listen! Dave!" It was Marta. She kept repeating my name.

"I hear you," I said. I waved a hand to show I had control of myself. "It's working! It's the other-sense again, better than before. I'm loving this, I can see everything!" I laughed loudly. "I can see your heart beating! You look strange."

"Professor, this is Cole. I think you're feeling some euphoria. In fact your brain activity is consistent with someone on narcotics."

"You mean I'm high?" I giggled. "That's great! People will pay for this!"

"Try not to get carried away with it."

I had my eyes back, untangled from the other-sense. I could see everyone looking back at me from inside the OCC. Drake looked like he just tasted something sour. Beth watched with hands clasped and eyes shining. Kyoko watched her screen, and her white-fire had a flicker to it that I didn't like, but I couldn't interpret.

"Kyoko, are you all right?"

"The hyperfields are stable," she said.

Before I could point out that wasn't what I asked, Beth came on: "Dave, your neurofield has increased in strength around twenty times. And its radius has almost doubled."

"Twenty times more than normal, or more than I was before?"

"Twenty times your previous reading. That makes it about two hundred times stronger than the normal range. Energy output's low, just like the alpha and beta fields, but a field this strong could, if you changed the configuration a little, it could, the energy—"

"Would be enough to burn my head to ashes?" I asked. That brought me down from my high a bit, but somehow I couldn't worry about it much. "So that's how those cases happened."

Cole came on again. "Professor, I'm going to have you try a series of tasks using this ability, so the scan can spot which region of the brain is involved."

"Right, go ahead."

He put Marta back on the intercom to do a few rounds of Beth's ESP test. I didn't need to ask to know I scored perfect every time. Then she had me describe objects at various locations around the dockyards, not bothering to check whether I got it right. Cole just wanted to watch the scans while I tried.

"It's hard to describe. Sometimes I can't really tell what I'm examining," I said. "The perspective is . . . well, there *is* no perspective. Objects aren't smaller at a distance, they're just . . . well, dimmer."

"I'd love to know what that looks like," Marta said.

"It doesn't look like anything," I answered. "That's what I'm trying to explain. It isn't sight. It's not visions. English doesn't have words for it."

It was really too easy. I started to get bored, and more interested in indulging the fascination of the other-sense itself. I suppose the euphoria contributed to my easy distraction. I caught a thought from Drake—an actual telepathic impression, I was sure of it—that brought a smile to my lips: *This is stupid. I can't believe they're buying it.* I thought about answering, just to give him a surprise, but didn't.

What else could I see? The auras reminded me of the medieval halos drawn on saints, making me wonder if Marta was right about some instinctive memory of past ESP. But the white-fires were bigger, a meter's radius or so.

I sensed movement; concentrating on my other-sense and ignoring my vision, it took me a moment to realize Marta had come out of the OCC.

"You shouldn't be out here," I said.

"I'm staying outside the field radius. I just came to give you this." She took out a small rubber ball and placed it carefully in the air, as motionless as possible. "You saw telekinesis during the Effect, let's give it a try now." She moved to one side.

I looked at the ball—with my eyes, I looked—and I studied it with the other-sense. The couple of times I'd moved objects during the Effect were accidental. Could I do it on purpose? I tried to give the ball a gentle nudge toward the OCC window.

The ball rocketed toward the transparency as if fired out of a cannon, and struck with a loud *THWOCK* hard enough to leave a little dent and make everyone behind the window duck instinctively. The ball ricocheted away, out of my sight, but I followed it with the other-sense until it hit the far wall of the hangar with a second echoing noise.

What if I'd tried to push it toward Marta for her to catch?

On the intercom, I heard Beth say, "Whoa!"

Kyoko turned. "What is it?"

"Energy output from Dave's field spiked when he did that, but, but there was no temperature increase. I think all the energy went into the ball."

"Marta," I said, "go back into the OCC."

"I'm all right," she said, though she sounded startled.

"I could have killed you. Go back in and nobody comes back out here until we shut this down."

Cole came on. "Do you want to shut it down now?"

"Do you have everything you need?"

"Well . . . we could use a little more data."

"Then keep it going. I'm not in any trouble, I just want to be safe."

Marta stared back toward the hatch.

Wait. Something was wrong.

With Marta out in the OCC, I could see her white-fire separate from the others, and it had something different about it. I closed my eyes, to see with the other-sense alone. Marta's aura was quieter than the others. It was—*asleep.*

Marta had slept through the Effect. Her vestigial psychic power remained inactive, and I could tell the difference. The other white-fires, the neurofields, they . . . vibrated. They were more alive. Some instinct told me that was how they should look.

The instinct knows white-fires that work. The quiet version only lives among the blind.

Marta's quiet field seemed inadequate. But something else was wrong, and it wasn't Marta's quiet aura. The problem was with the other neurofields.

Cole came on the intercom. "Professor, what are—"

"Wait." I wanted to concentrate.

The extra flicker to Kyoko's white-fire, that bothered me at first. I spotted something similar about Cole's. And, there! With Drake's as well, and a gleam from the guard in the back.

They all had it. They all had that little flicker, and it was *wrong.*

It didn't come from within the white-fires. It wasn't a disease, or defective machinery as Marta had speculated. It was like a candle when someone blows on it, not hard enough to blow it out, just enough to distort the shape of the flame and make it . . . flicker.

It shouldn't be that way. Some ancient instinct knew it. I sensed something ugly and destructive here. Was this what was driving people crazy? It must be, though it seemed so subtle.

"It's not in the brain," I said, forgetting the others couldn't know what I meant. "It's external, tampering with the neurofield. Maybe I can tell—"

During the Effect, I could tell where it came from. I knew it was the generators. Could I do the same now? A destructive force pushed on the neurofields. Where did it push from? If I could sense the direction—

There was movement in the OCC. They had the intercom off, but if I concentrated all my mind on studying their white-fires, I could pick up fragments of what they were saying:

"—not making sense—"

"—something going wrong—"

"—you have to shut it down!"

"Don't shut it down!" I shouted. "I'm all right, I just have to find out where the flicker comes from—"

I stretched the other-sense as far as it would go. At such a distance, everything seemed dim and foggy. I identified the Wheel more by its motion than its shape. To the other-sense it was a weirdly nongeometric mass of decks and bulkheads going round and round. Faint sparks scattered through it—human white-fires just barely detectable at this distance. Was one of them brighter than the others? But it wasn't what I was looking for.

Debate in the OCC. They were about to shut everything down.

I frowned. "What's that?" Something different—a red spark, not a white one, and it was bright. "There's—"

I could bring it into clearer view by concentrating on it. With all my attention on the other-sense, sight and sound faded. There was a room. A large room, with a cluster of white-fires in it, and—and—*Shock! Pain! Rage!*

It was like sticking my hand into a pool of molten steel. There was no warning. I tried to draw back but I was caught, trapped. The whole force of the other-sense was focused on that terrible red flame. It was a neurofield, but not like the others. It was strong, too strong, shrieking with power, with *wrong* power, the same power distorting all the white-fires around it. But instead of creating a gentle flicker, I felt it as a wave blasted right into my head, spewing blistering emotions into my mind. Rage! Hate! Pain! A mad, gleeful laugh! Flame ran in my veins instead of blood.

It knows I've found it!

What was it? Even as it burned me, I had to know. I couldn't look away. I couldn't withdraw my mind. There were others around it but they were normal, candles around a furnace. What was it? Who was it? I must know! I would find out! I tried to read it, but it was so distorted by the Picasso-world perspective that belonged to the other-sense, I could hardly tell the shapes were human. But they were small, about a dozen of them, and the Inferno was among them, barely human, but still a person.

The red fire bore down on me, searing my mind. It wanted me dead before I could tell anyone, and it could do it! I was burning, burning, dying, and—

Suddenly the vision was taken away. The other-sense ceased and I felt as if I'd been stricken blind. I screamed and thrashed. People closed in, trying to hold me still. Someone called my name.

Then it was over. I could see again. I gasped for air. My skin was clammy, and I felt suddenly freezing cold. I recognized Dr. Cole applying some instrument to my chest. The others crowded around, faces pale and horrified. There were no auras. The other-sense was gone.

"W-wha hop?" I panted. "Wha happen?"

The careful webwork of sensors was wrecked, a trail of tangled wires. Either the others had ripped it aside to reach me quicker, or I'd ruined it thrashing around while I was . . . while I was . . . under attack.

Something had attacked me. It attacked my mind. Something out there. I tried to remember what I had sensed.

"B-burning." For some reason I couldn't talk quite right. "It burning."

"You had a seizure. Try to relax." Cole's voice was soothing, bedside manner in place.

"Y-your field's energy output spiked," Beth said. "And I think, I think all of it w-went into heat. The hangar temperature went way up. We, we, we think you were about to catch fire like Eric and Mark in the Effect."

"Herring. No. Hurting. Hurting nerve fields. Find it." Words came but I couldn't make a sentence out of them. I clenched my fists in frustration. I had to tell them!

Remember, dust it! It was red . . . the Red Light and Shadow from my nightmares? No, it was different from that. A red hyperfield. Yes! My concentration started to come back. A neurofield, but red and bright. And the body behind it . . . it had been small.

"Not seez . . ." I said. "Seizure. Wasn't me. From outside." The words started to come easier, but not easy enough. "Okay. Attacked. But I'm okay."

I concentrated hard. I had to get this out. I searched the faces around me until I found Marta. I met her eyes and managed to put the words together: "Something is horribly wrong with the children."

CHAPTER EIGHTEEN

They took me to the infirmary. I didn't protest too much, though I tried to explain that what had happened wasn't a seizure but an attack from outside. The doctor didn't buy it.

"Even if you're right, that doesn't prove no damage was done," he said.

I didn't push the point. I had the idea if I talked too much about psychic children attacking me, my next stop after the infirmary might be in my quarters. That phrase had lost its power to terrify after what I'd just faced. Still it would be an unpleasant irony if I managed to keep my Beast hallucination a secret, but got myself locked up for seeing the real danger—and lost the only chance to warn everyone and stop it.

So wait, let Cole do his exam, let him see I'm not delirious or hysterical. Then we'll talk.

And after that? My impulse was to run to the Admiral's Suite and interrogate the kids. But what would I ask them? "Hey kids, which one of you just tried to kill me with your mind?" Yeah, that would work.

I didn't know if it was safe to go near them. That red-flame neurofield was pure poison. It might be dangerous even without the Effect lighting up my other-sense. Thinking it over, I wondered if it had even been a deliberate attack. The child might be completely unaware of what it had done. I had the feeling that just peering into that fire was enough to kill me.

Of course, I had been near the children before without—my headaches! That piece fell into place; I was amazed I hadn't realized before that a headache developed every time I went near the Admiral's Suite, and faded again when I went away. Each time I'd just thought myself lucky it hadn't lasted.

I could tolerate a headache, so if I needed to go talk to the children, I could. It seemed only with my other-sense boosted was the child's neuroflame—I mean neurofield—dangerous enough to really hurt me. And no one else had said anything about headaches near the children. Perhaps my stronger field made me vulnerable. But now we could deal with the problem. Now that I knew the source of the epidemic on the Alley, we could put an end to the madness as well. With that reassuring conclusion firmly in mind, I lay back on the stretcher and let myself relax as the medics carried me to the infirmary.

Once they had me in one of the exam rooms, Cole checked me over. Marta leaned silently against the wall by the door. She had a poker face; I couldn't guess what she was thinking, ESP or no ESP. I lay back with an exhausted sigh. The desire to sleep flooded my brain, but I held it back.

"Well, it looks like you escaped any brain damage," Cole said, sounding maddeningly impartial about the possibility. He shook his head slowly. "I hope we got all the data we'll need, because I'm not allowing anyone to do that again."

"How did the data look?"

"Complex. The computers will have to chew on it, compare it to the neurology database, see if they can find a critical pathway to whatever might be generating this other-sense."

"At least we know what's happening now," I sighed. "Marta was half-right."

"Oh?" Marta's blank expression didn't change. "Was I?"

I shook my head to keep it clear. "The Effect woke up a vestigial sense, yes. But people aren't going crazy because the machinery's gone bad. There's an external influence distorting the neurofields. Marta—it's one of your kids. One of them is . . . broadcasting. It's beaming insanity straight into every mind that can receive it." I went on to describe what I'd sensed, in as much detail as I could muster.

"You got all that from your other-sense?" Marta asked.

"What I got from the other-sense was that it almost killed me just to look at it. The rest I can figure out."

"I think you should consider that your perceptions might be false," Cole said.

I tried to sit up, but a fresh wave of dizziness took me back down. It was very difficult to sound forceful under those circumstances, but I tried. "Dr. Cole, during the original Effect I sensed the direction of the influence causing all the trouble, and I was right."

"I know that," he said. "I also know from your account that you felt nothing like the euphoric state you had this time. So this time was different, which means those perceptions could be distorted. At the very least, you were high—as you put it yourself—and that means unreliable."

"I see the point," I admitted. "At least check out the children."

He barked a laugh. "You can believe I'll check! And I hope your crazy theory is right. Assuming we do find a way to suppress ESP, it'll be much easier to treat one child than everyone on the Alley."

"We still need to find out how to do that. So we've got a lot of data to examine." I tried to sit up again, and it didn't work any better than before. "Can you give me something to get me back on my feet?"

"Yes," he answered. "It's called rest. Get some. Go to sleep."

"I don't need to sleep, I just need to stand up," I said.

"Listen. You've recovered quite well, given an episode of such magnitude. Your heart rate returned to normal right away. You were lucid and speaking clearly within minutes. Those are all good signs. Your blood sugar is down but we can fix that with a glass of fruit juice. However, the seizure has weakened you on top of several days' sleep deprivation. You told me the pills I gave you to sleep didn't stop your nightmares. Well, I've got stronger stuff than those. You need sleep."

Nothing he could give me would stop the Red Light and Shadow from returning; I can't say why I was so sure of that. Cole's pills might keep me from waking up but the sleep would not be pleasant. Even so I'd be willing to face it if not for a more important factor: "How many more people will go insane while I get a good night's sleep? How many are coming in per hour now?"

He frowned, and glanced from me to Marta and back again. Finally he said, "We're not even bringing them in anymore. We're just locking them in their quarters, violent or not, and trying to get around to check them as fast as we can manage."

"I don't have time to sleep. We have to start going over that data right now. I know there must be some kind of stimulant or something you could give me."

"Sure, if I want you to have a stroke or heart attack," he said. "I wouldn't recommend even a cup of coffee right now." He sighed heavily. "But you're right. Everyone else on board needs us both working. So I'll make a deal with you. Give me two hours resting here. Drink some juice, eat something, sleep if you can. Two hours. Then if everything seems good, I'll hold my nose and avert my eyes and give you something to keep you going. But only if you rest now. Deal?"

"Okay."

"Good." Cole took a final look at the readings from the instruments, then went to the door. "I'll send an orderly in with something sweet. Get that blood glucose back up. And I'll see you in two hours."

"Send someone to examine those kids," I said.

"I will." He nodded at Marta and left.

There was a long silence. Marta still wore her poker face.

"I'm not going to change into a hospital gown with you watching," I said.

She didn't smile. "*Dust!* Dave, that was really scary."

"I'm okay."

"I've worked with kids with epilepsy," she said. "I've never seen a seizure that bad. The doctor downplayed it. Whole-body convulsions. You stopped breathing. Your heart went into fibrillation. Your brain activity looked like you had high-voltage wires attached to your skull. It all went back to normal the moment they shut down the generators, and lucky it did because you were seconds from dying. *Seconds.* Think about that before you ignore Cole's instructions." Her eyes met mine. She was deadly serious.

"The child did that to me. We have to stop what it's doing to everyone else."

She stared at me hard for a few more seconds, then stepped away from the wall and let herself fall into a chair. Her face fell, her shoulders slumped, and she looked tired and weak. "You really think one of them attacked you? On purpose?"

"At the time, I thought so. But I'm not sure. Maybe it was just . . . *what it was.*"

Marta stood up again and paced the room slowly. "Just like how you were broadcasting during Beth's ESP test, allowing people to get high scores without even knowing you were doing it."

227

"Right. It was bright, Marta. Far stronger than me even with the generators boosting my neurofield up. That was part of what made it burn, just that it was too bright. Like getting too close to a flame."

She stopped pacing and turned to look at me. Her voice was unusually flat. "And the other part? Don't tell me about white-fires and neurofields and flickers. What did it feel like?"

Just remembering it hurt. I spoke with an effort. "Rage. Hate. Pain. It was full of them. Was made of them, in a way."

Marta looked at her fingertips. "What else?"

I thought about it. Why was she so sure there was more? But she was right. "Confusion. Chaos."

She nodded without looking up. "How could you do this to me?"

It took me a second to realize she wasn't asking me the question. She sighed. "Abuse is the ultimate betrayal, anger and fear and pain coming from someone who a child is biologically designed to expect love and care from."

Now she looked at me again, shadows behind her eyes. "I believe you. God help my kids, I believe you. All of that emotion, blasted right into people's heads with so much power it almost killed you just to look at it. What would that do to someone?"

"I know you must hate the thought that one of your kids is causing all this."

"I hate the thought of anyone feeling what my kids feel," she said, very softly. "They were going to be okay. We get them back to the Colonies, they get all our best treatment, and they don't have to feel that way anymore. Now everyone has to feel it."

I thought I knew what most bothered her. "I've been there," I said.

She blinked, surprised. "What?"

"'How sharper than a serpent's tooth,' remember? You're the one who pointed out what my hyperfields meant to me, and I know your work meant as much to you. Now it's turned on you."

She gave me a thin, weak smile. "Right." She went to the door. "So, I'll talk to the children." She left before I could say anything more.

◀ ◀ ◀

An orderly brought in a tray with cookies and fruit juice. He had to help me sit up to drink it—blast this weakness! But I felt a good deal stronger after eating.

There was a computer screen in reach. I called up the intercom and paged Drake, on audio only. He answered after a few pings.

"Dave?" I heard him speak aside to someone else, "It's Dave!"

Then back to the intercom. "We've been waiting for news, but I didn't expect you'd be the one to call. It, uh, didn't look good in the hangar."

"Where are you?" I asked.

"Rec center. Everyone's here. How are you?"

"Tired but okay. Have you had a chance to go over the data we recorded?"

There was a brief silence. "Well, no. We've been kind of worried about you."

"Oh. Right. Well, tell everyone thanks for the thoughts. I'm okay. They're going to let me out of here in a couple of hours. But listen, we've got a lot of work to do. I need you to run the data through the analysis routines. I want a model of what the Effect does to a neurofield."

"Why the rush? It's late, we can work on it tomorrow—"

"Drake, have you been paying attention? There's no time for that. This place is melting down. Cole said they're not even bringing the crazies in anymore, there's so many of them. We've got about two days before it's everyone, and no guarantee that any of our group will make it that far. Now we've got a lead on what may be causing it, and we've got to move."

Just trying to sound forceful left me out of breath. It probably violated my deal with Cole just to make the intercom call instead of lying quietly.

Never mind, I'll lie quietly once I get the wheels turning.

"What lead?"

"One of the children with Marta has some kind of abnormal neurofield. It's broadcasting a kind of telepathic signal that's driving everyone crazy. We need to find—"

"Dave, have you got dust in your filters? First you buy into all this psychic nonsense and now it's—what? You think you've got a kid possessed by demons or something?"

Dusted hell, is he still on this? Was he in the OCC when I pranged that ball against the window or wasn't he?

I tried to sound patient. "No, I think I've got a kid with an abnormal neurofield, one that's damaging to others. That's what knocked me out during the experiment. So we need a way to suppress neurofields, and we need to measure the kids' to find out which to shut down."

"Oh, you don't know? Your magic crystal ball didn't give you the kid's full name?"

That used up all the patience I had. "Drake, I don't have time for your dust. If you have an alternate explanation for what's happening, I'm glad to hear it. Until then we test the hypothesis we have. If it's wrong, we'll find out. Now run the data, and get the equipment ready to measure the kids' neurofields."

"You smashed the new instrument array."

"Then get Kyoko and her group on rebuilding it."

"Kyoko's gone to bed."

I closed my eyes and counted to ten. "Fine. In the morning then. I suppose we can't get the kids in to be tested before then anyway. But you get that analysis under way now."

"Fine."

I shut off the intercom and fell back into the pillows, exhausted. I was sweating and out of breath, and my heartbeat felt funny. All the energy I'd regained from eating had gone into arguing with Drake. Dust him, couldn't he see the evidence in front of his eyes?

I looked around the little exam room. It was an interior room, thankfully, no windows, no walls along the outside bulkheads. That was nice. No claw sounds. No Beast. All bedrooms should be interior rooms. Maybe if I slept, just a little, there'd be no Red Light and Shadow either. I let my eyes close.

How much time before the two hours were up? I wondered if I should even try to sleep, with so little time left. Dust in space, I needed to. I felt my mind begin to drift.

Marta said the children thought the Effect was funny. I wondered if that meant something. Children. Flexible minds. Minds thinking.

Something.

Sleep.

Kids playing. One of them with a flashlight.

A Red Light.

With a Shadow in it.

It found me! The Red Light and the Shadow poured out of the Child's flashlight like oil on fire, filling the air, extending thick, foul-smelling tendrils of liquid darkness over my face, choking me, drowning me, and burning me all at once. Burning, burning, burning—

I woke up.

Son of a bitch, I thought. *Bloody dusted hell.* There was nowhere I could sleep. I shook my head, sending little drops of sweat to patter on the pillows.

No matter what Dr. Cole's next exam showed, I would demand he give me something to keep me awake. I sat up, fighting off the wave of dizziness that followed. I still had another half hour or so before Cole returned, assuming he was prompt. But when was a doctor ever prompt? Especially under these conditions. I had to do something to keep myself awake until then. I could check with Marta, see if she'd learned anything from the kids. That was good. I looked up the Admiral's Suite and hit the intercom.

"Dave." Marta appeared on the screen, and gave me a critical look. "Not resting like the doctor said? I'll tell on you."

"I just had a nice little nap," I lied. "Is Cole examining the children?"

"No one's turned up yet. I talked to them, but nothing seems unusual. I've got them drawing pictures of 'the game.' That's what they call the Effect."

"I remember."

"Maybe one of them will draw something revealing. Like your Picasso-painting description of the Alley. But that's all I'm going to do tonight. I have to put them to bed soon."

How many more will be insane by morning? But it would be morning before we could do anything anyway, and I couldn't ask her to interrogate the children all night. "In the morning we're going to measure their neurofields. That'll tell us which one it is."

"I hope so."

"Cole or I will find a way to shut down the child's neurofield, and then all this is over. It's going to be okay." Another thought occurred to me. "Have you been having any headaches since going back to the children?"

"No. Why?"

"Since the Effect, I've had headaches anytime I went near them. I didn't put it together until after what I saw tonight."

"Dust, Dave, you wait to mention that until now? Why mess with your equipment if you can spot the right child just by interviewing them one-on-one to see who gives you a headache?"

"Oh!" I felt very foolish. "It didn't even occur to me . . ." I covered with a brief laugh. "Well, we should measure their neurofields anyway, for the data, but I'll be sure to talk to the kids when we do it."

The door pinged. "Cole's here," I said. "Put the kids to bed, then meet me when I get out of here."

"Sure." She signed off.

The door opened but it wasn't Cole who came in. It was another medic—actually a doctor, going by his shoulder insignia. He checked his handscreen with a brisk air. "Your chart says to release you if you feel up to it. Frankly, even if you don't, I'd rather you rested in your quarters. We need the bed."

"Yeah. Where's Dr. Cole? Is he still analyzing the data?"

"What analysis?"

"Didn't he tell you about this? We just did an experiment with my hyperfield generators, trying to find the cause of the breakdowns—"

"Oh yes," he said. "I wasn't involved in that, I've been busy with the patients. Let me see what Dr. Cole wanted to do . . ." He studied the handscreen.

"If you're not familiar with it, maybe I should talk to Dr. Cole."

"I'm afraid that's not possible."

"Why, what's he doing?"

The moment I asked the question, I knew the answer.

The new doctor looked up with a bland expression in his eyes. "Dr. Cole," he said, "is in his quarters."

CHAPTER NINETEEN

But he was fine. Just two hours ago. He had no symptoms.

But did I know that? No. Just because Cole hadn't let anything slip in front of me didn't mean anything. Wasn't I keeping the Beast a secret from everyone, for fear of getting locked up before I could finish my work?

No doubt it was the same for Cole, but he finally broke. He must have started raving, because his staff wouldn't put him in his quarters without very good cause. Because if they did, they could do it to me too. Just because I seemed nervous, or had said some strange things about a certain child . . .

They'll come for you any moment. What's this new doctor reading so carefully on his instruments? In an instant he'll pronounce judgment: Ah! I see from this we need to send you to your quarters.

The euphemism had regained all its power to terrify. I had a picture of the Beast whispering in the doctor's ear, right before he came in, "You just send him to his cabin, I'll wait for him there."

The infirmary had become enemy territory through which I moved as a spy in danger of discovery. I would find no more help here; I had to get out before anyone noticed anything wrong—like the fact that I was becoming paranoid about the medics themselves.

I told the new doctor about what Cole and I were hoping to accomplish (but said nothing about the Child).

He seemed to think it was a sign his boss had already gone over: "He wanted to identify a previously unknown brain pathway, using only the equipment we have on board, and then target it with radiation treatments?"

I itched to get out of the infirmary, to get far away. I tried to hide my impatience as I asked for a prescription for some stimulants. The doctor was reluctant. "Chief Cole did enter the prescription, but I'm not sure he was . . . thinking clearly."

"Look, I get that you think Cole and I were chasing fantasies. Have you found any way to treat these cases? No? Then I want to keep working on the idea I've got, and I need to be awake to do it." I then made what, in hindsight, was the most erroneous statement of my life: "If I'm wrong, no one but me gets hurt because I took a few pills."

In the end he gave in, more to get rid of me than any other reason. With Cole gone, he was now CMO and he had too many other worries to keep arguing with me. He entered a prescription into his handscreen. "No more than two of these every six hours," he said. "And I'm only giving you enough for two days."

I picked up the pills at the dispensary on my way out, and took the first dose immediately.

◀　◀　◀

I found Marta in the rec center around midnight. She sat alone on a couch far from the door, in the dark except for a single reading light on the table beside her. Normally, a Friday night would have found the place still crowded at that time. But those days were gone.

The stimulants had kicked in by then. They produced a hard-edged, metallic sort of wakefulness, like a toy running on an overcharged battery. It wasn't comfortable, but the drugs had me on my feet and alert, and that was all I needed.

With the jazz of energy came a new realization: I now had the other-sense all the time. Just a trace of it, and only when I really concentrated, but I did have it. I first noticed right after leaving the infirmary. I went out to the hangar and found Beth and some others already setting up for neurofield measurements. Turned out she'd overheard my conversation with Drake. While we talked I realized I could see their white-fires, just barely. If Beth had told me *then* I was psychic, I wouldn't have argued.

I was eager to find Marta and tell her about it. It fit her hypothesis that the Effect taught the brain how to use its psychic power. I'd had my second piano lesson, and now could play better. Once we had taken care of the danger posed by the Child, it occurred to me this could open a new use for my hyperfields. Repeated treatments to safely build up the ability. Think what people could do with it! I didn't pause to wonder if there might be consequences to something like that.

All these ideas were bursting in my brain, foamed up by the stimulants, as I went looking for Marta. But when I found her, silent in the dark, all my enthusiasm drained away.

She leaned back, studying a sheaf of papers in her hands. As I entered the rec center, she glanced up, studied my face for a few seconds, and said, "Well, you look wired. I see you talked Cole into putting you on speed. You'll pay for that later, you know."

"Not Cole," I said. "Not anymore."

She gave me a questioning look, and then understood.

She looked down at the papers. "Dust," she whispered. There was something cloudy and black about her that I took for depression.

I walked over but didn't sit down, instead standing in front of the sofa, rocking back and forth on my heels. "Did you find out anything from the children?"

"Nothing they said seemed out of the ordinary for children in their situation. They're all asleep now. But what do you make of these?" She held out the papers.

I looked at the top sheet and froze. All the breath went out of me.

It was a child's drawing. The artist had filled the center of the page with an irregular blob of solid black, and then filled in the rest of it with red. I went to the next page. This child drew the red in the form of rays coming from a central black spiral. The next one had something that looked like a black asteroid with red flames all around it. Another was a crude black silhouette of a spacecraft that seemed to be exploding in clouds of red gas. The Red Light and the Shadow. The image from my nightmares, drawn on one sheet after another. A dozen of them.

I couldn't say anything. I went through the pages a second time, and again, as if some magic would change them into pictures of something else.

"I asked them to draw what happened during the Effect and that's what they came up with," Marta said. "They'll talk about seeing through walls and making things fly around, but ask them to draw it and they come up with—*that*. What do you think it means?"

"I don't know."

"You described the power you sensed as red. Could that be what they're drawing?"

"I call it a red flame, but it wasn't like this." I paced, just a little circle in one spot. What I saw during the experiment wasn't the Red Light and Shadow, though it had a resemblance. These drawings showed me my nightmares, not what I'd sensed from the Child. Could I explain that to Marta? I hadn't told anyone about the Red Light and Shadow, any more than I'd told them about the Beast.

"Oh, sit down already, Dave." Marta pointed at a spot next to her. "I know stimulants give you a buzz, but those of us *not* on drugs are getting tired watching you stand there and vibrate."

"Sorry." I sat down beside her, and tried not to fidget.

Everything was silent in the large, empty room. I could hear the whisper of air circulating through the vents. Off in the distance, just faintly, someone shouted. Someone else on his way to his quarters, the new final destination of the damned. Marta heard it too, because I felt her shudder and she edged a little bit closer to me. I caught the scent of Navy-issue soap, a nice routine smell that belonged to calmer days.

Apart from that one shout, I could've believed we were the only two people left on the Alley.

"In the morning we'll find out which child is the one," I said. "Maybe then we'll learn what the drawings mean. Beth and a couple of others are setting up the generators now for testing, and we'll even let Beth give them her ESP test."

"While you check which one gives you a headache," she said, with a half smile.

"That too. We'll figure it out."

She twiddled her fingers and looked at nothing. "And then what do we do? Once we know which child is driving everyone crazy. How do we stop a telepathic broadcast?"

"There'll be a way. Now we know we don't have to shut down psychic powers in everyone, just the one child, it'll be simpler than we thought. I'll be working on it tonight, going over the data from this afternoon. It's going through the analysis software right now and it'll be ready for me to look at in an hour or so. I am going to figure it out. The data will show just what the Effect does to a neurofield and from there, I'll find a way to stop it."

239

You're not fooling anyone. The thought pushed its way into my head. *She knows you haven't got a clue. Your mind is an open book these days, or have you forgotten?*

And yes, Marta knew. "You're going to spend the night stabbing in the dark," she said. "What happens if you can't solve the physics?"

I hesitated, unsure. "Well . . . maybe there's . . . some other approach . . ." I trailed off because that train of thought led in only one direction.

Marta nodded. "Yeah. That's what I thought." The cloudy darkness thickened in her white-fire.

"It's just a few days until the relief ships arrive," I thought aloud. "And the Child can't hurt them. Our evidence is only people exposed to the Effect are vulnerable. If worst comes to worst, maybe we could keep the Child sedated, just for that long . . ."

"Still pretty dangerous, given a child's physiology," she said. "But that's where we'll come out, isn't it? Harm an innocent child to save everyone else. The end justifies the means."

"We'll find another way."

"Sure." She took a deep breath and let it out slow. "Do I have to jump up and do a striptease to get you to put your arm around me?"

"Oh!" I hesitated just because I was so caught off guard, but then I put my arm across her shoulders and she leaned against me.

"Here's a clue," she said. "When a woman is sitting alone, feeling sad, and then asks you to sit next to her, she's not inviting you to an academic conference."

"I'm sorry," I said. "I guess I'm slow on the uptake."

"*Pfft!* Your head's all full of hyperfields and equations; there's no room for anything else." She rested on my shoulder. "It's all right. If you weren't clueless you wouldn't be Dave. It's actually one of the things I like about you." Another pause, and then she said, so quietly she might have been talking to herself, "I like being with people who don't know what I'm feeling."

Silence fell between us, thick and heavy. I didn't say anything, certain if I did, it wouldn't be any good. Some psychic I was! The other-sense was apparently good for reading icons on handscreens, not hearts.

When she spoke again it seemed to be on a tangent. "Ten years ago, when I was in college, they approved a new treatment for traumatized children. It involves neuro-stimulation on the brain centers that control emotional development. Combined with therapy designed to complement the procedure, the child literally grows healthy emotions over the old scars. My classes were abuzz with talk about it. It's wonderful seeing how much it does for the kids I work with. They don't forget what their abusers did to them, but the memory stops hurting them. They get to be the people they would have been without the abuse."

A few days earlier she would have lit up when talking about this, but her dark mood didn't lift. I kept my tone neutral. "It sounds like good news."

She shifted her position slightly. "You can't do the treatment on grown-ups. The relevant brain centers break down at puberty; the neurons get reassigned to adult brain functions."

"I see." I waited for her to say whatever she had to, but by now I had guessed.

"Do you know what used to happen to abused children before they invented that technique? Mostly they turned out okay. But there was a pattern that a lot fell into. The abused became abusers in their turn."

For once, I had guessed correctly, apart from a butterfly. "You're not an abuser," I said.

241

She stiffened and pulled away from me, but her reply was at first cryptic. "My mother used to have this old family heirloom. It was some kind of art piece, abstract. Made of metal. I don't know what it was, but its base looked exactly like this." She pushed up one sleeve to reveal an odd-shaped scar on her upper arm. "I have plenty of scars just like it, in all sorts of places." Her voice had drained of all emotion, but she was dark.

I said nothing.

"I was about five when my dad died," she continued, so flatly she might have been talking about an interesting video she'd recently seen. "After that, Mom started to put the old family heirloom on a heating coil and then using it to give me new tattoos. That's what she called it, giving me a tattoo. Whenever I did anything to piss her off, like spilling my drink or being late home from school or breathing too loud." She remained frozen, blank of face and of voice, but at that last thought, the black cloud in her aura flared up with a swirl of red. A familiar red, the same that had nearly killed me in the OCC, though her neurofield was so faint and dim it was nothing more than an impression, harmless. At least to me.

She took a deep breath. "She got caught, of course. A teacher at school noticed one of the burns, and they took me to a doctor, and then they took me away from her. Screaming and crying for Mommy despite everything. They invented neurotherapy too late for me. I had to get over it the old-fashioned way."

"I'm sorry," I said. It was too little, but it was all I could say.

She laughed jaggedly. "I never talk about that. I don't like anyone knowing about it. I make my friends among people who'll never ask. But it has to come out now. Because I still have all the scars."

She stood up suddenly and walked a few paces away, her fists clenched. "The abused become abusers."

I got up and grabbed her by her upper arms, making her look at me. "No. You care about those kids. You haven't done anything to hurt them."

"You still don't get it," she said. "I've spent my life making sure no one else has to suffer like that, and I'm not going to change now. One of those kids is beaming all that pain into everyone on board and I will do whatever it takes to stop it. Even *some other approach* as you so delicately put it. And don't lie to me and pretend we don't both know what that other approach might have to be."

"We'll find another way," I said. "We only need time, just a few extra days—"

"Really? If the Alley goes to hell, will anyone live long enough for the ships to get here? With no one watching the lifesystems? If we don't find a way, then God help me, I'll do what I have to. I can hate myself for that, but I'll do it anyway."

"Come back and sit down," I said, and pulled her back to the sofa. She might have been made of wood. She wasn't crying or anything so obvious (I had the idea that she never cried; maybe she used up her life's supply of tears back in her childhood) but her face was that of someone being tortured. I didn't try to put my arm around her again. I sat and faced her.

"Listen to the clueless physicist now, because this time I have a clue. You're not talking about taking it out on the kids because you're angry or impatient or disappointed with your life. You're imagining the worst-case scenario and the worst you might ever do, and you hate it. The fact that you hate it shows who you are, not the fact that you can imagine it. You'll do whatever it takes to avoid the worst. Know that about yourself."

Another long silence fell between us. The stimulants had me twitchy, but I managed to sit still until, little by little, she began to relax. She met my eyes, and for once in her life, all the old wounds showed in them, not hidden beneath a grin and a smart-ass remark.

So I kissed her.

It was probably the wrong thing to do. Wildly inappropriate. Foolish. Ridiculous.

I felt her surprise, but then she leaned in and kissed me back. We stayed that way for a long time, and then settled down side by side, my arm around her shoulders again.

It didn't go any further than that one kiss. It wasn't the right time for it to go further. Among the things I will regret for the rest of my life is that the time never came.

The silence was better now. I thought about secrets, and knew where the conversation had to go next. Dust, I didn't want it to. I debated with myself in dizzy, stimulant-fueled spirals:

Trust her. The Beast seemed so trivial now, a childish fantasy I ought to just get over. *She'll help.*

The frightened side of me rationalized. *She'll be insulted I even brought it up. How self-indulgent am I?*

She needs you to trust her like she just trusted you.

Or maybe she'll call the medics and tell them I'm crazy.

She'd only do that if it really had to be done. Trust her.

No.

Trust her.

"I need your help."

She turned slightly, to look at me. "What with?"

I had the feeling of someone about to jump into an ice-cold swimming pool. "Do you remember, a few years back, all those news reports about a monster in the Asteroid Belt? They called it the Beast of the Belt?"

"Yeah. Something like a big ape-man in space without a pressure suit, that would come look in at people from outside their lifesystem domes." She waited for me to explain why I'd brought it up.

"After the Effect, when Beth first suggested we might have found the basis for ESP, I started thinking about old stories like that. And I thought, if ESP is true, why not those stories? I thought, if I look out the window now and see that Beast, it would prove that everything I think I know is false, and science is nothing but a blind alley."

She straightened up and shifted so she could face me directly. "That's the phobia about windows you mentioned to Dr. Cole. You're afraid you'll see it."

"It's worse. I *have* seen it."

"The other night in the Observation Gallery, when we saw the first crazy officer. Something startled you right before he showed up."

I nodded. "That was the first time. I only saw something out of the corner of my eye; I could just about convince myself it was a trick of the light. But later I saw it staring in at me through a window. It disappeared right away, but there was no denying what I saw. Then I heard—*thought* I heard—its claws ticking on the bulkhead outside. The sound followed me to my cabin, and ticked right by my ear all night."

It was easy to go on once I'd taken the plunge. Marta nodded as I talked, her expression composed.

"Now I have the idea that if I see it one more time, just one more, I will finally go crazy," I said. "So—no windows."

"Given the situation, it's pretty rational to be afraid of going crazy," she said.

"But hallucinations?"

"Yes, you're having symptoms. Who isn't? It doesn't mean you're crazy. You still know what's real and what's not."

"For now."

She frowned, disliking the defeatism.

"There's one more thing," I said.

"What? Is the Beast planning to blow up the base?"

For some reason the return of her irony made me feel better. "No. Something different. I also told the doctor that his pills didn't stop my nightmares. They seem to have worked for everyone else, but not me. The nightmares all revolve around a single image." I picked up the stack of children's drawings. "This image. I call it the Red Light and the Shadow."

Marta's brows drew together in genuine wonder. "And the children drew it?" She took the drawings from my hand and browsed through them. "Can't be a psychological state of your own, then . . . Hum. They said these showed what the game looked like. Some common image that psychically receptive minds pick up from the Effect, maybe?"

"There's a word that goes with it. *Eiralynn.*"

"Hate all men?"

"No, it's *hey—RAH—lin.* Except without the *H*. Eiralynn."

She tried it out. "Eiralynn." Hearing her say it made my skin crawl. But she shrugged. "Means nothing to me."

"Whatever it means, it's part of the reason I asked the medics for stimulants. Until this is over, I don't dare try to sleep."

She put down the papers and looked at me. "Well, that's not good for your health."

"Will it kill me?"

"Quite possibly."

I shrugged. "Anyway, that's it. I haven't told anybody about this. I'm scared of winding up in my quarters with no chance of solving this. Maybe more scared than I am of actually going crazy. So no one knows. No one but you."

She tilted her head back, and for a moment grew darker. "Why are you telling me? You feel the need to reciprocate in the secrets exchange?"

"No!" I shook my head. "Maybe that's the reason I *could* tell you, but it's not the reason I *did*."

"Then why."

"I told you: I need your help. You're immune. You're not going crazy. I need you to keep an eye on me. Pull me back from the edge if you see me start to go over it. And—" I hesitated before plunging into the iciest part of the pool. "And if it comes to the point you can't, make sure I do get sent to my quarters before I can do any more damage."

Marta cocked her head, and suddenly the smart-ass gleam shone in her eyes, and I knew it was going to be all right. "You don't have to ask twice," she said, and her trademark grin spread comfortably across her face.

CHAPTER TWENTY

Twelve names. Twelve children. One of them had a secret, and might or might not be aware of it.

The list had first names and ages only, due to Colonial Services confidentiality rules. "I don't know their last names myself," Marta said.

Aaron, 5	Akira, 7
Andrew, 10	Elise, 10
Laurie, 7	Mira, 6
Molly, 9	Nia, 7
Rick, 6	Samuel, 5
Sharon, 10	Thomas, 7

We were a little fuzzy on whether we had permission to take the kids out to the hangar, since the Alley's dockyard section was technically a sensitive area, but we went ahead and did it, hoping that anyone who might object would be too busy to notice. That seemed to be the case. The medical staff declined to even send an observer, clearly thinking the whole idea was just some delusion Cole and I had been chasing. The ever-present security guard with his hand on the main breaker was the only crewman around, and he didn't offer any opinions.

Marta got her roommate Teresa along with Brown and a couple of other stewards to help herd the children to our hangar. She and her helpers managed to get them into an empty room near the

OCC, where they would bring them one by one into the hangar for their measurements.

I had spent the entire previous night poring over the data, popping another pair of pills along the way. My nerves hummed like high-tension wires but I couldn't let myself slow down.

Overnight, Drake had worked late enough to give me the analysis I had demanded. I don't know how late Beth and the others from Kyoko's group worked in the hangar. I had my students with me—those that were left—for a while, but they dropped out one by one. Tom Markov stayed up the longest; he seemed to have recovered from his depression over Anne. Together we ran the data from the experiments—over and over, backward and forward, in real time and slow motion, until we could almost recite every number from run 37 through run 41 by heart.

"Look at this," Tom said at one point, looking over the data from run 41 after everyone else had given up and gone to bed. "The instant of transition when the beta field stabilizes and your neurofield shoots up to two hundred times normal. See this configuration shift in the alpha field at the same moment? It suggests an energy spike but none was recorded. Could that energy be going to strengthen your neurofield?"

"Seems likely," I said.

"And then here, when you performed your telekinetic trick." He scrolled forward. Tom believed in the ESP connection but, to my relief, showed none of the eerie fanaticism Beth had developed. "Beth did record an energy spike, but apparently it all went into the ball as kinetic energy, none into heat. Look at your neurofield at that moment—it's the *exact same* config shift the alpha field showed earlier. I think this is diagnostic of a hyperfield diverting its output into some kind of potential energy, whether it's a kinetic potential or a voltage potential—or even the potential to strengthen another hyperfield. I don't think anyone's ever described a potential energy state for that."

"They haven't," I said. "We've always described hyperfields emerging from EM fields, never from other hyperfields. But something like that happened in run 37—the energy buildup between the generators, like a third field had formed there."

"Think of the possibilities! Hyperfields made by other hyperfields, without generators—what if you could set up some kind of network of fields all sustaining each other? We could build hyperfield machines, technology with no material component."

Tom was filled with a student's wild enthusiasm for the radical idea. I wondered briefly where the depressed young man who had blamed me for Anne's death had gone.

But I said, "How would you control something like that?"

"You'd control it psychically. It'd be a machine made of psychic power, really."

The night went on like that; several times Tom or I would become excited by some fascinating detail that promised new horizons of research. But nothing we found helped our immediate problem; we didn't know how the generators boosted my neurofield, or the Child's, and we didn't know how to do the reverse. Nor did we come any closer to finding the missing piece to the Ryder equations, which continued to present a face that seemed complete and seamless.

Eventually even Tom's enthusiasm waned. As the clock counted toward 0700, he said, "You know, we really don't even know if these run files are right. The Ryder equations are built into the software that translates the instrument readings into a hyperfield model."

"Nothing we can do about it," I answered. Those files contained billions of separate values for every second of recording, data on voltages, temperatures, subatomic excitation states, and hundreds of other variables. No human could make anything of them unaided. "Once we figure out the new equations, we can rewrite the software accordingly. Until then we just have to hope the models we have give us what we need."

I rubbed my eyes; time for another dose of stimulants. "Let's call a halt for now, Tom. Go try to get some sleep. We're going to be checking the kids in a couple of hours; we'll get back to this after we see how that turns out."

"Okay," he said. He stood up, but paused at the door. "Oh, by the way, are you still using Anne's handscreen?"

I frowned. "Well, yes. I'm sorry if it bothers you—"

"No, no, it's okay, she just asked me to tell you she needs it back."

About five seconds ticked by while I realized what he had just said. Finally all I could say in reply was, "What?"

"Anne has some work to do and she needs her handscreen back. She wanted to know if you could borrow someone else's for a while."

My skin crawled at the thought of him conversing with Anne. Even though it must have taken place only in Tom's mind, I couldn't help picturing a scene between him and some rotting, horror-video specter. I let seconds pass, while I pushed down the image, until I could say with seeming calm, "Sure. I'll get it back to her next time I see her."

"Great, thanks." Tom gave me a cheerful smile and then left.

I thought for a moment about calling the infirmary, and having Tom sent to his quarters. But I rejected the idea at once. If he was happy in his delusion, more power to him. I wished mine were so pleasant.

251

The Beast had ticked its claws against the bulkhead throughout the entire night. Now, as we prepared to check the children's neuro-fields, I wondered why I couldn't hear it clattering about the hangar. The whole place was outside wall. The Beast ought to have plenty of opportunity, but it was silent. Only the hollow echoes of the hangar itself filled the air.

Beth worked Kyoko's station while Drake and I settled in front of ours. Drake couldn't stop himself from repeating his opinion of the whole thing, muttering under his breath, "We're wasting our time," as I settled at my computer station in the OCC.

"Dave knows what he's doing," Beth said. "Didn't you see what happened in that experiment?"

"Yeah, he came out of an epileptic fit claiming the kids were evil spirits or something. Let's get right on that."

By now their ongoing debate had become a kind of background noise. They'd given up shouting at each other or getting angry, and had settled into a steady grumble that was easier ignored than listened to.

I didn't notice any headache when I helped get the kids to the ready room, but I was so buzzed on stimulants that I wasn't sure I'd have felt anything anyway. I'd most likely notice when I saw the kids one-on-one. In the meantime, I watched the group for a moment as Brown told them about how during the War pilots would assemble here to board their fighters. The kids all knew him, and he made a point of talking to each child individually.

"He's been really good with them," Marta whispered.

So, there was an unexpected side to the drab little man. I wondered what symptoms he was suffering, or was he among those who had slept and were now immune? No, he couldn't be—the Effect happened right after lunch and he'd have been at work. What nightmare now crept up in the back of his mind? Or was it a happy delusion, like Tom's? He gave no sign of anything wrong.

Almost thirteen hundred people on board the Alley, between the crew and the *Lunar Explorer* survivors, and I knew almost nothing about what was happening to any of them—except that apart from the two hundred or so who had been asleep, they were all on the edge of insanity. And all because of a telepathic broadcast coming from one of the harmless little kids in this room. It seemed impossible, and yet the other-sense had been clear.

I still had no clear idea of what I would do about it when I found out which child was the one.

Just find out, I thought. *What to do about it can come next.*

We took the kids in alphabetical order—having no clear reason to suspect one over another—and that put five-year-old Aaron up first. Marta brought him in from the ready room. He stared in wide-eyed fascination at the generators. Marta told him they were going to take a "sort of picture" of him and got him settled in.

Instead of taking the beta generator apart again, as we'd done for the original neurofield measurements, Beth and the others had managed to salvage the setup used for my own test. They'd yanked out all the brain activity and medical monitors, leaving only the hyperfield instruments.

Aaron looked around with interest as Marta helped him clip himself to the guide rail. The alpha field was already in place, using the same settings as when we measured the adult crew. The beta generator remained dark.

When Marta was clear, I started the clock. But even two minutes was a long time for a boy that young to stay still. As he grew impatient, Marta kept him entertained with smiles and distracting chatter, all the while keeping the distance I told her we'd need to get a clean reading.

I watched as the variables settled down, and the running average yielded a view of Aaron's neurofield. It looked just about the same as the data we'd recorded for the adults. The field was neither stronger nor weaker, falling comfortably into the normal range (in fact it hit right about average), and there weren't any distinctive configuration differences that I could see. I looked particularly for some of the features Tom and I had noted from run 41 during moments I'd really exerted my other-sense, but there was nothing that resembled those configurations in the child's data.

Well, it was only a one in twelve chance that the first child we measured would be the one. So the result wasn't unexpected. Still, it was hard not to feel disappointed. And somewhere at the back of my mind, a little worm of disquiet began to writhe. I think I already knew how this would turn out.

I hit the hangar intercom. "Okay, all done."

Marta waved an acknowledgment. As we'd planned, she brought Aaron into the OCC. I called up a visual model of Aaron's neurofield, just to have a picture to show him. The computer model produced an elaborate image, something like a mixture of crystals and soap bubbles, all made out of glowing fog. It didn't look anything like the white-fires as they appeared to the other-sense but that was because the computer produced a visual model, and the other-sense was not vision.

"There you are," I said as Marta brought Aaron over to the screen. "That's you."

He stared wide-eyed at the screen. "That's me?"

"That's a part of you that's invisible," I said. "But all these machines let us take a picture of it so we can see it."

He thought this over for a while, and then said, "You didn't say *cheese*."

I smiled. "Oh, sorry. But I think the picture would look the same."

"Aaron," Marta said, "I want to ask you about the game a few days ago. You know, the one where things flew through the air?"

Drake made a noise, and I silenced him with a glare.

"Uh-huh?" Aaron said.

"Have you felt different since then? Felt funny or seen strange things?"

"You ast that before," Aaron said.

"Yes, last night we talked about it, didn't we? But maybe you changed your mind?"

"Uh-uh."

Marta pointed at the screen. "Have you ever seen anything like that before? Maybe during the game, or since then?"

He frowned and considered the question with great care. "I got a glow-in-the-dark ball for my birthday."

"But during the game?"

"No."

"How about this." Marta pulled Aaron's drawing of the Red Light and the Shadow from a folder and showed it to him. "Remember drawing this?"

"Yeah, that's the game," he said.

"Yes. I asked you to draw that. But you said the game was about things flying through the air, and seeing through walls and things. Why didn't you draw that?"

"Cause that isn't what it *looked* like." Aaron seemed to think this was obvious. "I can draw the flying stuff too if you want."

"Sure, if you'd like to," Marta said. "We'll go back to the other room and you can play, or draw whatever you like."

"'Kay."

Marta met my eyes for a moment, asking a wordless question. I shook my head. No headache. No sense of anything unusual at all. She led Aaron away, and a few minutes later, was back with Akira. A few years older than Aaron, he asked a lot of questions about the generators and the instruments and what we were doing.

But his results came up normal, and again, I had no headache or any other unusual sensation from him. He had a little more to say in Marta's interview, and recognized his neurofield portrait on the screen as "something they showed us in school once." But nothing he said sounded unusual.

Andrew and Elise both recognized the image on-screen as a hyperfield from their schoolbooks, and were unconvinced that it was a picture of *their* hyperfield. Both were normal. And so was Laurie. And Mira. And Molly, and Nia . . .

Thomas was the last. Drake's sarcasm had increased with each child who showed negative results. "Always the last place you look, isn't it?" he asked as Marta settled Thomas—Tommy, he went by— in for his "picture."

"Shut up," I said, too frustrated to be diplomatic, or even polite. My latest dose of stimulants was wearing off. I'd been taking them faster than the doctor prescribed: In twelve hours I'd taken a full day's worth. The crash, when it came, would be hard.

And making it twelve for twelve, Tommy had an average hyperfield, nothing interesting to say in his interview, and did not give me a headache.

I floated there, clipped to the computer station, and paged through the results, one after another, several times through. They were all normal—normal—*normal*!

Marta reappeared after taking Tommy back to the ready room. "Well?" she asked.

"Nothing. Nothing from any of them." I pounded a fist against the console in sudden anger. "Why does *everything* I look at come up nothing? *Something* is actually happening here. People are going crazy all over this base. What am I missing?"

Of course Drake was quick with his I-told-you-so. "You're not missing anything because nothing is going on here," he said. "The Effect caused brain damage, end of story. Let the medics deal with it, and let's get back to our research. All this psychic stuff you've been chasing, it's just dust."

"But you *saw*," Beth said. "You were here when Dave moved that ball without touching it. Look!" She pointed to the dimple in the OCC window. "You can still see where it hit, hard enough to do that!"

Drake waved a hand. "Probably some kind of conjuring trick."

"Oh, you're, you're, you're impossible! Can't you see what's happening here?"

"Obviously, I was wrong," I said, cutting off their futile debate. "Whatever I sensed under the influence, I was wrong."

Beth protested. "No, Dave, you're the one who can *see*! You must trust what the power has shown you!"

"Beth, I agree with you about neurofields and ESP but these kids are all normal. Whatever my power showed me was wrong." I felt depression settle over me. "And I don't know what to try now."

"Let's just get back to proper research," Drake said. "Our generators achieved stable overlap not once but twice—during the

Effect, and again yesterday. Maybe you've forgotten that's what we came out here to do. Let the medics handle the crazies, and let's get on figuring out how it worked."

I had no reply. *Let the medics handle the crazies?* They could do nothing; Cole's successor had been as clear about that as Cole himself had been. They weren't even treating the crazies anymore, just locking them away so they wouldn't disrupt the base. But I could do nothing either; the only real lead I had turned out to be a red herring.

Marta's children were exonerated. The Child driving everyone crazy wasn't hers, it was mine: my work, my generators. They'd done something to us all, and I couldn't stop it now.

They had beaten me at last.

CHAPTER TWENTY-ONE

As of noon on Saturday, the Alley still functioned. Madmen did not roam the halls. Crew manned their stations and did their jobs, as far as I could tell. They even served lunch as scheduled, for what it was worth.

With Cole out of the picture, I no longer had access to the precise number on the doomsday clock. But by my calculation, unless the rate had slowed, then there must be around two hundred and fifty cases among the crew now. The three factions—the insane, the at-risk, and the immune—would be about the same size. Soon the second category would pour itself into the first, and along with new cases from the near six hundred survivors of the *Lunar Explorer,* the ranks of the mad would swell still further. And then? Could the skeleton crew, the "custodial shift" as Lieutenant Leighton had called it, keep the Alley running until help arrived in four more days, while over a thousand maniacs rioted across the base? I suppose it depended on whether they managed to get enough of them secured in their quarters as the cases arose.

I could do nothing about it.

At lunch Ellen Patton, one of Kyoko's technicians, jumped to her feet and began clawing at the cast on her left arm. She'd received the cast after breaking the arm during the Effect; now she screamed that spiders were crawling out of it and all over her. Two crewmen got up from their table and took her by the arms. They tried to be gentle about it, but as they escorted her toward the door she began to struggle.

"Not that way!" she screamed. "Can't you see the web? Not that way not that way OH MY GOD, THE WEB!" She kept screaming all down the hall, on her way to her quarters, where, no doubt, some giant eight-legged horror waited to toy with its prey. I hoped they'd find a medic to sedate her before they locked her in with it.

I could do nothing about it.

Half the research group failed to show up for lunch. I didn't know who was doing something else and who had already gone Ellen's way.

I could do nothing about it.

"We'll figure something out," Marta had said, before taking the children back to the Admiral's Suite.

Sure.

I shuffled back to my office, feeling numb and dull. I was coming down hard off the stimulants and saw no use in taking more. I thudded into my chair and stared at my desk screen. I didn't even activate it. What would be the point?

Tik-tik-tik-tik.

Starting at a distance, and then eagerly rushing closer, the sound of scrabbling claws outside on the hull came to take up station right behind my head. They started drumming happily right in the center of the window.

Tik-tik-tik-tik.

I shot to my feet, snarling in rage. The room spun around me as I whirled to face the blank panel. I staggered and fell back against my desk, then straightened again as I screamed my fury against the nightmare on the other side of the wall.

"Shut up, shut up, SHUT UP!" I slammed my fists against the window. "Aren't you satisfied yet?" Another fist slam. "Aren't things bad enough?" SLAM. "What more do you want?" SLAM. "Do you want me to come out there, is that it?" SLAM. "That's what you'd like! Get your claws into me! Not enough for you to drive me crazy, is it!" SLAM. "You want to rip me apart yourself, don't you!"

I pounded the window, my shouts becoming incoherent, until a wave of pain from my bruised knuckles lanced up my arms. In one instant, with no transition, I went from burning hot to ice-cold, and I stopped in midswing.

The claws did not change their constant, maddening rhythm. *Tik-tik-tik-tik. Tik-tik-tik-tik. Tik-tik-tik-tik.*

My breath came in ragged shards. I could feel my heart pounding against my ribs. But the wild rage had gone. I listened to the ticking with a more glacial kind of anger. There was only one thing left to do: Face the Beast head-on. I'd clear the window and look right into its red eyes—*which would have shadows in them*—and let it take me down into final madness—or else beat it, watch it vanish beneath my gaze and trouble me no more.

That won't happen, you know. You'll see it and the last thing you'll ever feel is your mind being sucked right out into the vacuum with it. This is the Hour of the Beast, triumphant!

I didn't care. I reached for the button that would clear the transparency.

"Don't."

I spun around, staggering like a drunk. Marta stood at the door. I don't know what I looked like, but she took a step backward and fear crossed her face. She reassembled herself in an instant. "Don't," she repeated.

I turned back to the window, then back to Marta. I was utterly confused. I reached for the button again.

"Don't do it," she said. "Don't look."

"I—" I frowned. What was I doing?

I have to face the Beast.

Why?

Because . . . because it isn't real. And I have to know that. I have to see that, or go mad.

"If I see it's not out there, I'll know it's not real," I said.

"But if you see it, that'll be the end of your ability to defend your mind," she answered. "Confronting your fears is a great strategy for dealing with a phobia, but to fight a delusion the answer is: Stay away. Avoid anything that triggers it."

I remained frozen, my willpower torn in half, the two halves fighting it out:

Trust Marta.

Look out the window!

No.

You have to know!

I do know.

"Dave, you trusted me enough to tell me about *that*." Marta nodded toward the window. "Trust me now. Come back from the edge."

I hung there, balanced, for another few seconds. Then all the strength went out of my legs, and I fell into the chair. Slumping forward over my desk, I put my hands to my temples. "I can't fight it anymore."

"Yes you can. You have to. We still have to fix this."

"Fix it? What can I do to fix it? Everything I thought was wrong."

"*Pfft!*" She sat on the edge of the desk. "Everything? Don't be ridiculous. Your friend Drake can say what he likes, you and I know it wasn't any cheat when you guessed the butterfly or pushed that ball around. The security video showed you were right about what happened during the Effect, and your experiment proved it did boost neurofields, explaining the phenomena. Have I left anything out? Wrong about everything? Dave, I'm not sure you've been wrong about anything."

I refused to be encouraged. I looked up at her. "I was wrong about the Child."

"One point to you. Do you want a round of applause?" Marta cocked a mocking eyebrow at me.

"Where has any of it gotten me? Maybe new frontiers of research for the next thirty years. That doesn't help any of us here. I don't know why people are going crazy or what I'd do about it if I did." I put my head down. "God, I wish I could sleep."

The ticking continued behind the bulkhead.

Marta watched me silently for a few moments, then stood up and came around the desk. She crouched down beside my chair and put her hand on my shoulder, pulling me around to look directly into her eyes. "I wish you could too," she said. "But unless you find out how to stop this, I don't think you can. Even if not for the nightmares, what if taking that time is what allows some maniac to get control of the lifesystems, or something else vital? Then we're all dead. Can you let that happen?"

No, I couldn't. I looked up and saw the aura around her head, calm, asleep, but sane. My other-sense was getting stronger, perhaps as my mind emptied of everything that would rival it.

Suddenly, for just one instant, I had the impression that I looked right into her mind, as if every thought and feeling was written in the shape and flicker of that white-fire.

There was a storm inside her. She was desperately tired; I caught an image of sleepless nights watching over the children since the *Lunar Explorer*, her one brief sleep the nap that had saved her from the Effect.

Behind that: a swirling chaos of memory and past pain, perhaps stirred up by the idea that one of her children was the cause of all the madness, and by the dreadful thought of what might have to be done to stop it. It was a storm that might have burst out on its own accord, if she hadn't released some of it, just briefly, with me the night before.

All that, and *she* had to keep *me* going? I felt monstrously self-ish, but I couldn't say anything to make up for it. She would hate it if she knew what I'd seen. She'd probably make some joke, laugh it off, but it would wound her inside. I felt embarrassed; it may have been involuntary, but I'd invaded her privacy. I turned away from the whole line of thought.

She was still waiting for an answer to her question. What had she asked? "Can you let that happen?"

From somewhere I dredged up a fake smile that wouldn't have fooled a factory robot, and put it on my face as if I thought it could fool Marta. "I guess *yes* would be the wrong answer."

She answered my fake smile with her own, far more convincing one. "Dust yeah—my next step is slapping you in the face."

◀ ◀ ◀

We'd moved to the conference room. My friend was still click-ing its claws against the window, and when I mentioned it Marta said at once, "Then let's go away from it." The conference room was an interior space. No windows, no outside walls. No Beast, nor any sound of it. Convenient, that my delusion had so simple a weakness.

But it'll find a way in sooner or later, won't it? You know that.

On the way to the conference room, I stopped by the bathroom and took two more pills. Medically disastrous, I'm sure. Also necessary. I'd soon have to get more, somehow.

Marta took charge, well aware that for the moment, at least, I needed someone prodding me along. "I'm not convinced you were wrong about the children. What I've seen tells me that other-sense of yours is reliable."

"The children were normal," I said.

"Maybe we should be looking for a subtle difference. Maybe one child's hyperfield has just the right frequency—or whatever hyperfields have—"

"Configuration. Hyperfields have configurations."

"The right configuration, then, to be damaging. You might have mistaken the harm it did you as an indication of raw power, but maybe it's not so obvious as that."

"Maybe." The stimulants started to kick in, and I felt more alert. Already the black depression of my crash was receding, and I didn't want it back.

My thoughts raced but not in the right directions. *You're already an addict.* Could that happen so fast? Maybe so.

Just let me get through this and I'll gladly face withdrawal when it's over.

The pills gave me energy, but I had to supply concentration. I sat down opposite Marta and activated the wall screen, calling up the data from run 42 that morning, and tried to hide my reluctance about wearily returning to work.

"Okay," I said, "let's go over the children's measurements again. See if any of them have any unique features." I displayed the first file.

Marta laughed. "Well, I can read Aaron's name on it. That's about all I get."

"As we go through all the kids, look for any value with a sharp difference from all the others. Here—" I split-screened the display and put Aaron's "portrait" beside his numbers. "Eyeball the graphic, too, see if anything jumps out. I always imagine hyperfields visually before I work out the math."

"Really?" She gave me an interested glance. "I've read that a lot of famous scientists in history worked that way. I think that makes you a genius."

"No, mediocre scientists work the same way."

She flashed a grin and I paged to the next file, Akira's. The numbers, and the picture, looked pretty similar.

"I don't know whether to hope we find something, or hope we don't." Marta squinted at the screen as if memorizing its details.

I went to the third file. Andrew. "I was expecting to see a major difference in field strength. If the difference is subtle, it could be swamped out by statistical variation."

"It doesn't seem like much variation," Marta observed. She pointed. "That one, didn't Aaron's file have the same number there?"

I looked. "That's apparent temperature inside the event horizon. Pretty similar for all neural fields—it's probably a coincidence." I flipped back to the first file. Sure enough, the number was the same.

Then I frowned. A lot of the numbers were the same. I switched back, and there it was.

"They're identical," Marta said.

"But that's impossible," I answered. "There's a margin of error—you wouldn't get a perfect match even if you measured the same field twice." I put the two files side by side. It wasn't just a few variables: Every number matched.

"So how does that happen?"

"Wait." I worked the console. "I should have done it this way from the first, it's the smart way to compare—" I put up a table of all twelve files in parallel columns, only leaving room on screen for the first twenty or so variables in each file, but it was enough to see the pattern.

There were only three different sets of numbers, scattered at random across the columns to make up the twelve files. Marta and I stared at each other. "Well this is just brilliant," I growled. "How in dusted space a screw-up like this happens—"

"How?" she asked. Her voice had gone strangely flat.

"I don't know. Someone goofed somewhere." I studied the files. "All twelve kids' names are on them. If the files were just duplicated by accident, the names would be duplicated as well. It must have happened right while we took the measurements. Which means no proper files were ever saved—" I glared at the console, my hands screwed up into fists. "Which means no backup copies. Dust! Of all the times for something like this to happen! Any of those kids could have an abnormal field and we'd never have seen it."

"How did it happen?" Marta asked again.

And again I answered, "I don't know." I thought it over. "It'd take more than a missed keystroke or two."

"Not a likely accident, then?"

"What does *likely* mean anymore?" I shrugged. "It's starting to seem like our computers have a mind of their own. The Effect, now this—" But I got her implication. "You think someone faked this data on purpose?"

"Don't you?" Marta's voice went flat and hard. "I think one of the children did it. *The Child.*"

"To keep us from finding it?" I shook my head slowly. "Even if you assume the Child read our minds well enough to learn *how* to tamper with the computers, none of the kids had access."

"We already think that one of the children is broadcasting its emotions." She had gone pale, and looked like she was about to be sick. Her aura had colors of dread. She stood up and paced the room slowly. "What if the Child becomes frightened, has only one thought: *Hide me.* What does that thought do if beamed into your head with the same power as the go-crazy signal?"

"You think one of us covered the data, without knowing it. Responding to a telepathic command."

"I think the Child knows what we talked about last night. I think he read straight from my mind the whole conversation we had about 'other approaches' and is terrified we're planning to murder him—or her."

She started to go dark again, and I cut her off. "If it thinks so, it's wrong. Don't beat yourself up again. We had this conversation already. We'll do anything to find another way."

She stopped pacing and faced me. "All right." There was more resignation than agreement in her voice. But I'd pulled her back, returning a small part of what she'd done for me earlier.

Practical matters. A search of the project database revealed that the three files copied over the children's results came from the original study we did with Rothberg and Wilson, before ever coming to the Alley. No help there.

I thought it over, then the light came on. "Run forty-two!" I said. "That's it!" I worked the keyboard.

"What?" Marta asked.

"The alpha field stayed on while we brought the kids in to sit beside it one at a time. I may have thought I was saving each child's data to a separate file, when in fact I was actually looking at these copies, but the run file records everything the generators do. Everything."

But all I got when I called up the file for run 42 was an error message. The file was corrupted.

I didn't even feel like cursing. The frustration was too perfect for such cheap commentary. I let my breath out in a disgusted puff. "Well, there it is. This is beyond accident, as if we needed any convincing. The run file's automatic. You can't decline to save it, or copy any data into it manually. So they crashed it. Whoever did this was clever enough to cover every angle."

I leaned back, and Marta put a hand on my shoulder, giving it a gentle squeeze. But I sat back up in an instant. "No. Not every angle. Whoever did this couldn't be that clever, not while working under the Child's hypnosis or whatever it was." I hunched over the console and started calling up software. "Drake is better at this kind of thing. I should call him." But I didn't. I kept working.

"What are you doing?" Marta asked.

"File recovery. The run file's trashed, but I bet it's not physically erased. Drake can dig into the memory itself with more advanced techniques than I know, but let's see what we get with the basics."

What we got were fragments. I looked through those that dated to the morning's tests on the children. There were headers from some of their files, scraps of data. I ran a pattern search and found some chunks that the analysis software could work with. The file was in pieces but it wasn't gone.

"Drake will be able to get the rest of it," I said. "It hasn't been erased anyway. We can—" I stopped, and stared.

"What is it?" Marta asked.

"Proof," I answered.

The analysis routines on one of the fragments with recognizable field data had come up with about a third of the parameters for one field.

I pointed. "That's a neurofield, and look at the strength."

"Stronger than normal?"

I gave a short laugh. "Try *three hundred times* stronger than normal. And that's without any boost from the Effect. I only got up to two hundred even under the influence."

We both stared at the partial data for a few seconds.

"We have to talk to the children," Marta said. "Tell them we know, try to reassure them, reassure the One, that we aren't going to hurt them."

"Let me call Drake first. Get him to work on recovering the rest of the log."

I paged Drake and Beth to the conference room and showed them the duplicated files. Marta watched silently, sitting in the far corner of the room.

"How did this happen?" Beth asked.

Drake frowned. "Could be the debugging sims, I suppose. They use old data files for testing, but it'd take a dusted big glitch to get the sims to write over genuine data . . ."

"What matters is getting the data back," I said.

"Well, it'll be in the run file," he said.

"The run file crashed."

"It crashed? That's a hell of a coincidence. Did someone do this on purpose?"

I exchanged a glance with Marta. "I don't know how it happened," I said. "But I was able to pull up a lot of fragments with a recovery program. Do you think you can get the rest?"

"Sure, assuming you didn't overwrite it by saving those fragments. Should have called me before you tampered. It'll take some time."

"Can you get on it?"

Drake shrugged. "Why bother? We already know there's nothing unusual about the kids."

For an answer I put the important fragment on the screen, and pointed at the field strength.

Beth gasped, then trembled in ecstasy. "It *is* true! Dave was right!"

"Seems like it," I said. "We need the run file back, Drake. We need to know which child that number belongs to."

Drake was silent for a long moment, staring at the screen, and when he turned back to me there was an expression of defiance on his face. "That is a file fragment. Corrupted data. It doesn't prove anything."

"Oh, dust!" Beth exclaimed. Drake and I turned in surprise. It was probably the first time I'd ever heard her use an obscenity. "How long are you going to, to, to keep your head in the sand trying to deny what's right in front of you?"

Drake turned back to me with a derisive snort. "See, Dave, this is why we should stop wasting our time on this neurofield psychic business." He pointed at the screen. "This sort of thing always sets them off. A simple computer glitch and they spin a whole fantasy world out of it—"

At this point I made a real mistake. I asked, "They? They who?"

I saw Marta shake her head *no*, with an amused gleam in her eyes, but it was too late. Drake was off.

"Them! People like her!" He jabbed his finger at Beth. "The great mass of gullible, superstitious, dust-brained, medieval-thinking morons that always gather around to believe any crazy thing as long as it's unscientific! And then deny every genuine discovery because it upsets their narrow little minds! The Army of the Night, I call them. They'd rather we stayed in the Dark Ages, and they'll do anything to drag us back!"

"Narrow little minds!" Only a few days before, Beth would have been completely cowed by Drake's rage. Now she drew herself up, shoulders back, chin raised, getting right in front of him to meet his glare with one of her own. I would have been proud of her, if I didn't suspect she was going crazy.

"Narrow little minds!" she repeated. "What about yours, blinkered against anything that doesn't fit your straight-edged little formulas! You'll, you'll deny every scrap of evidence, you'll imagine medieval conspiracies, but you won't admit what's right in front of you unless you can f-find it in a physics textbook! But Dave knows." She found me with shining, disturbing eyes. "Dave's seen it, the world beyond. He's the only one who knows how to deal with it. You should be listening to him instead of arguing. But you'd bury it all, wouldn't you? I bet you covered up that data yourself, rather than admit you were wrong!"

"I did?" Drake laughed. "How about you? All you psychic freaks are the same, ready to pull any fairground trick, fake any evidence you have to. Maybe you tampered with the files to make it look like some miracle happened, and crashed them by accident. You're incompetent enough."

"All right, stop!" I shouted. "It doesn't matter who screwed up, all that matters is getting those files back. Drake, if you think I'm wrong about the Child, find me the data and prove it. Marta and I are going to talk to the kids and when we get back I want those files restored."

Drake glared at me, smoldering. "I don't think I like the tone you've taken the last few days, Dave. You're my colleague, not my boss."

"I'll get the files if he won't," Beth said. "I know you know what's best, Dave."

I waved my hands. "Fine, you do that. Better yet, why don't both of you work on it? That way you can check each other and make sure nobody fakes anything."

They glared at each other. "Oh, there won't be any faked evidence while I'm here," Drake promised.

"Won't be any cover-ups either," Beth answered.

"Fine. Good. Great. Marta, are you coming?"

I sighed with relief as soon as the conference room doors closed behind us, and glanced at Marta. "Maybe it wasn't the Child at all. Maybe one of them really did do it."

"Be nice to think so, wouldn't it?" she said.

"Do you think they might . . . actually hurt each other?"

"They're heading in that direction. Do you want to call the medics?"

"Dust, no." I sighed. How much worse could things get?

"It might be better not to let them work together. It's the same principle as you not looking out windows: Stay away from what triggers their delusions."

"If they can still work, I need them working." I rubbed my eyes. "Kyoko can get between them; she's around somewhere. But let's go talk to the kids, and hope we find a way out of this nightmare before it gets any worse."

As we approached the Admiral's Suite, I waited for another headache to appear. None did. I mentioned it to Marta.

"It makes sense if the Child is trying to hide," she said. "He or she is holding back the power you've been sensing." Her eyes lit up with a new hope. "We should check the infirmary. If there've been no new cases in the last few hours, maybe it means the Child can control itself. Maybe we won't have to do anything at all . . ."

"Be nice to think so, wouldn't it?" I echoed her earlier words.

She gave me a look. "This Child is a victim, not a villain."

"I hope you're right. When we go in, you talk to the kids, and I'll try to look at them with the other-sense. It's faint but what I saw yesterday wasn't subtle. I should be able to spot it."

We reached the door. Marta hit the opening panel and we entered.

And froze.

All twelve children danced in circles, in three groups of four, holding hands as if they were playing ring-around-the-rosy. But they were singing: "Which one is it? Which one is it? Can you tell? Can you tell?"

Marta and I stood in the doorway, astonished. The Child had found a new way to hide.

CHAPTER TWENTY-TWO

Marta recovered first. She walked into the middle of the group with a wide smile. "Well, this looks like a fun game. Who thought of it?"

"I did!" said one of the older boys, Andrew if I remembered right.

But one of the girls echoed at once, "I did!"

"I did!" said another.

"I did! I did! I did!" Every one of them chimed in.

Marta laughed and played along, but I could see she was unnerved. "Seriously now, whose idea was it?"

The children stopped dancing and formed themselves into one circle around her.

"You don't get it, do you?" a boy asked.

"There is only me," said another.

There was something menacing about that circle, all facing Marta. She sensed it too. She turned this way and that, trying to watch them all. I stayed outside the group, but started moving slowly around, getting a look at all the kids. I don't know what Marta thought, but my mind echoed her words just before we'd entered: "a victim, not a villain." She was wrong. There was an enemy in this room.

In perfect unison, all twelve children turned to look at me.

"Dave gets it," said a girl.

"Marta's too slow," said one of the boys.

Marta looked at me questioningly. She understood what was happening, she just didn't want to face it.

I said it for her, speaking to all the children, but to the Child in particular. "You're controlling them."

"Good! Give him a sticker, Marta!" The children giggled, mockingly.

Marta's mouth opened in a shocked O but then she gathered herself. She swept her eyes around the circle. "Let them go."

"Or what?" They giggled again.

The children circled Marta, and I paced in a circle around the children. I put the faces together with the names I'd learned that morning. The boy who last spoke was Rick. Before that, the one who mentioned the sticker was Molly. I studied each child in turn, not just with my eyes. I pushed the other-sense as far as it could go. It wasn't much, but there was a faint white-fire around each child's head. One of them should be brighter than the others, and red.

"You'll never spot me that way," said a girl, Sharon, standing directly behind Marta.

"Not unless I want you to," said Thomas, off to one side.

"Dave thinks he's a big man with his little power," said Nia.

"You're blind without your machines to help you," said Rick.

"But I don't need machines," said Elise.

Every time Marta turned to look at one child, another would speak up. They kept her off-balance, unable to gain control of the situation. She said, "You don't have to do this. All I want is to help you."

"Aw, Marta thinks I'm scared," said Mira.

"Poor Marta, guilty, guilty about her bad thoughts," said Andrew.

"Oh no, what if we have to hurt them?" cried Aaron in a falsetto mockery of Marta's voice.

Molly put her hands to her eyes and pretended to cry. "Boo-hoo, boo-hoo, poor things, poor things, I feel so bad for them."

I let Marta do the talking. She knew the children, maybe she'd get through. But I kept studying them with the other-sense. The Child said I couldn't find it that way. Even if it told the truth, it might let something slip while its attention was on Marta.

Marta, meanwhile, changed her tactics. She stopped letting herself be turned around and stood still, speaking to one child in particular—it was Andrew, the oldest. "If you're not scared, then why are you hiding? Let the others go and talk to me yourself."

He grinned at her. It took me a moment to recognize the almost perfect imitation of Marta's own grin. "Do you really think I'm Andrew or are you just trying to look tough?"

"Let them go," Marta said.

"No."

"But I'll let you talk to one of them, if you want," Laurie said. "How about this one?" Her face went blank for a moment, and then she went rigid, her eyes clamped shut and her mouth opened in a long, horrible scream of pain and terror. She threw herself at Marta, her hands fluttering and her clear, piercing voice filling the room with terrible cries. "Marta, Marta!" she wailed. "Make it stop! It's all in my head all the time and it burns! Make it stop! No more, no more!"

Marta's face crumpled with pain, as if Laurie's cries physically hurt her. She crouched down and wrapped the little girl in her arms, then picked her up and carried her out of the circle to a couch along the wall. The children made no move to stop her or to surround her again. They just stood in their circle and coolly turned, watching.

Laurie clung to Marta with fierce desperation, her hands clasped behind Marta's neck, face buried in her shoulder. Her whole body convulsed with the force of her sobs. Marta sat down with her on the couch. "Shh, shh, it'll be all right." Over Laurie's head, her eyes met mine in desperation. "It's all over now."

"Oh no it isn't." Laurie stiffened suddenly and pulled away, and smiled at Marta with cold, glittering eyes and an entirely unchild-like expression. Laurie's tears still moistened her cheeks, but it was not Laurie who spoke. "I guess now you know I'm not Laurie."

"Or maybe I am, and I just act really good," said Elise.

Marta jumped to her feet and glared at the circle, face white, fists clenched. "Stop this! Don't you see that you're hurting them?"

The Child continued to speak through the children, and I couldn't even make a guess at which voice was truly its own.

"So what?"

"They don't count."

"They're not really alive. None of you are. Not like me."

"I've been seeing into your tiny, blind little minds, all trapped inside your own heads, since I was born."

Twelve pairs of eyes found mine. "That's right, Dave. I didn't need your machines to give me power. I had power already."

"No one is awake like me," it continued. "No one ever has been. I know everything that happens around me, right down to the dust in the air. I know every thought in every mind. I know everything you know. You're all just shadows next to me."

Laurie climbed off the couch and resumed her place in the circle. Marta stood and faced the children. I went to stand at her side, and I could feel her shaking.

"Aw, look at the two of you, standing shoulder to shoulder against the bad guy."

"That's so cute. But do you know what Dave's been up to?"

"He looked inside your mind. Didn't even ask."

"That's kind of like sneaking up behind you and ripping all your clothes off, isn't it?"

Marta, surprised, glanced my way briefly.

I felt my face redden. "The other-sense flashed," I said. "I wasn't expecting it. It wasn't intentional."

"You don't have to explain," she said. I saw her anger, but she turned her glare on the circle.

"Uh-oh!" The children giggled. "Marta's mad at me! I'm in trouble now!"

"Yes, you are," she said. "And I don't feel sorry for you anymore. But I feel sorry for the others, the ones you're hurting, and I will take them away from you."

"You can't do anything."

"Yes we can," I said. "You can't control us the way you're controlling the children, or you would have already done it."

"Can't I? Who messed up the files when you were measuring us? You did, Dave. I told you to do it, and you did. You don't even remember."

The Child's shot struck home, and I didn't try to hide the fact. What would have been the use? The Child could see into my mind. Instead, I turned it around. "Okay. Do it again. Make me do something. Right now."

There was a silence and the children looked sullen. I'd scored a point in return. Marta's eyes darted between me and the children. I could see by her white-fire that she was concentrating hard, but I couldn't read anything else and didn't try.

I stared at the children. "You can't. You can get me when I'm unprepared for you, maybe. When I'm thinking of something that gives you a window. But not while I'm resisting you."

"You're right," the Child admitted. The voice did not sound upset. "But you'll be mine soon. It's harder with grown-ups than with kids. I have to scrape your minds open first. The crazies are mine already; I just haven't used them yet. You'll be mine soon too."

"*Tik-tik-tik-tik.*" Several of the children made the noise, and all laughed.

"You're trying to hurt us," Marta said. "Which just proves how afraid you really are. You're still hiding, because you know if we find you we can stop you."

"Maybe you can drive me crazy," I said. "But Marta's immune to you, and so are the midwatch crew and so are the crews on the relief ships that'll be here soon. Sooner or later you'll be among people that you can't hurt."

"I don't have to be able to drive you crazy to hurt you." Something cold and deadly glittered in the children's eyes, like frozen flames. "Ask Teresa."

Marta drew in a quick breath and looked around the room.

I had completely forgotten the *Lunar Explorer* steward who should have been there watching them. I suppose Marta had as well. Now a chill of fear settled over my heart. I knew that whatever the Child meant, it wasn't bluffing.

Marta's eyes lit on a door into another room of the suite. In two fast strides she reached it and hit the panel. I was right behind her as the door opened into a bedroom. On one of the beds lay the body of a woman. The smell of burned flesh filled the air, but there was almost no sign of smoke, and the fire alarms had not gone off. It was exactly the same as I'd seen during the Effect. Teresa's head and upper torso were gone. There was nothing left but a mound of ash on the mattress.

It felt like a kick in the stomach. I had imagined that Marta and I were gaining the upper hand in the confrontation. If the other children reflected its moods, then it had been petulant and sullen when its taunts had failed to intimidate us, which made me think whatever power it had, it was still just a child. We could handle it. But that was all gone now.

It can kill with its mind, I thought.

Marta whirled around and screamed, "Why did you do that?"

"I didn't need her anymore." The children's voices were now cold as the dead Sun, and there was a new, horribly alien quality to them. They sounded like the high voice from my nightmares. Their eyes focused, glittering, on Marta. "Now about these ideas you're having. Such busy heads, trying to think up ways to get at me. You have to be close for me to make you die, but that's not a problem. I have all my toys"—the children spread their arms to indicate each other—"right here, and if you try to do anything to hurt me, I'll start burning them. I can spare a couple and still have enough to hide in. Want to see?"

"NO!" Marta leaped forward, panic in her eyes and in her mind. But then she froze, looking around wildly, helpless. The children laughed.

"Good, you know who's boss," the Child said. "The two of you are going to go away now, and if either of you come back here, I'll burn you. And I'll burn one of the kids first, just so you'll die knowing I did it. Tell that to the other one who keeps coming around trying to find me with his mind games."

The children left their circle and drew together into a tight knot in the center of the room. I knew what was about to happen. The Child opened up its power.

I thought my head had exploded, so sudden and intense was the pain. It was the same headache I had when I went near the children before, but now so gigantic and crushing I screamed and clutched at my head. With each heartbeat, I felt every capillary pound little hammers into my skull. Staggering, I fell to my knees.

At the same instant, visible to my other-sense, the Child's red aura flared into existence. At close range, it blazed almost as fiercely as it had when I'd encountered it under the Effect. I tried to see through the pain to spot which child it came from, but it was impossible. It was like staring right into a searchlight. All twelve, the Child and its victims, clustered together in the heart of the glare. I could see nothing but its own killing flames, which built up in an instant—a fever—an oven—burning—

Flames! Oh God, flames! Heat pulsed through the pain.

I felt the power of the other-sense, which had so easily shoved a rubber ball around the room, move on instinct: In defense, it tried to hold back the heat, but the Child's power battered it down. I lost control over the power, over my own neurofield that now poured out uncontrolled energy. I couldn't fight back. I couldn't defend myself.

Marta screamed out and fell. I could see her white-fire brightening on its way to becoming true flame. The Child was going to burn us both.

I staggered toward her, stumbled, picked myself up. I managed to reach her and grab her hand. Dimly, I heard the children laughing. The heat was savage now, inside my head and out. Was my hair already curling into ash? I yanked hard on Marta's hand. Scrambling, we dragged each other toward the door, and managed to throw ourselves through.

We fled down the corridor, and the heat began to subside. Still farther, stumbling, bumping the walls. The heat was gone. The headache faded.

We collapsed to the hard metal deck, shuddering and gasping, while the power withdrew from our minds and left only choking emptiness.

CHAPTER TWENTY-THREE

We lay there, spent, for several minutes. Marta was pale, her skin clammy, her clothes soaked with sweat, plastered to her skin. I was no different. She pushed herself up on all fours, moaning, "Oh God, oh God, oh God," over and over. Suddenly she threw up. When she was done retching, she crawled back away from the mess and sat up against the wall, gasping for air.

I dragged myself over to sit next to her. I felt my head, expecting to find my hair burned away, but apparently it hadn't really gotten that hot. The Child had only made us feel it. Still, I knew it could supply the lethal reality just as easily: There was Teresa's body, back in the suite, to prove it.

"There . . . there are a lot of pathologies that can . . . result from child abuse." Marta struggled for a detached, clinical tone, but failed. "You've just heard the worst. The Child . . . the mind we heard, speaking through the . . . it's a sociopath. It's a . . . a rare . . . outcome. Fortunately. Sometimes they can be treated. But the worst ones . . . I've only seen a few cases in my career, none as bad as this." The words were rambling and barely coherent, but I understood her. She shuddered. "A mind like that, with that kind of power . . . Oh God, what's it doing to my children?" She let her breath out in a heavy, despairing sigh, and leaned her head against my shoulder.

Even now she didn't cry, at least not openly, but I could tell her white-fire wept. I put my arms around her.

Back the way we had come, I sensed the Child's fiery presence. I could feel the intensity of it from here; it hurt even from a distance. I think it was exerting itself on purpose, extending its power to create a barrier that I could not cross. I knew I could go no closer without burning. Could anyone? It hurt Marta too, but perhaps those without any ESP of their own would be safe unless the Child targeted them.

"We'll think of something," I said. "I think it lied about not needing the generators to gain power. Maybe it could read minds before, but all this"—I waved a hand in an all-encompassing gesture—"all this didn't start until after the Effect. And if my generators gave it power, there's a way for them to take it back."

"It won't let us get close enough to do anything," she said. "It'll kill the children. I can't let it kill the children." I noticed that she didn't say "he or she" or just "he" anymore. The Child was "it" to her now, as it had been for me since I first sensed it. And that was right. The Child might have been human once, but there was nothing human left in the mind we just met.

"There has to be a way," I said. "By now, Drake should know which one it is. He'll have recovered the run file and we'll know. Then we can figure out how to get it away from the others. Let's get back to the conference room."

But we didn't move. We were still too shaken; we couldn't do more than sit and wait to recover. The silence stretched.

Finally Marta asked, "What did it mean by 'the other one who keeps coming around'?"

I had no answer.

◀ ◀ ◀

Drake was still in the conference room when we returned. He sat at the computer console, facing the wall screen. When Marta and I entered, he gave me a strange look.

Beth sat in the corner, away from the table. She jumped to her feet. "Dave, I want you to know I don't believe it."

"What?" I looked from her to Drake and back again. "Believe what?"

"I think you know," Drake said.

"He doesn't know what he's talking about," Beth said. "He's paranoid. I don't believe it."

"It's a switch, isn't it?" Drake said in a coldly conversational tone. "I thought she'd believe anything. Unless, of course, it proves she's been wrong all along."

Marta went to the table, sat, and put her head down on her crossed arms. She already knew that whatever this meant, another hope was about to be snuffed out.

I didn't get it yet. "What are you talking about? Did you recover the children's files?"

"Yes I did," said Drake. "As well as the user logs that let me know you're the one who trashed them in the first place. So what was the point, Dave? Destroying the data and then asking me to get it back?"

Oh bloody dusted hell. I took a deep breath and made the futile attempt. "Okay. I know you won't believe this, Drake, but here it goes. One of those children has an abnormal neurofield. Three hundred times stronger than normal. That means it's powerfully psychic. Telepathic. The Child is what's driving everyone crazy on the Alley. Do you get it? It's real, Drake. It's trying to hide, so it sent out a telepathic signal saying *hide me* and I was influenced. I knew one of us was; I didn't know who. So it was me. That doesn't change anything. I have no memory of doing it, I didn't mean to do it, and I need those files."

"I knew it," Beth sighed, folding her hands in blissful relief. "I knew it!"

"Do you think I'm as gullible as Beth or some crackpot cultist?" Drake snorted.

"I don't care," I answered. "I don't care whether you believe me or not. Just show me the data."

"Oh, I've got more than that! You remember the logs from before the Effect? There were a series of garbled entries that the computer accepted as proper commands?"

"Yes," I said. "I suggested you give it to the coms department to see if their decryption software could untangle it."

"I suppose you didn't think it could. Clever way to divert suspicion, suggesting it yourself."

"Suspicion? Drake, do you think—"

"I don't think, I know. They called while you were gone, and sent me the file. It wasn't a crash; it was just a simple encryption algorithm, the same type people use to keep their home directories private. Not hard for the Navy's computers to crack, once someone found a minute to do it."

With a sinking feeling I realized what Drake must have seen in that log.

But how? I couldn't understand how it was possible. *That was before the Child gained power from the Effect!*

Drake kept talking, confirming my fears. "The commands are all there. And so is the ID of the person who entered them. You. You set up the Effect, and then you ran a privacy lock to hide what you'd done. You just didn't hide it well enough."

I dropped into a chair. Somehow the Child must have made someone in the communications division insert my ID into the log. *All the crazies are mine*, it had said.

So it must have taken control of one, I thought.

I couldn't help debating myself. *But from such a distance? From a room in the Wheel all the way to the Hub? It couldn't have that kind of range, could it?*

Maybe it happened when we took the children to the hangar. Perhaps, at the same time it made me hide the data, it also reached out to an officer, making him insert my ID into the earlier run, just as they were going through the Hub.

That must have been what happened. But Drake would never believe it.

Beth tried to come to my defense. "Drake, don't you see? The same thing happened twice! The Child must be possessed. This is all the work of evil spirits! We have uncovered the path to enlightenment! Dave can help us open our minds to the psychic vision, and the evil ones are trying to stop him!"

Beth was not helping.

Drake jumped to his feet, wearing an expression of triumph. "It all makes sense now," he proclaimed, looking directly at me. "You're the one with the knowledge necessary to create the Effect. So you set it up, lay it like a trap for Charles and John, so you can be elsewhere when it goes off. Then when it starts, you miraculously know the generators are causing it, and rush to save the day. You spin a wild story about ESP that no one else can confirm and trot out your made-up theory about how hyperfields can explain it all. You stage a few magic shows, cheat on Beth's test, work with her"—he jabbed a finger at Marta—"on a cheap mind-reading gag. Then you come up with this bit about a psychic Child. Only you trash the data, allowing you to insert some fake numbers into one of the file fragments without any evidence of tampering, and get me to—"

"Wait!" I had to shout to override his harangue. "Insert fake numbers? So you saw the files and one of them *is* abnormal? Which one?"

"Don't even bother, Dave. You don't really care. You know it's all fake."

I got to my feet and leaned over the table, glaring at him. "Drake, dust it, show me the bloody dusted files!"

Drake leaned toward me, our faces inches apart. "*I ERASED THEM!*"

My mouth dropped open and I fell back, sitting down hard as my legs lost all strength. "You *what?*"

"Did you think I'd help you pull off this hoax? I've got to hand it to you, it's probably the most elaborate scam in the long history of psychic charlatan hoaxes, but it's over now. I'm not letting you put that data out on the net to turn yourself into some kind of guru idolized by every gullible idiot in the Colonies." He pointed at Beth, then turned back to me. "I'm shutting you down, and I'm going to see to it that you're prosecuted for every death that occurred in your little stage show."

"Drake, for God's sake, why would I want to do such a thing?"

"Because you're one of them!" Drake's eyes went wild at this point, and I realized that he really had, finally, lost his mind. "The Armies of the Night! Organized to bring an end to all knowledge! Marching against the truth! I thought Beth was one, but she's just one of the rabble they always dupe. When did they recruit you, Dave? Did they promise you a priesthood in their new Reign of Darkness? I've found you out! Everyone will know! Science will triumph in the end, as it always has and always will!"

Marta lifted her head and met my eyes. She silently mouthed the words *no use.*

Drake went on shouting in the same vein for some minutes. I let him play himself out. When he finally got tired of arguing without drawing a response, he subsided into a fuming silence and glared at me.

"Just tell me one thing, Drake," I said slowly. "Before you erased the files, did you look at them? Which one was abnormal?"

"Who cares?" he shot back.

"Just—tell—me."

"I didn't bother to look." Drake turned on his heel and walked out.

All the crazies are mine, the Child had said.

After a moment, Beth said, "I believe in you, Dave. You'll know what to do."

I sighed. "Did you see the files, Beth?"

"No."

I went to the computer just in case Drake was lying, but the files were gone. Without any hope, I tried some recovery tools. Of course Drake had anticipated that—hadn't he just used them himself? He'd zeroed all the file space. Run 42 had ceased to exist.

Every path is blocked. There's no way out. I almost regretted that I'd let Marta talk me away from the edge. I slumped in the chair and rubbed my eyes.

I felt a touch and looked up. Marta had her hand on my shoulder. "I was thinking," she said softly. "What if we take each child to a separate room, far apart, all over the Alley? If they're out of range of its power, they'll tell us who it is. Eleven children will point to one, and even if the one tries to pretend and points to another, we'll still know the truth."

With a tired sigh I put aside the idea of just giving up. "How do we get close enough to take them?"

"They still have to eat," she said. "The Child will have to let the stewards in with food. If we get a sedative from the infirmary . . . we'd have to get it into the food without the stewards knowing, or the Child will read them . . ."

"Might work." My thoughts were getting foggy; the latest dose of stimulants was wearing off, too soon. Maybe the confrontation with the Child had burned through their effect. I only had two pills left. The prescription for two days' worth had lasted only one. "I'll . . ." Utter exhaustion filled my mind at the mere thought of what I had to say next, but I plowed on. "I'll get back on the physics. There must be some way to use the generators to suppress or cancel out the Child's neurofield. If we can couple that with hyperfields that blanket the whole base like the Effect, we wouldn't even have to go near it."

"Okay." Marta headed for the door. "I'll go to the infirmary, find out about tranquilizers."

"Pick up some more of these while you're there," I called after her, holding up my remaining packet of stimulants.

She looked back, and her forehead creased in a slight frown. But she said, "Right. I think I could use a few myself."

Beth came to the table. "What do you want me to do, Dave?"

I wasn't sure she'd be any use. Even if she was more cooperative than Drake, she was still talking about evil spirits and paths to enlightenment. But she wasn't ranting and raving, and right then I'd take all the help I could get.

"We need to get everyone together," I said. "Everyone who's left, anyway." I frowned. "Where's Kyoko, by the way?" I hadn't thought about her absence from the OCC when we'd measured the children. I realized I hadn't seen her all day.

"She's around," said Beth. But her tone was a little vague.

The only symptom I'd seen in Kyoko was fatigue, which she'd seemed to get over with a few hours' extra rest yesterday. I'd gladly share my drugs with her if she needed help to perk up. She, Drake, and I were the only three faculty on the project; with Drake out of the picture I needed Kyoko. I needed her more than Drake, really. The generators were our babies.

"She wasn't in the OCC this morning," I said.

"I figured I'd let her sleep in, 'cause she was so tired last night, and 'cause I was the one who set things up for the measurements." Beth smiled at me. "And I wanted to work with you. You have the sight, you know how to—"

I hit the intercom and spoke without waiting for Beth to finish. "Kyoko, this is Dave. Are you in your office?" There was no answer. I paged the electrical engineering lab. "Kyoko?"

"Maybe she's in her quarters," Beth said. Then, catching my look, she added quickly, "I don't mean it *that* way."

I flipped the intercom to page the entire lab section. "This is Dave. Kyoko, call in please."

There was still no answer.

With sudden dread, I got to my feet and ran for the door, colliding with Drake, who was coming in at the same moment. We stumbled back.

"I heard the page. Is Kyoko all right?" At least for the moment his suspicion and hostility had been displaced; he was concerned.

"I don't know," I said. "She's not answering."

I turned left out of the conference room, heading up the corridor to her quarters, with Drake and Beth following.

At the door I pinged. No response. I pinged again. Nothing. "Kyoko? Kyoko, are you in there? Are you all right?"

Beth pushed between me and Drake to reach the door. "I know her entry code," she said. She hit a quick series of numbers on the pad, and the door slid open.

There was blood everywhere. Splashed on the walls, pooled on the floor, most of it already dry. A faint decayed smell already poisoned the air, making my stomach turn.

Kyoko lay in the middle of the room, sprawled on her back, eyes glassy and filmed staring at the ceiling. The table knife she'd shoved into her own throat stuck there, gleaming in cruel silver.

Her handscreen lay right by the door, at my feet. The screen glowed soft blue. I picked it up. There were two paragraphs of Japanese text I couldn't read, but at the bottom of the page, she'd written in English: *Can't be crazy.*

CHAPTER TWENTY-FOUR

In a normal world, a sane world, there'd be impassive officials to take care of the cold business of death. Emergency calls would be placed, medics or police would arrive, the machinery of civilization would swing into action to wrap the situation in protective layers of official business. Those left behind need not be troubled with the ugly physical details.

How much of that civilized machinery was left on the Alley? We'd have to report what we'd found, but I suspected that little would be done. The shrinking crew had enough on their hands dealing with the living.

Beth covered her mouth with both hands and stared, eyes wide and shocked. A strange whimpering noise escaped from behind her fingers. Drake turned away, and stumbled a few paces down the corridor. He slumped forward facing the wall, his fists clenched, pressing against the metal, his head down. I wanted to go to Kyoko and close her eyes, remove that obscene knife from her throat. But I couldn't bring myself to approach the body. I was ashamed of my cowardice, but there it was: I couldn't do it.

I took Beth by the shoulders and pulled her back out of the room. It was like moving a piece of furniture. She stumbled slightly as I pulled her and just kept staring. I closed the door. She blinked, glanced at me as if she'd forgotten I was there, and then crumpled. She would have fallen if I hadn't been holding her. I let her down gently as her legs folded. She sat on the deck, bent forward, gasping for air between choking sobs. I sat down next to her, supporting her weight as she slumped against me.

I looked up at Drake. "You believe I caused the Effect." I pointed at the closed door. "Believe I didn't want this!"

But there was no accusation in his eyes as he turned to me. They were wide, red-rimmed, and haunted. And the wildness of insanity had vanished altogether. "What have I been thinking? What have I been thinking?"

Shock therapy. The phrase swam into my mind. Finding Kyoko had jolted Drake back to reality. At least for the moment.

"I destroyed those files." He sounded astonished. "I thought it was the right thing to do. Destroying data! What was I thinking?" He stared at me. "If I'd worked with you, we could have prevented—"

"No," I said. "By the time we argued, it was too late." I thought about the blood already dry, the smell already in the air. "She must have done it last night."

"I read this article once," Drake said. "The author used the phrase *Army of the Night* to describe people always chasing after the latest quack theory. Since all this ESP business came up, I keep remembering that. Now I'm losing track. I keep thinking there's a real army out there . . ."

I almost asked why he hadn't said anything, but then thought, *What a ridiculous question! The same reason I didn't, of course.* I realized then what a mistake my paranoid secret-keeping had been. We should have helped each other all along.

"I keep thinking I'm going to see a monster outside the windows," I said. I was surprised how easy it was to admit, now. "We're all losing track of what's real. It's happening to everyone on board. But we're not all gone, not yet, and we still have work to do."

"What work? What can we possibly do about any of this?"

I remembered what Marta had told me, "Avoid what triggers the delusion," and picked my next words like steps in a minefield. I couldn't avoid Drake's trigger as easily as telling him not to look through windows.

"This all started with the Effect. Whatever damage has been done to us, that's where it began, and that's where it will stop, if it can be stopped. No one but us is going to find a way."

Drake looked at his shoes, and didn't answer.

"Beth," I said. "Lock Kyoko's door, would you?"

She looked up, brows drawing together as if she didn't understand me. "W-what?"

"Lock the door. Use Kyoko's code."

"But, shouldn't we, we call someone?" Like Drake, she was herself again. The acolyte of the church of ESP had retreated for the moment.

"We will, but let's make sure no one disturbs the scene until they get here."

"Oh. Oh yes." Beth climbed slowly to her feet, moving like a very old woman instead of a young student. As she entered the code with trembling fingers, I thought of someone sealing the door of a tomb, and was suddenly convinced that no one would ever open that door again. *Here lies Kyoko Fujiri, in her quarters now and forever, amen.*

◀ ◀ ◀

The officer who took my report about Kyoko didn't even try to hide his indifference, and I knew her body would lie there until the relief ships arrived, if the Alley survived that long.

Only four people showed up when I paged for a lab meeting in the conference room. Bill Lee and Teri Frank from Kyoko's group,

Bob Taylor from Drake's, and Tom Markov. Including Drake, Beth, and myself, we totaled seven people, out of the thirty we had only a week ago. And the rest? In their quarters. One way or another.

Tom smiled and sometimes engaged in whispered conversation with no one. It appeared Anne stood to his right. Bill also muttered under his breath to someone who wasn't there, but in his case, he didn't seem as pleased to see them. Teri stayed quiet, her eyes constantly darting back and forth. Bob clutched what looked like a napkin from the mess hall and twisted it unceasingly in his hands. God knows what I looked like to them.

We had our goal: a generator configuration that would suppress neurofields just as the Effect had boosted them. And, we had, in the cold light of reality, no idea how to find it. We tried various ideas. Running computer simulations. Going back to the data. Trying to pin down exactly how it differed from the Ryder prediction. Trying to find the math to describe it. These were all things we'd been doing since the day after the Effect.

If we had years to work on it, I'd have been excited by the opacity of the problem; the harder it was to solve, the more significant the new discovery would likely be. But we didn't have years.

My other-sense continued to grow stronger and I was very aware of the halos around every head. But the white-fires gave me no scientific insight; they were just there. It was frustrating that I had this new, miraculous ability to sense hyperfields, and yet it was no help.

At least I was free of the Beast so long as we worked here in this interior room.

Marta returned a few minutes after we started working. She paused at the door, her eyes passing over the scene, and then approached me.

"Is this everyone?" she asked.

"Yes." I told her about Kyoko, speaking in a low voice.

Marta looked appropriately sympathetic, but had other things on her mind. I resented that for a moment, but that was both foolish and unjust. She never knew Kyoko.

I saw she didn't have any tranquilizers. "No good at the infirmary?"

"No," she said, and her white-fire colored with dark clouds. "It's chaos up there. I don't know how many of the medical staff are left, but they're overwhelmed. The place is lunatic central. Best I could gather, people keep going to the infirmary looking for help—you know, when they feel themselves slipping—but there's no help to give them, and now it's just a mob scene. People running around, fights breaking out, patients strapped to their beds screaming—"

She broke off, and I saw her tremble. Her face was pale. I stepped forward to hold her, but she pulled away.

"So I sneaked into the dispensary on my own. It's been cleaned out of every kind of sedative I know about. I guess they've been trying to knock out everyone who comes by. I did find these, though." She pulled a small packet from her lapel pouch and handed it to me. A glance at the label showed me they were the same stimulants the medic gave me before. "Try not to OD, by the way. I'd feel just awful."

"Yeah." I smiled briefly but couldn't manage a laugh. "Is it that bad all over? I shouldn't have sent you off to the infirmary alone—"

Marta did laugh. "Don't get all chivalrous on me, Dave, it's too corny for my taste. And no, it's not so bad. I saw crew on duty, mostly the night shifts by now, I suppose. There are a few places with a lot of crazies wandering around—the section with the *Lunar Explorer* survivors is one. Mostly it's quiet though." She frowned. "Probably just my imagination, but I'd almost say spooky . . . I know the Alley's mostly empty, so you expect lots of quiet sections, but it's . . . well, spooky."

She fell silent, her eyes thoughtful, and then the intercom chimed. We both jumped. It was the base-wide announcement signal and everyone looked up, expecting something momentous. Instead, we heard a bland voice announce that food service had been consolidated to the mess hall on deck 3.

Marta burst out laughing. "Oh that's wonderful! Listen to me, 'Ooh, it's so spooky out there,' and then we get that! Well, that's how bad it is, Dave: It's so spooky they've had to close the extra mess halls."

I had to laugh with her.

"I thought about something else," she said, growing serious again.

"What?"

"The other one." Marta's eyes narrowed and her brows drew together. "The Child said, 'the other one' kept coming around with 'mind games, trying to find me.' Do you think it could be someone like you? Someone who gained some amount of ESP from the Effect, and sensed the Child like you did?"

I thought about it. "When I was undergoing the Effect for the second time, I did sense a neurofield much stronger than normal. Brighter. Right before I spotted the Child. But if that was the other one, I gather they've had no more success than we have."

"We still ought to get in touch with him, if he exists."

The other-sense was still too dim without the generators' aid. The white-fires faded beyond perception except at close range. Only the Child showed from a distance, a red flame, a little spark of pain even from here. Still, I tried to see more.

"There's nothing," I said after spending some time trying. "I don't find anyone."

"Okay then." Marta sighed. "It was just a thought. But—keep looking."

"I will. But we have to focus on what's within reach. If we can't tranquilize the Child, we're down to what we can do with the generators."

In my memory now, that day in the conference room remains in a kind of limbo, a no-man's-land claimed by what came before, and what came after. It was the last gasp of the research project, working on a scientific question about hyperfield physics. It was the last day of the Alley still under control; outside the conference room doors, it was already dissolving. Not gone entirely—we broke for dinner and saw routine operations still intact—but it ended soon thereafter.

The stimulants covered my exhaustion but did not get rid of it. I was as energetic as a toy spaceship, but my limbs trembled and my heartbeat acquired a rattling, overloaded kind of feeling. The pills kept me going, and I shared them with anyone who needed them.

Marta plied her trade as a counselor, circling the conference room, keeping an eye on everyone, offering a whispered word here, a reassurance there, holding us all together. Drake was just happy we were working the one part of the situation he believed in. Beth soon resumed her mystical pronouncements, but since she believed I was some kind of ESP prophet, she gladly did whatever work I asked of her.

We made progress of a sort. With a lot of computer assistance, we pinned down the mathematical *form* of the divergence between the Ryder equations and our three unexplained data sets. But I couldn't attach any physical meaning to that form. It was like having a jigsaw puzzle with one huge piece missing; we knew the shape of the piece, but not the picture.

A little after two in the morning, Bill Lee, without saying anything, just stood up and left. We never saw him again. Not long after that, I happened to look over Teri's shoulder and see that instead of computer code, she was typing nursery rhymes over and over. Marta gently led her from the room, suggesting she get some sleep.

At 0700 Sunday morning the intercom pinged again. A voice followed immediately: "Stand by for an announcement from Commander Warren. All hands attention to orders." The message repeated a couple of times, and then the Commander came on.

"This message is to all crew and civilians on board. You are all aware of the deteriorating conditions on base. For the safety of all, it is a necessity that the vital functions of this base continue to operate, and that requires orderly conditions in which the crew can work. In the interest of maintaining such conditions, I am ordering all personnel on board, except designated members of the evening and mid-watches, to be placed under sedation until the relief ships arrive."

Warren ended his statement and another officer came on, giving out details of where duty sections were to report to be issued their pills. He spoke as if he expected everyone to line up like it was a routine exercise.

"That's why the dispensary was empty," Marta said. "They were planning this."

"It's crazy," Bob said. When our heads turned, he reddened, but added, "Well, it is."

"He's right," Marta said. "The only ones who'll obey the order are the ones who *aren't* crazy yet." She thought about it. "They won't even get all the sane ones to obey. Would you take pills from someone trying to put you to sleep for two days? People will be afraid they're being poisoned."

"Who says they're not?" Drake asked. "Warren could have gone nuts."

"He's got Lieutenant Leighton from the midwatch as executive officer now," I said. "Leighton would have taken command if Warren had lost it."

"Desperation," Marta said. "No one can think of a better plan."

"I'm going up there," I said. I glanced at one of the table screens but shook my head. Better see him in person. "We *have* a better plan. It's the Child we need to sedate, not the crew."

"The Child?" Drake snorted. "Dave, are you still on that? I thought you got better."

"You're right, it was just a stray thought." I pulled Marta aside and spoke quietly. "If I tell him what we know, what happened in the Admiral's Suite—"

"Even if Warren believes you, the children will have heard his announcement too. The Child won't trust anyone now, not even the stewards bringing food. It's liable to kill anyone who gets near it on general principle."

"Well, we have to try something. I'm going to see the Commander. Keep an eye on everyone here, right?"

"All right." She leaned in and lowered her voice to a whisper, as if afraid of eavesdroppers. "Remember, we don't really know the Commander's mental state. If he has lost it, don't push. Humor him, and then get away."

"I will."

"We'll still be here when you get back," she promised.

I looked once around the room. Drake, Beth, Bob, and Tom. All that was left. Would they be here when I got back, or would it just be Marta, immune and alone, the last holdout? There was nothing to do but go to Warren. When I returned, I'd find out.

CHAPTER TWENTY-FIVE

Up ahead was a sideways jog where the corridor skirted a larger room, running for a bit along the outside wall, with windows looking into space. The last time I passed this spot, I saw the Beast outside, staring back at me. I stopped before I reached the turn, hovering while I argued with myself. Then I turned and retraced my steps until I found a cross corridor to take me over to the parallel corridor on the right-hand side.

That corridor didn't pass any windows, and I followed it all the way to the elevator lobby. Only after the elevator began to rise did I realize my mistake.

I hadn't even thought about it. I had let habit lead me right to the same elevators we always used: those in spoke E. The same spoke I'd climbed during the Effect. The same spoke that let out into the center of the Observation Gallery, with floor-to-ceiling transparent walls three decks high on either side. I couldn't be more exposed to the Beast if I put on a pressure suit and went outside. Ever since the Beast, I'd gone the longer way around to reach the OCC, via spoke D opening to the Hub among the low-gravity machine shops—nice windowless rooms. How did I forget this time?

The Beast tricked me! It lulled me into forgetting with all those safe hours in the conference room, knowing I'd take the wrong elevator out of habit!

No it didn't. I snarled at myself. *Because it's not real!*

But I knew, if I saw it, I'd go crazy, once and for all. I should stop the elevator, go back down, take the long way around. But the control deck had the same floor-to-ceiling windows! One way or another, I had to face it.

Okay then, just keep your head down. Like before.

Ridiculous! How was I going to have any conversation with Warren with my eyes fastened on my shoes? I thought about going back down and calling him on the intercom.

No! I am not so far gone that I can't even walk through an empty room. Surrender to it now and I really am crazy.

I broke out in a cold sweat as the elevator slowed to a stop.

As the doors opened I heard, distantly, the sound of gunfire.

Dust, what now?

It wasn't loud, but it had to be close or I wouldn't have heard it at all: The electric snarl of a sidearm's beam doesn't carry that far. It seemed to be in the opposite direction from the control room. Perhaps among the machine shops—maybe it was a good thing I didn't go that way after all.

Or maybe getting shot would be the lesser of two evils.

I gritted my teeth. *I will not be defeated by an illusion. I still know what's real.*

Keeping my head down, I started walking, cupping my hands around my eyes to cut off any peripheral vision. Still, I felt the openness all around me, and the other-sense showed me the vast, smooth transparencies with the vacuum outside endlessly tugging at them.

And the sound! It was right there, instantly, matching every step.

Tik-tik-tik-tik. Tik-tik-tik-tik.

Look at me, it said. *Look at me, look at me, look at me.*

304

No! I won't! I wanted to run to get that awful room behind me as fast as possible. But I held myself back. If I gave in to panic, I'd never come back from it. I kept to a brisk walk.

If anyone's watching, you look like an idiot. Put your hands down. Look at me.

The Beast had been talking to me for some time, I realized. At least the last few days, those little whispers I thought were my own thoughts. It had tried to get me to look at it before—back in my office, before Marta had stopped me—and it had almost succeeded then. It was more determined now, but so was I.

I won't listen, I thought.

You're already crazy. I'm not real, remember? Look at me and you'll see.

Not looking where I was going, I ran into a chair and fell over. In the low gravity I wasn't hurt but I sprawled in a heap, my hands coming down instinctively to brace myself against the fall, while my head turned and I got one brief, sweeping glance across the room and out into space.

I saw no Beast. It wasn't there. But I clamped my eyes shut anyway, before the delusion could catch up. Because it was a delusion. Nothing else. *Not real.*

There was no reason for a chair to be there. They were all lined up in theater rows facing the transparency. How did the chair get in my way? The Beast must have put it there, to trip me up!

No, it can't come inside. The Child must have done it. Or one of the crazies. I was no longer clear on the difference. Which was the one that wasn't real?

My heart thudded as I struggled to my feet, keeping my eyes shut. I cupped my hands into blinders again and walked. Just a little bit farther.

The other-sense could not see the Beast. No white-fire around its head, no Picasso-type distorted figure. Nothing at all, even though I could hear it and *knew* it was there.

It lies, I thought, and I wasn't sure whether I meant the other-sense or the Beast itself.

And then, the bulkhead in front of me! I changed course and jumped through the door into the corridor leading through the operations offices. The windows were behind me. I was safe. Safe until the control deck.

I gave myself a few moments to recover, feeling a certain sense of accomplishment: I had passed by the worst windows, and survived. But I had come so close to giving in. With a shock, I realized that for most of that short walk, I'd believed the Beast was really out there, only realizing the truth in brief moments. Clearly windows were a severe threat to mental health. Windows should be banned altogether. Maybe it was all the windows everywhere causing people to go insane. *No! Do not give in to such thoughts!*

The other-sense was more reliable than sight or hearing. It never showed the Beast even when I believed it was real. ESP was immune to hallucinations, how about that? I wondered what Drake would have to say.

There were still the windows in the control deck, where Warren should be. I'd have to speak to him without looking like a total lunatic, or he'd never believe anything I had to say. I summoned my strength, and continued.

Two guards wearing sidearms flanked the door into the control deck. The extra security made sense with a gun battle going on nearby. They patted me down for weapons before they let me go in.

There were more guards inside, several surrounding the Commander. Perhaps because I wouldn't raise my eyes above waist level so as to avoid the windows, I noticed that everyone present was also armed.

"Professor." Warren nodded at me as I came in. "I'll be with you in a moment."

He studied a handscreen while a junior officer looked on. After a moment he nodded briskly and gave the screen to the other man. The officer saluted and moved off, and Warren turned his attention to me.

He looked exactly like always, like he'd been carved out of granite. Nothing in his demeanor sounded the faintest alarm bell about his mental state.

"I'm glad to see you're all right," I said. "I heard the gunfire when I got to the Hub."

I kept my eyes focused on him, careful not to look to either side. It seemed to work okay.

"Don't worry, Professor, we will soon restore order to this command."

"I may be able to help with that."

"Oh?" Warren gave me a sharp look, and now something odd entered his expression, but I couldn't pin it down.

Something is wrong here. My thought, or the tricksy voice of the Beast? I frowned. Nothing to do but continue.

"Yes. I'm sure you're aware how hard it's going to be to get everyone on board sedated." Warren's eyes narrowed, but I went on. "If I'm right, you won't have to. We just have to sedate the children who came on board from the *Lunar Explorer*."

That caught him by surprise. He cocked an eyebrow at me, suddenly interested. "The children?"

I explained, or tried to. I told him about my first glimpse of the Child, under the influence of the generators. How just seeing it brought on a seizure. I covered what Marta and I found in the corrupted run file, and what we'd witnessed in the Admiral's Suite. But my words limped and wandered, and my whole account foundered against the stony crags of Warren's closed expression. He didn't believe a word of it.

"Well, that's a very fanciful tale, Professor," he said, "but I must say, not plausible. What's happening here is far more straightforward than that."

"It is?"

Warren paced the deck, calm and in control. "My officers and I have been conducting our own investigation of these incidents, of course. My coms division has uncovered a clear pattern in recent message traffic. I now have absolute proof that a major smuggling operation is under way. Precious metals from the Asteroid Belt are being shipped to the Colonies off the books, in exchange for illegal drugs as well as foodstuffs without proper tariff seals, at prices to undermine the products of legal farming. This is a major operation. We also have reason to suspect human trafficking may be involved, taking underage girls to serve against their will in illegal gambling casinos operated by several criminal organizations in the Belt."

Oh no. Oh no. Warren had just hit every crime headline from every slow news day. He wasn't describing an imminent plot, he was reciting the laundry list for ratings-period journalism. The "com traffic" his men had monitored was probably a tabloid newsnet.

And he wasn't done yet. "A party of saboteurs employed by the crime cartels infiltrated the base to prevent our interdiction of the smuggling, by destroying order in this command. Fortunately the criminals have been unmasked. They resisted arrest. That was the gunfire you heard."

"Commander, that's—" I cut myself off before saying the word *crazy*, remembering Marta's advice: Humor him and then get out.

"That's very good news, Commander. It puts my mind at ease to know all this has been resolved."

"It will be very soon," he said. "Lieutenant Leighton proved to be the leader of the sabotage party. He opposed my plan to sedate disorderly personnel and so restore order to this command. After I announced my discovery of Leighton's true identity to the crew, he attempted to unlawfully relieve me of duty, with the aide of his accomplices from the midwatch crew. Fortunately enough men remained loyal, and the mutineers were driven off. They will soon be arrested and disposed of, and then we will restore order to this command." He leaned forward and fixed me with steel eyes. "Now let's talk about you, Professor."

I paled. *You know where this is going, don't you.*

"Among the communications my officers transcribed was a computer log decrypted at the request of your colleague, Professor Williams. The file clearly shows your role in engineering the accident which first disrupted order in this command."

Dust, I wish he'd stop saying order in this command*!*

"No, Commander, I didn't—"

"Computer logs do not lie, Professor. Your ID code implicates you in this plot. You might even be the ringleader."

How do you argue with a lunatic in command of armed men? I tried. "Commander Warren, the Effect was an accident. I didn't cause it, I don't even understand it! For God's sake, Commander, my own friends died—"

Warren didn't even appear to hear me. "Accordingly, Professor David Harris, I hereby place you under arrest." His tone was implacable. "And I sentence you to death—sentence to be carried out immediately."

CHAPTER TWENTY-SIX

At the Commander's gesture about a dozen officers and crew-men, all armed, surrounded me.

"You can't do that," was the best I could come up with.

"Yes I can," Warren replied.

I turned to the men surrounding me. "He can't—you know that! You must know that! The Colonies don't have a death penalty. He has no legal right to give an order like that!"

"This is a combat situation," Warren said. "Suppression of smuggling and piracy is part of this base's mission, and my ships and my men have authorization to use lethal force in defense of themselves or civilian bystanders."

"Defense against what? I'm unarmed! You have me in custody! Here I am, under arrest! You don't have a right to execute prisoners!" I felt more indignation than fear. I just couldn't believe any of this.

Warren ignored me. "Accordingly you will be taken to the nearest air lock for immediate execution."

Air lock? *Air lock?* But that would mean—

They were going to eject me into space. *The Beast was out there!*

Acid panic twisted in my guts. Sweat beaded my skin, icy cold. I looked around wildly. "Which of you men are from the midwatch? You must see he's lost his mind!"

But they didn't. Some of the officers looked at me with knowing grins. Some with angry grimaces. Some with vacant expressions, almost hypnotized. There wasn't a sane man among them.

"Your accomplices will not help you now, Professor." Warren nodded in satisfaction.

"Commander Warren, *listen*—"

"I have no more time to waste on you. Take him away."

"No, wait—I can still find a way to fix all this!" The men closed in.

I backed away from the guards, turned, and—it was there. Outside the window.

The Beast splayed out against the transparent wall, long fingers and toes grasping at invisible seams, a dark man-shaped figure covered in shaggy fur. Goblin ears rose from its head, twitching this way and that, and red goggle eyes stared directly at me, while its mouth stretched in mad laughter. It ran a long tongue over its broken, jagged teeth, and its breath fogged the window.

How can it have breath in a vacuum?

But of course it had breath. It didn't have to make sense. It had no rules, no logic, no rationality. It was madness, come for me at last. Its gaze froze me on the spot, stopped my breathing, until I felt Warren's madmen grabbing me by the wrists, lifting me off my feet in the faint gravity, while others grabbed my ankles to keep me from kicking.

I arranged all this. They're bringing you out to me. You're coming out here and then we'll PLAY!

I screamed. I thrashed in the grip of the guards until several more crowded around, wrapping me in their arms. "No! NO! Don't you see it? Look!" I tried to point but my arm was tightly held. "You have to kill it," I shrieked. "You have to kill it! Cover up the windows before it gets you next! Nothing can live in a vacuum!"

They must understand! They must! Didn't they see the danger? The Beast was an impossibility, a paradox! While it lived, the Universe made no sense!

"It's insane, don't you get it! It can't be! Make it not be before we all fall apart!" It was useless. "Look!" I screamed again. "You have to believe me!"

Warren paid no attention. Other men laughed. They looked right at the Beast but didn't see it. They carried me out of the control room, and as we passed through the door, it waved good-bye. *Goodbye, but not for long.*

They carried me up the stairs. I tried to think. There was no way out. No way out. Up and through the transfer room into the dockyards. My struggles were no more effective than a baby's. The guards knew their work, crazy or not. No way out. We continued out into the main dockyard corridor.

I kept screaming until one of the squad got fed up. "That's enough of that, pirate!" he snapped, and punched me in the face. I stopped yelling. The man who hit me had braced himself against a handhold to make sure his fist had impact. He hit hard enough to loosen my teeth on that side. I tasted blood. I wouldn't put it past my captors to kill me with their bare hands if I kept it up.

The pain snapped me out of my screaming hysteria, but fear still squeezed my heart. I tried to think. There must be a way to get through to them. Maybe I should provoke them. *If they kill me first, then I'll be safe from the Beast.*

But I was too afraid to do it.

We turned into a side corridor and found signs of combat. Burn scars on the walls, spatters of blood. And then, after another turn, bodies. Some living crewmen moved among them, but they paid no attention to us and my captors paid no attention to them. I saw one of them with streaks of blood smeared on his face like war paint.

"Watch yourself, men," said one of the squad, evidently the senior. "The mutineers were last seen in this area."

Mutineers? That means Leighton and the midwatch crew. If they found us—did I dare call out for help? What would the guards do if I tried? Their fists, that's what. How could I—

The other-sense! I had it still; it was getting stronger. I remembered Beth's ESP test. Sixty percent accuracy if they took the test from me. *You don't just see, you can send!* But who would hear? I reached out with the other-sense, harder and more desperately than ever before, trying to summon up the power I had during the Effect.

I sensed the Child's mind and it burned. There it was, a virulent red flame in the distance. It was laughing. It must know exactly what was happening. *Naturally—it's in league with the Beast. They've been working together all along,* I thought. There was no white-fire near it: no living mind. Had it already killed the other children, or was I just too far away to sense them?

The auras of my captors' minds were bright, close and vivid. They all had that diseased flicker. Stronger now. The other-sense could clearly see their madness.

I searched wider. The farther I looked, the more everything faded, becoming gray and then disappearing. I needed to find a group of white-fires without the flicker, people moving with purpose. That might mean they were still sane—and then, somehow I'd try to call out. My surroundings faded, sight and hearing ignored while I poured all my attention into the other-sense.

There! What was that? I found a white-fire, like everyone else, but so bright! Almost as bright as the Child's but with no red in it, and no pain. Before I could look closer, it vanished, as simply as turning off a light. As if its owner had noticed my observation and quickly hid.

The other one! Marta was right! The Child's other one was someone like myself, someone with power and—and the ability to hide it. That's why I couldn't see it before.

But if the other one wanted to hide, would he or she answer my call? In desperation, I made the best attempt I could to send a thought in its direction: *Help!*

I felt no power behind that call. I had no power to send. Just a last, futile gasp.

And then I was out of time. The men carrying me stopped. I jerked back to the immediate, using my eyes and ears again. The squad had reached an air lock. One man worked the controls and the inner door slid open, revealing a dark, metal cave, cold air rolling out.

My last attempt: "Don't do this. Some part of you must realize this is wrong. Don't do it!"

"We're not mutineers, pirate," said the crewman who had punched me. "Commander Warren protects us from the Ugly Men. We will always be loyal to him!"

Another crewman grinned at me, nodded in the direction of the first, and waved his forefinger in a circle at his temple. "He's nuts." He obviously expected me to laugh right along with him.

It couldn't hurt to try. I managed some ghastly imitation of a chuckle and said, "Yeah, what can you do? But we know better, right? So you're not going through with this?"

"Now, now," he said. "You've got nothing to worry about. All a matter of discipline. We do what we're told, and everything will be all right."

And with that, they pushed me inside, sending me flailing across the chamber. I grabbed wildly for a handhold to stop myself and swing around and back out before they sealed me in.

But I didn't manage to grasp anything until I hit the outer doors on the far side. I scrambled away from them in panic. The outer doors were death, ready to open as soon as the guards pushed the button. I twisted around and leaped back toward the inner doors, trying to get through into the corridor before they closed. But they were already sliding shut, closing and sealing with a dreadful hydraulic hiss.

In the silence of the small metal chamber, I heard a hateful voice, but not with my ears.

I heard you call for help, Dave.

It was the Child, its mind alive with alien glee. *So I've sent your friend to give you a hand.*

And then, *that* sound. *Tik-tik-tik-tik—tik-tik-tik-tik—tik-tik-tik-tik.* Right outside, ready to come in the instant the doors opened. The claws tapped impatiently. It waited.

My insides turned to water. The strings between brain and body broke so my movements became loose, useless flailing. I clawed at the inner doors and screamed and pounded until my knuckles were bloody. I braced myself with a handhold and kicked at the doors and stabbed at the control panel hard enough to crack it. It had an emergency stop button, but they'd locked it.

I was going to die with the Beast's shaggy arms wrapped around me, its claws digging into my flesh, its eyes leering into my own. I would feel its breath on my face—even in space, I'd feel it. It would be hot and smell like ozone. The Beast would open its mouth in gibbering triumph and lick my face with its fiery tongue—

Tik-tik-tik-tik.

Come on out, Dave, it's time to play!

No no no no no no no! I clawed at the inner door with my fingernails.

There was a metallic sound from the air-lock mechanism. It was going to open! I clutched at the handholds. If I could just hang on, and not be blown out into space, then maybe explosive decompression would kill me before the Beast got to me. But I knew that was hopeless. It would just come into the airlock after me. And it could keep me alive for as long as it wanted to play.

Because it didn't have to make sense.

Hearing the sound of the hydraulics, I closed my eyes. My last scream tore my throat raw.

Nothing happened.

I clutched the handholds, stared wildly at the sealed doors. My breath came in great shuddering gasps. It took me long, slow minutes to finally understand that it was the inner doors, not the outer, that had opened.

I turned. A man was framed in the door. My eyes had adjusted to the dark air lock, and at first he was just a silhouette against the corridor lights. It was Brown, the bland little steward, his presence so inexplicable that I just stared in confusion.

"I heard you call for help, Dave," he said, perhaps unaware that he echoed the Child's words. "I'm impressed. I didn't expect you could do that."

Did I call him bland? His white-fire blazed with blinding power. His eyes were a brilliant green, though I recognized a moment later they weren't green, but another nameless color of the other-sense. This was the mind I'd sensed, the white-fire brighter than all the others. This was the other one.

The men who had dragged me to the airlock now floated limp in the corridor outside, apparently dead or unconscious. I squinted at them, baffled. Was this just some last hallucination as the air rushed out of my lungs?

But Brown said, "Come out of there before someone else comes along. The Commander may have gone nuts, but he's still good at his job, and when these guys wake up and report back, he'll have them all out searching for you."

I shook my head, still dazed.

He became impatient. "Move it, Professor," he snapped. "I've got to get you out of sight. You're the last hope I can see of getting out of this mess."

So the Beast still reigned, because the Universe still made no sense. But then why did it let me get away? Maybe Brown didn't make sense either. Commander Warren had turned into a sort of pirate king sending people to walk the plank, and a waiter had just single-handedly rescued me from a dozen psychotic military men. Brown. The mild little mess steward who said "Good morning, Professor" every day when I got my coffee had rescued me because I was the only hope of fixing the situation. So then, I was crazy. Okay.

I followed Brown on autopilot, not caring where he led me. There didn't seem to be much use in trying to think on my own.

How did he do it? He wasn't armed. The men had no marks on them I could see. All he had was that aura, that white-fire that blazed like nothing I'd sensed from anyone else, bright enough to sense from halfway across the Alley and sensitive enough to hear my pathetic little call for help. If anything I'd come to believe about neurofields was true, he must be some kind of immensely powerful psychic. Had he overcome the guards with some telepathic sleep signal?

Dust it, what's the use of clinging to scientific terms in a Universe where reason has no place? Powerful psychic? Call him a wizard! A magical elf! He'd knocked out the men with a magic spell. That made as much sense as anything else did now.

The Beast followed us. Its claws clattered along just on the other side of the corridor walls. I could feel its frustration and disappointment. It wanted another chance at me. Maybe Brown could fight it off. Maybe he knew the right spell to make evil shaggy trolls go away.

I was about to ask him when he stopped and faced me. "All right, before we go any farther you've got to guard your mind. You're no help to anybody wandering around with it wide open for that kid to stomp on at will."

What? Guard my mind? Because that kid was stomping on it? The Child! Monsters, wizards, and demons. That was the world now, and everything I thought I knew was futile. So this wizard wanted me to do a spell to guard my mind. Sure! Why not?

I laughed hysterically. "Great! You mix up the newts' eyes and I'll draw the mystic runes!"

"Concentrate, dust it!" he snapped. "It's trying to destroy your mind before I can get you to protect yourself. Close down your *misharen.* What you've been calling the other-sense. Shut it down. Do it now!" He shouted his final words, and I shouted back.

"How?"

"How do you close your eyes? You can. So do."

I tried. I closed my eyes as if to give myself an example to follow. I could sense Brown watching me, watching my mind with his power. His white-fire had colors that I knew to be emotions. Frustration and impatience. And fear.

I was aware of the Child again. It really did burn. Red fire around it, not white. Demon or dragon, it breathed flames at me. How could I shut it out? I tried to look away, but the other-sense had no direction. More like hearing than sight in that respect, so how did I shut it down?

And there, beyond the Child.

My breath left me in a long, shuddering sigh. There beyond the Child, vast beyond belief, alive with flame that made the Child's burning look like a harmless candle, the *Thing* from my nightmare, the Red Light and the Shadow. First the Beast, and now this!

The Red Light was chaos. Madness. Pain. Death. And the Shadow, less than nothing. Emptier than vacuum. Size measured in negative numbers. It drew me in, a yawning, devouring pit leading to the One True Void.

Don't look at that! Brown's shout was not with his voice. His white-fire vibrated in a way that had words in it. It had the color of panic. And it was loud, like a slap in the face. I reacted on instinct, without conscious decision. I drew back. I closed my "eyes." Instantly the other-sense receded and became nothing. I felt blinded. Everything around me was suddenly nothing but a surface. Then I opened my eyes, my real ones.

Brown had gone pale, and sweat beaded his forehead. "Sharu help us if you'd attracted *Its* attention," he said. But he nodded. "At least something good came of it. You've closed your mind. Well done. Feel better now?"

I did. It was astounding: The result was instant. I had my mind back. In one stroke, I could think again. Only just then did I realize how bad it had been. It had been like trying to have a conversation in a room with loud music, while the volume increased so slowly I never noticed it. Now it was switched off, and the silence was beautiful.

The Beast was gone, and I understood at once that it had never been there. What I had imagined as the ticking of claws was just the routine sound of relays and valves. No wonder I'd thought it was following me: The sound of the Alley's machinery formed a constant background everywhere on the base. I was embarrassed at having been so gullible.

I studied my rescuer. He had power, that much was obvious. I still thought *wizard* might be a better word for him than any other, but the thought no longer had a hysterical edge to it. I could ask the obvious question and be only a little afraid of the answer. "Who are you?"

"Not now," he said. "Follow me. I have a place."

He moved on and I had to follow or be left behind. Brown's manner made it clear he would say nothing more until he was ready. So I kept my peace, and followed. But my question was only delayed, not forgotten. I was grateful for the rescue, but he *would* explain himself.

We went deep into sections of the Alley I'd never visited. We were going into a deserted region of the dockyards perhaps unused since the War. Lightpanels were dim, status indicators dark. The air smelled dry and antique.

Eventually, we reached a small room inside a triangle of docking hatches. The pyramid-shaped chamber had once served as local control for the three docks, judging by the deactivated consoles on the walls.

"Be a while before Warren's crew looks here," Brown said. "This section hasn't been used in years."

Windows looked out over the empty docking spires into space. I enjoyed the freedom of looking out with no fear of any shaggy ape-men outside. But Brown hit a control to blank them all.

"Don't get overconfident," he warned. "You've shut off the attack, but the damage already done will take time to heal. For now, it's best not to give the delusion a way back in."

"Marta said something like that."

"Yeah, seems like she knows her business. I'm not sure about her, though; she hides a lot."

I took offense. "I know what she's hiding, and it's none of your business."

I pushed over to the control panel and attached my belt clips to the rail, so that I could talk without drifting. Brown didn't bother. He had the casual freefall skills of any Navy man. It was time for my questions. "Who are you?" I asked again.

He considered his answer. "Do you recall saying to Drake that maybe real psychics don't want to be noticed? You were right. We don't."

"You heard that?"

"I've been watching you, Professor. That's why I was sent to the Alley."

"Sent. Then you're some kind of government agent?"

Brown shook his head, smiling without humor. "No. We're nothing to do with your government. We've studied your civilization, but we have a civilization of our own."

"Oh my God, you *are* a magical elf." It was an attempt at a joke. But I half-expected him to answer yes.

This time he laughed. "No. I'm as human as you are." Then he looked thoughtful. "Although it's possible such myths among your people come from encounters with us. We've been around a long time." He shrugged. "It doesn't matter. In our language, we call ourselves the Mi'vri. It's a contraction of *misharen o lyvri*—that is, 'people of misharen.' Espers might be a good translation into your words."

"And misharen is—?"

"Exactly what you think. Psychic power, ESP, neurofields. Your ancestors would have said magic."

I shook my head. "This is very hard to believe. Some kind of hidden civilization living among us for centuries without anyone—"

"No, not living among you. We have a world of our own, not even in this Solar System."

"Now wait, that's impossible. No manned spacecraft has ever left the Solar System. So how could human beings get—"

"We don't use spacecraft," he said, and something in his tone told me he'd say no more on that subject.

Maybe he's just crazy. Another of the Alley's maniacs, telling me a fairy tale born of his delusions. But no. He had some kind of real power. He wasn't crazy—or not just crazy, anyway. But that didn't mean he was telling the truth. I told myself to reserve judgment on him.

"Okay, say I believe you," I said. "Psychics live in another Solar System with your own civilization. Fine. Why come here? Why spy on me?"

"Because you're dangerous. Frankly, Professor, your research is appalling. All hyperfields are *like* misharen, enough to worry us, and we've been tracking your Colonies' development of the technology from the beginning. But your hyperfields *are* misharen. Mindless machines with psychic power." He shuddered openly. "What's happened on the Alley is the least of what could go wrong with *that.*"

An angry reply rose to my lips, but I suppressed it. Still, I resented his accusation. I wasn't making bombs or weapons. The list of useful possibilities ran through my mind—hyperfields that generated electric current directly, no need for white-hot temperatures and photoelectric panels. Spaceships running without rockets, no need for reactors and explosive drive plasma. Sensing devices, medical instruments, artificial gravity—all beneficial. All a boon to human safety and prosperity. And Brown called it appalling?

He was still speaking. "What worried us wasn't the technology itself anyway, it was you. You were born with a little misharen—the wrong amount. Enough to open your mind, not enough to control it. You were open to being . . . influenced. Used."

The word hung in the air for a moment. The next question was hard, but I had to ask. "Used by who?"

"By the Enemy."

"What do you mean—the Child?"

"No. The Enemy—the Mi'vri's enemy, the one we've been fighting for millennia. The Child is just a pawn. Like you."

"Like me." I stared at him. "What are you claiming that I've done?"

"Not *you*, not really." He frowned, and frustration showed in his eyes. "That's where I failed. Everything I could sense told me you were acting on your own, under no influence. I never considered that the Enemy might be manipulating circumstances *around* you. Then the kid came on board, and the Enemy moved before I even realized it. It made you set up your generators to create the Effect."

"I didn't!" I protested. First Drake had accused me, then Warren, and now Brown. "I don't know how my ID got into the computer logs, but I didn't—"

"You did, but not of your own will. You blacked out, and under the Enemy's direction you set up the generators."

And then I remembered. That morning, before the Effect, I had dozed off in the transfer room, on my way back from the generators. And—*and I had a dream of the Red Light and Shadow*! It hadn't yet become a nightmare. I had shrugged it off and forgotten about it.

Brown said, "The Effect boosted the misharen of everyone on the Alley who was awake to receive it. The Child most of all because it had power already. I sensed it when the kids came on board. That was *why* they were brought on board."

"The accident with the *Lunar Explorer*—"

"Was no accident. Do you think it was a coincidence that the children came on board just in time to be exposed? The Enemy arranged it."

"What is this Enemy?"

Brown hesitated a long time. Finally, he said, "*Without* opening your mind, tell me what you sense from your misharen. Your other-sense, as you call it. Don't reach out. Be passive. Look. What do you see?"

"Nothing," I answered. But then I realized I did sense something. The Red Light and Shadow was still there, so faint I could barely detect it. As if it was so bright that no closing of the other-sense could shut it out completely. I shied away from it.

"Go ahead and look, Dave," said Brown. I understood he knew exactly what I was sensing. "So long as you don't reach out, don't use any power, it can't tell that you're looking."

Faint as it was, the image carried the whiff of my nightmares. I shuddered. "Why do I still see it? The other delusions—"

"Because it's not a delusion," he answered. "Misharen will never show you a delusion."

"You just told me having misharen is what allowed the Child to drive people crazy."

"Yes, it opened your mind to attack, but the misharen itself never lies. You can rely on it. What you're sensing now is real. That is the Enemy."

"What is it?"

"It's called Eiralynn." His voice hardened as he said it, and his lips curled as if just pronouncing the name left a foul taste in his mouth.

I knew it. My stomach twisted at the word from my nightmare.

"It's a creature made entirely of misharen. It's the Enemy of everything that lives, and the last time it came to your Solar System it snuffed out your Sun."

"What! The Catastrophe!" I stared at Brown, my eyes going wide. "It *caused* the Catastrophe?"

"Yes. We weren't able to stop it."

"But ten billion people died! Why would it do such a thing?"

"Because it likes it when human beings suffer pain, terror, and death." He paused, taking time to choose his next words. When he finally spoke, it was in a language I did not recognize: "Se the in thystrum bad thæt he dogora gehwam dream gehyrde hludne in healle."

"What's that?" I asked, annoyed by the riddle. "Something in your language?"

"No, it's an ancient Earth language. It's a line from a poem about a deadly beast and a hero who defeats it. The poet says of the creature: 'That which lived in darkness was harrowed by the rejoicing in the hall.' He's describing something evil, the sort of thing your civilization tries hard to disbelieve in. Something so inimical to human life that the existence of happiness actually hurts it. That poem was written around fifteen hundred years ago, in a time with less knowledge than yours, but with more wisdom. They knew however bright the lights in the hall, outside in the dark, there are monsters."

CHAPTER TWENTY-SEVEN

I believed him.

I didn't want to. I didn't want to follow him into some mystical universe where evil spirits could turn off stars like lightpanels. But I didn't have a choice. It explained everything. All the coincidences. The impossible accident of the *Lunar Explorer*. The impossible accident of the Effect. The presence of the Child at just the right time.

And it was *there*, the Red Light and the Shadow. The Killer of Billions. I'd feared it since it first showed up in my dreams. Now I hated it. It used me. It used my work, *my* hyperfields, perverted them into something horrible.

Is it moving closer? No. Just my imagination.

I had a thousand questions. But only one that mattered. "How do we kill it?"

"Kill it? Us? Forget it, that's far beyond our reach. But we may be able to stop what it's doing here."

"How?"

"I don't know," he said. "I'm hoping you know."

I shook my head. "Me? I don't know anything about this Eiralynn. Why would I be able to do something when you can't?"

"Because you have knowledge that I lack." My face must have revealed my skepticism, because he continued at once: "Having a heartbeat doesn't make you a cardiologist. I can tell you all about using misharen as a skill, but I'm not a scientist. No Mi'vri is; we don't approach the world that way. You're the one who knows how your machines work, how to fix what they've done."

My frustration welled up. "I don't. I've been trying to figure it out ever since the Effect. I've gotten nowhere."

"Until now you've been trying to work with your mind subject to tampering. The Enemy will have stopped you from thinking of anything useful. That's why I never contacted you before."

Now my frustration changed to anger. "You could have helped, and you didn't? If you'd come forward at the beginning, maybe we could have solved this before things got so bad. Maybe before Kyoko died, or God knows how many others. Instead you sat back and did *nothing*!"

"I've done more than you think." He answered my heat with some of his own. "More than I can explain to you unless you want to spend a few months studying Mi'vri skills. But contacting you was out of the question. Understand this, Professor: You were nothing but a danger. So long as your mind was hanging open, anything I said to you I'd be saying to the Enemy, and anything you did would have been what the Enemy wanted. Since the Effect, you haven't taken a single step it didn't allow you to take." His expression was harsh and without sympathy. But he paused, and his face softened. "But when you called out for help, that changed everything. If you had enough power to do that, you had enough power to guard your mind. And so, you might be able to find a solution. I hope you can, because I've tried everything I know."

I frowned, disliking the claim. Disliking him. How could he put this on me? He was the wizard, the expert. He'd known what was happening all along and he left me to wander in a fog of confusion and fear. He should be the one to stop this Enemy of his.

He'd have let Warren throw me out the air lock! I wallowed in my resentment, relishing every sullen thought: *Beth's ESP test wasn't enough for him—I had to pass his entrance exam! And now he comes to me for help? Now? After everything has fallen apart? After he's run out of options, he wants me to provide some deus ex machina for him?*

A god from the machine! *Yes, that's exactly what he wants: for my machines to rescue him.* My misharen-making machines that were so appalling—until he needed them.

I folded my arms. "What's your interest in all this, anyway?" I demanded. "If you're off living in some other Solar System, what do you care what Eiralynn does to this one?"

He didn't like me saying its name. He'd avoided saying it himself, I noticed, except for the one time. I felt a sudden urge to yell it in his face, over and over.

"It would take a long time to explain, longer than we have," he said. "There are laws of nature that operate on another level from the ones you know. You need misharen to access them, so you've never discovered them, although your philosophers and mystics have vaguely sensed them. One of them is this: There is such a thing as destiny. Call it fate, or karma, whatever. The Universe is going somewhere, and your species is a part of it. When the Enemy nearly wiped you out in the Catastrophe, it was like destroying one of the supports of a building. Destroy too many, and the whole structure comes down. History itself collapses and the Universe falls into chaos. We won't survive any more than you will. Nothing will survive, not even the Enemy itself."

"Then why would it want such a thing?"

"I doubt that it does. I doubt that it cares one way or the other. It's not about what the Enemy wants, it's about what it is. It's a cancer on Time, and the disease will be fatal if left untreated." Brown leaned forward, and his eyes bored into mine. "So it's no use, you standing there resenting me. I don't know what the Enemy wants with this Child. I don't know whether its success here will be the fatal blow to History or not. But I can't take the chance. Whenever the Enemy does *anything*, the Universe dies a little more. It has to be stopped. Are you going to help, or not?"

I didn't like Brown, but I still believed him. So what choice did I really have?

"All right," I said. "What exactly do you expect me to do? You do have some plan, I hope?"

"You built a machine that gives people misharen. Make one that takes it away. Remove the kid's powers and whatever the Enemy wants with it is over."

"I don't know how."

"Figure it out."

I frowned at him. *Just like that. Figure it out. No problem.* Maybe the Enemy had been keeping the right ideas out of my head, but it was no simple question even without interference.

But it would feel good to use my generators against the Red Light and Shadow. I'd pay it back for turning my children against me.

Maybe, despite what Brown said, I could even damage or destroy Eiralynn itself! Brown said it couldn't be done, but he admitted he knew nothing of science and technology. That would open his eyes, and those of his Mi'vri, if my "appalling" research defeated the creature they'd been fighting for centuries!

I even smiled as the thought crossed my mind: *Drake will love this. Science triumphs over the Armies of the Night.*

I studied the Red Light and the Shadow, keeping my other-sense passive as Brown had warned. Did it wonder what I was thinking, now that my mind had closed to it? One pawn was now off the board. What was its countermove?

It's definitely closer now. I hadn't been sure before but was now. Did that mean anything?

"I can't get near the Child," I said. "Can you?"

"No. I can stop it from reading me but I can't stop it from burning me, same as you. And there are worse things it can do."

"So anything we figure out has to be done remotely. If we blanket the entire Alley with my hyperfields, just like the Effect, but so they'll suppress psychic power, then they'll suppress everyone's—including yours." I made this point with a certain relish.

He wasn't bothered. "I've risked my life in the war against the Enemy. Risking my misharen is a smaller price."

"Oh, losing it doesn't cost you your immortal soul or anything?" I needled him.

"No more than losing my sight or hearing would. I won't like it. But if that's what it takes."

Now he sounds like some clichéd hero from a video thriller, I thought. But I was just looking for more reasons to dislike him, and that accomplished nothing.

There was a . . . a *movement* from the Red Light and the Shadow, like people might have sensed on Earth when a shark's fin cut past them. Some movement like that.

"Did you see—"

"Yes," Brown answered. "It may have nothing to do with us."

"What can we do against a thing like that anyway, a thing that can kill a star?"

"It doesn't always win. The Enemy's power is . . ." Brown hesitated, searching for the right word. ". . . indirect. It works from Outside. It manipulates—events, situations, people. Some people it uses without their knowing it, and there are some who serve it willingly. Eiralynn has its Mi'vri too." Brown's mouth curled. His eyes took on a smoldering expression of remembered anger, and I knew he was thinking of someone specific he had known. I wondered how many battles he had fought against his Enemy and its servants, and how many he had won or lost.

After a moment the mood passed, and he continued. "We think it worked on your Sun for centuries to arrange the Catastrophe, and it only could because something natural happened that created an opportunity. It's the same reason it doesn't just wipe you out by destroying your Colonies: It couldn't do it by brute force. It would have to find a way in, and work to move the pieces into place. It makes mistakes. If it can achieve a goal by killing ten people, or by killing ten thousand, it'll pick the ten thousand every time—even if that requires a more complex plan with more that could go wrong. That's how it loses. If we can see what it's doing in time, we can block its moves. It's a chess game, and it's been going on for thousands of years. You'd be surprised how much of your History is really a record of battles you know nothing about."

"I might not be," I said. "You only have to read a history book to know something's always been wrong with the world."

"Yeah." Brown shrugged. "We need to stay focused. Take out the kid's powers and we stop whatever the Enemy is doing *here*, whether it's part of a larger plan or just some petty act of sadism. Now that it's moving, we have to hurry. It has enough brute strength to kill us, if it wants to. So let's not wait while it decides."

"I need more," I said. "Any details about misharen might be helpful."

"I told you, I don't know much about your scientific terms."

"Forget numbers or equations. Tell me how you use it, what it does. Anything that might help me understand it physically."

"There's one thing that may help," he said. "Linda Ryder's equations. She didn't publish all of them."

"What!" I gaped at him. "What do you mean?"

"When she tested her first hyperfield, every Mi'vri in your Solar System felt it. Until then, we had no idea that her research had anything to do with misharen. As I told you, we're not scientists, so we had no way to connect the two until after the fact.

"We had failed to prevent the Catastrophe, but we worked all through the Dark Years to help your people survive. There were hundreds of Mi'vri in your Colonies then, doing anything they could. When that first hyperfield went off like a—like a *misharen bomb*—some of us wanted to suppress the whole technology. But we were failing. Your people were on the edge of extinction, and we knew this technology could save you. So we compromised. We contacted Linda Ryder."

Compared to all I had heard, this should have been only a minor surprise. Somehow I found it more shocking than all the rest. "Linda knew about you!"

"You grew up in the Dark Years, Dave, but you were a child. Linda Ryder saw the Catastrophe itself, and when she learned about the Enemy, she was happy to do anything she could. Your people needed hyperfields, but she agreed to suppress . . . certain aspects. The ones we thought were most dangerous."

I leaned forward, now very intent. "What aspects. Specifically." I unclipped my handscreen and held it, fingers poised, ready to note every syllable.

"I don't know anything about the math of it. But—"

Brown's sentence hung there, unfinished, without even a breath to signal its interruption. It took me a few seconds to realize he had stopped speaking, and a few more to realize it was more than just a pause. I looked up from the screen.

"Brown?"

He floated there, seemingly unchanged, but made no response to my call, not even a flicker of his eyes.

"Brown!"

What was wrong with him?

I only realized Brown was unconscious when I saw he was drifting, slowly turning in place, and not correcting himself.

No, not unconscious. There was no white-fire around his head anymore. None.

"Dust! Brown!"

Heart pounding, my fingers fumbled at my belt clips as I unhooked from the rail and pushed across the room toward him. When I reached him I had to clutch at the front of his uniform with one hand, while grabbing for a nearby rail with the other, to prevent us from tumbling apart again. He was completely limp.

He must just be unconscious. *Must* be. I shook him. "Brown! Wake up!"

His head rocked back and forth, but he made no response. Holding my breath, I let go of the rail and felt for a pulse. There was none.

I recoiled on instinct, pushing him away with a sharp cry. The breath I'd been holding whooshed out of my lungs, and I gasped for oxygen.

Brown's body hit the far wall with the same soft thud as the body in the OCC right after the Effect. But this time I could see the rag-doll flopping of limbs as the body's motion was arrested, and the aimless drift as it rebounded.

"What happened?" I asked aloud, as if Brown could continue his explanations. "What happened?"

It was so quick, and so silent, that it hardly seemed like death. He had just . . . ceased. Like hitting the button for the next page of a book, and finding it blank. There was no attempt to defend himself, however futile. No last words, no cry of pain. Just an uncompleted sentence.

I would be next. I breathed in shallow pants and waited to die, muscles so tense I might already have been in rigor mortis. The Enemy killed Brown first; obviously he was the greater threat, but my own death could be seconds away.

But instead came the voice.

I know you can hear me.

It was faint, a mere flutter against the edges of my closed othersense. I strained to anticipate whatever death would come. I desperately desired some warning, even if I could do nothing about it. I didn't want to just end without even knowing it was happening.

I know you can hear me.

It was an alien voice. For a wild, hopeful instant I thought it might be Brown, still alive in some astral form. Who could say what happened to wizards when they died? But it was not his voice. Then I thought that the Red Light and the Shadow might be talking, but it was not that voice either. It was the Child. Barely detectable, and yet it had the quality of a shout—as if yelling to get through to someone with his fingers in his ears.

I know you can hear me.

I could not sense the Child itself. Its flame was not as bright as the Enemy's, and to detect it I would have to reopen the other-sense. Even at that moment, I retained enough sanity not to do so.

Clever of you, to hide your mind, but I don't need to read your thoughts to hear everything you say. I can pluck the words out of the air.

It was lying. I didn't believe it knew what Brown had told me. I wondered if that was why I was still alive: Maybe it wanted to know. Maybe it wasn't sure if there were other Mi'vri on board, or on the relief ships.

I spoke aloud. "He said there's a million Mi'vri on the way right now."

I killed him. It was easy.

It *was* lying! It didn't know that I had just spoken, or what I had said. It also lied about killing Brown. Eiralynn did that, not the Child. Perhaps it didn't know that Brown had told me about the Enemy.

I can kill you too. But it will be more fun to see you crazy. Open your mind.

I shook my head in denial, but made no attempt to reply. I kept the other-sense shut down. Better to die than to let it into my mind again.

Open your mind! It'll be easier for you that way.

There were colors in the mental voice. Anger. Hate. And a delicate shade, just detectable—fear. Could it possibly be afraid of me, of what I might do, with my mind free? More likely it was afraid of Brown and what he might have told me. That's why it wanted my surrender. It would enjoy seeing me insane, no doubt, but what it needed was to read my thoughts and memories, to know what Brown said.

I knew Eiralynn would kill me the moment it was sure I wouldn't do what the Child wanted. I doubted if it would wait very long to make up its mind. But even with the imminence of my death, I felt less fear. I would die with my mind my own: a small victory, but a victory nonetheless. And if not knowing what Brown had said left a seed of doubt gnawing at the Enemy, so much the better.

A small victory, and all I had to do to win was wait. Maybe that's all I had to do. Wait, and be silent.

I can do more than kill you. I can make you hurt. And I will. I will make you hurt until you do what I want.

I won't deny its threat frightened me. I believed it could do what it said. But I was also encouraged: Its threats were a sign of weakness. It couldn't simply *make* me do what it wanted, and so it threatened.

Open your mind! You are my toy so you have to do what I say!

Its toy? How completely had it controlled me these past few days? But that no longer mattered. I was winning! I was beating it! Even as my defiance brought me closer to death, I still triumphed at hearing the petulance in the Child's voice. It sounded now like what it was: a bully, swollen with power beyond all reason but still nothing more than a schoolyard punk.

I almost let myself tell it so, but my sanity prevailed.

Do it! Do it now!

I did nothing. I waited until the Child's voice stopped. It had given up. Now the Enemy would kill me. I tensed once more, but without the paralyzed fear of a few minutes earlier. I wondered if I would feel or know anything about the end when it came. I wondered if I would find myself in some kind of afterlife. Why not? I now lived in a Universe of myth and legend.

But I didn't have a chance to find out. Death did not come. The Red Light and Shadow hovered, the Child remained silent, and nothing happened. I was very slow to realize that nothing would. No death, no pain. The tension ebbed away, drop by drop, until I was just myself, waiting. The Enemy wasn't going to kill me. Was it biding its time, waiting for me to slip and open my thoughts to it once more? Let it have a long wait then.

I pushed over to the body. I did what I'd been too cowardly to do for Kyoko: I closed Brown's eyes, and then attached his belt clips to one of the zero-g couches so he wouldn't drift. It was the only gesture of respect I had time for. "I hope you told me enough," I said. Maybe just to have my mind free would be enough.

I had won my small victory; now it was time to win a big one. I kicked off from the bulkhead toward the hatch into the corridor, completely oblivious to the thought that the Enemy might have had some other reason for letting me live.

CHAPTER TWENTY-EIGHT

I worried about going back to the Wheel. I'd have to go through the Hub and I expected Commander Warren's men to be all over it.

But my fears about the Hub proved groundless; after a tense moment when I came face-to-face with a group of guards, both wondering if the other was crazy, I learned they were from the midwatch. They'd retaken the Hub and had control over the Alley.

"The Commander's crazies had us pinned down," one of the men said, "but then they all split up into small squads for some nutcase reason and went searching all over the dockyards. That let us take 'em down squad by squad."

Strange that Warren's search for me should prove the means to get the Alley back under control! Had the tide turned everywhere, thanks to my small victory out in the docks?

Leighton had died in battle and his second, Chief Warrant Officer Wyatt, was now in command. She warned me about going down to the Wheel. Apparently somebody had overridden the security locks and everyone formerly locked in their quarters was loose and roaming around. With a skeleton crew further reduced by battle casualties, Wyatt concentrated on holding the Hub and left the Wheel to chaos, until the relief ships could arrive.

The inflexible laws of orbital mechanics set the timetable and no emergency could alter it: Three more days remained until the next window for rendezvous, and no ship could reach us before then.

I learned Commander Warren was also dead. After being dislodged from the Hub, he and about a dozen men had wandered the dockyards grabbing random victims and blowing them out the air locks. About an hour ago, they apparently got bored and went into an air lock themselves. Just like that.

I recalled Warren as I'd known him before all this started: the genial host who always bet in Drake's pool. Clenching my fists and gritting my teeth, I vowed that I *would* strike back, and I would strike at Eiralynn itself. The Red Light and Shadow loomed everywhere now, a constant background to my every perception. Brown said it was made of misharen. It must be something similar to what Tom had mentioned in an offhand remark: a network of hyperfields all sustaining each other. Fine, then. If there could be hyperfield organisms, there could be hyperfield poison for them. I'd find it.

I believed I knew its plan. Brown said it couldn't destroy the Colonies by brute force. It manipulates. It needs a way in. What better way than the Child? I could imagine a thousand ways the Child could spread destruction across the Colonies. Huge and secure as they seemed, the Colonies remained space stations requiring complex systems to sustain life. So—there's a wave of mysterious burning deaths among the lifesystem engineers. Someone adjusts the settings on the hyperfield power systems and a million people suffer the Effect. Hundreds of children start dancing in circles, spreading panic. That was the Enemy's plan. I was certain of it.

Against it, I had only one, slim hope: Linda had hidden something, some aspect of hyperfield theory the Mi'vri wanted suppressed. On one level this wasn't news: I'd known the published Ryder equations were incomplete since run 37. For the past week I'd tried to pry open those equations without success. Knowing they were *deliberately* incomplete was only a thin clue, but a clue nonetheless. The best place to look would be in the long list of false assumptions Linda rejected in order to repair Marshenko's flawed theory. That list was an ideal place to bury something that needed hiding.

Why had no one ever noticed before? But no ancient evils were needed to explain that. After Linda's demonstration, the Colonies praised her work as the salvation of humanity from the Dark Years. Scientists enshrined her equations atop a magnificent pedestal, and in the thirty years since, never asked a research question that didn't fall within their framework.

Until run 37 showed they didn't include everything, and alerted the Enemy to its way in at last.

◀ ◀ ◀

The elevator chimed, slowed to a stop, and the doors opened. I heard someone shouting, not far away. A man's voice, but I didn't recognize it.

All the crazies are mine, the Child had said. What if it could control them to put them in my way now?

I moved cautiously out of the elevator, trying to look in every direction at once. Some of the crazies were out in the dockyards, but there must be close to a thousand down here in the Wheel, once locked in their quarters, now free.

There were people in view. They didn't seem violent. One woman sat huddled against a wall off to my left. A man shuffled past, walking aimlessly and slowly as if he'd been drugged. Another man lay sprawled, unconscious or dead, on the deck. None of them wore uniforms. None were from the research group. They must be *Lunar Explorer* survivors.

I ignored them, and they ignored me. I headed down the corridor toward the conference room. The corridor ran straight through a block of unoccupied cabins and then hit a little lobby before entering our office and lab section. Seeing a crowd of people milling about in that lobby, I went forward cautiously.

There were some people I recognized. Brian Souter from the research group. Victoria Martens and Carol Pierce, who I knew had been sent to their quarters back when there was still order on board. The rest of the little crowd was a mix of uniforms and civilians. They all milled about aimlessly. Some talked to each other. From a distance, it looked like a cocktail party. Only when I got close enough to see their faces did their expressions, vacant or frightened or angry or manic, reveal the truth.

I tried to push through with as little fuss as possible. Even with my other-sense carefully closed, I could see the ghosts of their whitefires, all flickering, jumbled, and wild.

Someone grabbed at my elbow. I turned, and it was Brian. "Dave!" he exclaimed, in great delight. He announced it to the crowd. "It's Dave!" Victoria and Carol came over, but no one else was interested.

"Dave, have you figured it out yet?" Brian asked. "We should have a lab meeting."

"We're still working," I said. Could he be all right? I didn't recall seeing him break down; he had just dropped out of sight. "Do you have something?"

"Of course! It's the worlds beyond the fish, Dave," he answered, dashing my momentary hope. "Do you see? *Beyond* the fish. That's where the convergence sings."

"Yes, of course, I understand. We'll get right on that." I tried to disengage but Victoria and Carol now crowded close, clutching at me.

"Dave, I'm sorry I'm late," Carol said, in a weeping little-girl voice. "I tried to come to the lab but they rearranged the rooms and now I'm lost. Lost, lost, all lost. Can you tell me where to go?"

Victoria giggled. "You're melting."

All three of them pressed close around me, blocking my attempts to move on. Some of the others started to notice the commotion and come closer. Suddenly there wasn't enough oxygen in the room.

"Let me go," I said, keeping my voice calm. "I have to go now, all right?"

I was the center of the crowd now and they all squeezed in against me. "It's the bringer of darkness!" cried one voice. Another said, "He's the spider! I was trying to tell you! Don't you see, he's the spider!"

Pressing even closer, they'd smother me if I didn't get away. Or I would go down and be trampled. Voices raised in shouts became animal snarls. Glaring, empty eyes faced me every way I looked. I pushed and struggled and shoved, trying to break loose.

"Call the Beast for him! He belongs to the Beast!"

I froze, my attempt to break free forgotten. I tried to spot whoever said that. *All the crazies are mine.* The Child was attacking me through these people.

I looked for the cold, alien glitter I'd seen in the children's eyes. But there was only madness. They still pressed in further; my moment of surprise had cost me the little space I'd won. Hands grabbed at my arms, my head, covering my face.

"Let me go!" I shouted. "I can help you! Let me through and I can still help you!"

"No one can help us," said a pale, elfin-eyed woman in civilian clothes, her face inches from mine. She gave a half smile. "We're the walking dead."

I picked up my feet, trusting the clutching hands to support my weight for just one moment, braced them on the chest of a man directly in front of me, and kicked as hard as I could.

It worked. The man flew back one way, I went the other. Everyone fell like dominoes, and the hands relaxed their grip. Scrambling to my feet, I ran for it.

I rounded another of those sideways jogs, maybe the same one I'd avoided on my way up, and just past it, I saw an open door on my right. I dove through it and slapped the control hard. The door slid shut.

I listened. I couldn't tell if the crowd was chasing me. If they were, the bend in the corridor might have hidden where I'd gone.

I heard nothing.

Turning around, I found myself in one of the grad student offices. Another door stood closed along the opposite wall. I went to it and listened.

Quiet.

I opened it and looked out, trying to show as little of myself as possible.

No one was in sight. Even if the crazies were looking for me, they might not think to check over here. The conference room where I'd left Marta and the others was about thirty meters away. Its door opened onto a cross corridor—a high-risk spot for meeting any of the crowd roaming from the opposite side.

No option left but to try. That's where I had to go. As I moved down office row, I darted from one doorway to the next, ready to open each door and dive for cover if I had to. My own office wasn't much farther than the conference room. I was tempted to go there, lock the door, and just hide.

I stopped at the corner and peered cautiously around. It was clear, but I heard muttered voices farther down. I shuffled over to the conference room door and hit the entry pad. It buzzed a refusal signal. The door was locked. I tried my code, which should have opened any door in our lab space, but still nothing. Whoever was inside had changed the code. That wasn't very easy. It must have been Drake; he and the others must still be in there.

I knocked softly. There was no answer. I knocked again.

I could hear the voices down the corridor becoming louder, just around the corner now. Whether they were the same crazies who'd attacked me or not, I didn't want to draw their attention. But I had to get the attention of whoever was inside. So I tried a whisper, as soft as I thought possible to still be heard through the door.

"Open up. It's Dave."

Still nothing. Dust it, this was useless. Abandoning caution, I knocked loudly and called, "It's Dave! Let me in!"

I heard a commotion inside. The voices around the corner stopped, and a moment later several people came into view. They were the same group as before, and seeing me they let out shouts of rage and charged forward. More came from around the corner behind them.

The conference door moved and I leaped through before it fully opened. "Close it! Close it!"

Drake was at the keypad. He punched it hard and the door started to close, but not before one of the crazies got close enough to stick an arm through. Faithful to its safety systems, the door opened again. I swung a fist and punched the madman in the stomach. He doubled over and fell backward, and Drake got the door closed before another could enter.

Marta threw her arms around my neck. "Dave, thank God! There was a PA announcement that they'd killed you!"

"They tried," I said. I looked around.

Drake, Beth, and Marta were present. There was no sign of Tom or Bob. I looked at Marta, and didn't need to ask the question. She shook her head. "Bob went right after you left. We took him to his quarters. That was before things got bad outside. Then Tom—there's a kind of gang out there now, attacking people—"

"Yeah, I met them."

"We think they killed Tom but we're not sure. We lost him, anyway, when the mob chased us on our way back from Bob's cabin. We locked ourselves in here. Then Commander Warren came on the PA to say you'd been executed, and issued orders that all members of the research project were to be arrested. So Drake hacked the security and changed the entry code on the door, in case they came for us. But they never did. Just the crazies."

"Are you all okay?" I asked.

Someone pounded on the door and I heard shouting and screaming outside.

"Everything's fine now that you're back, Dave," Beth said. She stared at me with worship in her eyes.

Drake paced restlessly. "The Army of the Night has taken over! Like they've always wanted! What can we do now?"

"We can beat them," I said. "It's not too late. We can still beat them. With science, Drake. We're going to beat them with science."

That got through to him. He stopped pacing and his eyes lit up. "With Science! Yes! The light of knowledge will always beat back the darkness!"

I lowered my voice and spoke to Marta. "How bad are they?"

She shrugged, and answered in a whisper. "Like you see. They've got their peculiar ideas but they're functional. They're not fighting each other anymore, for whatever that's worth. Drake seems to think Beth is an innocent dupe of his Army of the Night, and Beth thinks Drake is too blind to be worth her notice. But what happened to you, Dave? How'd you get away?"

"Okay." I raised my voice to include Drake and Beth in the conversation. "You all need to hear this. You need to know what we're really up against."

I told my story as quickly as I could. Beth listened with wide eyes and folded hands. Drake didn't seem very interested. But Marta frowned when I repeated all that Brown had told me, and when I finished with the news of how Eiralynn killed him, she looked very troubled.

"It's the Dragon that guards the Path to Enlightenment!" Beth breathed.

"Just some god delusion that the Army of the Night believes in," Drake said.

But Marta pulled me aside. "Dave, you don't mean to say that you believe all this?"

I was surprised. "Why wouldn't I?"

"Isn't it obvious that Brown was just delusional, like everyone else?"

"No! He took out those guards. He showed me how to defend my mind. He had real power."

"I believe he was psychic," Marta said. "So are you, and you aren't immune."

"What made him immune was knowing how to defend his mind, just like he taught me."

"Think about it, that doesn't even make sense. If all you have to do is shut off your psychic power, then why is everyone else going crazy when they have none in the first place?"

The question startled me, and I scrambled for an answer. "It must be," I said after some quick thought, "that by boosting everyone's hyperfield the Effect made them all susceptible. It's the vestigial sense waking up, like you said. But it takes more power to be able to defend your mind."

"You just made that up. You're bluffing your way through any objection because you don't want to give up the delusion."

I grew frustrated. Why wasn't Marta with me on this? I couldn't understand it. "Look, the Beast is gone. I know it was never there. I understood that right away. How do you explain that, if Brown was just crazy?"

"Who knows what happens when two telepaths meet? Maybe your minds synched up somehow, and his delusion just replaced yours. Maybe it was a fifty-fifty chance that he'd have started believing in the Beast instead of you believing in this Enemy."

"Now *you're* just making it up."

"So I don't have all the answers. I don't believe you do either. This story of Brown's, there's no sense in it. An evil force manipulating all of history with a secret society opposing it? That's classic conspiracy-theory stuff. *Think.* The Enemy can snuff out the Sun but it can't destroy the Colonies? It can kill Brown but doesn't hurt you?"

I had answers to all that . . . didn't I? Or had I just made them up to explain the new delusion? Why exactly *did* I believe Brown? I started off saying I'd reserve judgment . . . and then, a few minutes later, I believed him. Could Marta be right? What if Brown's stronger ESP just imprinted part of his mind on mine?

No. It couldn't be. The way my mind cleared when he showed me how to close the other-sense. I couldn't mistake that. And Eiralynn—it was there. I could still sense it. The one constant in the whole experience was this: The other-sense was reliable, as Brown had said. Now it showed me there *was* a Red Light and Shadow.

"Marta, look at me. You're the impartial observer, so you tell me. Am I crazy? Am I acting like I did about the Beast?"

She sighed. "No. You seem better."

"I am better. Even if I'm wrong about Eiralynn, at least I'm thinking clearly again. Brown did that much. As for the rest—it doesn't matter. What we have to do is the same, either way: shut down the Child's psychic power." I turned to Drake and Beth. "We have to get back on the problem. Let's get to work."

"We will succeed with you to lead us," Beth said. "It's your destiny to open the Path to Enlightenment. As we open our minds to the Great Outer Realms, we will Ascend. Your precognitive vision will show the way—"

She was practically praying to me now. It was horribly uncomfortable, and I couldn't help but try to argue.

"Beth, try to remember all these psychic powers come from hyperfield properties. They're not supernatural. And precognition is certainly not—" I stopped.

The final jigsaw piece dropped into place.

"Dust in space, that's it!" I all but leaped for the chair in front of the computer screen. I called up my home directories and the mathematical software with the Ryder equations.

"What? What is it?" Marta came up behind me. Drake and Beth looked on.

"Precognition is a psychic power!" I worked the keyboard breathless with excitement, my fingers flying. *Brilliant! That's it!* "There is such a thing as destiny," *and misharen can see it!*

I glanced up at my audience. "Seeing the future, if it can be done, would violate causality. We physicists are pretty sure that's impossible. Well, I'm pretty sure we've been wrong."

If I add a time extension to the field geometry . . . The first subset of the Ryder equations, the dimensional series, described hyperfield shape in all three spatial dimensions and ten of the quantum dimensions. The series included no terms concerning the time dimension, but I saw now where they'd go. I added the terms and had the software solve the equations. The hyperfield models flowed into new shapes. I smiled. I was on the right track.

"A hundred years before Linda Ryder's work," I said, "Marshenko published the first theory of hyperspace. It had a number of flaws, but the biggest was that it implied causality violation. Linda's greatest insight—according to what she published—was to find a way to exclude the time dimension."

I was right here the first day after the Effect, right at this point! If Marta hadn't interrupted . . . But I couldn't blame her. I had dropped the matter easily enough, failing to realize what was right there in front of me.

I would need some new terms in the quantum excitation series. I continued my monologue as I worked. "Only she didn't. What she did was solve for a hyperfield design that *included* the causality violation, but published a 'flat' hyperfield with zero radius in the time dimension, and hid the fact by leaving out every expression with the time variable in it." I felt like I was teaching a group of freshmen. What a great lecture this would make when we got back to the university! "No one ever questioned the omission, because physicists don't believe in causality violation in the first place."

It all fits in so easily, how did I not see it before?

There! The final addition, and still the equations held up: internally consistent, properly derived, and new. I leaned back.

"So there it is. Hyperfields react to future events, not just present ones. Bloody dusted hell, no wonder the Mi'vri wanted it covered up! If destiny is real as Brown said, technology like this is exactly what could destroy it." And now that technology was in my hands.

I should have been alarmed by that. I wasn't.

"Are you sure it's right?" Marta might have been doubtful because I kept mentioning Brown's "delusion."

"Yes, but let's test it anyway. Drake, give me some simulations. Have the software reference these new equations."

I gave him the file name. "Let's start with the Effect. Use the settings you got from the self-diagnostics."

Drake spent a few minutes at the keyboard. It didn't take him long.

On screen, two monster hyperfields blossomed out from the generators. Drake scaled back the display. Ten kilometers' radius, according to the computer—the same that the run files showed for the Effect.

"Copy a neurofield from the Rothberg-Wilson study and stick it in there," I told Drake.

He typed some more. The model neurofield instantly inflated to twenty times its previous strength.

"One test passed," I said. "Let's try run 37. Same software and settings we used then but with the new equations."

Now the screen showed normal-size alpha and beta fields moving together—and then the ripples, the field shape projected on the event horizons, even the bright point of energy directly between them. The animated graphic looked exactly like what we'd seen in real life—was it only a week ago? I sat down beside Drake and called up the run 37 file, putting it side by side with the simulation. Within the margin of error, the numbers matched.

"Second test passed," I said. "This is it. These are the *complete* Ryder equations! We have it!" It was my moment of triumph. Victory! The answers mine at last! And I could *see* again—now that I knew the one missing piece, I could unfold those fields in my imagination once more, and see how they had to work exactly as we'd found them!

Beth fell to her knees, hands folded, eyes staring heavenward in ecstasy. "The Path to Enlightenment! Dave has found the Way!"

Marta, alone among us, remembered the present concerns. "Does it help us? How do we use it to stop the Child?"

"Let's find out." Buoyed by confidence, I bent over the screen once more to look into exactly how the Effect had boosted our neurofields.

Yes. It all came easy now, so easy it was almost disappointing. These two parameter sets—if solved for overlapping fields the energy assumed exactly the geometry needed to boost a third. And how naturally the new equations allowed a hyperfield to produce kinetic energy! No wonder the neurofields were telekinetic; it was almost as simple as producing light and heat.

But enough gloating. What about the practical question? The new model showed the boosted neurofields would return to normal as soon as the Effect ended, but we already knew that—it was the brain that changed, gaining superior ability to use its vestigial ESP, as Marta had proposed.

I had no way to force the brain to unlearn its skill; I had to suppress the misharen itself, give that new skill nothing to work with.

Shut down the neurofield then—but how? The Effect increased it, so what would decrease it? Perhaps some kind of phase change in the overlap . . . no, that wouldn't work.

I frowned harder. A canceling signal, then. Something to make the neurofield collapse, like artificial fields collapse in overlap. No.

This can't be right. But it was. The wonderful clarity which the new equations provided made it impossible to deny the truth. I suddenly felt sick to the point of throwing up.

"Marta," I said. "Marta, it can't be done."

CHAPTER TWENTY-NINE

"Don't be silly. You've barely started looking," Marta said.

"I don't need to keep looking." I got to my feet and started pacing. "It's not that I can't think how. The new equations say it's theoretically impossible. I can use energy to strengthen a field, but I can't weaken it, except by shutting down what generates it in the first place." I stopped pacing and stared at her. "The Child isn't being boosted by the Effect right now. There's nothing to take away. The idea we had with Cole, find a way to shut down the part of the brain that creates the field—that could work. But my generators can do nothing."

"No!" Drake roared in protest, startling everyone. "Science always finds a way to defeat the Army of the Night! Our technology will triumph!"

"It's your destiny, Dave." Beth's whisper was as quiet as Drake's shout had been loud. "Let the Path to Enlightenment guide you. There is a Way."

How about that. Drake and Beth agree with each other at last.

"I suppose we could just shoot the little sociopath between the eyes. Its neurofield would go with it." I looked at Marta. "I think it's already killed the other kids. Last time I looked, I saw no normal white-fires near it."

Marta winced that I would be so blunt. The other approach we had talked about had come round at last, and it hung in the air. But she didn't back away from it. "The Child would kill anyone who

354

came near it with that thought in their head. We'd never get close enough to try."

I was tempted to try anyway. Not just on the tiny chance I'd succeed. If the Child really had killed the others, then when I burst through the door to the Admiral's Suite, I'd see it for who it was. I would know which one it had been. Andrew? Molly? Samuel? At least I'd die knowing its face, instead of a distant red flame and a cold voice. But no, it wouldn't even let me get close enough to open the door.

That's not the way.

And there was still Eiralynn. The Red Light and Shadow was close now, watching. I could feel it, like Death looking at me. Anything the Child could not stop, it would. Unless I found a way to hold it back. Unless I found hyperfield poison.

I caught a flash from one of the screens. "What was that?"

It was the simulation of run 37. In real life, the experiment ended when the generators burned out. But theoretical model generators couldn't burn out, so the simulation had kept running until just then. The screen read: *Hyperfields collapsed. Simulation ends.*

"Drake? What happened there? Run it back!"

Everyone watched the screen as Drake backed up the sim to an earlier time index. It was the third hyperfield, the one I'd called the gamma field that formed between the other two. It just kept getting brighter and brighter until that final flash, and then all three hyperfields vanished. What had happened?

Looking at the numbers, I worked the math.

"That's interesting," I said. A little rebirth of hope blossomed in my mind.

"What happened?" Marta asked.

Drake answered before I could. "The middle field hit theoretical maximum."

"It kept drawing energy from alpha and beta to get stronger and stronger, until it hit the max." Seeing her puzzled look, I explained further. "Theoretical maximum hyperfield output: a wide-open, unrestricted rift between the normal universe and hyperspace. All the energy that can flow through does. There's none left over for any other hyperfield. The alpha and beta collapsed, and since they created the gamma, it stopped too. You could say it sawed off the branch it was sitting on."

I thought it over. "Yes. It would work."

"I don't understand."

What did Brown call Linda's first hyperfield? A misharen bomb. Yes. That's what we need here. A misharen bomb, to kill the Child and Eiralynn itself in one blast.

"No other hyperfield can exist within the radius of that gamma field once it reaches maximum. If we can blanket the entire base with it, like the Effect—it'll shut down everything. No more psychic power for anyone, including the Child."

Marta smiled. "Then that's it! You've found it!"

"There's a catch."

"What?"

"Theoretical maximum . . . that's energy on a thermonuclear scale. It'll go off brighter than the Sun used to be, if only for a few microseconds. We'll stop the Child, and Eiralynn too—but we'll vaporize the Alley and everyone on it."

"Pfft!" Marta showed her disappointment. "So much for that plan, then."

But her eyes widened when she saw my expression. "Dave? That idea's out, isn't it?"

My mind raced. "The Enemy couldn't stop it. It couldn't do

anything, it couldn't come near it. It's made of hyperfields—it would have to retreat or be destroyed."

"Dave, don't joke about this. You're talking about killing everyone."

I faced her. "You said you'd support whatever turned out to be necessary."

"To *save* everyone from the Child! If you had a plan to kill the Child and save the rest, then God help me, I'd go along with it. But not this. Not this!"

"We can't get the Child itself." I circled the room, ticking off points with my fingers. "It'll burn us before we get close. It has the crazies to defend it. It has Eiralynn to defend it. We can't use any conventional means to kill it because Eiralynn could step in. No. We can't wait for the relief ships. They'll take it back to the Colonies and whatever the Enemy plans for the Child, it will succeed. There's no way to use my generators to reduce its neurofield alone. No. This is the only way to stop both the Child and the Enemy."

"You haven't even *looked* for another way!" Marta shouted, desperate.

"I don't need to." I was filled with righteous certainty. I would strike back! I'd found the hyperfield poison that I needed to attack the real Enemy. Even if some lesser alternative presented itself, I'd reject it.

How easily the method presented itself! How readily it emerged from the new equations. Someone might as well have whispered the answer in my ear.

"Linda's hyperfields saved the human race from the Dark Years," I said. "Now mine will save the human race from its greatest Enemy!"

"Yes!" Drake pumped his fists. "We burn the Army of the Night here and now, and they'll never spread their superstitions again!"

"You have shown us the way!" cried Beth. "We follow you to our Ascension!"

I looked Marta in the eye. "You're outvoted. We do it."

The pounding on the door had stopped, and the shouting was distant. The crazies had moved on for the moment. Inside the conference room, nobody said anything.

What an inspiring group we were! Beth began to chant softly in some kind of ecstatic trance, while Drake quivered with suppressed fury, eager for battle with his Army of the Night. Marta collapsed into a chair at the conference table, her head bowed. I dry-swallowed another couple of stimulant pills. One final burst of energy, that's all I would need.

Did the Enemy know what I planned? That was now a vital question. It had killed Brown. I had to assume it could just as easily kill me—and would, if it thought I was a threat. I had kept my mind closed, and if Brown was right, even Eiralynn couldn't read my mind. So I could assume it didn't know. But it might kill me at any moment. I couldn't waste time worrying about it.

I resumed pacing. "Drake, we'll need software. If we set the generators for a base-wide radius, the gamma field should be so dispersed that the generators won't burn out until the whole show goes up."

Drake did not answer. I raised my voice. "Drake."

"It's always been them," he said, looking down at the deck. "Generation after generation, they always come again, waving their Ouija boards and their Bibles, opposing every attempt at knowledge, trying to drag humanity back into the Dark Ages of superstition.

The Inquisition tortured Galileo! The Armies of the Night! But they won't succeed!"

Catching me off guard, he lunged for the door and slammed a fist into the locking panel. Released, the door slid open and Drake leaped into the corridor shouting, "Do you hear me? Your day is done! Reason and Science will always triumph!"

"Dust!" I went after him. "Drake, listen to me! Get back here!" I grabbed him by the shoulders and shook him. "Science triumphs when you *use* it, right?" I pointed at the screen. "There. On the computer. Use knowledge against them. We need settings for field parameters from run 37 and the field radius from the Effect. You have to set up the control program. That's what stops the Army of the Night, right?"

Drake stared at me wildly, but then he seemed to calm down and understanding flickered in his eyes. "Software. The control program. Yes."

He relaxed and I let him go. Slowly, he walked to the screen and sat down at the keyboard.

I tried to close the door again, but Drake had broken the panel. I looked out, up and down the corridor, afraid that his shouting would bring the gang down on us. But for the moment, there was no sign of anyone. I thought I heard the echo of distant shouts, but that was all.

I wondered if we should move, find somewhere we could barricade ourselves in if we had to. The computer lab, maybe. But I dismissed the idea. We'd have to move soon anyway. I turned back to face the room.

"Beth, you're the only one left from the electrical engineering group," I said. "We'll need to set up the hardware when we get there. Can you do that?"

"I'll do whatever you want me to," she said. "You will lead the way to our Ascension. We have only to open our minds to the Path of—"

"Yeah, you told me all about that already," I said, more sharply than I intended.

Beth took no offense. She just kept watching me with the sort of expression normally reserved for cult leaders.

I kept my voice level. "What we need to do can't be done with ESP or Paths to Enlightenment or anything like that. We have work to do on the generator circuitry, and it'll need to be done with precision. All right?"

"I know," she said. "I can do it."

"Right, good." I sat down heavily beside Marta and let out a long, slow breath. The room fell silent, the only sound Drake's fingers on the keyboard. What if he was just typing "Army of the Night" over and over again? Nothing I could do about it. He knew the software; it'd take me hours to make the needed changes.

"Dave." Marta lifted her head slowly, revealing a pale, haunted face. Her eyes met mine. "Dave, don't do this."

I looked away, unable to hold her gaze. "You had your say. We've decided."

"Decided?" She waved a hand at Drake and Beth, and leaned in to speak in a whisper. "None of you know what you're doing! Fighting imaginary armies, following imaginary gurus, waging epic war against the Evil Out of Time! Can't you see that's just as much a delusion as what Drake and Beth believe?"

"No," I said. "No. It's real."

"It's a hallucination, just like the Beast outside the window."

"That *was* a delusion, but it's gone now. Brown showed me how to block out the Child's influence."

"He traded you one delusion for another. You asked me to keep an eye on you, remember? I'm immune to what's happening and you asked me to warn you if you started to lose it. Dave—*you're losing it.* Everyone will die."

"I'll get on the PA system the moment before we activate. I'll warn everyone to get to the escape pods."

"And what about the ones who are already too crazy to understand? They don't deserve to die. For God's sake, Dave, the relief ships will be here in just a few days!"

"That's why we have to act now."

"It's why we can afford to wait. We can warn them about the Child. They won't take the children back to the Colonies right away. They'll get treatment for the victims. They'll stabilize the situation here. You'll have time to find a better way."

"They won't listen to us!" I shouted, jumping to my feet. Drake and Beth turned to look. "You know they won't. They won't even listen to you. You'll just be another lunatic. They'll take the children straight back to your colleagues, and then it'll be too late. Don't you get it? Right now it's contained here on the Alley, but once the relief ships arrive, it'll be loose in the Colonies. Eiralynn wants this Child for some purpose, and whatever that is, it has to be stopped!"

In desperation, Marta shouted back, *"There—is—no— Eiralynn!* Don't you understand?"

And then I did. With a sudden flash of inspiration, I understood everything. I actually gasped out loud. "Yes," I said. "Yes! I understand perfectly. 'Eiralynn has its Mi'vri too.' That's what Brown said. And you're one of them."

Her eyes widened in shock. "Dave!"

All the pieces now fell into place. I leaned over Marta, glaring down at her. Drake and Beth watched. "The *Lunar Explorer* strikes a meteor big enough to destroy it. The odds are millions to one against an accident like that ever happening, and it happens right when the ship's radar is down. Coincidence, or did you sabotage the radar while Eiralynn steered an asteroid into the proper collision course?"

Marta cringed back in her chair, eyes wide and face pale, frightened by the anger in my voice and the aggressive way I leaned over her. She tried to answer. "I wouldn't even know where the radar was. I didn't—"

I rode right over her, talking fast and getting right in her face. "You and your kids are walking on the lifeboat deck when the accident happens. Lucky break, there. Just in time to get brought to the Alley, the one place in the Solar System where there's a piece of equipment that'll give one of the kids supernatural powers, and no sooner are you on board than the required accident happens—and you're conveniently asleep during it, so you escape the effects."

"I lost *friends* in the shipwreck. I wouldn't—"

"You've had friends killed, right. And you've got a dozen kids to take care of, but instead of worrying about that you keep bumping into me, winning me over until I'm spending more time with you than with my own colleagues, right when I should be investigating the Effect. Leaves you ideally positioned to stop me from finding out about the Child, doesn't it? And when I do, you're right by my side to help me figure out which one it is—only somehow we can't."

"You and I met a couple of times in the mess hall. *At mealtimes.* Where else did you expect me to be? I didn't start working with you until you asked me to."

"And now I've discovered the truth about Eiralynn and how to stop what it's doing, and you're trying to convince me it's all in my head. So we either have a string of unbelievable coincidences, or else you've been working for Eiralynn all along."

I'd never seen her look so frightened. She must have thought I was about to attack her, right there. But of course she'd always been confident before, with her cocky grin and smart-ass humor. She'd always been in control, the willing agent of history's master manipulator. Now she was caught.

"I—Dave, I, I—" she stammered. She took a deep breath and composed herself. "I didn't cause any of this any more than you caused the Effect. Don't you see you're doing the same thing to me that Drake did to you when he found your ID in the computer logs? *You* were the one who set up the generators for the Effect. Are you working for Eiralynn?"

"It used me without my knowing it," I said. "I wasn't defending myself against it. I didn't know then there was anything to defend against. Maybe it's the same with you. I'll give you the benefit of the doubt; maybe you don't know what the Enemy's made you do. I'm not crazy like Warren and the proof is: I'm not going to throw you out an air lock. I'm not going to hurt you at all. Unless you try to stop me." I jabbed a finger at her. "So stay right there, and don't say another word."

I turned away. "Drake, get back to the software. We need that program."

It didn't take him long. I spent the time keeping watch at the door to check if anyone came our way. But the entire area now seemed deserted. I couldn't hear anything even in the distance now. Beth sat down cross-legged on the floor and meditated, her eyes closed and her face blissful. Marta watched me with frightened eyes.

Drake said, "I've got it. It's done."

I rushed to his side. "Okay, plug it into the simulation routine and let's see if this will work. Use the engineering sim—we'll need to factor in the durability of the generators."

Ten kilometer–radius hyperfields sprang into existence on the screen. On that scale, they appeared as one. Only the sim's numbers showed they were two fields . . . no, three! The gamma field appeared, also so huge it engulfed the entire Alley.

With the energy spread out, everything in the Alley would heat at once. By the time the heat was enough to shut down the generators, the gamma hyperfield would be only milliseconds from maximum, and the tiny lag between generator burnout and field collapse would be enough to hit theoretical max. Or so I hoped.

And so it was, according to the sim.

"It's going to work. We can do it!" I clapped Drake on the shoulder. "Save the new software and upload it to the OCC!"

"Dave!" Beth shouted.

I turned. Marta was gone.

"Drake, follow me, we've got to stop her!"

I launched myself out the door. Marta had already disappeared around a corner, but in which direction? She would either destroy the generators before I could use them, or else smuggle the Child into an escape pod, putting it safely beyond my reach.

She knows which child it is, and it'll let her into the Admiral's Suite with no problem.

I hesitated. If I was wrong and she was innocent, it'd be the generators. If she was guilty, it might be either one. Two chances generators, one chance Admiral's Suite. So be it.

At the corner I turned in the direction of the elevators, and with Drake at my side, we pursued the spy from the Army of the Night.

CHAPTER THIRTY

I didn't see Marta ahead. Had I guessed wrong?

At the next cross corridor, a woman appeared just in time for us to collide and fall over in a heap. I grabbed her, but it wasn't Marta.

"The singing!" she cried. "It has to be in the air! But the colors are all wrong!"

Drake ran past, not slowing down. I tried to disentangle myself. "All right," I said.

She began to sob. "I need the singing but I can't find it. It's in the air."

"I'll help you find the singing, but later. Let me go."

I pulled myself loose and ran on, without a backward glance. Drake was now about ten meters ahead. I lost sight of him at a jog in the corridor, but I heard a sudden bellow of rage. I put on a final sprint to catch up.

As I rounded the corner into the elevator lobby I saw Drake and Marta. He'd grabbed her by the front of her shirt with one hand, and drew back the other in a clenched fist. Her eyes were wild with terror. At the moment I came in sight, he shouted, "Army of the Night! You're finished!" and slammed his fist into her face.

"Drake! Stop!"

Marta crumpled, stunned. Drake released her shirt and she fell to the deck in a heap. He drew back a foot to kick her, but I dove for his legs in my best attempt at a tackle. I'm no athlete, but neither was Drake. As he stood on one foot preparing his kick, I knocked his leg out from under him. Thrown off-balance, he came down on top of me. I felt something break, a rib I suppose, because there was a sudden jagged pain in my chest when I tried to gasp for air.

Drake rolled over me, and the broken bits in my chest ground together, making me yell with the pain. Ignoring me, he went after Marta again, crawling on his knees as he swung his fists. Marta curled up into a ball, trying to protect herself.

"Army of the Night!" he shrieked. "No more Dark Ages! Reason prevails! The ignorant will be destroyed!"

I threw my arms around him and dragged him off her. The pain in my chest increased with every move, but I was blind to it. "Stop!" I screamed. "Stop it!"

Drake and I grappled in a horrible, incoherent moment of animal snarling, clawing, and pounding. My peripheral vision went blood red. Suddenly Drake was on the floor and I was sitting on his chest, punching him over and over again, shouting at the top of my lungs, "You do not hit her! You do not hit her!"

Someone spoke to me, pulled at me. I snarled and shook them off. They tried again. The red faded. Drake was unconscious, his face a bloody mess. There was no telling how long I had been pounding him uselessly. My hands were covered in blood. I could feel I'd reopened the wounds on my knuckles from when I had pounded on the air-lock door, but most of the blood must have been Drake's.

Marta pulled at my shoulder. Beth stood nearby, watching, eyes perfect circles, fists crammed against her mouth like a frightened little girl. Marta's lip was bleeding, and one of her eyes was already starting to swell shut. "Dave, it's over. Stop. It's over."

I went limp—then stiffened again as the broken rib shifted. Breathing hard, I dragged myself away from Drake's unconscious body. I started shaking as the animal rage drained out of me. Fighting the pain in my chest, I struggled to my feet. I looked down at Drake. He was out cold, but he wasn't dead. His chest rose and fell evenly.

Thank God I didn't kill him. What had happened to me? I had to stop him from hurting Marta . . . but then I lost all reason in primal rage. Why? Brown showed me how to defend my mind. I wasn't crazy anymore . . . was I? Maybe it was the drugs, stimulants driving me forward on overcharge for—what? Was it two days or three? Time had blurred.

Marta got to her feet, swaying slightly. She put a hand to her forehead. All the energy seemed to have drained out of both of us. She looked at me. Even with my other-sense closed, I could read the thought in her eyes: *Has he come to his senses?*

"Dave . . ."

"This doesn't mean I've forgotten who you really are," I said. "Don't try to stop me again."

She sighed and leaned against the wall. "It's just a nightmare," she said, as if to herself. "In the morning I'll wake up."

◀   ◀   ◀

Time passed. There was silence. Where was everyone? Where was the gang that had attacked me before? Now the corridors were deserted without even a sound of distant trouble. Had they all killed each other? Or retreated behind the closed doors of offices and cabins, each to his own imaginary little world? It was as if the Alley was holding its breath, waiting to see what I would do.

After a while I summoned up the will to move again. Breathing was like fire, moving not much better. The elevators took forever before the doors at the far left pinged and slid open. I grabbed Marta by the arm and pulled her along. She made no effort to resist.

Drake moaned and shifted his position. Marta stopped and looked back, then at me. "Are you just going to leave him?"

I hesitated. "I think it would be dangerous for us to be nearby when he wakes up," I said.

"This time yesterday, would you have found it so easy to abandon your friends?" She wasn't going to miss any opportunity to make me doubt myself.

"Nothing about this is easy," I snapped. But I also looked back. Muttering something unpleasant under my breath, I let go of Marta and went back to Drake. I took his handscreen, called up a memo pad, and entered "Get to an escape pod" in the largest letters that would fit, then pressed it into his hand.

"There," I said. "That's all I can—"

There was a shuddering jolt and the floor moved sideways under my feet. Beth, Marta, and I all fell sprawling. I yelled again as the fall punished my broken rib. The deck bucked and shuddered, and I felt a pronounced swaying. Crashing sounds accompanied the groaning of overstressed metal as loose objects rattled, toppled, and shattered. Washing over it all, alarm sirens began to sound a deafening, doomed wail.

"What's happening?" Marta shouted over the noise. Even Beth seemed shocked out of her trance, and stared around the lobby with wide eyes.

"Someone's tampering with the Alley's attitude controls," I shouted back. "The same thing happened during the Effect."

After the initial jolt, the noise and the shaking subsided a bit. But they didn't stop completely, and the swaying increased; the Wheel wobbled like a bicycle tire on a loose axle.

A recorded voice—obviously recorded from its maddeningly neutral tones—interrupted the sirens. "Disaster alert. All hands to evacuation stations. Repeat, Disaster alert. All hands to evacuation stations." The message repeated at intervals between siren screams.

I wondered why that never went off during the Effect. The damage must be worse this time. But it didn't feel like the Alley was shaking itself apart. The swaying was worse than during the Effect, but it seemed—*seemed*, at least to me—that it was a stable oscillation that wasn't doing much further damage. I staggered to my feet. Marta made no effort to rise, but she looked up at me.

"It's over!" she shouted. "You'll never make it to your equipment now. It might all be ruined anyway. Let me go to the children, get them to the evacuation—"

"No!" I shouted. "No! You're not getting the Child away! We're going on!"

I grabbed her arm again and yanked her to her feet. My ribs screamed their protest, but I ignored them. The elevator doors had closed. I hit the button again, willing the cab to still be there.

I had avoided the elevators during the Effect, taking the stairs for fear the elevator would jam. Now I had no choice but to risk it. I'd never make it up those stairs now.

The doors opened. I threw Marta into the cab and went in after her, yelling at Beth to follow. She tried to stand up, fell over, and then crawled into the elevator on all fours. I slapped the control for the Hub. The noise muted as the doors slid closed, and I breathed a sigh of relief when the cab started moving.

The cab shook and banged against the walls of the shaft, but it kept moving. Gravity diminished as we rose toward the Hub, as did the swaying sensation. I could hear, from overhead, the deep electric hum of the maglev bearings straining against the Wheel's wobble.

369

Just like in the Effect. As the elevator slowed to a stop and pinged its arrival, I heard gunfire.

Marta seemed resigned now. It's only with hindsight that I can recall the terror in her eyes. Beth smiled in supreme confidence that everything would obey the destiny she imagined.

The doors slid open.

The hum was louder than it had been during the Effect, a sign I suppose that the Wheel's deviation was worse than before. Metal groaned as the Hub's bulkheads bent and crumpled under the strain. But the loudest noise was the crackle of guns, and the air was thick with the ozone smell of spent charges. The fighting was close by.

"Be careful," I said.

No one was in sight as we emerged from the elevator. The gunshots came from ahead, screened from view by the facing pair of elevators. I heard shouting.

My ribs caused less trouble in the low gravity, though breathing still hurt like dusted fire. I kept a grip on Marta's arm and pulled her along, even though she was no longer resisting, as I peered around the corner. Beth followed serenely.

A ragged line of armed crewmen stretched across the width of the observation gallery, their backs to us, facing down a mob of crazies waving pieces of metal or broken furniture like clubs. Bodies littered the deck; bloodstains colored it red. Most of the dead must have fallen from the crewmen's gunfire, some perhaps from the mob itself. Little groups of madmen, distracted from their conflict with the soldiers, surrounded many of the bodies, battering and tearing at them with unrestrained fury. All of the crazies shrieked and howled, snarling in rage at the line of soldiers still standing against them.

This was far beyond any of the madness I'd seen before. There were no elaborate delusions here, no schizophrenia. Only raving animals, all traces of even deranged intelligence erased. The tele-pathic poison spewed out by the Child must have entered a new phase, escalated to a new and terrible level.

There seemed to be hundreds of the maniacs, filling almost the entire gallery in a struggling mass, trampling on the bodies, surging back and forth. Some were in uniform. Some were civilians. Some had clothes so torn and disarrayed I couldn't tell. Seeing them, Drake's phrase came to mind: *the Army of the Night.*

I had wondered where everyone had gone. It appeared they'd all come here. Why? What common thread of their madness would lead them all to the same point, right in my path?

In my path, that was it. Had the Child, or the Enemy itself, sent them to stop me? Blasting out what remained of their minds and turning them into a pack of rabid animals ready to tear me to pieces? But that couldn't be—if the Enemy knew what I planned, it would kill me outright, just like it did with Brown. I knew I had no strength to resist such an attack.

I saw Officer Wyatt issuing orders. The last of the midwatch, the immune, who were supposed to take over when the rest of the crew succumbed, were now making their final stand.

Why didn't they retreat, head for the elevators or through the secured doors into the control room? But the madmen must have taken the control room—someone caused that jolt to the Wheel.

You're wasting time watching this. The stairs to the mezzanine rose just behind the line of crewmen. If they were forced back at all, that route would be cut off.

"Come on," I said.

I tried to sprint for the stairs but I had forgotten the fractional gravity. My first step turned into a long, ungainly leap which pulled Marta off her feet and sent the two of us tumbling head over heels.

The impact wasn't hard but we ended up in a tangle, and I screamed, the broken rib again.

There was a roar from the mob. They'd seen us. The crewmen didn't, but the madmen surged forward, howling in mindless rage.

"Here they come again!" shouted one of the crewmen. Guns began to crackle in ragged volleys.

The crew's fire was ineffective: Men and women in the front line of the mob fell, but those behind just poured over them. I tried to get to my feet while retaining my grip on Marta's arm, but it was an awkward attempt.

"You're hurting me," she said. She spoke quietly and seemingly with no emotion, but I heard her clearly despite the noise.

"Get up," I said.

"Let go of my arm. You don't have to drag me with you. Do you think I want to stay here?" She waved her free hand at the battle line.

"All right," I said, letting her go.

Beth had come up behind us. I estimated we had seconds before the mob overran the armed line. A crewman went down, bleeding from his scalp as something thrown struck him in the forehead.

"Head for the stairs," I said. "Fast."

Marta leaped for the base of the stairway, Beth right behind her. I followed. But then Marta sidestepped, bypassing the stairs and running toward Wyatt.

"You've got to stop him!" she yelled, pointing back in my direction. "He's going to kill everyone!"

I cursed and changed course to grab her. Wyatt turned in Marta's direction, surprised, her mouth open to say something. Beth stopped on the stairs, looking back.

THE CHILD

The Army of the Night reached the line of crewmen.

Dozens of crazies went down before the crew's last volley of gunfire, but dozens more poured over them, and the last of the crewmen were buried under the stampede, screaming as they were battered to death or torn apart. The howling of the mob rose in ugly triumph. One lunatic swung a broken-off chair leg at Wyatt, shattering her skull. She went down in a bloody heap. Three or four swarmed over Marta. I heard Beth scream and then the lunatics were all over me. Someone had got hold of my arms and legs, throwing me off my feet. Teeth bit at my throat.

What I did next was pure instinct. I could never have done it if I'd had time to think about it.

I used the other-sense. The other-*power*. I opened my mind, dropping the defense Brown had taught me. I opened myself up and I *pushed*. Hard.

An unseen force threw my attackers back. I felt myself doing it. I added another push, poured every bit of energy I had into a telepathic scream, as loud as I could make it:

FEAR.

It worked like a charm. Or like black magic. The howls of insane rage turned to screams of insane terror, and all at once the mob was pulling away from me, the crazies pushing, shoving, clawing, trampling each other in desperation to get as far away as possible. Within seconds I found myself in the center of an empty circle with those nearest me in the crowd pressing back against the pack of bodies blocking their further retreat.

The Red Light and Shadow knew what I did! In my nightmares I was the focus of its attention, but in waking life it was just there, indifferent. But now Eiralynn turned in my direction.

With my mind wide open, I could, at last, sense that it too was a mind. Vast, seething, and depraved beyond comprehension, yet still a mind. It burned, like the Child's, but with a strange and alien fire. Just to sense it was to reel on the edge of joining the mindless pack of the insane. And a voice came from it, the Voice, speaking the same words I had heard over and over in the Dream: "Mi'vri! Alan ayanvishar! A simai lansar ire ayangemar a ima lan a'ayan y'poro. Eiralynn ayansar a lanres ra'ayan seshar!"

The words were still a mystery, except for two: its own name, and it addressed me as *Mi'vri*. It thought I was one of Brown's people! Eiralynn had noticed my use of power and thought I was a Mi'vri. Surely it would now destroy me, as it had Brown! I had opened my mind, it must now know—

Stop that! I clamped down on my thoughts. If it was going to kill me, it would. Panic wouldn't save me, and perhaps it hadn't read my mind yet. I took a few more seconds to risk sending out another telepathic yell to anyone who might still be receptive:

ESCAPE PODS. NOW.

Then I closed off my mind.

There was a strange ripple through the crowd as it huddled back away from me. I didn't know if any of them were capable of responding to the message, but if there were any rational minds left on the Alley then perhaps they'd get it, and get out. I had to hope that some had already obeyed the alarm sirens.

The mob wouldn't hang back for long, now that I'd shut down my misharen again. Already a mutter rose from the pack. I picked myself up and ran to Marta. I couldn't leave her behind, even then.

She was unconscious but alive. When I felt her neck for a pulse, it was strong. The low gravity made it easy for me to pick her up, and although my broken rib screamed, I carried her to the stairs.

Beth stood halfway up the flight, her arms spread wide. "The demons that bar the way fall back before your power," she half-said, half-sang. "Truly you are the Bringer of Ascension! A being of light in human form, sent to lead the Way along the Path to Enlightenment!" I felt sick. Nothing I planned deserved her adulation.

But she was now the only help I had. So I choked off what I wanted to say, and kept it to, "Let's go. Hurry."

I leaped up the stairs. Behind me I heard the mob growing bold again; seeing me run encouraged their aggression. The mutter became a snarl of renewed rage. When I reached the mezzanine I couldn't help but pause for a look back: They were charging, almost to the foot of the stairs.

I turned away. "Go! Go!" I shouted. Beth was at least capable of recognizing the danger, because she took one look behind me and leaped for the next stairwell.

Up those stairs and we were on the inner Hub deck, right in between the Wheel's bearings. The bass hum of their overloaded circuits drowned out all other noise, but I knew the others followed. Up again to the Transfer Room. The entire room shuddered and banged with the Wheel's wobble and I could see the bulkheads shifting and bending.

How long before metal fatigue just tears them apart?

Beth grabbed a handhold and let it pull her into zero-g. I just jumped. Coriolis force pushed me sideways, and I came down in a tumble, clutching Marta's limp form to my chest. Now weightless, I put out my feet to stop my motion and kicked off toward the main passage.

Mercifully, the towline still ran. I held Marta with one arm around her waist and grabbed a handhold with the other. Beth was just ahead of me. The electric hum faded as we moved away from the Hub, and I could hear the crazies again. I looked back.

They followed, the Army of the Night. Wild, screaming faces peered into the passage from the Transfer Room. Some grabbed for the towline. Others scrambled after us bouncing from handhold to handhold along the cylindrical walls.

We reached the turnoff for our hangar. Where all of this began, and where it would all end. No towline here—we had to use the handholds. Beth was getting farther ahead. Carrying Marta made me awkward. Behind, I could hear the crazies gaining on me.

There! The hatchway to the hangar! Beth was already through. I dove after her and immediately let go of Marta, letting her unconscious body drift into the cavernous space. I whirled around to slam the hatch.

"Beth! The hatch in the OCC! Lock it, lock it!" Beth jumped through the door into the office. I punched the locking code into the door panel and the hatch sealed. A moment later I heard pounding on the other side of it. Letting out a deep breath, I began to tremble with the realization of how close our escape had been.

I took a look to see where Marta had ended up. She wasn't moving, just floating in the middle of the hangar. I followed on one of the handholds and caught her before she hit the far wall. She was still unconscious—when she went down under the mob she must have gotten a bad blow to the head. But her pulse was steady. I towed her back to the OCC and clipped her belt to a rail away from the computer screens.

"Okay," I said. Beth watched me expectantly. "Okay. Okay. Set the generators."

My heart pounded, my breath came in gasps that grated the pieces of my rib against each other, and my nerve endings vibrated. The fight-or-flight response mixed with an overdose of stimulants in a cocktail that sang warning sirens in my blood. I had to slow down now. I had work to do, one last time.

The generators didn't need much work. The software would do most of what we required. I pulled away the extra instruments for neurofield measurements. The generators needed a few components switched out to return them to run 37 status.

Marta was still unconscious when we finally moved into the OCC, and I started to worry about her. How bad a concussion had she received? But if she woke up, she'd only try to stop us.

"Beth, take Kyoko's station and start priming the generators," I said.

"Yes." She could hardly restrain her excitement now that the moment of Ascension was at hand. But she began the start-up routines as efficiently as Kyoko would have.

I took Drake's station and hoped he'd configured the software correctly. It had worked in simulation, but how many times had an experiment gone another way than what the sims predicted?

Not this time. It will work. I entered the new settings. Through the window, the webbed spines of the hyperfield generators moved as the computer settled them into their final configuration. From outside the noise of enraged screams and pounding on the hatches continued.

The variables on Drake's screen went green one by one. "Debugging sims complete, everything's okay," I said.

"The generators are primed," Beth answered.

The old, familiar smell of ozone drifted in from the hangar.

I looked at my screen displaying the usual array of graphs. "Instruments are running." The computer stood ready to record the data into a run file that no one would ever read.

"It's going to feel like the Effect, but maybe stronger," I said. "Brace yourself."

Beth smiled in supreme confidence. "We will defeat the Dragon, and we will be rewarded with our Ascension. We will become Spirits of Light and rise to the highest plane! I am ready!"

"I hope you're right," I said. It would be so much better than what I expected.

I poised my fingers over the keyboard. Normally, Kyoko's station had control over final activation. But I called up the program on Drake's screen instead; I had to be the one to push the last button.

And then, I hesitated. Some last shred of sanity tried to warn me off, one final chance to avoid my fate.

If it can kill ten people or ten thousand it'll pick the ten thousand every time. That's how Brown had described the Enemy. Wasn't that exactly what I was going to do? Blow up the entire base? Kill everyone on board, when the goal was just to shut down the Child's misharen?

"Dave." Marta was awake. "Dave—don't. Please."

But there was no other way.

Are you sure about that? Really? Did you even really look? Are you SURE?

No. No, I wasn't sure. I looked at the screen, the computer waiting for me to tell it "go," and suddenly doubted myself.

What am I doing here? This is insanity, no different from the mob that tore those crewmen apart!

But then, all my wrath rose up in righteous opposition. No, it wasn't just to stop the Child. Eiralynn was the key, and this was how I'd strike back at the true Enemy. It used me, manipulated my life! It perverted my work, my wonderful hyperfields, into something terrible!

It haunted my nightmares, sent the Beast to destroy my mind, and killed my friends. It caused the Dark Years *and it must pay!*

Beth unclipped from the rail and straightened out into a ceremonial pose, floating in front of Kyoko's station like some ancient priestess before an altar of sacrifice. She flung out her arms and tilted her head back in rapturous expectation.

Marta screamed her last effort, "Dave! Don't!"

For no reason except that it was the thing to say, I shouted out, "THIS IS RUN FORTY-THREE!" and hit the button.

And the skies ripped open like the Wrath of God had torn them apart.

It was the Effect times a hundred. Times a thousand. My mental defenses went down in an instant, blasted apart by the power of the other-sense that could not be denied or ignored. The real world, the world of eyes and ears and taste and touch, vanished before a new reality where I walked in eternity with all of time and space stretched out around me. The Alley was laid bare to my inspection, every wire, every fitting, every seam. And every person. They ran and struggled aimlessly, their white-fires blazing out of control.

And there was Eiralynn! No hiding from it now, no looking away. It poured its rage on me like molten metal trying to burn my mind from inside out. The sheer agony of it almost killed me. The misharen, the power, was too much! I had to expend it, push it out of myself.

The window of the OCC shattered, blowing outward. The bulkhead around it bent and twisted. The fragments narrowly missed hitting the generators. They could have smashed them and undone everything. But they passed by and the power continued to build.

Beth achieved her apotheosis, but it cheated her. In her eyes and in her mind there passed triumph, doubt, confusion, pain, and then—her mouth opened in one, long betrayed scream, and she exploded into flames. Weightless, she could not fall, nor could the flames rise. She just hung there in a ball of fire, as her last scream died away and her body curled in on itself, until she was gone.

At that I returned Eiralynn's rage with my own. I sent my thought against it in blazing fire, and even though I knew I could not hurt it, I let my triumph show in furious bravado: *The last one, Monster! She was your last victim! I've beaten you! I've beaten you! It's over!*

And it was! It moved away! It retreated before the hyperfire I had kindled in the heart of the Alley. It couldn't stop me now. It couldn't remain close enough to do anything. It had to flee! It had lost!

But what of the Child? Had it escaped, perhaps getting to an escape pod? No, there it was! Still in the Wheel, still locked in the Admiral's Suite, soon to burn. It was red and furious in empty hate and fear. It howled and gibbered in final outrage. *You're my toy! You can't. You can't! Oh, no fair! No fair!*

I still had to get out. And Marta. She still lived; I saw her heart beating inside her chest. Saw her white-fire still bright. But she thrashed in wild convulsions, and I could feel the pain she was in. I could see it, lighting up her brain.

Finding my flesh-and-blood fingers took concentration. The world of matter and energy was so much less real than the world of the other-sense. But I managed to release my belt clips, and I kicked off toward her. I tried to grab her, but her struggles made it difficult. So I used the misharen, wrapping her in a blanket of telekinetic force to hold her still, while I unclipped her from the rail.

I didn't unlock the hatchway out of the OCC. I just blew it off its hinges. It felt good to release the energy. Perhaps if I didn't, it would build up until I, too, died in flames. The crazies outside no longer had any interest in us. Some had burned, and those still alive were in convulsions, or curled up in fetal balls, or just drifting, limp and aimless.

Still using the power, I drove myself and Marta down the corridor away from them. I didn't have to bother with the handrails. The power built up fast. Soon I would burn no matter what I did.

The other-sense showed me an evacuation station up ahead, with a cluster of escape pods. None had been launched that I could tell. Marta had stopped thrashing by the time we reached them. I pushed her inside, and followed.

It was hot, getting hotter. The misharen told me the worst heat was around the Hub. Why there, I didn't know. But the Alley's structure there had already begun to soften and melt. The Wheel would come apart in moments. It wouldn't stop the hyperfields. Nothing would stop them until the generators themselves vaporized.

The controls of an emergency escape pod are simple, by design. There is only one button: LAUNCH. I hit it.

Explosive bolts fired. A warning alarm sounded. And we were away. The pod accelerated hard, putting distance between itself and the base. Already the misharen faded as the pod moved out of the range of the hyperfields.

I turned to Marta, hoping she would recover, now that the Effect was behind us. But she was dead. I can't say when she died. Sometime while I was driving us down the corridor. I cursed, shouting my futile rage into the small space of the escape pod. I pounded my fists on the walls until the pain stopped me.

No one. I saved NO ONE!

I had only one final mistake to make, and I made it. It was the old mistake, the mistake humans have always made, at least according to the old myths and legends that, I suppose, contain more truth than we know.

I looked back.

The gamma field covered the entire Alley, just like the equations predicted. It tore space wide open, a full rift into hyperspace, pouring out energy just like a new Sun. They saw it all over the Solar System, I'm told. The Alley vanished into a whiff of vapor and with that the hyperfields collapsed and the rift vanished, leaving not even an echo.

But it was too late for me. I had looked back, and in the final seconds as the rift opened, I saw—I won't tell. I saw the truth, that's all I'll say about it. And that was what, finally, blasted my mind to pieces. I remember nothing more but howling darkness, and a nightmare that would never end.

So that's it. That's how a respectable physicist became the worst mass murderer in the history of the Colonies.

I have to rely on what I've been told for the rest: I have no memory of it. I was a raving maniac when they found me, days later, screaming inane horrors at the top of my lungs, shut up in the escape pod with a dead woman.

At first they assumed I'd killed Marta. And they were right. I'd killed her by switching on the generators. Just like I killed Beth, and everyone else. But the autopsy found no identifiable cause of death, and officially I was cleared—of that one murder, at least. So they tell me.

No one else launched any escape pods. No one else survived.

The Alley was in communication with the Navy until very near the end, so the epidemic of insanity was known. That, plus my condition when they found me, was enough to settle my legal status. Even after they'd worked out what I'd done, there was no question of a trial. So here I am, wearing pajamas and eating soft foods with round implements. And here I expect to remain for the rest of my life.

Was Marta guilty? I guess not, since she was right. I have to live with that.

Which of the twelve children was the One? I will never know. I have to live with that too.

Was Eiralynn real? Oh yes. I know you want me to deny it. If I finally admit that it was a delusion, then that shows the therapy is working, that I'm on the way to being "cured." But it was not a delusion. I'm not sure Humanity itself can live with that.

You just have to be satisfied with the progress I've made so far. A year later and here I am, not raving, able to tell my story. I've told it plenty of times already.

Ah, that's it! You want to know the part I've always refused to tell. You want to know what I saw when I looked back. You figure it'll be some kind of breakthrough if I can finally face the one detail that I've always left out.

It all has to do with time. I have no computer here, but I can still work with hyperfields in my head. I've played with them since waking up. Oh yes, what else do I have to do with all the hours? I've worked out exactly what it means that hyperfields extend into time. It means a being like Eiralynn, made entirely of misharen, could move anywhere it likes, not just in space but in time as well.

Are you beginning to understand?

You want to know what I saw when I looked back? All right. I will tell you.

I looked back as the Rift opened and the Alley was consumed, and I saw that I had failed. I realized, too late, that I had been Eiralynn's pawn from beginning to end. Brown was wrong; he should have let them throw me out the air lock, but in Eiralynn's chess game he never saw the endgame coming.

Here is what I saw: The Rift opened, and it came in contact with the snarling red-flame neurofield of the Child. But the Child's power wasn't snuffed out. It merged *with the Rift. The color of its hate and rage spread across the Rift; they folded together and just before it vanished out of the Universe I saw it fully formed, glaring red with a crawling shadow blacker than space at its heart. The Red Light and Shadow, newborn.*

The Child was Eiralynn. That was the plan all along. Eiralynn came back in time to arrange its own creation. A cancer on time, Brown had said, and he was right. It tangles up causality, makes chaos out of order, just by existing. Eventually, it will bring the universe down.

And I didn't stop it.

I created it.

ACKNOWLEDGMENTS

This book would not exist without the help and support of a constant parade of friends, teachers, and fellow students going all the way back to high school, when I first started building the world in which it lives. Too many friends to list have displayed heroic patience in listening to me expound on my "History," and offered both valuable comments and unwavering encouragement along the way.

Every teacher I ever had deserves thanks. But on the craft of writing, Anne Freeman and Joan Strassmann get a special mention: thank you both for your abundant red ink, which I often disliked at the time but now realize was more valuable than gold. When this story began to take shape, I had the further good luck to learn from Barbara Wedgwood, J. Suzanne Frank, and all the teachers and students of The Writers Path at SMU. Thank you all, without you this book would still be something I only thought about writing, someday.

Thanks to my agent, Miriam Kriss, who believed in the book, to Courtney Miller at 47North, who agreed with her, and to Eleanor Licata, who helped me make it better.

Finally, extra special thanks to my writing buddies Amanda, the other Amanda, Joe, Kay, Kristen, and Lauren. You guys are even better than coffee.

ABOUT THE AUTHOR

Keith F. Goodnight is a native of Texas and distant relative of famed cowboy Charles Goodnight—the inventor of the chuck wagon. Born and raised in Dallas, he didn't actually live in a library while growing up, but he tried. A graduate of Rice University and an alumnus of the Marching Owl Band, he once performed at half-time dressed as a Christmas tree. When not writing, he enjoys cooking and working on his model railroad.